"My name is Dr. Edward Royland," he said. "I do atomic power research."

"That's a lie," said the Nazi, standing in the New Mexico sunshine. "There is no such thing as atomic power. Which of our concentration camps have you escaped from?"

—from "Two Dooms"
by C.M. Kornbluth

# FANTASTIC WORLD WAR II

edited by
**FRANK McSHERRY, JR.**
introductions by
**S. M. STIRLING**

BAEN
BOOKS

# THE FANTASTIC WORLD WAR II

Copyright © 1990 by Frank McSherry, Jr., Martin Harry Greenberg, and Charles G. Waugh

A Baen Books Original

Baen Publishing Enterprises
260 Fifth Avenue
New York, N.Y. 10001

ISBN: 0-671-69881-8

Cover art by Ken Kelly

First printing, June 1990

Distributed by
SIMON & SCHUSTER
1230 Avenue of the Americas
New York, N.Y. 10020

Printed in the United States of America

# CONTENTS

# ACKNOWLEDGMENTS

# INTRODUCTION

## S.M. Stirling

It is a characteristic of the greatest historical turning-points that they cast a multitude of shadows across the consciousness of humankind. The myth-making mechanism that is the our species' instinctive response to events that shake our world swings into action, covering and re-covering the bare facts with legend and turning the everyday grubbiness of the participants into angelic and demonic transcendence. In the earliest surviving chronicles, we can only infer the originals from the later accretions. A Romano-British war-leader becomes the stainless Arthur of Camelot and the Round Table to the descendants of the Saxons who obliterated his people. The beer-swilling, beef-guzzling charioteer barbarians who conquered the Indus Valley are transformed in the *Vedas* to Indra, Varuna and their godlike followers; the civilized and urbane folk they destroyed are, naturally, shown as demons. And this to the vegetarian and abstementious Hindus!

In the end, each cycle of myth incorporates its predecessors; the original story is so compelling that it "sucks in" subsequent heroes and their tales. Charlemagne's legendary Ireland and the Elbe, and every notable figure of Northern saga visited Hrolf Kraki. The roll of sleeping hero-kings waiting to redeem their people includes Arthur, Charlemagne, Holger Danske, King Svatopluk and enough others to litter the subsoil of Europe with sufficient enchanted saviors to make subway construction extremely problematic.

The stories sink into the popular consciousness, layer upon layer, until they become a force in themselves; they provide the patterns, the lens of interpretation through which the popular consciousness interprets events. This process is not a medieval relic; it remains a real social and political phenomenon. In 1848, the nationalist rebels of Bohemia thought King Svatopluk (or his son) was returning to free them from the Hapsburgs. Ambrose Bierce turned the War for Southron Independence into a field for his own dark fantasies; in 1914, British soldiers saw spectral longbowmen and angels above the machine-gun fire and shellbursts of Mons.

And we can still observe the process at work—with some modifications introduced by literacy and historical consciousness. The best recent example is World War Two, the second crisis of the great 20th-century civil war of Western civilization. Even with fifty years of perspective and the (recently!) opened archives of the Great Powers, historians are still arguing over the origins, the course, the outcome of the Second World War. Long before the conflict was over, the ordinary people involved knew that something far more was at stake than the usual war. The modern equivalent of the tribal bards, fiction writers, were hard at work from the beginning, integrating the events of their day into the myth-structures that lived in their audiences' minds, given fact meaning and resonance. The Nazis' own skillful use of Germanic myth, the torchlight parades, the death's-head badges, the crooked cross, all the twisted nihilistic symbolism of their political cult, made them a natural subject for this treatment.

Parachuting stormtroopers disguised as nuns and insidious "fifth columnists" were the staple of the first year of the war, together with the sinister Nazi spy, the quisling, and the monstrous armored giants of the Panzer divisions. In fact the paratroops (none in wimples) were a minor nuisance, the fifth column did not exist, Viskund Quisling an embarrassment to the Germans, Nazi secret intelligence largely a joke through which Allied and Soviet moles and codebreakers ran rampant, and German tanks inferior in numbers and armor to their Allied counterparts . . . Yet the instant legends, like those about Dunkirk, the Battle of Britain, and Stalingrad, served to structure and explain otherwise vast and incomprehensible events. Appeals to national popular history (the Armada legend in Britain, or the Danish resistance groups which called themselves after Holger Danske) gave participants a feeling of continuity, of connection with ancestors who themselves had struggled against comparable evils and triumphed.

In the postwar period, as more of the contours of the struggle became known, it joined earlier historical nexus points as a source of the common stock of metaphor and image. The Holocaust was instantly (and justly) an effective shorthand for absolute evil; the Nazi, now safely dead and in no position to inspire cautionary fear, a villain everyone could agree to hate—unlike contemporary devils as bloodstained but possessed of multimegatonne persuaders. High culture gives us "Shoa"; popular culture Hogan's Heroes and Action Comics. The mythmakers of the scientific age, the science fiction writers, went to work on the Second World War, bringing to it their peculiar combination of realism and wild imagining. Particularly attractive was the *alternate history*— that most useful way of throwing a unique light on the present by the shadow of *what might have been*.

*Frightening as the evils of National Socialism were, it was the sheer speed and thoroughness with which they seized political and moral control of a great and civilized nation that bewildered and disheartened many. For some—even as intelligent a man as Kipling—some inherent fault of the German people could be blamed; the "beastly Hun" was up to his old tricks. Given the huge contributions of Germany and Germans to the cultural and political heritage of the West, this was unsatisfactory for most; and since the purported experts are still engaging in scholarly jousts, ordinary men and women were left groping for an explanation. Given the nature and extent of the evil, and the genuine anti-Christian element in Nazi doctrine, the most traditional Source of all was called into play . . .*

# THE HOWLING MAN

## Charles Beaumont

The Germany of that time was a land of valleys and mountains and swift dark rivers, a green and fertile land where everything grew tall and straight out of the earth. There was no other country like it. Stepping across the border from Belgium, where the rain-caped, mustached guards saluted, grinning, like operetta soldiers, you entered a different world entirely. Here the grass became as rich and smooth as velvet; deep, thick woods appeared; the air itself, which had been heavy with the French perfume of wines and sauces, changed: the clean, fresh smell of lakes and pines and boulders came into your lungs. You stood a moment, then, at the border, watching the circling hawks above and wondering, a little fearfully, how such a thing could happen. In less than a minute you had passed from a musty, ancient room, through an invisible door, into a kingdom of winds and light. Unbelievable! But there, at your heels, clearly in view, is Belgium, like all the rest of Europe, a faded tapestry from some forgotten mansion.

In that time, before I had heard of St. Wulfran's, of

5

the wretch who clawed the stones of a locked cell, wailing in the midnight hours, or of the daft Brothers and their mad Abbot, I had strong legs and a mind on its last search, and I preferred to be alone. A while and I'll come back to this spot. We will ride and feel the sickness, fall, and hover on the edge of death, together. But I am not a writer, only one who loves wild, unhousebroken words; I must have a real beginning.

Paris beckoned in my youth. I heeded, for the reason most young men just out of college heed, although they would never admit it: to lie with mysterious beautiful women. A solid, traditional upbringing among the corseted ruins of Boston had succeeded, as such upbringings generally do, in honing the urge to a keen edge. My nightly dreams of beaded bagnios and dusky writhing houris, skilled beyond imagining, reached, finally, the unbearable stage beyond which lies either madness or respectability. Fancying neither, I managed to convince my parents that a year abroad would add exactly the right amount of seasoning to my maturity, like a dash of curry in an otherwise bland, if not altogether tasteless, chowder. I'm afraid that Father caught the hot glint in my eye, but he was kind. Describing, in detail, and with immense effect, the hideous consequences of profligacy, telling of men he knew who'd gone to Europe, innocently, and fallen into dissolutions so profound they'd not been heard of since, he begged me at all times to remember that I was an Ellington and turned me loose. Paris, of course, was enchanting and terrifying, as a jungle must be to a zoo-born monkey. Out of respect to the honored dead, and Dad, I did a quick trot through the Tuileries, the Louvre and down the Champs Elysées to the Arc de Triomphe; then, with the fall of night, I cannoned off to Montmartre and the Rue Pigalle, embarking on the Grand Adventure. Synoptically, it did not prove to be so grand as I'd imagined; nor was it, after the fourth week, so terribly adventurous. Still: important to what followed, for what followed doubtless wouldn't have but for the sweet complaisant girls.

Boston's Straights and Narrows don't, I fear, prepare

one—except psychologically—for the Wild Life. My health broke in due course and, as my thirst had been well and truly slaked, I was not awfully discontent to sink back into the contemplative cocoon to which I was, apparently, more suited. Abed for a month I lay, in celibate silence and almost total inactivity. Then, no doubt as a final gesture of rebellion, I got my idea—got? or had my concentrated sins received it, like a signal from a failing tower?—and I made my strange, up-Ellingtonian decision. I would explore Europe. But not as a tourist, safe and fat in his fat, safe bus, insulated against the beauty and the ugliness of changing cultures by a pane of glass and a room at the English-speaking hotel. No. I would go like an unprotected wind, a seven-league-booted leaf, a nestless bird, and I would see this dark strange land with the vision of a boy on the last legs of his dreams. I would go by bicycle, poor and lonely and questing—as poor and lonely and questing, anyway, as one can be with a hundred thousand in the bank and a partnership in Ellington, Carruthers & Blake waiting.

So it was. New England blood and muscles wilted on that first day's pumping, but New England spirit toughened as the miles dropped back. Like an ant crawling over a once-lovely, now decayed and somewhat seedy Duchess, I rode over the body of Europe. I dined at restaurants where boar's heads hung, all vicious-tusked and blind; I slept at country inns and breathed the musty age, and sometimes girls came to the door and knocked and asked if I had everything I needed ("Well . . .") and they were better than the girls in Paris, though I can't imagine why. No matter. Out of France I pedaled, into Belgium, out, and to the place of cows and forests, mountains, brooks, and laughing people: Germany. (I've rhapsodized on purpose for I feel it's quite important to remember how completely Paradisical the land was then, at that time.)

I looked odd, standing there. The border guard asked what was loose with me, I answered Nothing—grateful for the German, and the French, Miss Finch had drummed into me—and set off along the smallest, dark-

est path. It serpentined through forests, cities, towns,
villages, and always I followed its least likely append-
ages. Unreasonably, I pedaled as if toward a destination: into the Moselle Valley country, up into the desolate
hills of emerald.

By a ferry, fallen to desuetude, the reptile drew me
through a bosky wood. The trees closed in at once. I
drank the fragrant air and pumped and kept on pumping,
but a heat began to grow inside my body. My head began
to ache. I felt weak. Two more miles and I was obliged to
stop, for perspiration filmed my skin. You know the signs
of pneumonia: a sapping of the strength, a trembling,
flashes of heat and of cold; visions. I lay in the bed of
damp leaves for a time, then forced myself onto the
bicycle and rode for what seemed an endless time. At
last a village came to view. A thirteenth-century village,
gray and narrow-streeted, cobbled to the hidden store
fronts. A number of old people in peasant costumes
looked up as I bumped along, and I recall one ancient
tallow-colored fellow—nothing more. Only the weakness, like acid, burning off my nerves and muscles. And
an intervening blackness to pillow my fall.

I awoke to the smells of urine and hay. The fever had
passed, but my arms and legs lay heavy as logs, my
head throbbed horribly, and there was an empty
shoveled-out hole inside my stomach somewhere. For a
long while I did not move or open my eyes. Breathing
was a major effort. But consciousness came, eventually.

I was in a tiny room. The walls and ceiling were of
rough gray stone, the single glassless window was arch-
shaped, the floor was uncombed dirt. My bed was not a
bed at all, but a blanket thrown across a disorderly pile
of crinkly straw. Beside me, a crude table; upon it, a
pitcher; beneath it, a bucket. Next to the table, a stool.
And seated there, asleep, his tonsured head adangle
from an Everest of robe, a monk.

I must have groaned, for the shorn pate bobbed up
precipitately. Two silver trails gleamed down the corners of the suddenly exposed mouth, which drooped
into a frown. The slumbrous eyes blinked.

"It is God's infinite mercy," sighed the gnomelike little man. "You have recovered."

"Not as yet," I told him. Unsuccessfully, I tried to remember what had happened; then I asked questions.

"I am Brother Christophorus. This is the Abbey of St. Wulfran's. The Burgemeister of Schwartzhof, Herr Barth, brought you to us nine days ago. Father Jerome said that you would die and he sent me to watch, for I have never seen a man die, and Father Jerome holds that it is beneficial for a Brother to have seen a man die. But now I suppose that you will not die." He shook his head ruefully.

"Your disappointment," I said, "cuts me to the quick. However, don't abandon hope. The way I feel now, it's touch and go."

"No," said Brother Christophorus sadly. "You will get well. It will take time. But you will get well."

"Such ingratitude, and after all you've done. How can I express my apologies?"

He blinked again. With the innocence of a child, he said, "I beg your pardon?"

"Nothing." I grumbled about blankets, a fire, some food to eat, and then slipped back into the well of sleep. A fever dream of forests full of giant two-headed beasts came, then the sound of screaming.

I awoke. The scream shrilled on—Klaxon-loud, high, cutting, like a cry for help.

"What is that sound?" I asked.

The monk smiled. "Sound? I hear no sound," he said.

It stopped. I nodded. "Dreaming. Probably I'll hear a good deal more before I'm through. I shouldn't have left Paris in such poor condition."

"No," he said. "You shouldn't have left Paris."

Kindly now, resigned to my recovery, Brother Christophorus became attentive to a fault. Nurselike, he spooned thick soups into me, applied compresses, chanted soothing prayers, and emptied the bucket out the window. Time passed slowly. As I fought the sickness, the dreams grew less vivid—but the nightly cries did not diminish. They were as full of terror and loneli-

ness as before, strong, real in my ears, I tried to shut
them out, but they would not be shut out. Still, how
could they be strong and real except in my vanishing
delirium? Brother Christophorus did not hear them. I
watched him closely when the sunlight faded to the
gray of dusk and the screams began, but he was deaf to
them—if they existed. If they existed!

"Be still, my son. It is the fever that makes you hear
these noises. That is quite natural. Is that not quite
natural? Sleep."

"But the fever is gone! I'm sitting up now. Listen! Do
you mean to tell me you don't hear *that*?"

"I hear only you, my son."

The screams, that fourteenth night, continued until
dawn. They were totally unlike any sounds in my experience. Impossible to believe they could be uttered and
sustained by a human, yet they did not seem to be
animal. I listened, there in the gloom, my hands balled
into fists, and knew, suddenly, that one of two things
must be true. Either someone or something was making these ghastly sounds, and Brother Christophorus
was lying, or—I was going mad. Hearing-voices mad,
climbing-walls and frothing mad. I'd have to find the
answer: that I knew. And by myself.

I listened with a new ear to the howls. Razoring
under the door, they rose to operatic pitch, subsided,
resumed, like the cries of a surly, hysterical child. To
test their reality, I hummed beneath my breath, I covered my head with a blanketing, scratched at the straw,
coughed. No difference. The quality of substance, of
existence, was there. I tried, then, to localize the screams;
and, on the fifteenth night, felt sure that they were
coming from a spot not far along the hall.

*The sounds that maniacs hear seem quite real to them.*
I know. I know!

The monk was by my side, he had not left it from the
start, keeping steady vigil even through Matins. He
joined his tremulous soprano to the distant chants,
and prayed excessively. But nothing could tempt him
away. The food we ate was brought to us, as were all

other needs. I'd see the Abbot, Father Jerome, once I was recovered. Meanwhile . . .

"I'm feeling better, Brother. Perhaps you'd care to show me about the grounds. I've seen nothing of St. Wulfran's except this little room."

"There is only this little room multiplied. Ours is a rigorous order. The Franciscans, now, they permit themselves esthetic pleasure; we do not. It is, for us a luxury. We have a single, most unusual job. There is nothing to see."

"But surely the Abbey is very old."

"Yes, that is true."

"As an antiquarian—"

"Mr. Ellington—"

"What is it that you don't want me to see? What are you afraid of, Brother?"

"Mr. Ellington? I do not have the authority to grant your request. When you are well enough to leave, Father Jerome will no doubt be happy to accommodate you."

"Will he also be happy to explain the screams I've heard each night since I've been here?"

"Rest, my son. Rest."

The unholy, hackle-raising shriek burst loose and bounded off the hard stone walls. Brother Christophorus crossed himself, apropos of nothing, and sat like an ancient Indian on the weary stool. I knew he liked me. Especially, perhaps. We'd got along quite well in all our talks. But this—*verboten*.

I closed my eyes. I counted to three hundred. I opened my eyes.

The good monk was asleep. I blasphemed, softly, but he did not stir, so I swung my legs over the side of the straw bed and made my way across the dirt floor to the heavy wooden door. I rested there a time, in the candleless dark, listening to the howls; then, with Bostonian discretion, raised the bolt. The rusted hinges creaked, but Brother Christophorus was deep in celestial marble: his head drooped low upon his chest.

Panting, weak as a landlocked fish, I stumbled out into the corridor. The screams became impossibly loud.

I put my hands to my ears, instinctively, and wondered how anyone could sleep with such a furor going on. It *was* a furor. In my mind? No. Real. The monastery shook with these shrill cries. You could feel their realness with your teeth.

I passed a Brother's cell and listened, then another; then I paused. A thick door, made of oak or pine, was locked before me. Behind it were the screams.

A chill went through me on the edge of those unutterable shrieks of hopeless, helpless anguish, and for a moment I considered turning back—not to my room, not to my bed of straw, but back into the open world. But duty held me. I took a breath and walked up to the narrow bar-crossed window and looked in.

A man was in the cell. On all fours, circling like a beast, his head thrown back, a man. The moonlight showed his face. It cannot be described—not, at least, by me. A man past death might look like this, a victim of the Inquisition rack, the stake, the pincers: not a human in the third decade of the twentieth century, surely. I had never seen such suffering within two eyes, such lost, mad suffering. Naked, he crawled about the dirt, cried, leaped up to his feet and clawed the hard stone walls in fury.

Then he saw me.

The screaming ceased. He huddled, blinking, in the corner of his cell. And then, as though unsure of what he saw, he walked right to the door.

In German, hissing: "Who are you?"

"David Ellington," I said. "Are you locked in? Why have they locked you in?"

He shook his head. "Be still, be still. You are not German?"

"No." I told him how I came to be at St. Wulfran's.

"Ah!" Trembling, his horny fingers closing on the bars, the naked man said: "Listen to me, we have only moments. They are mad. You hear? All mad. I was in the village, lying with my woman, when their crazy Abbot burst into the house and hit me with his heavy cross. I woke up here. They flogged me. I asked for food, they would not give it to me. They took my clothes. They threw me in this filthy room. They locked the door."

"Why?"

"Why?" He moaned. "I wish I knew. That's been the worst of it. Five years imprisoned, beaten, tortured, starved, and not a reason given, not a word to guess from—Mr. Ellington! I have sinned, but who has not? With my woman, quietly, alone with my woman, my love. And this God-drunk lunatic, Jerome, cannot stand it. Help me!"

His breath splashed on my face. I took a backward step and tried to think. I couldn't quite believe that in this century a thing so frightening could happen. Yet, the Abbey was secluded, above the world, timeless. What could not transpire here, secretly?

"I'll speak to the Abbot."

"No! I tell you, he's the maddest of them all. Say nothing to him."

"Then how can I help you?"

He pressed his mouth against the bars. "In one way only. Around Jerome's neck, there is a key. It fits this lock. If—"

"Mr. Ellington!"

I turned and faced a fierce El Greco painting of a man. White-bearded, prow-nosed, regal as an Emperor beneath the gray peaked robe, he came out of the darkness. "Mr. Ellington, I did not know that you were well enough to walk. Come with me, please"

The naked man began to weep hysterically. I felt a grip of steel about my arm. Through corridors, past snore-filled cells, the echoes of the weeping dying, we continued to a room.

"I must ask you to leave St. Wulfran's," the Abbot said. "We lack the proper facilities for care of the ill. Arrangements will be made in Schwartzhof—"

"One moment," I said. "While it's probably true that Brother Christophorus's ministrations saved my life—and certainly true that I owe you all a debt of gratitude—I've got to ask for an explanation of that man in the cell."

"What man?" the Abbot said softly.

"The one we just left, the one who's screamed all night long every night."

"No man has been screaming, Mr. Ellington."

Feeling suddenly very weak, I sat down and rested a few breaths' worth. Then I said, "Father Jerome—you are he? I am not necessarily an irreligious person, but neither could I be considered particularly religious. I know nothing of monasteries, what is permitted, what isn't. But I seriously doubt that you have the authority to imprison a man against his will."

"That is quite true. We have no such authority."

"Then why have you done so?"

The Abbot looked at me steadily. In a firm, inflexible voice, he said: "No man has been imprisoned at St. Wulfran's."

"He claims otherwise."

"Who claims otherwise?"

"The man in the cell at the end of the corridor."

"There is no man in the cell at the end of the corridor."

"I was talking with him!"

"You were talking with no man."

The conviction in his voice shocked me into momentary silence. I gripped the arms of the chair.

"You are ill, Mr. Ellington," the bearded holy man said. "You have suffered from delirium. You have heard and seen things which do not exist."

"That's true," I said. "But the man in the cell—whose voice I can hear now!—is not one of those things."

The Abbot shrugged. "Dreams can seem very real, my son."

I glanced at the leather thong about his turkey-gobbler neck, all but hidden beneath the beard. "Honest men make unconvincing liars," I lied convincingly. "Brother Christophorus has a way of looking at the floor whenever he denies the cries in the night. You look at me, but your voice loses its command. I can't imagine why, but you are both very intent upon keeping me away from the truth. Which is not only poor Christianity, but also poor psychology. For now I am quite curious indeed. You might as well tell me, Father; I'll find out eventually."

"What do you mean?"

"Only that. I'm sure the police will be interested to hear of a man imprisoned at the Abbey."

"I tell you, *there is no man!*"

"Very well. Let's forget the matter."

"Mr. Ellington—" The Abbot put his hand behind him. "The person in the cell is, ah, one of the Brothers. Yes. He is subject to . . . seizures, fits. You know fits? At these times, he becomes intractable. Violent. Dangerous! We're obliged to lock him in his cell, which you can surely understand."

"I understand," I said, "that you're still lying to me. If the answer were as simple as that, you'd not have gone through the elaborate business of pretending I was delirious. There'd have been no need. There's something more to it, but I can wait. Shall we go on to Schwartzhof?"

Father Jerome tugged at his beard viciously, as if it were some feathered demon come to taunt him. "Would you truly go to the police?" he asked.

"Would you?" I said. "In my position?"

He considered that for a long time, tugging the beard, nodding the prowed head; and the screams went on, so distant, so real. I thought of the naked man clawing in his filth.

"Well, Father?"

"Mr. Ellington, I see that I shall have to be honest with you—which is a great pity," he said. "Had I followed my original instinct and refused to allow you in the Abbey to begin with . . . but, I had no choice. You were near death. No physician was available. You would have perished. Still, perhaps that would have been better."

"My recovery seems to have disappointed a lot of people," I commented. "I assure you it was inadvertent."

The old man took no notice of this remark. Stuffing his mandarin hands into the sleeves of his robe, he spoke with great deliberation. "When I said that there was no man in the cell at the end of the corridor, I was telling the truth. Sit down, sir! Please! Now." He closed his eyes. "There is much to the story, much that you will not understand or believe. You are sophisticated, or feel that you are. You regard our life here, no doubt, as primitive—"

"In fact, I—"

"In fact, you do. I know the current theories. Monks are misfits, neurotics, sexual frustrates, and aberrants. They retreat from the world because they cannot cope with the world. Et cetera. You are surprised I know these things? My son, I was told by the one who began the theories!" He raised his head upward, revealing more of the leather thong. "Five years ago, Mr. Ellington, there were no screams at St. Wulfran's. This was an undistinguished little Abbey in the wild Black Mountain region, and its inmates' job was quite simply to serve God, to save what souls they could by constant prayer. At that time, not very long after the great war, the world was in chaos. Schwartzhof was not the happy village you see now. It was, my son, a resort for the sinful, a hive of vice and corruption, a pit for the unwary—and the wary also, if they had not strength. A Godless place! Forsaken, fornicators paraded the streets. Gambling was done. Robbery and murder, drunkenness, and evils so profound I cannot put them into words. In all the universe you could not have found a fouler pesthole, Mr. Ellington! The Abbots and the Brothers at St. Wulfran's succumbed for years to Schwartzhof, I regret to say. Good men, lovers of God, chaste good men came here and fought but could not win against the black temptations. Finally it was decided that the Abbey should be closed. I heard of this and argued. 'Is that not surrender?' I said. 'Are we to bow before the strength of evil? Let me try, I beg you. Let me try to amplify the word of God that all in Schwartzhof shall hear and see their dark transgressions and repent!"

The old man stood at the window, a trembling shade. His hands were now clutched together in a fervency of remembrance. "They asked," he said, "if I considered myself more virtuous than my predecessors that I should hope for success where they had failed. I answered that I did not, but that I had an advantage. I was a convert. Earlier I had walked with evil, and knew its face. My wish was granted. For a year. One year only. Rejoicing, Mr. Ellington, I came here; and one night, incognito, walked the streets of the village. The smell of evil was strong. Too strong, I thought—and I had reveled in the alleys of Morocco, I had seen the dens of Hong Kong, Paris, Spain. The orgies were too wild, the drunkards much too drunk, the profanities a great deal too profane. It was as if the evil of the world had been distilled and centered here, as if a pagan tribal chief, in hiding, had assembled all his rituals about him . . ." The Abbot nodded his head. "I thought of Rome, in her last days; of Byzantium; of—Eden. That was the first of many hints to come. No matter what they were. I returned to the Abbey and donned my holy robes and went back into Schwartzhof. I made myself conspicuous. Some jeered, some shrank away, a voice cried, 'Damn your foolish God!' And then a hand thrust out from darkness, touched my shoulder, and I heard: 'Now, Father, are you lost?' "

The Abbot brought his tightly clenched hands to his forehead.

"Mr. Ellington, I have some poor wine here. Please have some."

I drank, gratefully. Then the priest continued.

"I faced a man of average appearance. So average, indeed, that I felt I knew, then. 'No,' I told him, 'but you are lost!' He laughed a foul laugh. 'Are we not all, Father?' Then he said a most peculiar thing. He said his wife was dying and begged me to give her Extreme Unction. 'Please,' he said, 'in God's sweet name!' I was confused. We hurried to his house. A woman lay upon a bed, her body nude. 'It is a different Extreme Unction that I have in mind,' he whispered, laughing. 'It's the only kind, dear Father, that she understands. No other will have her! Pity! Pity on the poor soul lying there in all her suffering. Give her your Sceptre!' And the woman's arms came snaking, supplicating toward me, round and sensuous and hot . . ."

Father Jerome shuddered and paused. The shrieks, I thought, were growing louder from the hall. "Enough of that," he said. "I was quite sure then. I raised my cross and told the words I'd learned, and it was over. He screamed—as he's doing now—and fell upon his knees. He had not expected to be recognized, nor should he have been normally. But in my life, I'd seen him many times, in many guises. I brought him to the Abbey. I locked him in the cell. We chant his chains each day. And so, my son, you see why you must not speak of the things you've seen and heard?"

I shook my head, as if afraid the dream would end, as if reality would suddenly explode upon me. "Father Jerome." I said, "I haven't the vaguest idea of what you're talking about. Who is the man?"

"Are you such a fool, Mr. Ellington? That you must be told?"

"Yes!"

"Very well," said the Abbot. "He is Satan. Otherwise known as the Dark Angel, Asmodeus, Belial, Ahriman, Diabolus—the Devil."

I opened my mouth.

"I see you doubt me. That is bad. Think, Mr. Ellington, of the peace of the world in these five years. Of the prosperity, of the happiness. Think of this country, Germany, now. Is there another country like it? Since we caught the Devil and locked him up here, there have been no great wars, no overwhelming pestilences: only the sufferings man was meant to endure. Believe what I say, my son; I beg you. Try very hard to believe that the creature you spoke with is Satan himself. Fight your cynicism, for it is born of him; he is the father of cynicism, Mr. Ellington! His plan was to defeat God by implanting doubt in the minds of Heaven's subjects!" The Abbot cleared his throat. "Of course," he said, "we could never release anyone from St. Wulfran's who had any part of the Devil in him."

I stared at the old fanatic and thought of him prowling the streets, looking for sin; saw him standing outraged at the bold fornicator's bed, wheedling him into an invitation to the Abbey, closing that heavy door and locking it, and because of the world's temporary postwar peace, clinging to his fantasy. What greater dream for a holy man than actually capturing the Devil!

"I believe you," I said.

"Truly?"

"Yes. I hesitated only because it seemed a trifle odd that Satan should have picked a little German village for his home."

"He moves around," the Abbot said. "Schwartzhof attracted him as lovely virgins attract perverts."

"I see."

"Do you? My son, do you?"

"Yes. I swear it. As a matter of fact, I thought he looked familiar, but I simply couldn't place him."

"Are you lying?"

"Father, I am a Bostonian."

"And you promise not to mention this to anyone?"

"I promise."

"Very well." The old man sighed. "I suppose," he said, "that you would not consider joining us as a Brother at the Abbey?"

"Believe me, Father, no one could admire the vocation more than I. But I am not worthy. No; it's quite out of the question. However, you have my word that your secret is safe with me."

He was very tired. Sound had, in these years, reversed for him: the screams had become silence, the sudden cessation of them, noise. The prisoner's quiet talk with me had awakened him from deep slumber. Now he nodded wearily, and I saw that what I had to do would not be difficult after all. Indeed, no more difficult than fetching the authorities.

I walked back to my cell, where Brother Christophorus still slept, and lay down. Two hours passed. I rose again and returned to the Abbot's quarters.

The door was closed but unlocked.

I eased it open, timing the creaks of the hinges with the screams of the prisoner. I tiptoed in. Father Jerome lay snoring in his bed.

Slowly, cautiously, I lifted out the leather thong, and was a bit astounded at my technique. No Ellington had ever burgled. Yet a force, not like experience, but like it, ruled my fingers. I found the knot. I worked it loose.

The warm iron key slid off into my hand.

The Abbot stirred, then settled, and I made my way into the hall.

The prisoner, when he saw me, rushed the bars. "He's told you lies, I'm sure of that!" he whispered hoarsely. "Disregard the filthy madman!"

"Don't stop screaming," I said.

"What?" He saw the key and nodded, then, and made his awful sounds. I thought at first the lock had rusted, but I worked the metal slowly and in time the key turned over.

Howling still, in a most dreadful way, the man stepped out into the corridor. I felt a momentary fright as his clawed hand reached up and touched my shoulder; but it passed. "Come on!" We ran insanely to the outer door, across the frosted ground, down toward the village.

The night was very black.

A terrible aching came into my legs. My throat went dry. I thought my heart would tear loose from its moorings. But I ran on.

"Wait."

Now the heat began.

"Wait."

By a row of shops I fell. My chest was full of pain, my head of fear: I knew the madmen would come swooping from their dark asylum on the hill. I cried out to the naked hairy man: "Stop! Help me!"

"Help you?" He laughed once, a high-pitched sound more awful than the screams had been; and then he turned and vanished in the moonless night.

I found a door, somehow.

The pounding brought a rifled burgher. Policemen came at last and listened to my story. But of course it was denied by Father Jerome and the Brothers of the Abbey.

"This poor traveler has suffered from the visions of pneumonia. There was no howling man at St. Wulfran's. No, no, certainly not. Absurd! Now, if Mr. Ellington would care to stay with us, we'd happily—no? Very well. I fear that you will be delirious a while, my son. The things you see will be quite real. Most real. You'll think—

how quaint!—that you have loosed the Devil on the world and that the war to come—what war? But aren't there always wars? Of course!—you'll think that it's your fault"—those old eyes burning condemnation! Beak-nosed, bearded head atremble, rage in every word!—"that you'll have caused the misery and suffering and death. And nights you'll spend, awake, unsure, afraid. How foolish!"

Gnome of God, Christophorus, looked terrified and sad. He said to me, when Father Jerome swept furiously out: "My son, don't blame yourself. Your weakness was *his* lever. Doubt unlocked that door. Be comforted: we'll hunt *him* with our nets, and one day . . ."

One day, what?

I looked up at the Abbey of St. Wulfran's, framed by dawn, and started wondering, as I have wondered since ten thousand times, if it weren't true. Pneumonia breeds delirium; delirium breeds visions. Was it possible that I'd imagined all of this?

No. Not even back in Boston, growing dewlaps, paunches, wrinkles, sacks and money, at Ellington, Carruthers & Blake, could I accept that answer.

The monks were mad, I thought. Or: The howling man was mad. Or: The whole thing was a joke.

I went about my daily work, as every man must do, if sane, although he may have seen the dead rise up or freed a bottled djinn or fought a dragon, once, quite long ago.

But I could not forget. When the pictures of the carpenter from Braunau-am-Inn began to appear in all the papers, I grew uneasy; for I felt I'd seen this man before. When the carpenter invaded Poland, I was sure. And when the world was plunged into war and cities had their entrails blown asunder and that pleasant land I'd visited became a place of hate and death, I dreamed each night.

Each night I dreamed, until this week.

A card arrived. From Germany. A picture of the Moselle Valley is on one side, showing mountains fat with grapes and the dark Moselle, wine of these grapes.

On the other side of the card is a message. It is signed *"Brother Christophorus"* and reads (and reads and reads!):

*"Rest now, my son. We have him back with us again."*

After the fall of France in 1940, England's position was truly desperate. Under no circumstances could Great Britain alone ever defeat Germany, a power which had shown itself as strong as all the other European states combined, and the most likely prospect was defeat after terrible losses. Many of the former appeasers in the British government were ready to do a deal; the intellectuals (see, for example, the sardonic quotes in the war diaries of George Orwell) were in a funk. Churchill's oratory was magnificent, but speeches alone did not rally the population. There is some merit in the French complaint that the English were simply too stupidly irrational to know they were beaten. They were also the heirs of an unbroken tradition of victory stretching back 900 years, in which "England always lost every battle but the last." Many invasions had threatened, but the Channel's guardians had always prevailed . . .

# "Take My Drum To England..."

## Nelson S. Bond

*"Take my drum to England, hang et by the shore,*
*Strike et when your powder's runnin' low . . ."*

It wasn't so much the retreating that got Thompson. That was bad enough. But leaving the heavy ordnance; that was what griped his guts. Even grenaded tanks, damaged cannon, stripped caissons and lorries were valuable booty to the steel-starved Jerries; they would melt down what weapons they could not repair, recast them, and one day use English arms to war on English people.

But it was unavoidable, just as this dogged retreat was unavoidable. The collapse of the Belgian left wing gave the trapped B.E.F. bitter alternatives: flight or surrender . . . and they had already had a bellyful of the second in Leopold's sudden, devastating capitulation.

Thompson trudged on. Above him high shells screamed and whined, unseen behind the slow, dripping pall of a gray mist and the blacker smudge from a hundred unfought fires now tightening like an eager, crimson

claw about Dunkerque. Overhead the roar of airplane
motors merged in thudding cacophony with the bite
and chatter of machine guns; pompoms fretted raggedly
from the shelter of emplacements about him. There was
no moment of silence, no rest for ears beaten sicken-
ingly acute by an interminable torrent of sound.

How long his world had been like this Thompson no
longer knew. Days . . . weeks . . . he could not remember. He had not slept for centuries; had not shaved
or washed in an aeon. There had been no canteen since
the battle began; he had long since eaten the last of his
emergency rations.

Yet one supply line had been maintained. In spite of
everything, an inexhaustible stream of ammunition fought
its way up from behind to feed hot, hungry guns. The
Nazis were paying in human coinage, Thompson thought
grimly, for every inch of terrain reluctantly granted by
the British. He had seen with his own eyes the havoc
created amongst fast, tiny advance tanks by Allied artillery, had seen decimated foray parties consolidate new
gains behind gray-green breastworks that still bled.
Yet they still advanced. And now . . .

And now there was a messenger wrenching to a stop
beside the barbed nest which was Thompson's post.
Waving, motioning, shouting words half indistinguish-
able to tumult-deafened ears.

The word "beach" was distinct, and that made the
entire message clear. It meant that Thompson now left
the ranks of those dwindling few who under cover of an
incessant barrage from the navy guns maintained a de-
fensive rear-guard action for their retreating comrades,
and became himself one of those who fled.

Others about him were rising from strategic covers;
from doorways, from rude barricades and shelters fil-
tered a slow stream of weary troops. Thompson knew a
vague wonder that this formless battalion should yet
uphold order in its forced withdrawal. Wonder and
strengthening pride. In this company were soldiers of a
dozen divisions, many leaderless, yet there was little
confusion and no panic. Blue, gray and khaki uniforms

formed one ordered column headed by officers who gave commands in different tongues.

They were no longer Britons or Frenchmen, Dutch or Norwegians. They were Allied soldiers, fighting in an allied cause.

Thompson found a place in the column. Overhead the sky droned with the hum of invisible motors; the coughing of cannon from the nearby shore was like the thunder of massive waves. Not all the defenders fell in. A skeleton force remained to cover this last retreat. They stuck to their posts with full knowledge of what must follow. One of these found Thompson's eye upon him, parted his stubbled lips in a grin, and gestured with closed fist, thumb stiffly erect.

Thompson answered the gesture in kind.

"Thumbs up!"

Then a command, and the motley column shrugged into motion . . .

The men on the front defense line had not been kept in ignorance as to their purpose. Word had sifted to them of the miracle transpiring on Dunkerque beach. But somehow the legend of that mass embarkation had seemed to Thompson a far implausibility until he saw it with his own eyes.

The city of Dunkerque was a smoking ruin. Thompson found no reminder in this shell-warped town of the Dunkerque he had once visited in the happy days before Warsaw. Rosendaël was a suburb peopled with ghosts who peered from behind shuttered windows, ghosts of women and children and aged men wakened from hiding by the dry *sough-sough* of marching feet.

The once wide, well-paved streets were crater-pocked where bombs had dropped and mountainous with crumbled debris where shells had found a mark. Unchecked fires had withered whole rows of deeprooted homes. In the Place Jean Bart the statue of David d'Angers stared fiercely, defiantly, out upon a vista of chaos. The belfry of St. Eloi was fallen, and one priceless cornice of the chapel of Notre Dame des Dunes, bomb-struck, had sheered away, exposing the sacred shrine . . . anomalously chaste and quiet in the murderous heat of battle.

But it was not these sights that quickened Thompson to new life. This was war; this was war's normal, wasteful toll. It was his first sight of the sea that wakened in his throat an echo of the murmur that swelled through the column of marching men.

The sea . . . and the fleet!

Short months ago this had been a brave harbor with docks and quays beside which great ships might make mooring. Now it had felt the force of the Nazi air armada. Its docks were ribbons of shredded timber, its miles-long quays broken and bent as if crumpled in a giant fist. The harbor channel bristled with the shards of sunken craft; not the most agile merchantman could thread that unnatural shoal to take aboard a human cargo.

And yet the evacuation was taking place.

From north and south and east, from St. Pol-sur-Mer and blazing Malo-les-Bains, from the canal banks and the low hills, came the retreating columns. Not in confusion nor in rank disorder, but in smooth, accomplished withdrawal, their lines converging on the open beach.

There, sheltered by rolling dunes to the northward, the column marched out into the waiting sea. Their line was a gigantic S writhing through the shallows to where in the gray distance a galaxy of craft stood by to take them on.

To north and south, so far as the eye could see, in two unyielding lines stood the warships of the fleet: grim, gaunt bulldogs of the sea, now welded prow to stern. And on each fighting vessel the guns had been so faced as to form a corridor between the rows. Skyward boomed the cannon; their ceaseless bombardment wove an arch of raking crossfire through which not even a gull might fly.

And in the broad avenue of safety thus created rescue vessels plied tirelessly back and forth, on each trip scooping another handful of the human flotsam that breasted the gray sea.

Beside Thompson someone murmured. It was young Owens who—or so Thompson had heard—was a poet of sorts. A sort of second Brooke, perhaps, though he didn't much look the part now, what with a weeks' growth of beard and that filthy bandage about his head.

"And they said the spirit of Nelson was dead," said Owens. "The spirit of Nelson and Drake—"

Then there was no time for reply, for the order was still forward. The sand gritted beneath Thompson's boots, the water was icy cold about his ankles and calves and thighs.

When his brain was so benumbed that it quite forgot the cold, when he could no longer remember why or how he had come here, or any world other than this breast-high grave of water into which, forward, he endlessly wallowed, Thompson's eyes lent him a sudden, startling knowledge. He had reached the tip of the sea-groping column. Somehow, few by few, the men in the queue before him had melted into the bee-swarm of yachts, dories, skiffs, shuttling back and forth beneath the curtain of gunfire. Soon, now, it would be his turn.

The realization was a shock stirring Thompson into his first considered action for hours. He turned and looked back at the falling city, saw that the thick, black, greasy smoke was now a solid wall about Dunkerque, and that an ever-narrowing band of flame tightened about the town, spiraling scarlet fingers into the creeping dusk.

The sea, which had been leaden-gray, was now a dull jet-purple, and the black night sky pressed heavily upon the lingering line of horizon daylight. The coughing naval guns spat salvos of orange flame; black hulks loomed suddenly in brief relief, were swallowed in instant darkness; rain began to fall, its freshness warm and sweet upon Thompson's salty, blue-cold lips.

The last thin lines of light snuffed out, and it was starless night.

For the first time a sort of panic swept over him. A lost, cold, lonely terror. Muted flashes dotted the water before him, behind him a voice moaned softly, and once there was a muffled splashing of oars at his side though his straining eyes saw nothing. He cried aloud, his voice strange and harsh to his ears.

"Here!"

Then a hand groping at his arm, a familiar voice.

"Thompson? That you, old boy?"

It was Owens. His nearness, the commonplace sanity of his question, calmed Thompson. It was so weird and silly and brave, so altogether damned British. For the emotion he showed they might have met at Piccadilly, not breast-deep in water where Dunkerque basin joined the choppy Channel rip.

"Right," said Thompson. "Damned cold, eh?"

"Filthy. We're almost out, though. Thumbs up!"

"Thumbs up!" said Thompson.

It was as if their voices were a beacon in the dark emptiness. Something brushed Thompson's shoulder, a grating oarlock whimpered, a dim flashbeam dazzled him momentarily, and warm, strong hands were beneath his armpits.

" 'Ere you are, mitey! A little 'oist does it. Up you come, now!"

After the swaying sea, the dory's boards were hard and firm and wonderful. He lay there panting heavily, not hearing the whispers about him nor feeling the bitter cold, the damp, bruising crush of other bodies clambering aboard. He hardly knew when the little boat, so laden that its gunwales cupped the breakers, heeled slowly on the last leg to safety.

He only knew the journey took long, the rowers were making heavy weather of their task. The dory wallowed in the trough, gulping water with each forward surge. More than thirty souls crammed space planned for a score. There was barely room for the oarsmen to pull. Men began bailing with pans and trench helmets and cupped hands, but the rain and washing breakers laughed at their efforts. Slowly but inevitably the dory dipped deeper, heavier.

And the fleet too far away to help. Thompson felt a slow sense of despair creeping over him. This had been a losing fight from the beginning. Dunkerque had been a lost cause, the mass evacuation a madman's dream. Even the gods of sun and sky pledged the swastika banner; even the god of the sea, whose realm had been Britain's pride for more than four centuries. Still he bailed; he did not know his hands were cracked and cold and bleeding.

The thunder of the guns rolled tumultuously. Once a great, winged bird of prey burst into flame high above them, flashed like a meteor into the stifling caldron of the sea, hissing in stricken agony. Far across the water a sailboat limned its brief red outline against the sky, spewing black motes into the water about it.

Still he bailed.

And then suddenly there was no longer need of his efforts. A last great breaker welled over the dory's prow. A score of voices lifted as one; the small boat trembled and rolled. Struggling bodies returned to the waters from which they had been taken . . . but this time there was no sand bottom on which to stand. Strange hands clutched at Thompson as if he were a buoy. He broke free, struck out for the far safety of the fleet, not hoping to make his goal. Choking for air, he gulped a lungful of water; he strangled and spat. Salt was bitter in his throat.

He felt himself sinking, and a strange lethargy was upon him. He found himself wondering if this were to be the end, if thus he were to escape the Dunkerque shambles? Once more he fought his way to the surface, essayed a few feeble strokes. There was a maddening, dull throbbing in his ears like the distant roll of summer thunder . . . or the rumbling of a far and ancient drum . . .

Then the miracle was complete, for once again there was a ship beside him. Only this time it was a tiny

sailing vessel. Its longboats were down, its sailors haul-
ing in the survivors of Thompson's sunken dory. The
refugees at last had found a haven.

What happened in the next little while was confused
and uncertain. There were great, rough blankets around
him, cutting the chill from aching bones; there was
grog, hot and fragrant in huge pewter mugs. Then
escape from the sea, the rain and the night into a bunk
room below decks, a wee cabin ill-lighted by a greasecup
lamp with floating wick.

Thompson slumped into a bunk. He must have
dropped asleep then, for when a hand shook him some
time later the concussive bellow of cannon fire had
faded into a dull, soft silence broken only by the groan
of straining planks and the shatter of waves on ancient,
sturdy wood.

It was Owens who had wakened him. An Owens no
longer grimy and bearded, but fresh and clean and
eager. The bandage was gone from his head, and his
voice was tense with excitement.

"How can you sleep at a time like this, old fellow?
Come on deck and watch. It's marvelous! Just like that
old poem of Newbolt's—remember?" His eyes shone;
he quoted:

"Yarnder lumes the island, yarnder lie the ships,
  Wi' sailor lads a-dancin' heel an' toe,
  An' the shore lights flashin', an' the night tide dashin'—"

They went up; Owens leading, Thompson following.
It was still black night when they reached the rail, but
it had stopped raining. The great, near stars of early
summer laid a frost of faint unearthly silver on the ship.
The port of Dover was a rising smudge marked by the
dimmest of beacons. And from the mainland Thompson
heard, as before, a dull and drumlike rolling.

About him, wraithlike in the gloom, huddled the
men who had been his companions at Dunkerque and
in the dory. A silence was upon them as they watched
the shore loom nearer. Somewhere abaft a slow winch

moaned; ghost figures in rolled pantaloons labored at
tasks unfathomable.

From somewhere high in the rigging came the warning cry of the lookout. A deep voice bellowed answer in
a sturdy Devon accent. Wood screeled on wood, sheets
flapped and wove and bellied again to the wind.

Thompson said shakenly, "We're safe, Owens. It's a
miracle. I never expected to see England again."

"He promised," said Owens softly, incomprehensi-
bly. "He said he would be waiting 'till the great Arma-
das come.'" He lifted his face to the stars. "Hear his
drum? There was need of him, the waiting drum was
struck, and he has come . . . as he said he would.
Remember, Thompson? He said:

"Take my drum to England, hang et by the shore.
 Strike et when your powder's runnin' low;
 If the foe sights Devon, I'll quit the port o' Heaven,
 An' drum them up the Channel as we drummed
    them long ago—"

"*Who* said?" demanded Thompson. "What are you
talking about? I don't understand—"

Then suddenly there were footsteps approaching
him, the firm, crisp grate of leather on salt-encrusted
boards, and a Devon voice, friendly but regretful in
his ears.

"There has been a mistake here, soldier lad. Ye ha'
no place aboard this ship. The shore is tha place, with
tha fellows."

And how it happened Thompson did not rightly know,
but of a sudden there was no longer strong planking
beneath his feet; there was instead once more the salt
and wet and frightful cold of churning Channel waters.
He cried out fearfully, and glimpsed for an instant the
white, startled face of Owens leaning over the rail above
him.

Beside Owens stood another figure, that of the captain of the sailing vessel. His cheeks were lean and
strong and bearded, and his eyes were filled with a

great pity, but with a great power, too. And he called a
message to Thompson, his clarion words half drowned
in the rolling crescendo of drums from the nearby shore.

"Tell England to be o' good cheer!" he cried. "Tell
England all will yet be well wi' her!"

Then he raised an arm in salute. The ship splashed
into the belly of a black-green trough, heeling about.
For an instant cold starlight glinted on its stern . . .
then the vessel and captain and crew alike were gone.

Thompson's flailing arm met and clung to a drifting
solid, and life was a flaming spark within his frozen
body. His strident cry lifted again and yet again. The
probing finger of a searchlight sought and found him . . .

When they had parted his cold, blue lips and forced
hot brandy between his locked teeth, Thompson tried
to give them his message. His voice was like the grating
of a blade on paper as he gasped the words.

"All will be well . . . with England."

The young doctor, red-eyed with fatigue, nodded and
motioned him to silence.

"That's right, soldier. Now rest a while." To his companion he murmured, "Keep him in hot blankets. He's
that far from pneumonia. He must have caught it bad."

"Rotten bad. Floated in on an overturned dory, the
only one of his boatload who made it. Hours in the
Channel, poor devil."

"The drums—" said Thompson.

"Of course, soldier. Try to sleep now." The man in
white shook his head. "Exposure. Cold. Surf beating in
his ears for hours. No wonder he hears drums."

Thompson stirred fretfully. His mind was beclouded
by alternate tempests of heat and cold that swelled over
him in fierce, devastating waves; the voices of his friends
were lost in thin, singing distances. And it angered him
that he could not seem to make them understand.

He wanted rest. But he could not rest until he had
told them of the boat that brought him here. He had to
make them understand about the boat and its captain.
He must let them know the drum had not been struck
in vain . . . that he had seen the sternplate of that

vessel as it vanished Channelward, and that the legend
gilded there had spelled *Golden Hynde* . . .

He tried again to bear the message given him.

" 'Tell England to be of good cheer,' he said. 'All will
be well with her,' *he* said."

"*Who* said, soldier?"

"It was . . . Drake. Sir Francis Drake. He has come
back . . . as he promised he would."

"Fever," said the young doctor, and laid a cool hand
on Thompson's forehead. "He's delirious, poor devil.
Keep him well covered . . ."

Fighting men have always tended to personalize their machines: witness the innumerable bombers with painted mascots. Ships have been more prone to this than most, since they are named as a matter of course. Many of the split-second decisions taken in combat are rationally unjustifiable, the products of the subconscious, of hunches and intuition. Projecting them on the equipment serves the same function as the dowsers' divining rod, giving an objective source for a prompting it might be uncomfortable to admit was simply welling up from the depths of the psyche. In World War Two, the involvement of the merchant marine—a front-line service in a war fought on the whole surface of a globe that is 75% water—made merchantmen as suitable for this treatment as warships had always been. The story-tellers found ways to put this dangerous but rather undramatic service in the formulae demanded by traditional heroics.

# VENGEANCE IN HER BONES

## Malcolm Jameson

The messenger from the Navy recruiting office found
old Captain Tolliver in his backyard. The crabby, sour-
visaged housekeeper took him as far as the hedge back
of the house and pointed the retired mariner out to
him. Captain Tolliver was reclining in a ragged canvas
deckchair taking the sun. He had on faded dungarees,
soft and pliant as linen from hundreds of scrubbings,
and the stump of his handless left arm rested carelessly
on his lap. The peg leg that matched it lay in alignment
with the one good leg. The captain had his eyes closed,
comfortably drinking in the sun's good heat, when he
heard the crunch of the messenger's step on the gravel
walk that separated the vegetable from the flower beds.
The old skipper's hearing was still alert, though, and
at the sound he raised his lids and looked inquiringly at
the newcomer.

"Commander Jason's compliments, sir," said the blue-
jacket, "and would you please step down to the office.
He has a ship for you."

Captain Tolliver smiled feebly, then he closed his

eyes against the glare. His eyes were not overstrong these days—the doctors had said something about incipient cataracts.

"Commander Jason is confusing me with my son. He already has a ship, working out of West Coast ports. My sea-going days are over. Forever."

To emphasize his point he waved the stump of his left arm, and lifted the peg leg slightly.

"No, sir. It's you he wants. He was very clear about that. He has a ship that only you can command. She's a rogue. They say she will obey no other skipper. He says they have waived your physical defects and will give you all the help you need. But they've got to have you."

The captain shook his head.

"He's wrong, I say. There is no such a ship. There was one once, but she rotted her life away in the back channel. They sold her finally to a wrecking company and broke her up for scrap. All I have to say to that is whoever bought that scrap had better have a care as to how they use it. For she was a vindictive wench. The *Sadie Saxon* bore grudges and would have her way no matter what you did. . . ."

"Yes, sir," said the messenger, eagerly, "that's the ship—the *Sadie Saxon*—a cargo type vessel! They've put her back in commission but she won't leave port. They need ships now that America is at war. Every ship. That's why they need you. The commander says please come. If you want, he'll send an ambulance."

"The *Sadie Saxon*," whispered the old captain, suddenly rapt with nostalgia for World War days when he and she were in their prime.

Then aloud, "He needn't bother about the ambulance. I can get there under my own power, son. Give me a hand so I can get up and go dress. The old uniform still fits, thank God."

Captain Tolliver's senility seemed to drop from him as a cloak the moment the well-worn blue garments were back on his lean frame. He looked a little ruefully at the tarnished gold lace on the sleeves and at the cap

device the years had tinted with green mold, but nevertheless he brushed the uniform carefully, squared his
shoulders, and marched down the steps without avail-
ing himself of the sailor's proffered arm.

"So they didn't break her up after all?" said the
captain, as they waited at the curb in the hope a
cruising taxi would come by. "How come? I know she
was sold."

"Too expensive. She was part of a contract for scrap
to be sent to the Japs some months ago, but they only
worked three days on her. She killed nine men the first
day they brought their cutting torches aboard, all of
them in different ways. One of her booms crashed
down the second day and smashed five others. On the
third day seven suffocated in a hold, and two slipped
and fell overboard. The men said she was jinxed and
threatened to call a strike. So they put a tug alongside
and hauled her back to her old berth."

Captain Tolliver chuckled.

"For the Japs, huh? She knew it even before they
attacked Pearl Harbor, but I might have told 'em. But
what's this about her *refusing* to leave port. Doesn't
that sound a little silly to you?"

His faded old eyes twinkled when he asked the question. It was one that did sound silly, when a person
came to think about it. Yet he knew it was not silly and
one an experienced sailorman would answer as seriously as he could.

"There's no other word for it, sir," replied the blue-
jacket, soberly. "She was refitted at Newport News,
given a crew and loaded with cargo. They took her out
to make a voyage to Spanish Morocco, loaded with
grain and automobile tires. But she wouldn't pass the
Thimble. Her rudder jammed and she piled up hard,
and at high tide, too. It took four days to pull her off.
They took her back to the yard and looked her steering
gear over. It was okay. So they started her out again.
That time she sheered out to the other side and grounded
near Willoughby Spit. The third time they tried to take
her out, she piled up in the dredged channel and

blocked all shipping for hours. The yard still insisted there was nothing wrong with her steering gear and suspected sabotage—"

"I know," said the captain. "They didn't find any evidence of it."

"That's right. They gave her crew a clean bill of health and ordered to sea once more. She won't budge. She had steam up and stood a good dock trial, but once she was out in the stream her propellers quit turning over—"

"With full throttle, of course," remarked Captain Tolliver calmly.

"Yes, sir. With full pressure in the boilers and throttle wide open. All she would do was drift until she banged into a dock.

"The tugs got hold of her and tied her up again. The engineers swear her engines are all right and there is no reason why she won't run. She just won't—that's all."

A taxi rounded the corner and caught the sailor's hail. As it slid to a stop before them the captain made one final remark.

"I see. They looked up her record and found she was always that way. Except when I had command of her. Well, I know what is on that little tub's mind and what to do about it. It won't be orthodox, but if they want her in service it is the only way."

"What's that, sir."

"Give her her head," said the old man cryptically, then stiffly climbed into the cab.

It was a week later that Captain Tolliver arrived at Norfolk Navy Yard. An aide of the admiral in charge of transport took him to the dock where she lay. She looked spick and span and new and a painter's stage swung under her bow, and was to play her part in keeping supplies going Eastward in spite of havoc to the West. Tolliver climbed up onto it with some difficulty and patted one of the shiny plates of her nose.

"Up to your old tricks, eh, Sadie?" the astonished

aide heard him say. "Well, everything's going to be all right now. We'll go hunting together."

Was it the wash of a passing tug that caused her to bob suddenly up and down that way? The aide shrugged his shoulders and was glad he was in the regular outfit. He would hate to have to go to sea through the war zone on a rogue ship under the command of a decrepit and senile madman of a skipper.

"I am ready to take over," announced Tolliver when he was back on the dock, "whenever those three men whose names I gave you have been replaced by others more acceptable."

"Acceptable to whom, sir? I repeat that they are loyal American citizens despite their German ancestry. They have been investigated fully."

"Acceptable to me as representative of the ship," answered the captain with all his old dignity. "When they are off we sail. Not before. Perhaps it is prejudice— Sadie's funny that way—perhaps your investigation was not as comprehensive as you think. That's your problem."

The aide laughed. The old lunatic, he thought, but I'm stuck I guess. They said give him anything he asked for.

"Very well, sir," was what he said out loud.

Captain Tolliver waited patiently beside the bow until the last of the three scowling men had come down it laden with their bags and dunnage. Then he mounted to the deck and went straightway to the bridge. His hand reached for the whistle pull. A long, triumphant scream of a blast split the air.

"Stand by your lines," bellowed the old man through a megaphone, "and tell the tug never mind. We won't need her."

Two hours later the *Sadie Saxon* swept through the dredged channel, picked up and passed the entrance buoy to the bay. Throbbing with the vibration of her churning screws and rising and falling to the heavy swell outside, she shook herself joyfully at the smell and feel of the open sea. Cape Henry and Cape Charles Lights soon faded behind. The captain set a course for

Bermuda, for the ship's orders had been changed. After the long delay in setting out the situation was different. She was to rendezvous with a Gibraltar bound convoy at the island.

Mate Parker came up to take the watch. It was a cloudy, dark night and the ship was running without lights.

"Keep a sharp lookout," warned the captain, "and handle things yourself. I don't want to be called unless something extraordinary occurs."

"Aye, sir," acknowledged the mate surlily. By rights he should be the skipper of this cranky tub—not this doddering old fool.

The captain got down the ladder the best way he could and groped along the darkened decks until he came to the door of his room. He did not undress at all but lay down in his bunk as he was. The *Sadie Saxon* could be counted on to do the unexpected at any time. He closed his eyes wearily, for the excitement of the day had taxed his strength to the utmost. In a moment he was fast asleep.

It must have been well after midnight when he was roused from his deep slumber. Mr. Parker was standing over him with a look of concern on his face.

"She's gone crazy again, sir," he reported, "and we can't do a thing with her—"

"Don't try," directed the captain. "What she doing?"

"Turned sharp to the left about fifteen minutes ago and is turning up about twelve revolutions more than her proper speed. The helmsman can't do anything about it. Neither can the engineer. She won't obey her wheel or throttle. What do we do—fold up and call it a day?"

Captain Tolliver sat up in his bunk.

"Oh, no. By no means. You'll be awfully busy shortly. Turn out all hands at once. Man your lifeboats and have them ready for lowering. Shut all water-tight doors below and see that there is plenty of shoring handy in case the peak gets stove in. Have the collision mat ready. That's all."

"But the steering?"

"Just let the wheel go. She'll steer herself. She knows where she wants to go. I don't."

The mate left and the old man dragged himself to his mismated feet and began the laborious journey to the bridge. Once he was up there he made sure that the searchlight was ready to turn on in case he needed it. After that he could only wait.

The wait was not long. Fifteen minutes later there was a shock, a grinding, bumping of something under the fore-foot and along the keel. The ship's engines stopped abruptly, then began backing. Captain Tolliver reached for the engine room telegraph and rang it to "Stop."

The ship stopped.

"Collision forward!" shouted the lookout in the bow. "We just ran down a small ship of some sort."

Tolliver could hear the boatswain and his gang dropping into the fore hold to see whether the damage was serious. Then he spoke quietly to the mate who was on the bridge beside him.

"You may put your boats in the water now, Mister. I have a hunch we just ran down a Nazi sub. I'll put on the light as soon as you are lowered."

The mate left on the run, more mystified than ever. A man came up from forward and reported the peak was full up to the waterline but the bulkhead abaft it was holding and the ship seemed to be in no danger.

"Turn on that searchlight," ordered Captain Tolliver, "and sweep aft."

There was a chorus of gasps as the light stabbed out into the murk and almost instantly lit on a large black object rearing up above the waves. It was the bow of a submarine, and even as they sighted it it slid backwards into the deep. But in that brief glimpse they saw several men plunge overboard, and as the light swept to right and left the bobbing heads of a dozen or more men could be seen in the water.

"Pick up those men and be smart about it," yelled

Tolliver through his megaphones to the boats. Then he watched as they dragged the survivors into the boats and rowed back to the ship. He watched as they hoisted the boats in and housed them at their davits.

"Put those men under guard," he directed, "and get back on your course. Things will be all right now." And with that he went below to pick up his night's sleep where he had left off.

The arrival of the *Sadie Saxon* at Bermuda caused quite a stir. Many were the congratulations upon the ship's luck in blundering across a U-boat and ramming it in the dark. The two officers and eleven men rescued from the crash were most welcome to the British Intelligence officers. Hasty arrangements were made for quick repairs to the ship's damaged bow. She had missed the convoy for which she was intended, but there would be other convoys and the little delay was well paid for by the bag of the undersea wolf. Captain Tolliver took his praise modestly.

"It's not all luck," he said. "It is a habit of the *Sadie Saxon*. If you will look up her record in the last war you will see she has done that sort of thing before."

By the time the ship was ready for sea again the hubbub had died down. Captain Tolliver took the position assigned him with entire calm and confidence. It was a big convoy and made up three columns of ships. The *Sadie Saxon* was given the post of danger and honor as the lead ship of the right-hand column. But destroyers frolicked about ahead and on the flanks. It would be costly for any submarine to tackle that well-guarded flotilla.

For three nights they went eastward, steaming without lights and in formation. There was no alarm other than the appearance overhead one day of a trio of scout bombers marked with the black and white crosses of Germany. The anti-aircraft guns of the escorting warships kept them at too great a height to do any damage, and so drove them away. But after their appearance old Captain Tolliver knew anything might happen. The *Sadie*

*Saxon* had behaved most peculiarly all the while they were in sight, vibrating almost as if she had dropped a screw.

"Steady, old girl," whispered the skipper into the binnacle, "you'll have to get used to those. They're an innovation."

It was the night after that that the big attack occurred. The long triple column of ships was plowing along through a dark and misty night and thirty officers on as many bridges were staring anxiously into the murk striving not to loose sight of the tiny blue stern light of the ship ahead. Under the circumstances mutual collision was much more likely than a hostile attack. The orders were strict—maintain radio silence at all costs, never show a light under any circumstances, and above all, keep station.

But the *Sadie Saxon* cared next to nothing about commodore's orders. At ten minutes past four in the morning she balked, her engines churning violently at full speed astern, to the consternation of the black gang who had had no bells to that effect and were caught off guard. Captain Tolliver was on the bridge when it happened and called sharply to the forward lookouts:

"Look sharply close aboard! What do you see?"

The ship was turning rapidly to starboard, her rudder jammed hard over, while the helmsman strove wildly to bring the wheel back the other way.

"The wakes of two torpedoes, sir—no, four—five—nine! Coming from starboard, sir."

The streaks of phosphorescent light were visible now from the bridge. The *Sadie Saxon* was turning straight into them; she would pass safely between a pair of them.

The aged skipper acted with an alacrity that surprised even him. He yelled for the searchlight and with his own hand pulled the whistle into a strident blast of warning. The searchlight came on and threw its beam straight ahead. There, in a line, were three gray conning towers—three submarines on the surface and in fairly close formation. The nearest destroyer saw them too and at once plunged toward them with its guns blazing. Geysers of white water shot up about the nearest one. A couple of seconds later a bright flash told of a six-inch hit squarely at the base of a conning tower. The other two subs were diving hard, but the one that was hit did not dive. Or did not dive the regular way. It rolled slowly over toward the *Sadie Saxon*, spilling frantic men from its torn superstructure, then settled to its grave.

The leading freighter of the middle column suddenly blew up with a bang, lighting up the sea like day. A moment later the second ship of the left-hand column burst into flames. At least two of the nine torpedoes fired had found a mark. But the subs that fired them had no opportunity to fire more. They had been ambushed in their own ambush, and already three destroyers were racing back and forth over the spots where they had last been seen and dropping depth charges by the score. Similar activities were going on on the other side. Apparently there had been other subs waiting there as well.

The *Sadie Saxon* lay still where she was until the survivors of the two ships destroyed had been brought on board. Then she unaccountably turned due south and ran for an hour at full speed. There she stopped and refused to budge another yard. It was well past the dawn then and a destroyer could be seen on the horizon behind still searching for vestiges of their attackers.

"Signal that destroyer," the captain said, "and tell him to come over here. We've got one spotted."

The destroyer came up within hail, and its captain delivered a blistering message through what must have been an asbestos-lined megaphone.

"Will the second on that ship kindly relieve that blithering idiot in command and put him under arrest? The—"

"The sub's right under me," Tolliver yelled back, "playing possum a hundred feet or so down." The ship started moving ahead. "Come in and drop your eggs. Then lock me up if you want."

He turned to Parker who was in a quandary as to what to do. The performances of the ship had shaken his nerve. He had begun to wonder whether *he* was the crazy man. Tolliver ignored him. Instead he walked out to the wing of the bridge and watched the destroyer do its work.

Huge seething hummocks of water rose as the ash-cans exploded under the surface. Four of them had gone off and the destroyer was coming back for a second run across the same spot. But there was no need. A half mile away a black nose appeared for a moment on the surface, stuck its beak up into the air, then with a loud hissing of escaping air fell back weakly into the water. Where it had been were three bobbing heads. There *had* been a sub under there!

"Thanks," flashed the destroyer, "well done. Rejoin convoy."

They went past Gib without stopping and made the hazardous trip to Alexandria without incident other than a few sporadic and ineffectual raids by enemy aircraft. At Alexandria Captain Tolliver found this message waiting for him; it was from ONI.

*"You are a better guesser than some of our experts. The three men you tipped us off to are in jail. They planned to seize the ship and divert it to a Norwegian port. Congratulations."*

The skipper gave a brief snort and then crammed the message into a pocket with his one good hand. Then he learned that on the voyage home he was to carry the convoy's commodore. The "commodore," a retired Navy captain, came aboard and looked around.

He did not say much until they were out of the Mediterranean and well to the west of Portugal. By then they had been joined by many other ships and were steaming in a formation much like the one before, with the difference that this time, being flagship, they were more nearly in the middle of the flotilla.

"You seem to have a remarkable ability to spot submarines, Captain," he remarked. "What is your secret?"

"Me?" said the skipper indignantly. "Hell, I can't see a submarine in the dark or under water any farther than the next man. All the credit is due to Sadie. She *smells* 'em. She hates 'em, too."

"Yes. I know. She rammed several in the last war, didn't she? And didn't they make her into a Q-ship?"

"She did. She was. If you'll look down there on the pedestal of the binnacle stand you'll see some file marks. There are fourteen of 'em now. Each one stand for a U-boat. Or raider. I tell you, she don't like Germans. She was a German herself, you know, but they didn't treat her right. She has a grievance."

"Now, Captain," laughed the commodore, "don't you think you are carrying your little joke too far? After all . . ."

"Do you know the story of this ship?" asked Tolliver fiercely, "well, listen."

It was close to midnight then and a bright moon was shining. The silhouettes of the ships about were distinct as black masses against the glittering white-kissed sea. The two officers went on talking, but their eyes were steadfastly kept ahead. This was a night when anything might happen.

"In 1914 this ship was spanking new. She was the *Koenigen von Sachsen* or something of the sort, freshly turned out of the Vulcan Works at Stettin. The outbreak of the war caught her at Hoboken and they tied her up for the duration. But when we joined the war in '17 and took her over, her innards were something pitiful to see. Her crew had dry-fired her boilers and they were a mass of sagging tubes. The vandals cracked her cylinders with sledges, threw the valve gear and cylinder heads overboard, and messed up all the auxiliaries. They fixed the wiring so it would short the moment juice was put on it, and they took down steam leads and inserted steel blanks between the flanged joints. In other places they drove out rivets and replaced them with ones of putty. I tell you she was dynamite, even after they fixed up the boilers and main machinery.

"Naturally, having a thing like that done to you would

make you sore—especially if you were young and proud and the toast of the Imperial German merchant marine. But that was not all. On her first trip across—I was mate then—a sub slammed a torp into her off the north of Ireland and it took her stern away. Luckily she didn't sink and another ship put a hawser on us and worried us into Grennock where they fixed her up. That would have been bad enough, but on the trip home she smacks into a submarine-laid mine off the Delaware Capes and blows in her bow. We had to beach her near Cape May.

"They rebuilt her again and we set out. But her hard-luck—or mistreatment rather—wasn't at an end. In those days our Secret Service wasn't as good as it is now and a saboteur got aboard. He gummed up things pretty bad. So bad that we caught afire and almost sank in mid-ocean. It took some doggoned hard work to save that ship, but help came and we stayed afloat. Well, that was the end of her patience. She went hog-wild. After that, no matter whether she was in convoy or not, whenever anything that was German was around—sub, torpedo, raider or what not—she went after it, and never mind engine room bells or rudder. Her whimsies cost me a hand and a leg before we were through, but I didn't mind. I figured I could take it if she could.

"She broke the hearts of three captains. A lot of captains, you ought to know, object to having the ship take charge. They said she was unmanageable and chucked their jobs. That left me in command, though at the time I didn't rate the job. Knowing something of her history, I knew better than to interfere. Her hunches are the best thing I know. No matter what she does . . ."

"Hey!" yelled the commodore, thoroughly alarmed, "watch what you're doing."

The *Sadie Saxon* had sheered sharply from her course and was heading directly across the bows of a ship in the column to one side of them. It was too late then, even if the *Sadie* had been tractable, to do anything about it. A collision was inevitable. The commodore reached for the whistle pull, but Tolliver grabbed his arm and held it.

"Wait," he urged, "this means something. I know her."

An angry, guttural shout came from the bridge of the ship whose path they were about to cross. Then came the rending crash as steel bit into steel—thousands of tons of it at twelve knots speed. The other ship had rammed the *Sadie Saxon* just abreast the mainmast and she heeled over sharply, spilling deck gear over the off rail. At once pandemonium reigned in the convoy as ships behind sheered out to avoid compounding the already serious collision.

At once fresh confusion succeeded. The ship that was the victim of the *Sadie*'s caprice suddenly dropped her false bulwarks and the moonlight glinted off the barrels of big guns both fore and aft. Harsh orders sounded in German and the guns began spitting fire. Shells began bursting against ships on all side as the raider that had insinuated itself into the midst of the convoy began its work. Escort ships began dashing toward the scene, worming their way through the scattering freighters so as to get to a spot where they could open fire.

"I told you," said Captain Tolliver, serenely. "You can always trust her."

But she was sinking, and the crew were lowering what boats they could. The commodore was one of the first to leave, since he was in charge of the entire expedition and must transfer his flag to a surviving ship. Tolliver stayed behind. There was not room enough in the boats for one thing, and his faith in the durability of the *Sadie Saxon* was unlimited. He had seen her in worse plight many times before.

The raider had succeeded in backing away, but it, too was in a perilous condition. Her bows were torn wide open and she was fast going down by the head. She continued to fire viciously at everything within reach, paying especial attention to the crippled *Sadie Saxon*. A shell struck her funnel and threw fragments and splinters onto the bridge. One fragment struck Captain Tolliver in the right thigh and he went down with a brief curse. Another pair of projectiles burst aft among the rest of the crew who were engaged in freeing a little raft from the mainmast shrouds. It must have killed them all, for when shortly afterward a destroyer ranged alongside and hailed, there was no answering cry.

Tolliver hauled himself to the wing of the bridge and managed to cut an opening in the weather screen. He looked out just in time to see the flaming remnants of the raider sink under the moon-tipped waves. The freighters had all gone and the destroyers were charging off in a new direction. Apparently submarines, working in conjunction with the camouflaged raider, had made their appearance. Tolliver watched a moment, then was aware of a growing faintness. His leg must be bleeding more than he thought. In a moment everything turned black.

It was broad daylight when he came to again. Another peep showed him an empty ocean. The convoy must have gone on, as it was proper and correct it should. And then he heard the burr and roar of airplanes overhead. They swooped low, machine-gunning the decks systematically on the assumption men were still aboard. One, more daring than the rest, swooped in between the masts. *Sadie Saxon* was trembling in every plate and rivet.

"Steady, girl," murmured the now delirious captain, laying his cheek against the bridge deck and patting it gently with his one hand, "you can't handle those, I know. But we've done enough, you and I. We can't keep afloat forever."

Her answer was typical. He had no way of knowing how deep she was in the water, or what her trim, but she heeled violently to port—hung there a moment, then turned quietly over on her side. The instant she chose to do it was just as the daring raider plane was diving beneath her radio antennae, ready to drop its final bomb. Captain Tolliver heard its wings snap off and its body crash as the whipping, heeling mast struck it. There was a final burst of flame, and the rest was cool, green water. The old sea dog felt the waves close over him, but he was smiling and content.

"Bless her old heart," was his last thought, "she even got one of *those*."

Nobody had expected the Third Reich to be anything but a strong adversary: "Who has not fought the Germans does not know what War is." The appalling victories of Japan were another matter; even the experts were astounded. From the last decade of the 20th century, it is difficult to appreciate how shocking the Japanese triumphs were, in an era when the nations of Western Europe ruled most of Asia as colonial dependencies and there were still gunboats on the rivers of China. For an Asiatic power to outfight Westerners, design better planes, sink their ships and drive their soldiers into retreat or POW camps, was an outrage against nature; the ferocity of the Pacific war, equalled only by the savageries of the Russian Front, drew on this racial animosity. The images of war in the East were still formed by Kipling and the pulp-adventure tradition: valiant sahibs, stalwart blond love-interests, dusky maidens, loyal sepoys, besieged jungle forts and small forces of disciplined riflemen mowing down shrieking native hordes. Herewith an example, with a ghost from the early days of European expansion in the East called in to balance Japanese airpower . . .

# RED MOON ON THE FLORES SEA

## H. Bedford-Jones

It was the morning of the third day, and a mist covered the face of the waters, and overhead in the sky a cloud was smoking.

West was the only one who perceived this curious smoking cloud, and he thought it some sort of optical illusion. He sat with his arm over the tiller, holding the boat on her course as the light dawn airs bellied out the sail gently. The Javanese woman and the two Malays were huddled under the tarpaulin for warmth; they, like Broome, were asleep. Broome was a Dutchman, a wealthy planter from the Celebes shore. West was an oil man from the Balik Papan oilfield. Only five of them; the boat could have held a dozen more easily.

None of them knew anything about a boat, or where they were heading. Broome had produced a gold pocket-compass and took West's name as a good omen.

"Steer west," he said. "God knows where we are! Steer west, and we're bound to reach the islands."

Somewhere in the Flores Sea; this was all they could tell. The *Billiton*, a K.P.M. island steamer, had been bound for Amboina, the great naval base, when she got it—specks droned out of the sky, bombs straddled her, two direct hits sent her down in ten minutes. This was on the first morning. West reached the boat by swimming and Broome helped him aboard. The three natives were already in the boat. The rest died.

The boat had sail and oars, food and water, but being Dutch she was not up to Board of Trades specifications. For the five of them there was enough, however.

West cocked his eye at that smoking cloud: A cone-shaped cloud above the mist, with curls of smoke proceeding from the tips—fiery smoke. A sardonic glint came into his dark eyes. Might be a mirage of a volcano, he thought, if there were such a thing.

His gaze dropped to Broome, a solid piece of bone and muscle, who huddled asleep at his feet. Good man, this Dutchman; capable, unexcited, poised. West could appreciate such a man. He was pretty well poised himself; wiry, slow-spoken, a smile behind his eyes and thin lips under a bony nose. He had been out here two years with the Dutch oil people, and his last job had been to set off the blasts when the Japs got a foothold ashore and the oilfield could not be held against them. That had hurt; but his work was properly done.

"Hello!" Broome stirred, sat up and blinked at him. He spoke English with quite an English accent. "I was dreamin'. Saw him plain as I see you sitting there!"

"Saw who?" asked West, smiling slightly.

"Hendrik van der Broome. Hard-jawed feller. Ancestor of mine who adventured out here in the Spice Islands when the world was young and decent. He was talkin' to me. My word! He could swear like a—like a Trojan!"

"Trooper, you mean." West's smile widened. "Some dream!"

"Must have been," muttered Broome, frowning.

The tarpaulin moved and one of the Malays came to life. He looked at West, turned and looked at Broome, then was electrified. His thin brown arm waved.

"Karang Api!" he cried out. "Karang Api!"

"The hell you say!" exclaimed Broome, twisting about, looking up at the sky. "Karang Api—well, I'll be blowed! Sure enough! West, why didn't you say anything about it?"

"Thought I was seeing things. Karang Api—that means *Coral Fire*! Is it real?"

Broome scrambled aft to the thwart beside him.

"Man, oh, man! Of course it's real! Volcanic island—devilish queer effect, isn't it? That's the mist. We see the peak above it. There's usually mist this monsoon; dust blows up from Australia—"

He broke off short, staring at West with round eyes. The American laughed.

"Well, what it is? Do I look like a ghost?"

Broome lost his expression of astonishment. A twinkle came into his placid blue eyes, and he dug his elbow into West's ribs.

"I never heard of a ghost who needed a shave, and you do! I was thinking about that dream and my ancestor Hendrik. He was a tough old pirate by all accounts; Karang Api was where he died. He had a fort there. It is queer—queer how things come into the mind. Well, now we can have a drink all around!"

"I guess so. Measure it out," assented West.

Lucky, he was thinking, as he watched Broome at work over the water-breaker. Luckier than most in this war. Only two days afloat, and no hardships to speak of; he even had his chief personal belongings in his pocket. He took the water handed him and sipped it with blessed relief and appreciation.

The two Malays gulped eagerly. The Javanese woman, whose name was Muda, at least all the name they knew, handled hers delicately; she was a slim, golden creature, highly graceful and extremely intelligent, if not beautiful. Her garments were thin silken tissues; her feet were bare and on one big toe was a jeweled ring. On her forehead, between her eyes, was a vermilion dot, a caste mark. She had scarcely spoken all the time they had been adrift, though she spoke both French and Dutch. The two Malays were dish-faced little Malacca men.

The mist was thinning under the new sunlight. As usual at this monsoon, when the air was loaded with infinitesimal dust-particles brought up from Australia by the unending winds, distances were foreshortened and visibility was limited; but the wonder of Karang Api was unfolding momentarily.

Coral Fire—the Malays named things well, thought West. That smoking cone in the heavens had come down now, it was attached to earth and had become real. It had a queer whiteness not unlike coral. The island of which it was part was a tiny thing, and no other land was in sight—although, from a small boat, the horizon is strictly limited.

"It used to be an important place in the old sailing-ship days," mused Broome, his gaze on the island. "Like Singapore is now. It controlled the lanes of the spice ships, you see. Now it has nothing but an airfield and an old fort my ancestor built—"

"An airfield?" broke in West, with a grunt. "I'll bet it hasn't any now! From what the radio said, the Japs have bombed every airfield they could spot between Manila and Port Darwin!"

Broome merely nodded.

He had changed, West reflected; possibly he himself had changed. The actual environment of war, its accidents and perils, provoked a total change in most men. They lost their superficial aspects. Now Broome had thin lines from nostrils to lips; it gave him an oddly cruel look. His talk of dreams, too, was odd. West would not have thought him the sort of man to indulge in such nonsense.

The boat was headed for the island, under West's touch. It was still some miles off. The sight of it worked a change on everyone in the boat. Hitherto they had not cared about one another; each had been more or less wrapped in his own evil destiny. Now they were back in the world again. Broome dealt out the tinned food and biscuit and they made a square meal all around. Tongues clattered. Even the impassive Muda came alive.

She was a dancer, West learned, from Lombok, the island adjoining Bali. The two Malays had been house-servants in Malacca, going to Amboina to take a job there and bringing their former master's effects with them; he was a Dutch merchant and it turned out that Broome knew him slightly. Broome himself had been going to fight. He was a reservist with the Dutch defense forces, an officer.

"And you?" he asked.

West grimaced.

"Gimme a chance, that's all. I'll join up with the first outfit I see, sure. Karang Api! I like that name. Can we get a coaster here?"

"God knows," said Broome, with a shrug. "The Japs are striking everywhere, by air and sea, like a flood of ants overrunning the jungle—just as they struck our steamer. The world has become a place of destruction; the aim of everyone is to destroy, destroy!"

"Well, keep your spirits up," said West cheerfully. "If we're back to the age of the survival of the fittest, I aim to survive. Glad we've struck an important place. We can get sent somewhere to get to work."

Broome gazed at the misty island.

"Don't be too sure," he rejoined. "This place is not important. As in most of the islands, the spice trade has died out, and the natives have thinned to nothing. Everybody may have been called in when the war broke out. It depends on what has happened here."

"An airfield means planes," persisted West.

Broome shrugged again, silently, as though to say that nothing had any meaning, these days. A gloomy streak in him had come to the fore; a premonition, mayhap. The Dutch have ever been thus; dogged, implacable, gloomy when most bitterly moved, but efficient withal.

Details of the shore plan were disclosed as the boat came in closer. Surf broke heavily upon the hungry reefs, except where the little harbor came clear. It was a poor sort of haven, giving little shelter during this southeast monsoon. There was a native town, not large,

grouped about a white building near the water; this
would be the Residence of the Dutch Controller or
governor. Farther back was an enormous clearing, a flat
airfield, with what seemed a large white structure, in
ruins. Sampans and fishing-craft were drawn up along
the curve of the harbor, but nothing was afloat. A white
lighthouse pointed the haven.

"No boat here!" observed West. "What's that between the lighthouse and the Residence?"

"The fort." Broome gazed at the gray, solid structure.
"The old fort, probably the one my ancestor built."

One of the Malays hopped into the bow. "*Bakboord
uit!*" he cried in the pilot's call, and West obeyed
instantly, sending the boat's head, not the tiller, to
port. Well that he was prompt, for they slid within ten
feet of a reef and had a glimpse of wreckage and part of
a black truncated buoy amid the foam.

"Hello!" said Broome. "Harbor buoys destroyed! And
the upper part of the lighthouse has crumbled. . . . No!
Blown away!"

"And nobody in sight," added West.

This was true. The two Malays chattered in low voices,
the woman stared impassively, but neither Broome nor
West spoke again for a while. . . .

Over the town reigned the silence of death. From
the harbor waters, to their right, protruded the tips of
two masts; nearby was a funnel and another mast, and
along the shore a tremendous lot of wreckage. The
upper part of the white lighthouse was a crumbled ruin.
A large portion of the town showed itself now as blackened shells—fire had stalked here. The white Residence
—ah! Only a portion of it was erect, the rest lay in
ruins. And at the edge of the airfield was the wreckage
of barracks.

Both men knew without telling. The Japs had passed
this way.

The square gray fort, however, seemed solid and
untouched. From its walls, cannon frowned down upon
the harbor entrance; it was a massive structure. The
docks were deserted. The boat headed straight in for

the principal wharf, from which a short street ran up to the Residence; now the Malays fell silent, too, sniffing the air like dogs. On the shore to the left was an enormous blackened pile of something that still smoked and fouled the air.

"Bodies were burned there," said Broome. "It is like a plague-stricken town."

"Must be some natives around," West grunted, as they ran in. "Down sail, there!"

The Malays moved. The sail fluttered down. The boat faltered along the wharf and touched. One man leaped out, the other flung him a line to make fast.

Broome gained the wharf. He beckoned the two Malays.

"Look through the town. Go to the airfield. If you find anyone, bring them back to the Residence."

West joined Broome, and they moved up the way together. The Malays ranged afield. The Javanese woman, Muda, drew her head-scarf more closely about her and moved on with her slow, graceful step, going nowhere; no one paid her any attention.

Broome touched West's arm and pointed. From here, they could see the rear portion of the old gray fort—it was all blown to flinders. The massive front walls and platforms were all that remained. Broome turned his head as he walked, watching the scene in fascination.

The Residence, whose kampong and rear buildings were all ruins, stood apparently untouched in the front portion; the barred flag of Holland hung listless on the staff above the entrance. Only the burst window-panes evidenced what had happened. Fire had not touched here. The Chinese bazaars around were all smashed and looted, their gaudy signs hanging crazily, doors swung wide.

West stepped to the porch of the Residence, between the empty sentry-boxes. He had an absurd impulse to work the big brass knocker. Instead, he tried the door. It opened. The two men walked into a hall with stairs going upward, passed into reception-rooms; here was the big office of the Controller. It was in disarray, the door of the safe standing open, papers littering the floor.

West dropped into a big narra-wood chair and took a whitish cheroot from a box on the desk. Broome followed suit, bit at his cheroot, leaned forward and picked up a lighter, and struck flame. The two men smoked gratefully, looking at each other, around the place. A queer moment, a moment of readjustment, of silent appraisal.

"How d'you figure it?" asked West.

Broome cleared his throat.

"They struck by air and with a landing-party. Were beaten off, apparently. The few officials and the sepoy soldiers cleaned up the mess afterward, then some craft came along and they decamped in her. Probably the Controller was killed. The natives skipped out and haven't come back."

"Looks like a good diagnosis," said West. "A rain came up, to judge by the evidence, and put out the fires—perhaps drove off the Jap planes. Yesterday or day before, I'd say."

Broome nodded. "We came along just too late to be taken off, eh? Should find plenty of grub lying around, however—"

His words died. He looked at Broome, who returned his look, startled. A *creak-creak* of sound reached them.


## Two


Into the doorway came a woman, looking at them.

She was a young woman, well built, erect. A bandage was about her head, with golden hair massed above and about it. She wore handsome white slacks trimmed with gold, and on her feet were slippers. She looked at them, held on to the door, and wavered.

"Oh!" she said. "I did not know—"

They both jumped forward as she toppled over. West caught her and lifted her to a chair. It was still early morning; she must have been asleep.

A padding step came in upon them. There, like a

phantom of unreality, drifted the Javanese dancer. One glance showed Muda the situation. She spoke to Broome, low-voiced, and he exclaimed in relief.

"She'll take her in hand. I'll carry her upstairs—"

Muddled words, clear meaning. He lifted the sense-less young woman, and with Muda trailing him, went upstairs. West recovered his cheroot and went on into the next room. Here began wreckage—walls down, on beyond everything in a pile of timber, bamboo and furniture. He came upon a closet, and found clothes in it, uniforms.

This was something like. His shrunken garments and soggy shoes were quickly doffed. He slipped into foot-gear that fitted well enough and spruce whites, a five-button uniform jacket and white shirt. The insignia on the uniform were of no importance now. When his own belongings and money were transferred to his new pock-ets, he beamed.

"West! Ah, here you are. I say—good!" Broome came along. "Muda will look after her. We'd better find something to eat. Make some coffee, eh? Wait till I get into some of these togs. Splendid idea. You're a deputy controller, I see. Better take a topee."

He, too, was transformed in brief space, and each took sun-helmets from the closet and then went out. In the other room, West stuffed some cheroots from the desk into his breast pocket. Broome did the same.

"I'd like to get out of here," Broome began. "I need the sunlight."

"And I, a bath," said West. "Our skins are impregnated with salt; maybe that's what gives me a jumpy feeling."

"You've got it too, eh?" Booome nodded. "I was about to say—"

It remained unuttered. Into the room came an old native hag with a tray holding a silver coffee-pot and two tiny glass cups in filigree silver holders. She was an ancient crone, incredibly creased and wrinkled. She put the tray on the desk, paid absolutely no attention when Broome snapped questions at her, and walked out of the room again with her shuffling step.

"Looks half blind, acts deaf," said West in astonishment. "Am I seeing things?"

A laugh broke from Broome; he plumped into a chair.

"Look! Time for morning coffee. She's probably been doing that for years—bringing the *controleur* and his assistant their coffee! Blow me, but she does it just the same now; deaf, blind, witless! That explains it. Here, drink up!"

The coffee was good. They smacked their lips over it. Yes, that explained it—but, catching another shuffle from the hall, West darted to the door. The old bent figure was going up the stairs with another tray. He came back and poured more coffee and gulped it hot.

"It's all real," he said, scowling. The laugh was gone from his dark eyes; they looked savage under his downdrawn brows. "All real, but feels queer."

"That's because death lies all around," Broome said placidly. "Dead things, rather; men. No dogs, d'you notice? Everything's cleared out. I'm for a look at the old fort."

They went out together into the sunlight and walked down the silent street. The mist had lifted, but the air was thick with dust particles and nothing at a distance was very distinct. Even the smoking peak above them was not clear-cut as it should be.

From the end of the street along to the old fort there was a broad pavement of coral blocks, well above high tide. It took them past what had been the funeral pyre of many men. Broome nodded at it.

"I'll tell you what happened," he said. "Prob'ly the remaining officers and sepoys and chief traders cleared out in some boat that came along. The natives had taken to the bush. They came back, looted things, dared not touch the Residence, and someone among them had sense enough to take care of the dead. That's about it. So there are natives somewhere."

"And the young woman we saw?"

"She was probably thought dead when the others skipped out. Hello! This is curious."

They were approaching the carven, age-weathered

entrance of the ancient fort. Out in front of the open gates was a litter—rifles and equipment, empty shell-cases glittering in the sunlight, boxes of the shells, and a gun, whose long and elevated muzzle with the flare at the end told it was anti-aircraft.

"There was hell to pay here," said West. "Notice the bullet marks everywhere? Machine-gunned from the planes, eh?"

"Obviously." Broome peered at the gun. "This is one of the early Bren types—see, it can be depressed for general use! And plenty of shell-clips ready. Yes; thirty or forty shells per minute. Blood-patches here. The planes wiped 'em out. Let's look into the fort. I have a sentimental reason."

There was not much left to look at inside the fort, except rubble and wreckage and an odor of decaying flesh from beneath the masonry heaps. The old gun-platforms were intact; along the walls stood ponderous eighteenth-century pieces of huge size. Broome came back to the entrance, removed his topee, and mopped his brow. He pointed at the harbor.

"Complete command from here, if you'll notice. My ancestor Hendrik died somewhere about here. A native flotilla and five Portuguese galleons came from Timor. He had two ships here in the harbor and fought for three days. When his ships sank, he came ashore and fought his battery from this place where the fort is now. Finally blew up the Portuguese admiral and they went away."

"And he was killed?"

"No. Sunstroke," said Broome, and laughed. "He's buried somewhere in the fort—well buried now!" He gave West an odd glance. "You see? That explains why I dreamed about him."

"Maybe," said the American. "Well, what the devil are we to do? You're no seaman, nor am I. We're somewhere in the Sea of Flores. None of these native craft on the shore are any better than our boat."

"And we'd have to get charts before we'd know where to head for." Broome tossed away the stub of his cheroot. "Hanged if I want to trust myself to the empty horizon again!"

"Same here." West nodded. "There comes one of our boys."

One of the two Malays was coming on the run. He approached them and squatted down respectfully.

"Tuan! The news is good," he said in perfunctory words, then chattered on. Broome questioned him. The news was not, in fact, good at all. His companion had found a group of natives hiding out and was trying to bring them back into the town, while he had come back with his report. Broome got it all out of him by degrees.

The airfield had been bombed into chaos. No planes had been here but there had been a radio station. It was gone, with all else, barracks included. There had been a fight with a landing-party, who had been driven off, three days ago. The slaughter ashore had been ghastly. Only the waterfront had been cleared of dead; corpses were thick at the airfield.

As Broome had figured, the survivors had looted everything. Two whites had survived; they and the chief inhabitants and what was left of the soldiers had left in a hurry when a coaster showed up. Most of the natives had tumbled loot and food into their largest boats and made off, afterward. Only a handful remained, hiding out.

"So that's that," said West. "Let's look up the woman."

"Right! I had forgotten her."

They went back to the Residence. West was more himself now. He was adjusted to reality and back in the world of fact. As they approached the Residence, the other Malay and half a dozen frightened, chattering natives met them and flooded about the entrance. Broome gave them curt, decisive orders. His first natural idea was to get the house and its life running again. The two Malays took charge; food and service were assured. West would have foraged for himself, but Broome wanted things done for him, by dominant instinct.

They went inside, and in the unshattered reception parlor Helena van Heynck received them.

She was gowned now, in sedate blue, her bandage was gone, and her golden hair was arranged over the grazing wound a machine-gun bullet had inflicted. She was a quiet, calm, capable young woman, the sister of the Controller. Hit in the machine-gunning, she had been left for dead—and that was all she knew. Only by questioning the natives did she now learn all that had happened. Her brother was not dead, but gone.

"She's dazed and in bad shape," said West in English, which she evidently did not understand. "Get her back to bed; she probably needs food, too. Where's Muda?"

The Javanese woman came and led Helena upstairs again.

West took a look around for food, blundering through glass-strewn rooms across the hall, and found something better. He approached it cautiously, investigated the antique wet batteries, turned the knobs—and it worked! His whoop of joy brought Broome on the jump, and they listened almost incredulously to the voice from Batavia.

Their incredulity became ghastly reality as they listened, until at length Broome reached forward and turned it off.

"Hey!" cried West. "What for?"

"Natives. They're outside, all around—they must not hear." Broome suddenly looked ten years older, and his eyes were burning. "Manila gone, the Philippines as good as evacuated, Singapore going—good God, man! The Indies attacked, everything being occupied—do you realize what it means?"

"Damn the natives!" West was angry. "Pack of lies, probably—"

"No, no! Think of ourselves! It means they'll be back here, at Karang Api! They may come any time!" cried Broome. "There's no place to hide; this is the only village on the island, the rest is thorny scrub and volcanic ash."

"You're worried about where you can hide?"

"*Verdammt*, no! No! About what we can do! It's no time to sit here and listen and do nothing! I tell you, I'm going back to the fort and talk with Hendrik van der Broome and find out what we can do—we must do something, do something!"

He rushed out of the room. West looked after him, whistled between his teeth, took a grip on his cheroot, then reached out and turned the radio on again, very softly. He knew now that Broome was mad.

Unhurried, he listened to voices from the air—Sumatra attacked, Burma attacked, Singapore as good as lost, China flinging its legions on the brown men, the yellow seas turned to blood—and his hard, grim face became yet harder. At a pad-pad of bare feet on the matting, he looked around to see Muda, and turned off the radio. She spoke softly, composedly, and he knew enough Dutch to hear that Helena was asking for him.

She was in the reception-room again; she smiled and gave him her hand. The Malays were arranging a table; food was coming up. West got her a cigarette. She was no longer dazed, but all alive, her blue eyes full of dancing lights. Muda sat beside her, on the floor, watching West as he talked. Dutch came hard to him.

He found her quietly practical. She told him where to find a map in her brother's desk; he got it. She knew distances. She knew a bit about boats, even. She pointed out to him that it was quite hopeless to try and make Bantong or the other places south of Celebes, since the Japs were everywhere, like vermin, working southward.

"Muda says your boat is good," she went on. "Straight south, it is only a couple of hundred miles to Ombai or Flores or any one of the island chain; from there, we can get to Timor easily. If you do not want to tack against the monsoon, head a bit southwest and you'd make Flores certainly. It should be only two or three days at the outside."

"We?" said West, meeting her eyes. She smiled.

"Certainly. You and Mynheer Broome, I, Muda, any of the natives who care to go. We can put plenty of food and water aboard. Even if we meet Japs, they will not bother a small boat. We should leave at once."

"Hello! Looks good, Helena," said West, studying the map. "If we'd only known this before—well, we're here."

A pretty hand, he thought. Not a pretty face; but, like the hand, capable. A calmly sensible young woman. And if not pretty, she had a shining beauty from within that drew him.

The meal was ready. Rijstaaffel, the eternal rice background, abundantly served by a Malay; the old crone undoubtedly knew where to burrow amid the ruins for food. Helena asked where Broome was, and West grimaced.

"We'd better not wait for him. He thinks he's gone to talk with an ancestor of his, one Hendrik van de Broome—"

"Oh! A famous man in olden days!" Helena's face lit up; then her expression changed as she caught the look in West's eyes. "What? Imagination? Well, perhaps he knows; perhaps he is right. Captain Hendrik was buried in the old fort. We will not wait for him."

The three sat down to table. Muda ate with them; she was a great artist, said Helena, famous in the islands. The gentle brown woman beamed at her but said little. In the midst of their meal Broome came in, and he was vigorous, alive, like a strong wind. He brushed Helena's hand with his lips and settled into a chair.

"Well! It is all settled!" he exclaimed cheerfully.

"Right," assented West, pleased and a little surprised. "Two hundred miles or so to Flores, south of us. With this steady monsoon, we can make it in two days. The boat sails well across the wind—"

Broome looked up from his heaping plate, gave West a widening stare of of his blue eyes.

"What are you talking about? Go? *Nein!* We stay. It is all arranged."

"You're cockeyed," said West, and got the map. "Now look; here we are, here's Flores, and—"

Broome brushed it aside. His gloom was gone. He

wore an air of bright and jovial determination, as though he were a man among children.

"Let me explain," he said. "The Japs will not be here till tomorrow. I have six of those natives at work now. They're good men, burning to revenge the slaughter here. I've got them at work with the gun, and by tomorrow they'll be well-trained. You'll see."

He began to ball rice between his fingers, tossing it into his mouth.

"Besides," he added, "they say there's a machine-gun at the airfield. They're bringing it over. No end of ammunition, too. And they say there's another group of natives."

West gathered his shocked senses together.

"Listen, Broome," he said, and meant his words. "That's nonsense and you know it. If the Japs really return to occupy the place, two popguns won't mean anything. We must get Miss Helena out of here. We can all find safety."

Broome waved a finger in negation, jovially good-humored.

"*Nein!* I have promised, my friend; it is arranged. We stay, we strike a hard blow, we show those little brown devils a thing or two! My ancestor, Hendrik, says it will come out well. I have promised not to disgrace him. He will help us. I will take the big gun, you will have charge of the machine-gun. It is very simple. The flag will fly, you see."

"Be damned to you!" said West, angrily. Then he checked himself, and checked a groan as he met the gaze of Helena, smiling and unperturbed.

"Perhaps Mynheer Broome knows, *ja!*" she observed.

West gulped. Broome was stark, staring mad, and what was to be done about it?

### THREE

Muda leaned forward and spoke in her liquid accents that softened the harsh Dutch words. "Tell us, please," she said to Broome, "how you know so well? You did not see him?"

"No." The Dutchman smiled. He looked so very sure of himself, so very sane, so very dominant and cheerful, that West's heart sank. "No; but I sat among the ruins and talked with him. He was there. I heard his words in my mind. It will be a tough fight, a good fight, with help on the way. We shall strike a blow for the queen, he and I and you!"

It was as though he spoke of something real and actual. He was wolfing his food, in haste to get back; there was much to be done, he said. West caught a glance from Helena, a glance of warning, and held his peace. She was right. Any argument, any dissent, might turn this flighty brain to violence.

Broome wiped his lips, shoved back his chair, excused himself, and departed in a hurry, telling West to show up when ready. When he was gone, West looked from Helena to the Javanese woman in helpless dismay.

"You backed him up," he said. "You were right not to excite him; but now there's no handling him! I might have been able to knock him out and take him along— he's out of his head, of course."

"Of course," agreed Helena. "But he bears a famous name; he should prove a splendid fighter! And when all the world has gone mad, why not trust a madman? That is logical. At the same time, if tomorrow passes and no Japs come back, I think I can persuade him to go with us. It is worth trying."

"Trust a madman, an unbalanced brain!" West groaned. Then he saw that Muda was laughing, her brown eyes like jewels, her brown cheeks dimpling.

"What have we to lose?" she asked. "Is life so precious? We're certain to die sooner or later; why not do it bravely? You are not a child."

"No, but I'm sane," retorted the American. He felt baffled by these queer viewpoints. "I don't intend to die till my number's up. I want a show for my money."

Helena broke into a slow laugh at his odd handling of her language. He flushed a little and went on, stubbornly.

"If the Japs do come, you know we haven't a chance. All this poppycock about talking to his ancestor—why,

it's absurd! You must see it! Helena, you can't believe
that rot?"

The young woman regarded him reflectively, appraisingly.

"No," she said. "Helena van Heynck could not believe it. He is obviously touched in his head. But, my
friend, he believes it! That's the great thing. And I am
just Helena, a woman who has seen bombs and murder
and fire all around. I would get out to that gun gladly!
I, too, have only life to lose, and I am not in love with
it. However," she added with a slight smile, "let us
humor him until tomorrow passes. I shall talk with him
presently. He is so sure of himself, that he will agree to
leave, if no Japs come tomorrow."

West nodded slowly, grudgingly. "I see. You're wiser
than I, maybe. Only I hate to lose a day!"

"Why?" put in the Javanese woman, her eyes amused.
"Why? You Americans are in such a hurry! But what is
a day, after all? In the sight of Shiva, or Allah, or your
God, it is a mere nothing."

West gave up. Something in the woman was deeply
impressive; and the golden-haired Helena was even
more so, not being childish but rather practical. He
turned to her.

"Maybe you're right. I'll make a bargain with you. I'll
humor Broome, if you'll do something for me."

"Agreed," said Helena, her eyes warm and friendly.

"It's high tide; I noticed when we came in that the
wharf was very high. Get these two Malays to work.
Load water and food into the boat, plenty of it. Have
the sail neatly rolled. Put in cushions and blankets and
whatever duffel you want to take away; and a compass.
You must have one around. Then have the boat stowed
safely beneath the wharf among the piles, out of sight.
That blasted idiot is capable of sinking her if he takes
the notion," he added bitterly. "Whatever happens,
we'll have the boat safe there for our getaway."

"That will be easily done," said Muda. "You are a very
wise man, mynheer; you bend like steel but you spring
back as you were. Yes, the two Malays will obey us."

Helena nodded. "It is a promise; depend on it. And remember, he promised also—or thinks he did, which is the same thing. So do not be harsh with him. Is it not strange how we four people are here upon a day, and all our past lives are nothing? All the little things have faded out, do not matter a bit. A few days ago they would have been so important!"

West looked at her. "Right. What is important? I get your idea."

"I think you do. The greatest wisdom is to know what is really important, and what is not. Civilized life destroys this wisdom, this focus. Today, in a situation like this, we see things so differently! And if we can just see them aright, it matters so much!"

West took his sun-helmet and went out, feeling ineffectual and rather lost. His usual forceful vigor was for the moment dissipated; he felt in need of adjustment. At first he had been aghast before the realization of Broome's utter insanity; but he was the only one who regarded Broome as so insane. That shook him a bit.

He was not, actually, thinking of himself, and he faced this squarely. He did want to get Helena out of this hell to safety. He felt less strongly about Muda; she was not his own kind, but Helena was. He had a horror of the thought of Helena falling into the hands of these little brown barbarians. She, apparently, did not. Was she so brave, then?

"Or so dumb?" he muttered as he walked along. "No, damn it, she's not dumb. She's got a lot on the ball. Maybe her viewpoint is better than mine after all. She'll talk to Broome later; perhaps we can wangle him without any trouble. And am I so confounded sane and right as I think I am? Dunno. But you can't tell me he was talking with his blasted Hendrik! That just doesn't make sense."

When he reached the paved esplanade above the beach, he saw Broome and a group of natives at work around the gun, over by the fort; and another group were at work closer at hand, at one side of the wharf where stood the blackened wreck of a godown.

"What are you doing?" demanded West, joining this group. The half-dozen men grinned and saluted him.

"Tuan, we clear one piece of this wreckage away, here at the corner. Tuan Broome commanded."

West got the idea at last. A section of the cement floor of the godown was being cleared, without touching the blackened ruins around. At one side was waiting a machine-gun of the belt-feed type, with belts and drums of spare ammunition. From this cement platform it would have murderous command of the wharf and the beach. With a shrug, West passed on. All useless, of course. One swooping Jap plane would gun everything here out of existence.

Broome greeted him jovially, mopping his face and ordering his panting group of natives to knock off.

"We have the hang of this gun," he exclaimed, pointing to the clips of tiny, conical shells stacked at hand. "Ha! It is cleaned and oiled; it works beautifully. The plan is taking shape. My ancestor Hendrik knows his business, West; he has arranged every detail."

"Where is he? I'd like to see him," said West dryly. The fanatic glare in Broome's eyes was the only indication of the man's aberration, but it was enough. Broome laughed and took his arm.

"My friend, he cannot be seen: you are making fun of me, what? That will be your gun yonder at the godown. You'll have six men; I have eight here. It is enough. Do you know anything about machine-guns?"

"No more than I do about those cannon in the fort embrasures," said West, with a nod toward the old gray walls. "I'm surprised that you don't try to use those ancient cannon as well!"

"Oh! My ancestor Hendrik spoke of them," replied Broome soberly. "They are placed to have the whole of this little harbor at their mercy, you know. A number of them are strong enough to use without danger of bursting—we shall see. Perhaps you had better drill your men with the machine-gun and see that it's in order. Fire a few bursts; there's plenty of ammunition.

I must talk with Hendrik and learn where the powder is kept, to use in the old cannon."

Mentally, West threw up his hands.

"Oh, all right!" he said, turning. "You'd better have Hendrik tell you exactly what the Japs will do when they come. I'd like to get one good crack in before they blow us all to hell!"

Broome beamed and nodded energetically. "*Ja, ja!* Hendrik will tell me all that."

West, with a muttered burst of profanity, walked back to the godown.

With a sardonic sense of futility, he went at the job assigned him. The corrugated iron sides of the shed might afford a certain protection against bullets, true. The cleared corner was by the entrance toward the wharf, where the track for unloading handcars ran in; that this particular spot had a superb command of the beach and wharf was undeniable.

The gun was old, but worked like a watch. When he had the hang of it, West was surprised by the smooth competence of its working. He tried a few shots, and the half-dozen natives flung themselves into the game with wild enthusiasm; the probably figured they could beat off the entire Jap navy.

He had them at work getting the gun cleaned up, when Helena and the two Malays appeared. The Malays went on down to the boat and began their work with it. Broome apparently took no notice. Helena spoke to the natives, smiled, and stood watching; her white parasol threw a glint of reflected radiance about her face like a halo. West stepped aside with her, beyond the earshot of the men, who understood Dutch.

"There's no use arguing with him," said West, with a nod toward Broome and the old fort. "He's talking about loading those ancient cannon and using them. Says that his ancestor Hendrik will tell him exactly what the Jap program will be. Stark crazy, Helena!"

"Well, the whole world is crazy, as I say," she returned thoughtfully, looking over at the party around Broome. "I have heard my brother say that these Japs are superb fighters when accustomed operations are followed, but that they lose their heads when their opponents try new tactics. That is why the Chinese have whipped them. Perhaps Mynheer Broome is right to use the old cannon. They would not be prepared for that."

"Hm! That's an idea anyhow," said West reluctantly. "You haven't given up the plan of leaving, I hope?"

"Certainly not," she rejoined. "But as Muda says, what does one day matter? And this is something to be handled carefully. I am going to talk with him now. But please remember one thing, my friend." She turned to West, her look very earnest, and laid a hand on his arm. "To him, Hendrik is real. Not to us, perhaps; but this does not mean it is not so."

West grunted skeptically. "You don't believe in ghosts coming back and fighting?"

She met his gaze for a moment, as though hesitating for words.

"No. But he does. Perhaps Hendrik van der Broome is putting thoughts in his head; that may be another word for inspiration. We don't know it's not so, anyway! Therefore, my friend, be gentle, I beg of you. The boat will be prepared."

She smiled, and passed out into the sunlight, toward Broome's group of men.

West followed her with his eyes. Strange woman! Adorable woman! The strength of a calm spirit was in her; composure sat within her like a quiet force. The thought struck him of what life would mean in company with such a woman, lifting like a fluid wave of the sea above petty worries and cares. Practical in her way, too.

He went back to his job, breaking out ammunition for the belts, while the brown men chattered and laughed—men who would be dead tomorrow, he reflected, if Broome was right about the return of the Japs.

## FOUR

In the cool of the afternoon, West sat in the parlor of the Residence talking with Helena and Muda, while the deaf old crone served them cooling drinks. Broome still labored. It was like being in some nook of the destroyed world, some nook untouched. The cool drinks, the glasses, the conventional words and garments; more, there was no sense of blasted loss and ruin, here in this room with the flag of Holland waving overhead. An oil man, a wounded woman, a Javanese dancer—strange trio!

Yet they were old and intimate friends, as though they had known one another for years; this was the amazing thing, that nothing of the past remained among them, that life had suddenly begun this very morning. All backgrounds no longer mattered. They were down to essentials, to the things of real importance. "The greatest wisdom is to know what is really important, and what is not." Helena's words recurred to West, now and again, with new truth.

Broome came in, fresh from a dip in the surf; with his breezy, healthy vigor it was impossible to deem him out of his mind.

"We located the powder," he said, accepting a drink gracefully. "Used for salutes. And we've got those old cannon loaded. Aimed and laid, too."

"Who's going to fire 'em?" asked West dryly.

"Oh, two of the boys are dying for the job. I showed 'em how. Odd thing—those old guns are set to converge their fire on a certain spot; anything coming into the harbor will get blown out of the water at that one spot! Used stone and iron balls that were piled in pyramids."

"You and Hendrik are welcome. What's the Jap program?"

"They'll send over a plane in the morning. Everyone lie doggo, mind! They'll think the place deserted and send in their landing-party. Probably in the afternoon." Broome spoke as though he had actual knowledge; it was uncanny. "Any radio news?"

West jumped up; he had forgotten the radio. Broome made no objection now, in fact was eager for news. He had worked hard and done much, and was a different man from the gloomy Broome who had arrived here. Exercise, however, had not worked out his mental kink, as West took note.

The air gave little good news. Singapore's water lanes had been cut and the city was lost. The Dutch fleet was active, the U.S. Navy was active, but the Japs swarmed on sea as on land, regardless of losses. Amboina and its naval base were under constant air attack.

"Just as well we didn't get there," said Broome.

They dined early; the two Malays reported that the boat was laden, covered with a tarpaulin, and moored beneath the wharf, where it would rise and fall with the tide. Broome paid no attention. Muda had from somewhere obtained fresh silken garments and a striking sarong of gold.

Dinner over, Broome fell asleep over a cigar. West got him upstairs, where they would share a bed, then came down again to finish his own cheroot. Muda disappeared.

"There's a moon," said West, "and I hear flying-foxes barking. Where do they come from?"

"Timor, I think," Helena replied. "Moon? No, let us stay here. There's nothing I want to look at outside, even heaven. The old life is gone."

"It'll come again, or a better one," said West. "It's hard to realize we've only been here since morning. How long have I known you?"

"A long time," she said quietly. "I shall be glad when we leave. Yes, we've only to live for what's ahead, now. By the way, I reached an understanding with Mynheer Broome. If nothing happens tomorrow, we leave next dawn. None of the natives want to go; they remain. Muda and the two Malays, yes. She is an odd woman, this Muda. I like her."

"Oh, she's all right," said West carelessly. Helena regarded him for a moment.

"You are very weary," she observed. "Why not sleep?"

West smiled. "Yes, I'm a bit done up; when this cheroot is finished, I'll turn in. How's the head?"

"Oh, this?" She touched her hair. "All right. Do you know, this morning I wanted to die? Yes; I had quite given up. Everything was hopeless."

"This time tomorrow night we'll be loading your grips in the boat."

"Everything is already in that I care to take."

"Funny thing," said West. "Broome doesn't seem to give the boat a second thought."

"No. He said this afternoon it was a waste of time, that we would not use it—that help will come from the sea."

"What he says doesn't impress me." West smothered a yawn and rose. "Well, guess my time's come, after all. Anything I can do for you before turning in?"

A faint smile touched her eyes, as she looked up at him.

"You are very strong, aren't you? Stronger than Mynheer Broome."

"No, I think not," West replied, a bit surprised. "He's muscled like an ox."

"That was not what I meant," she said. "There is outward strength and inward strength, strength of the body and strength of the mind and soul."

"Oh!" said West. His eyes twinkled. "Same with beauty, I expect. Various kinds of beauty; you've given a new meaning to the word, Helena. Good night."

He went upstairs and was asleep the moment he touched the bed. . . .

Sunlight wakened him, and voices, and the odor of coffee. It was broad morning. The deaf old crone was here with her tray and little cups, and Broome was talking at her quite uselessly. Broome had found a razor and was shaving luxuriously. Shaving! West gulped the coffee, and chivvied Broome into giving up the razor after a once-over scrape.

The mirror startled him; then he went at the job, wondering that Helena had not been frightened out of her wits by those spiky blurred faces of theirs. This was something like, he thought, as he got into his clothes.

"Be careful," said Broome warningly. "When the Jap plane comes on reconnaissance—keep hidden. I've warned them all."

Good Lord! Broome and his ancestor Hendrik! This took away some of West's high spirits, but the twinkle persisted in his eyes. After all, there would be only the day to put in. No Japs would come—and he could well afford to enjoy the feel of solid land for another day.

He was dressed ahead of Broome, and downstairs. In the reception-parlor he found Helena, arranging flowers in a vase. Her eyes widened on him.

"You look different!"

"I am!" Naïve as a boy, West brushed his hand over his face. "See? Shaved, rested, ready for anything!"

"I didn't mean that. Shaving doesn't matter. You had dropped the load, that was it. I felt the same. I went into the kampong to get some flowers—and then I saw everything. But there were flowers, just the same!" The hurt came into her face. "They are gone, you see; all gone, so many forever!"

"And we mourn them!" Muda had entered, unheard. "Why should we? Because we're selfish—because we'll not see them again and regret it; or we think we'll not see them. All nonsense! You people of Europe are children who have been taught to think death is terrible! Yet you know it must come to us all. Why can't Christians accept it as a natural event?"

Helena turned on her with a touch of asperity.

"Because we don't know what comes after, that's why!"

"Well, you should know," said the Javanese woman. "Your wise men tell you. Ours tell us. We believe. And you think it is a wonderful thing because Mynheer Broome talks with his ancestor! What folly!"

"Never mind, girls, just forget it," intervened West, and his awkward Dutch brought a quick smile from them. "Ancestors be hanged! Helena, did you get that map and a compass put in the boat? Good. I'll gamble common sense against ancestors any day, and common sense tells me not to worry about the Japs, and that I'm hungry. Here's Broome. Morning, mynheer!"

"*Goeden dag, goeden dag!*" exclaimed Broome heartily. "*Gegroet!* What, flowers? That is wonderful! There's a mist on the mountain and on the sea. I am glad that I thought to have those guns covered over last night. Better leave them covered until the moment of use, eh?"

West was in too good humor to dispute the issue. During breakfast, he assented gayly to Broome's demand that they get in more practice with the guns; he resolved to take the man's obsession lightly and not cause any argument or dissension.

So they donned helmets and walked down together to the esplanade, and found the little group of natives. The latter were grotesquely attired in bits of uniform looted from the bombed barracks and were keenly eager to be at work; they proudly displayed rifles and ammunition salvaged from the wreckage, and West was astonished by their anxiety to fight.

"Rather, to kill," said Broome. "These island men are gentle, like the Malays, but they have a heritage of ferocity second to none. Wait and see."

West put his half dozen at work, drilling with the machine-gun. The peak gradually came clear of the mist, and presently he walked over to Broome's station and watched him at his task with the larger gun. Three of the natives were preparing linstocks and fuses to fire the ancient cannon from the fort—which, West privately decided, would be far more perilous to them than to any shipping in the little harbor.

Broome knocked off, to join him with a cheroot and to talk of his ancestor Hendrik and the fight here. At some comment from West, he shook his head.

"You have the name wrong in English—Karang Api is not Coral Fire, except literally. In English it is the other way around, Fire Coral. When the peak flows lava, as happens now and again, the name is most appropriate. Fire Coral! It is a good name. My ancestor Hendrik made it famous in history."

West was tired of hearing about ancestor Hendrik, and sauntered off. He looked back to see Broome getting the gun covered over with canvas, no doubt to camouflage it from sight of the Jap plane that was coming.

Back to the ruins of the godown again, where two of his men were excitedly calling him. Upon gaining the blackened iron walls, he found his half-dozen grouped about an opening. They had discovered a trapdoor and ladder leading down into a basement chamber, excavated from the coral rock. It was quite empty; it must have been used in the old days to store perishables.

The excitement of the men amused West, as he perceived how seriously they took the predictions of Broome. This cellar might have made a good refuge, he thought, during the Jap attack. As he inspected it, voices sounded above; he came up, to find Helena, Muda and the two Malays on hand, and showed them the opening.

"There's your best place of refuge," he said, smiling, "in case old Hendrik has correct information and the little brown rats do swarm again. It'll be safer than the Residence, anyhow—"

Muda checked him.

"What is that?" she exclaimed, her liquid eyes widening in sudden alarm. "Do you hear it?"

Eyes lifted, searching. West stood frozen. It was impossible—yet he heard it. Down the sky came a droning mutter. A man yelled, and pointed; then they all saw it—the shimmering sun-silvered thing flying in from seaward.

"Quick! Here, inside the walls, out of sight!" cried West.

FIVE

In a moment of time, everything changed for West—his whole viewpont was switched, his entire attitude altered.

Broome had said that a reconnaissance plane would come over, and there it was. A single plane, coming in low, so low that the Rising Sun emblem under the wings was clearly visible. And it was fast. From the ground, its speed seemed incredible.

"Everybody stand quiet," said West. The natives, all the group of them, were standing inside the roofless godown. Lack of movement was the main thing. West looked over at the fort, and saw that Broome and his natives had disappeared. A canvas was flung over the gun there.

West glanced up. Shreds of the roof of the shed remained, enough to shelter the party here from observation. It hid the plane from them, but the drumming roar of the engine filled the air. Now it flashed directly overhead, circling. The deserted place was being studied sharply.

As he stood, West tried to tell himself that this was merely an accident of fate. He tried, and failed; he found himself laughing at the notion. More likely, Broome's fantasy had somehow fallen in with the truth of things. Whether any landing-party would evolve out of that misty sea was dubious, but here was a plane, scouting the place. And the drumming of this engine, which might so easily have been the rattle of a machine-gun or the smash of bombs, spoke eloquently of winged murder.

Thus far, Broome had hit the facts—never mind how! West found his incredulity shaken, slipping, sliding away. The natives were muttering savagely, Muda was looking up openmouthed, a fury in her eyes; but Helena was watching him. He smiled, reading her thought.

"If we had left at dawn, we'd be a few miles out at sea now, eh? And that plane would have seen us, probably would have machine-gunned us," he said, lifting his voice above the dull engine-roar. She nodded. She had closed her white parasol and now held it loosely.

"Mynheer Broome is right so far. The morning's nearly gone. Do you think it will be safe to lunch at home?"

"Quite," said West. "Might be a good idea to cook up a bit of food ahead and make a lot of coffee, and get it somewhere safe. If any Japs come, their first job will be to destroy what's left of the Residence. With the flag, it stands out like a sore thumb. And there'll be all these natives to feed, you know."

"Rice," she said. "So you think Broome will be right!"

West laughed. "I've quit thinking."

The plane was satisfied now and was winging straight out to sea again. Everyone relaxed. The two women and the Malays started back to the house. West clapped on his topee and headed for the fort, his natives trailing.

Broome was coming and met him halfway, a frosty light of exultation in his blue eyes. The two groups of natives met and set up a great chattering.

"Well, you win," said West. Broome took his arm.

"Of course. My ancestor Hendrik knew. Now we have until three o'clock or so. You didn't believe me, eh? Don't blame you. Feeling more like pitching in?"

"Absolutely," said West. "That damned plane left a chill in the air, Broome. It'll blow us out of the sand when the landing-party comes—if it comes."

"No." Broome shook his head with a positive mannerism. "No. They will not send any planes with the landing-party. You'll see. Hendrik said to ask your advice, so give it."

West was inclined to laugh, but did not. That plane had chilled laughter. Besides, he had changed. He resolved suddenly to pitch in neck and crop. He took no stock in Hendrik, but a landing-party might be the logical thing now. That plane had come from the sea, had gone back to the sea; there must be ships out yonder under the mist.

"Okay, Broome," he said, a new crispness in his voice and air. "The two guns are placed right; couldn't be better. If these chaps land, they'll be under my machine-gun. I'd say for you to start in on 'em when they get close to shore—"

He paused, as reality flooded on him.

"Well? What is it?"

"They'll do for us, you know, in the end. Shell us, and send a plane or two. Most likely a cruiser is out there, carrying a few planes."

"Now, now!" Broome gripped his arm and chuckled. "Hendrik said there was help on the way, so cheer up!"

"Be damned to Hendrik! I'm with you all the way," snapped West. "I'm willing to check out, if I can help send a pack of those devils to hell ahead of me! Let 'em come in close, then cut loose with everything we have. Is that it? Better keep men on watch, and if ships show up, have everyone scuttle out of sight till we're ready to open. And my chaps have found a cellar under the godown; better put the women there when the mess starts."

"Good! Good!" exclaimed Broome, vigorously. "D'ye know, I've found the secret of working that gun? I have. It's quite a trick, but I've got it. Ha! My ancestor Hendrik will be proud of me before this day is past!"

He gave rapid orders to the natives, who saluted awkwardly and scattered. He came over to the godown with West, inspected the cellar, agreed that it should be proof against anything except bombs, then stood eyeing the surf and the little harbor with hungry, frenetic eyes that seemed to see strange things in this emptiness. He nodded toward the native boats drawn up on the shore.

"We should use these; I cannot see how. Do you?"

"No," said West. "Better ask Hendrik."

"A good idea! I'll do it. Hm! The tide should be at flood around three oclock. Yes, I'll go ask him. I'll be up at the house presently for *rijstaaffel*."

He stalked away in the direction of the old fort, where Hendrik presumably kept his headquarters.

West went to the Residence. By this time, the moment of elation, of swift decision, had ebbed. He began to think it was all nonsense about any attack coming!

Halfway up, he encountered the two Malays. Between them they carried, one by either handle, an enormous rattan basket covered over with cloth. They set it down.

"Tuan!" said one of them, earnestly. "Tuan West! We want to fight, too!"

West nodded. "Plenty of rifles lying around. Help yourselves. What have you there?"

"Food, tuan, for the cellar beneath the godown."

"Oh! Good work. Take it along."

At the Residence, he found the women helping to ready the table. Helena came to him and drew him into one corner, purposefully.

"I have a thing to say, my friend," she stated. "Call me a silly woman if you like. But you have deep sense; don't pretend to be cynical, and don't sneer at Mynheer Broome."

West met her gravely intent gaze, and smiled.

"I'm not. Nothing will surprise me now. What did you want to say?"

"Just this. Remember, please, that where one has faith, no evil can prevail! Don't tell me that's a sugared saying for children; it's not. It's most dreadfully practical. Be honest and admit it."

West looked at her, stirred by her eyes, her words.

"Okay, I'll be honest, Helena. This is a hard world; I've never seen faith move any mountains, in spite of what the preachers say. Did you mean it in regard to Broome?"

She nodded quickly.

"You have seen he was right. There are so many things we do not understand, my friend! It is much easier to accept them. It is easy to agree that perhaps Hendrik talked to him—"

"Well, I can't prove he didn't," said West, "but you can't make me believe he did, either! I'm not against him. I'm with him, all the way. If a Jap ship pokes up over the horizon, you can bet I'll give all I've got, too!"

She beamed. "Fine! And remember what I said. Mountains or not, it is a practical fact that evil cannot prevail against faith. I want you to understand it, because I have great faith in you and what you can do."

She bustled away, leaving him in frowning wonder. Faith in him! That was a new angle, he thought. What the deuce had he done to deserve any faith? Nothing. Well, that sort of talk was all very well, and good for morale and that sort of thing.

"But faith doesn't work against a machine-gun," he

reflected practically. "Faith didn't save China from Jap planes! Or—hold on, now! She said *prevail*. That means to win out. And China has won out, so far as the Japs are concerned—oh, hang it all! First thing you know, I'll be going dotty like Broome; and hearing voices! The hell with all that; stick to what you know, boy, and don't get blisters on your heels!"

He dismissed the matter, as Broome showed up, cheerfully confident. A quick wash, and they all sat down to another abundant noon meal after the island fashion. The two Malays were back, and grinned knowingly at each other as they served.

During the meal, Broome went to turn on the radio, and West caught the eye of the Malay serving him.

"What are you two boys so happy about?" he demanded. The flat-faced little man laughed and showed his betel-stained teeth.

"Tuan, we have found nearly twenty rifles, all loaded!"

"Oh!" said West, chuckling. "Take care of 'em, then."

The radio brought the usual indeterminate news, with a report from Batavia that the Allied fleets were striking savagely against the Japs, and combing the widespread islands for marauders, while the depredations went on wholesale by air and sea. It was a depressing report, and Broome savagely switched it off.

"Things are happening and they're not telling us," he snorted. "*Ja!* You will see. My ancestor Hendrik said that the Americans have destroyed the Jap base in the Carolines."

"Let's hope it's true," said West. "We've been wearing them down, no doubt, but that isn't winning battles, which is what the public wants. The hard, telling work isn't dramatic, I expect."

"When one has faith, evil cannot prevail," said Helena.

"*Ja!* That is so!" exclaimed Broome. "My friend West, you might argue it; but it is so. It has more meaning than appears."

"I'm not arguing it," said West, smiling. "Got any more coffee?"

The meal was prolonged until Broome, glancing at his watch, leaped erect.

"Ha! It is two-thirty! Time we were leaving!" he cried. "I'll be off. West, bring the ladies to your cellar—everyone! These Malay boys, too. No one is to show himself, when the enemy appears. They will be watching. They will be careful."

West, tempted to cynicism, was about to speak when the pad-pad of running bare feet sounded, and a panting cry. In upon the room broke one of the natives from the esplanade, with hoarse alarm.

"Tuan! Ships, two ships—they are in sight! They have come!"

Broome was off at a lumbering run, a trail of growling oaths in his wake. West got Muda and the two Malays off, loaded with blankets and cushions, and saw Helena appear with a bag.

"Bandages and supplies," she said. "And a bottle of schnapps. Ready?"

West went to her, took the bag, then leaned forward and kissed her on the lips.

"Ready, yes," he said. "And no illusions about it, either. Let's go."

A smile struggled into her face, banishing its startled expression. She caught his arm, reached up to him, and returned his kiss.

"I—I'm afraid not," she said unsteadily. "No illusions, after all; and I'm horribly frightened!"

"Thanks. so am I," said West. "Or I was. I'm not now. Do it again, will you?"

She complied, and he forgot all about being frightened.

SIX

Everyone was well in hand, even the deaf old crone being huddled in a corner of the cellar. For the present, Helena remained above, watching, arm in arm with Muda. All eyes were on the sea, the natives ready with ammunition-belts, and West at the gun. Nothing moved toward the fort; the quick-firer there was still covered, the men and Broome were out of sight.

Seaward lay what West knew to be iron destiny. All heartening talk aside, all pretense to the contrary, fate was upon them; there was no escape, there could be none, nor survival. The two drifts of smoke shredding on the wind grew into two craft standing in for the harbor. Due to the misty air, alive with dust particles from the Australian deserts, they were closer than appeared; they were within a mile when they swung around and halted.

"Afraid of the mines," said Helena, with a strained air. "The reefs and channels and harbor were all heavily mined when the war broke out—"

A light cruiser, thought West, and a troopship or tanker. No planes appeared, and he recollected Broome's prediction, with a mental wrench. Blast it, the man was right again! Not a plane in sight—the vermin were sure of their prey now. Sure, but very careful.

"Boats," said Muda, breathless. The men chattered; they were poised, set to feed the belts. West spoke to them quietly, then remembered the two Malays. He looked into the cellar. Not there. No one knew what had become of them. Gone with Broome to fight, he thought, and dismissed them from his mind.

Boats, yes. Half a dozen specks coming from the ships out there, one of them far in advance to scout the way. Not mere ship's boats, but barges, steam launches, great sturdy craft with a spot of color fluttering from each. . . . The Sunburst Flag was landing.

"Why don't you shoot?" demanded Helena nervously. "Why doesn't Broome—"

"Because that cruiser would then blow us to pieces before we accomplished anything," West rejoined. "Our aim isn't merely to make a gesture of defiance and then perish; we want to do something worthwhile before we're rubbed out!"

"Are you so sure about—about perishing?" she asked under her breath, startled.

"Of course. Why, my dear, each of those launches

carries bow guns; and once we start to work, that cruiser will blast everything here. Dying's part of our job; part of men's job from Hawaii to Sumatra, these days," he went on quietly. The twinkle had gone from his eyes. He was graver, yet he smiled slightly as he met her gaze. "We'll accomplish something first, that's the main thing. Now take Muda down, will you? God keep you!"

She put her hand out. He gave her a quick grip; a word to Muda, and they were going down the ladder. West himself lowered the heavy trapdoor. This marked the beginning of the end, he knew. He met the excited looks of the natives, and nodded cheerfully.

"Steady, now! Let Tuan Broome start the fun."

They crouched, tense and ready.

The first big launch, crowded with men, glittering with rifles, came nosing into the harbor, its draught too shallow to be worried about mines. Still the old Bren gun remained covered, the shore empty. The launches in the rear swept on. Three of them bunched in the lead, four others trailed—eight in all, several hundred men packed into them.

The first headed for the wharf, slowing speed, men standing with ropes to make fast. West controlled his pounding pulses; he met the rolling eyes of his men, could hear their whistling breaths. That wharf-end was directly before them, not a hundred yards away. The launch came drifting in upon it. A seaman sprang ashore, then another, to make fast. The three following launches were now within the harbor, turning for the wharf.

From the old fort burst a booming roar, a huge belch of powder-smoke—then another and another, as the ancient cannon let go. The sand shook to the detonations; the men yelled. Upon West rushed a feeling of incredulous awe. One could actually see those huge old balls in the air, as though hurled by giant hands. A final roar; two guns went off together.

Directly before the three launches, water spouted high. Time seemed to stand still. The launches made an effort to separate—too late. One was struck full amid-

ships and smashed like a toy boat. The next had her
bow stove in and began to settle at once. The third
caught a ball that raked along her side and left it crumpled; she still floated, but was a mass of disorganized,
screaming men. None the less, her bow gun swung
around and began to pump shells at the old fortress.

"Ready!" said West, and leaned forward.

Half a dozen men were on the wharf, others were
scrambling up, from the first launch. The machine-gun
began to rock and stutter and recoil. Slowly, deliber-
ately, West swept the wharf-end and the launch itself.
Exultant furies hammered in his veins; the wharf was
cleared, the bullets tore through the crowded mass of
men, through the launch itself. She began to fill before
his eyes.

West shifted the gun, aiming for the still floating
launch farther out, where the water was alive with
heads. His first burst went wild, then he found the
range and mercilessly sent a sleet of bullets into launch
and swimmers, spraying them with death. The launch
slewed around helplessly. Then the gun ceased to kick.

The natives fed in a new belt. Back to the first launch
now, to men scrambling on the wharf; they were torn
off like flies. Corpses littered the water. West ceased
firing. The four launches stringing along farther out had
slowed.

There was a shrieking whine overhead, another and
another. Dull reports sounded; the light cruiser was
jetting flame and smoke in the sunlight. Shells began to
burst. The walls of the old fort disintegrated and blew
apart. The guns of the four launches were spitting flame,
too.

Bursts ringed the shore, flamed in the town behind.
The Residence was blown into ruin. The walls of the
godown clanged under impact of shrapnel and bullet.
One of the natives leaped in air and fell, a bleeding
mass; a shell burst ten feet away and the concussion
blew out half of one wall with tremendous clangor.

West turned his gun on the Japs now wading ashore from the shattered launches, off to the left. The native next him was struck with thudding bullets and fell across the gun; he had to be removed.

Abruptly, the hacking cough of the quick-firer yammered on the air. Broome was at his gun, men clustered around him; he sent a stream of his deadly little contact shells out at the four launches. He was slow to get the range, but when he got it West stood up and yelled in mad delight. They were in too far to escape.

One of them went to pieces. The other three put on full speed in a frantic dash to make the shore. The shells missed them, struck all around them. One lost way, slewed around, and drifted; the other two foamed on.

Off to the left, one of the sampans that had been drawn up on the shore floated out; loose on the high tide, thought West. A shell burst with blinding, deafening concussion; sand and blood sprayed everything. Two of his natives remained alive and settled grimly down to feed in the belt. West wiped his eyes and steadied to aim anew.

The two launches were coming on, were close, but Broome had them now. His shells ripped into them. One was sinking, and went under in a cloud of steam as her engines blew up. The other held on. West looked for Broome—he and his men and his gun had disappeared in a cloud of explosive smoke and sand. A direct hit, apparently. So that ended Broome!

The remaining launch was heading in for the shore. West's gun bucked and roared. The bullets swept her savagely. The men about the bow-gun were down, the mass behind were in bitter agony. Rifles flashed in vain reprisal. The stuttering, yammering gun kept up its deadly work. The stern of the launch was settling as she came. She went under, fifty yards from shore.

Shell-bursts were still vengefully searching out everything in the town, along the shore, on the waterfront. West wiped sweat from his eyes, motioned his

two men to get in a new belt, then sprang up. Here was
Broome, running, laughing, roaring, darting into the
godown—Broome, naked to the waist, one arm dan-
gling, streaming blood.

"Every one! Got every one!" he panted exultantly.
"One still afloat out there, West! Put your gun on her!"

West got down again and obeyed, spraying that crippled launch until he got the range and poured a deadly
fire into her. Then he ceased, feeling sick as the crisis
passed.

"Ha! My ancestor Hendrik!" shouted Broome like a
madman, dancing and pointing. "Look! He is in the
sampan!"

West rubbed his eyes. That floating sampan was out
among the swimming figures in the water. They crowded
around her, made for her in droves. The sharp little
reports of rifles came from her, punctuating the deeper
bursts of shells from the cruisers; a laugh came from
West, as he looked.

"Like hell that's Hendrik! That's our two Malays at
work—"

So it was, indeed. Japs crowded over the stern of the
sampan; the Malays went at them with knives swinging
in the sunlight, with rifle-butts, then cleared them off
and began firing anew.

"Well, we're finished," began West, and went reel-
ing as a terrific explosion rocked him and sent him off
his feet. He fell against Broome and they went down
together. Another explosion covered them with sand
and blew the last of the godown walls away, and sent
the machine-gun down the shore, a twisted mass of
metal.

West clawed his way out of the sand, helped Broome
clear, and stripped off his shirt. He began to tie up
Broome's head and arm, while the Dutchman sat grog-
gily blinking at the water. The rifles in the sampan
were still at work, dropping the few Japs who got
close enough to wade in. There were very few left,
now.

"That cruiser is blowing hell out of everything," said West. "Hold still, will you? Hear those shells scream overhead?"

Broome grunted. "I don't understand it," he said faintly. "My ancestor Hendrik—told me there would be help."

"About time she got a plane or two off," said West, "to mop us up from the air. Well, we're done, anyhow. I had two men left—they're gone now. By God, those chaps fought like good 'uns! We've done something, that's sure—"

His words died. Broome gripped his arm suddenly; the man's eyes widened into a blue stare, his mouth fell open, he tried to speak and could only gasp. West swung around and looked.

"Told you!" The labored croak broke from Broome. "Told you! My ancestor—"

Where the cruiser had been a pall of smoke was lifting in the sunlight. The second ship had swung about, smoke was pouring from her funnel; then she heeled far over on her side, swung upright again, heeled again.

Across the water came a heavy thudding roar, and then two more.

"Torpedoes, by the Lord!" burst forth West. "A sub's got 'em both!"

SEVEN

Broome lay on the sand, his eyes fierce, claimed by exhaustion and hurt. The trapdoor stood open. Helena and Muda and the deaf old crone were taking care of the three wounded natives who had survived the shell-bath; one, like West, had remained unhurt. The sun was westing, the afternoon was nearly over.

The cracking of rifles from the sampan had ceased. The sampan itself was being rowed toward the long, slim shape that had come into the harbor, its super-structure crowded with men, the flag of Holland appearing at its staff. It took the sampan alongside and the small boat made for shore, heavy with white uniforms.

West got into his discarded uniform coat and walked over to Broome, and stooped.

"Let me give you a tip," he said. "Keep your mouth shut about your ancestor Hendrik. Other people might not understand. We know—that's enough."

Broome's eyes went to him. "Right. Thanks, old chap."

Two spruce young officers and a crowd of sailors hurried up from the wharf. The greetings were not ceremonious; there was no time. the lieutenant in command of the sub was in a tearing hurry, and said so. He spoke Frisian Dutch, of which West hardly understood a word. The sense was clear, however.

He was deeply regretful, but things were so crowded aboard the sub—a single person might be taken, no more. Even one would pack them to the limit. That one, he said, bowing, would of course be Mejuffrouw van Heynck.

Helena's resentment took everyone aback. She? When Broome was hurt, wounded, needed treatment? The second officer broke in helplessly.

"But what can you do? To remain here is impossible. These vermin will return; they are everywhere. This has been a glorious blow at them, but after all—"

"We'll go as we planned. We have a boat ready; we'll go to Flores." Helena was angry now. She commanded them to carry Broome to the sampan and get him aboard the sub. Broome himself tried to protest, but she silenced him. She dominated them all.

West scarcely noticed the congratulations and praise showered on them all. The curious fact of Helena's dominance was the big thing. He shook hands with Broome, Helena kissed his cheek, and he was helped away to the wharf. The officer in command threw up his hands.

"After all, it is war," he said. "Yes. You had better get off at once, before dark. I can give you a chart and mark the course for Flores; I'll send it back by the sampan."

He was in a desperate hurry; he had his sub to think about.

The whole scene, to West, was a rather incredible sort of dream, not at all what he would have expected. The Javanese woman, Muda, was rearranging the dressing of the three hurt natives. The sampan was coming back to the wharf, the two exultant Malays rowing her; the sub herself was turning and heading outward. West thought of the boat neatly secured under the wharf, safe from all harm—

"Well?"

Helena was standing before him, smiling as she regarded him. He started.

"Eh? What did you say?"

"Nothing. I was about to say, though, that now you understand perfectly? About Mynheer Broome?"

"And his fancies? No. They were right enough. But you can't convince me that he really talked with his ancestor Hendrik."

Her smile widened. "Strong man, stubborn man! It is what I told you to remember. You must get inside of his head. He thought it was Hendrik—perhaps his subconscious brain only hit upon the things that were to happen in a logical sequence—"

West made an impatient gesture.

"Have it any way you like. What does it matter? I can't believe in what we've just seen happen here. Those two ships blown up—this submarine—"

He checked himself. Her quiet strength, her poise, astonished him. She was unshaken, firm, assured.

"Look here," he said quickly, "are we leaving in the boat?"

"Of course," she replied. "Why not? My ancestors, too, fought in these seas. It will be an adventure, my friend, an adventure! But we cannot fail to reach safety. When one has faith, no evil can prevail. And—"

She paused, a color like the bloom of a roseleaf lifting in her cheeks.

"Yes?" prompted West. "And—"

"And," she repeated, with a faint smile, "there will be a moon tonight, on the wide sea."

*"Darkness, be thou my Light," Milton's Satan said; the symbolism of the Nazi movement often drew on like sentiments. The role of the Nordic pagan mythos in National Socialism is well known. Like much else in that incoherent ideological ragbag, it drew on the existing body of Pan-Germanist extreme nationalist and anti-rationalist mysticism, the ideas which had been a staple of the Mitteleuropan lumpenintelligentsia for a generation before 1914: bits of misunderstood Nietzsche, a little Gobineau, half-digested geopolitics flavored with Wagner and spiced with a corrupted Romanticism. A common image was the wolf/werewolf, from Hitler's Wolf's Lair headquarters in East Prussia to the Werewolf guerrillas intended to harass the Allied occupation forces. No doubt this prompted one author to speculate on the human werewolf's meeting with another East European myth. . .*

# THE DEVIL IS NOT MOCKED

## Manly Wade Wellman

*Do you not know that tonight, when the clock strikes midnight, all the evil things in the world hold sway? Do you know where you are going, and what you are going to?*

—Bram Stoker

Balkan weather, even Balkan spring weather, was not pleasant to General von Grunn, leaning heavily back behind the bulletproof glass of his car. May 4th—the English would call it St. George's Day, after their saint who was helping them so little. The date would mean something to Heinrich Himmler, too; that weak-chinned pet of the Fuehrer would hold some sort of garbled druidic ritual with his Schutzstaffel on the Brockenberg. Von Grunn grimaced fatly at thought of Himmler, and leaned forward to look out into the night. An armed car ahead, an armed car behind—all was well.

"Forward!" he growled to his orderly, Kranz, who trod on the accelerator. The car moved, and the car ahead took the lead, into the Borgo Pass.

Von Grunn glanced backward once, to the lights of Bistritz. This country had been Rumanian not so long ago. Now it was Hungarian, which meant that it was German.

What was it that the mayor of Bistritz had said, when he had demanded a semiremote headquarters? The castle along this pass, empty—ready for him? The dolt had seemed eager to help, to please. Von Grunn produced a long cigarette. Young Captain Plesser, sitting beside him, at once kindled a lighter. Slim, quiet, the young aid had faded from von Grunn's consciousness.

"What's the name of that castle again?" inquired the general, and made a grimace when Plesser replied in barbarous Slavic syllables. "What's the meaning in a civilized tongue?"

"Devil's castle, I should think," hazarded the captain's respectful voice.

"*Ach*, so—Transylvania is supposed to be overrun with devils," nodded von Grunn, puffing. "Let them defer to us, or we'll devil them." He smiled, for his was a great gift for appreciating his own epigrams. "Meanwhile, let the castle be called its German name. *Teufelschloss*—Devil's Castle."

"Of course," agreed Plesser.

Silence for a while, as the cars purred powerfully up the rough slope of the pass trail. Von Grunn lost himself in his favorite meditation—his own assured future. He was to establish an unostentatious command post for—what? A move against Russia? The Black Sea? He would know soon enough. In any case, an army would be his, action and glory. There was glory enough for all. Von Grunn remembered Wilhelm II saying that, in the last war.

"The last war," he said aloud. "I was a simple *oberleutnant* then. And the Fuehrer—a corporal. What were you, captain?"

"A child."

"You remember?"

"Nothing." Plesser screwed up his courage to a question. "General von Grunn, does it not seem strange that the folk at Bistritz were so anxious for you to come to the castle—*Teufelschloss*—tonight?"

Von Grunn nodded, like a big fierce owl. "You smell a trap, *nicht wahr*? That is why I bring two carloads of men, my trusted bodyguard. For that very chance. But I doubt if any in Transylvania dare set traps for me, or any other German."

The cars were slowing down. General and captain leaned forward. The car ahead was passing through the great open gateway of a courtyard. Against the spattered stars rose the silhouette of a vast black building, with a broken tower. "We seem to be here," ventured Captain Plesser.

"Good. Go to the forward car. When the other arrives, form the guard."

It was done swiftly. Sixteen stark infantrymen were marshaled, with rifles, bombs, and submachine guns. Von Grunn emerged into the cold night, and Kranz, the orderly, began to bring out the luggage.

"A natural fort, withdrawn and good for any defense except against aircraft," pronounced the general, peering through his monocle at the battlements above. "We will make a thorough examination.

"*Unteroffizier!*" he barked, and the noncom in charge of the escort came forward woodenly, stiffening to attention. "Six of the men will accompany me inside. You will bivouac the others in this courtyard, maintaining a guard all night. *Heil Hitler*."

"*Heil Hitler*," responded the man briskly. Von Grunn smiled as the *unteroffizier* strode away to obey. For all the soldierly alacrity, that order to sleep outdoors was no welcome one. So much the better; von Grunn believed in toughening experiences for field soldiers, and his escort had lived too softly since the Battle of Flanders.

He walked to where a sort of vestibule of massive rough stone, projected from the castle wall. Plesser already stood there, staring at the heavy nail-studded planks of the door. "It is locked, *Herr General*," he reported. "No knob or latch, bell or knocker—"

But as he spoke, the door swung creakingly inward, and yellow light gushed out.

On the threshold stood a figure in black, as tall as von Grunn himself but thinner than even Plesser. A pale, sharp face and brilliant eyes turned upon them, in the light of a chimneyless oil lamp of silver.

"Welcome, General von Grunn," said the lamp holder. "You are expected."

His German was good, his manner respectful. Von Grunn's broad hand slid into a greatcoat pocket, where he always carried a big automatic pistol.

"Who told you to expect us?" he demanded.

The lamplight struck blue radiance from smooth, sparse black hair as the thin man bowed. "Who could mistake General von Grunn, or doubt that he would want this spacious, withdrawn structure for his new headquarters position?"

The mayor of Bistritz, officious ass, must have sent this fellow ahead to make fawning preparations—but even as von Grunn thought that, the man himself gave other information.

"I am in charge here, have been in charge for many years. We are so honored to have company. Will the general enter?"

He stepped back. Plesser entered, then von Grunn. The vestibule was warm. "This way, excellency," said the man with the lamp—the steward, von Grunn decided to classify him. He led the way along a stone-paved passage, von Grunn's escort tramping authoritatively after him. Then up a great winding stair, and into a room, a big hall of a place, with a fire of logs and a table set for supper.

All told, very inviting; but it was not von Grunn's way to say as much. He only nodded, and allowed Captain Plesser to help him out of his greatcoat. Meanwhile, the steward was showing the luggage-laden Kranz into an octagonal bedroom beyond.

"Take these six men," said von Grunn to Plesser, indicating the soldiers of the escort. "Tour the castle.

Make a plan of each floor. Then come back and report. *Heil Hitler.*"

"*Heil Hitler*," and Plesser led the party away. Von Grunn turned his broad back to the fire. Kranz was busy within the bedroom, arranging things. The steward returned. "May I serve the *Herr General?*" he asked silkily.

Von Grunn looked at the table, and with difficulty forebore to lick his fat lips. There were great slices of roast beef, a fowl, cheese, salad, and two bottles of wine—Kranz himself could not have guessed better what would be good. Von Grunn almost started forward to the table, then paused. This was Transylvania. The natives, for all their supple courtesy, disliked and feared soldiers of the Reich. Might these good things not be poisoned?

"Remove these things," he said bleakly. "I have brought my own provisions. You may eat that supper yourself."

Another bow. "The *Herr General* is too good, but I will sup at midnight—it is not long. Now, I will clear the things away. Your man will fetch what you want."

He began to gather up dishes. Watching him stoop over the table, von Grunn thought that he had seldom seen anyone so narrow in the shoulders—they were humped high, like the shoulders of a hyena, suggesting a power that crouched and lurked. Von Grunn was obliged to tell himself that he was not repelled or nervous. The steward was a stranger, a Slav of some kind. It was von Grunn's business to be scornful of all such.

"Now," he said, when all was cleared, "go to the bedroom and tell my orderly—" He broke off. "What was that?"

The other listened. Von Grunn could have sworn that the man's ears—pale and pointed—lifted voluntarily, like the ears of a cat or a fox. The sound came again, a prolonged howl in the distance.

"The wolves," came the quiet reply. "They speak to the full moon."

"Wolves?" The general was intrigued at once. He was a sportsman—that is, he liked to corner and kill beasts almost as much as he liked to corner and kill men. As a guest of Hermann Goering he had shot two very expensive wild bulls, and he yearned for the day when the Fuehrer would graciously invite him to the Black Forest for pigsticking. "Are there many?" he asked. "It sounds like many. If they were not so far—"

"They come nearer," his companion said, and indeed the howl was repeated more strongly and clearly. "But you gave an order, general?"

"Oh, yes." Von Grunn remembered his hunger. "My man will bring me supper from among the things we have with us."

A bow, and the slender black figure moved noiselessly into the bedroom. Von Grunn crossed the floor and seated himself in an armchair before the table. The steward returned, and stood at his elbow.

"Pardon. Your orderly helped me carry the other food to the castle kitchen. He has not returned, and so I took the liberty of serving you."

He had a tray. Upon it were delicacies from von Grunn's mess chest—slices of smoked turkey, buttered bread, preserved fruits, bottled beer. The fellow had arranged them himself, had had every opportunity to . . . to—

Von Grunn scowled and took the monocle from his eye. The danger of poison again stirred in his mind, and he had difficulty scorning it. He must eat and drink, in defiance of fear.

Poison or no poison, the food was splendid, and the steward an excellent waiter. The general drank beer, and deigned to say, "You are an experienced servant?"

The pale, sharp face twitched sidewise in negation. "I serve very few guests. The last was years ago—Jonathan Harker, an Englishman—"

Von Grunn snorted away mention of that unwelcome people, and finished his repast. Then he rose, and stared around. The wolves howled again, in several directions and close to the castle.

"I seem to be deserted," he said grimly. "The captain is late, my orderly late. My men make no report." He stepped to the door, opened it. "Plesser!" he called. "Captain Plesser!"

No reply.

"Shall I bring you to him?" asked the steward gently. Once again, he had come up close. Von Grunn started violently, and wheeled.

The eyes of the steward were on a level with his, and very close. For the first time von Grunn saw that they were filled with green light. The steward was smiling, too, and von Grunn saw his teeth—white, spaced widely, pointed—

As if signaled by the thought, the howling of the beasts outside broke out afresh. It was deafeningly close. To von Grunn it sounded like hundreds. Then, in reply, came a shout, the voice of the *unteroffizier* uttering a quick, startled command.

At once a shot. Several shots.

The men he had encamped in the courtyard were shooting at something.

With ponderous haste, von Grunn hurried from the room, down the stairs. As he reached the passageway below, he heard more shots, and a wild air-rending chorus of howls, growls, spitting scuffles. Von Grunn gained the door by which he had entered. Something moved in the gloom at his very feet.

A chalky face turned up, the face of Captain Plesser. A hand lifted shakily to clutch at the general's boot top.

"Back in there, the dark rooms—" It was half a choke, half a sigh. "They're devils—hungry—they got the others, got me—I could come no farther than this—"

Plesser collapsed. Light came from behind von Grunn, and he could see the captain's head sagging backward on the stone. The side of the slender neck had been torn open, but blood did not come. For there was no blood left in Captain Plesser's body.

Outside, there was sudden silence. Stepping across Plesser's body, the general seized the latch and pushed the door open.

The courtyard was full of wolves, feeding. One glance was enough to show what they fed on. As von Grunn stared, the wolves lifted their heads and stared back. He saw many green-glowing eyes, level, hard, hungry, many grinning mouths with pointed teeth—the eyes and the teeth of the steward.

He got the door shut again, and sagged upon it, breathing hard.

"I am sorry, general," came a soft, teasing apology. "Sorry—my servants were too eager within and without. Wolves and vampires are hard to restrain. After all, it is midnight—our moment of all moments."

"What are you raving about?" gasped von Grunn, feeling his jaw sag.

"I do not rave. I tell simple truth. My castle has vampires within, wolves without, all my followers and friends—"

Von Grunn felt for a weapon. His greatcoat was upstairs, the pistol in its pocket.

"Who are you?" he screamed.

"I am Count Dracula of Transylvania," replied the gaunt man in black.

He set down the lamp carefully before moving forward.

Science fiction is the mythology of a rationalist and scientific worldview. Paradoxically, this made it more difficult for science fiction to deal with the real-world phenomenon of Nazism. Fantasy more easily deal with the irrationalism, the fetishistic blood-hunger, the farrago of nonsense translated into cold reality by the power of Will that was at the heart of National Socialism. Science fiction, particularly in the 1940s, was heir to the traditions of the Enlightenment, in their Anglo-Saxon form; committed to an optimistic, technophile view of reality. But the converse was also true: by their contempt for objective reality, their fantasies of "racial science" and persecution of Germany's finest minds, their disdain for order and long-term planning, the Nazis fatally weakened themselves. Until the 1930s, Germany was the world leader in science and technology; Adolf Hitler gave the Allies the lead which proved crucial in winning the war. Even the crippled remnants of German's technical skill produced the first jets and IRBM's. What might the full flower of it have done? In this story, the author uses metaphor to show with telling effect that science is not a tool that anyone can use. Only a mind attuned to its demands can grasp and use it . . .

# SECRET UNATTAINABLE

## A.E. van Vogt

The file known as Secret Six was smuggled out of Berlin in mid-1945 when Russia was in sole occupation of the city. How it was brought to the United States is one of those dramatic true tales of World War II. The details cannot yet be published since they involve people now in the Russian zone of Germany.

All the extraordinary documents of this file, it should be emphasized, are definitely in the hands of our own authorities; and investigations are proceeding apace. Further revelations of a grand order may be expected as soon as one of the machines is built. All German models were destroyed by the Nazis early in 1945.

The documents date from 1937, and will be given chronologically, without reference to their individual importance. But first, it is of surpassing interest to draw attention to the following news item, which appeared in the New York *Sun*, March 25, 1941, on page 17. At that time it appeared to have no significance whatever. The item:

### GERMAN CREEK BECOMES RIVER

London, March 24 (delayed): A Royal Air Force re-connaissance pilot today reported that a creek in north-ern Prussia, marked on the map as the Gribe Creek, has become a deep, swift river overnight. It is believed that an underground waterway burst its bounds. Sev-eral villages in the path of the new river showed under water. No report of the incident has yet been received from Berlin.

There never was any report from Berlin. It should again be pointed out that the foregoing news item was published in 1941; the documents which follow date from 1937, a period of four years. Four years of world-shaking history:

April 10, 1937

From    Secretary, Bureau of Physics
To    Reich and Prussian Minister of Science
Subject    10731—127—S—6

1. Inclosed is the report of the distinguished scien-tific board of inquiry which sat on the case of Herr Professor Johann Kenrube.
2. As you will see, the majority of the board oppose emphatically the granting of State funds for what they describe as a "fantastic scheme." They deny that a step-up tube would produce the results claimed, and refute utterly the number philosophy involved. Num-ber, they say, is a function, not a reality, or else mod-ern physics has no existence.
3. The minority report of Herr Professor Goureit, while thought-provoking, can readily be dismissed when it is remembered that Goureit, like Kenrube and Kenrube's infamous brother, was once a member of the SPD.
4. The board of inquiry, having in mind Hitler's desire that no field of scientific inquiry should be left unexplored, and as a generous gesture to Goureit, who has a very great reputation and a caustic pen, suggested

that, if Kenrube could obtain private funds for his research, he should be permitted to do so.

5. Provided Geheime Staats Polizei do not object, I concur.

G.L.

Author's Note: *The signature G.L. has been difficult to place. There appear to have been several secretaries of the Bureau of Physics Research, following one another in swift order. The best accounts identify him as Gottfried Lesser, an obscure B.Sc. who early joined the Nazi party, and for a period was its one and only science expert. Geheime Staats Polizei is of course Gestapo.*

MEMO                                            April 17, 1937
From    Chief, Science Branch, Gestapo

If Kenrube can find the money, let him go ahead. Himmler concurs, provided supervision be strict.

K. Reissel

COPY ONLY                                       June 2, 1937
From    Co-ordinator Dept., Deutsche Bank
To      Gestapo

The marginally noted personages have recently transferred sums totaling Reichsmarks four million five hundred thousand to the account of Herr Professor Johann Kenrube. For your information, please.

J. Pleup.

June 11, 1937

From     Gestapo
To       Reich and Prussian Minister of Science
Subject  Your 10731—127—S—6

Per your request for further details on the private life of J. Kenrube since the death of his brother in June, 1934, in the purge:

We quote from a witness, Peter Braun: "I was in a

position to observe Herr Professor Kenrube very closely when the news was brought to him at Frankfort-on-Main that August, his brother, had been executed in the sacred blood purge.

"Professor Kenrube is a thin, good-looking man with a very wan face normally. This face turned dark with color, then drained completely of blood. He clenched his hands and said: 'They've murdered him!' Then he rushed off to his room.

"Hours later, I saw him walking, hatless, hair disarrayed, along the bank of the river. People stopped to look at him, but he did not see them. He was very much upset that first day. When I saw him again the next morning, he seemed to have recovered. He said to me: 'Peter, we must all suffer for our past mistakes. The tragic irony of my brother's death is that he told me only a week ago in Berlin that he had been mistaken in opposing the National-sozialistiche Arbeitspartei. He was convinced they were doing great things. I am too much of a scientist ever to have concerned myself with politics.' "

You will note, Excellency, that this is very much the set speech of one who is anxious to cover up the indiscreet, emotional outburst of the previous day. However, the fact that he was able to pull himself together at all seems to indicate that affection of any kind is but shallowly rooted in his character. Professor Kenrube returned to his laboratories in July, 1934, and has apparently been hard at work ever since.

There has been some discussion here concerning Kenrube, by the psychologists attached to this office; and the opinion is expressed, without dissent, that in three years the professor will almost have forgotten that he had a brother.

K. Reissel.

MEMO AT BOTTOM OF LETTER:

I am more convinced than ever that psychologists should be seen and not heard. It is our duty to watch every relative of every person whose life is, for any reason, claimed by the State. If there are scientific developments of worthwhile nature in this Kenrube affair, let me know at once. His attainments are second to none. A master plan of precaution is in order.

Himmler.

October 24, 1937

From      Secretary, Bureau of Physics
To        Reich and Prussian Minister of Science
Subject   Professor Johann Kenrube

The following report has been received from our Special Agent Seventeen:

"Kenrube has hired the old steel and concrete fortress, Gribe Schloss, overlooking the Gribe Creek, which flows into the Eastern Sea. This ancient fortress was formerly located on a small hill in a valley. The hill has subsided, however, and is now virtually level with the valley floor. We have been busy for more than a month making the old place livable, and installing machinery."

For your information, Agent Seventeen is a graduate in physics of Bonn University. He was for a time professor of physics at Muenchen. In view of the shortage of technicians, Kenrube has appointed Seventeen his chief assistant.

G.L.

May 21, 1938

From      Science Branch, Gestapo
To        Reich and Prussian Minister of Science
Subject   10731—127—S—6

Himmler wants to know the latest developments in the Kenrube affair. Why the long silence? Exactly what is Professor Kenrube trying to do, and what progress has he made? Surely, your secret agent has made reports.

K. Reissel.

June 3, 1938

From     Secretary, Bureau of Physics
To       Chief, Science Branch, Gestapo
Subject  Professor Johann Kenrube

Your letter of the 21st ultimo has been passed on to me. The inclosed précis of the reports of our Agent Seventeen will bring you up to date.

Be assured that we are keeping a careful watch on the developments in this case. So far, nothing meriting special attention has arisen.

G.L.

PRÉCIS OF MONTHLY REPORTS
OF
AGENT SEVENTEEN

Our agent reports that Professor Kenrube's first act was to place him, Seventeen, in charge of the construction of the machine, thus insuring that he will have the most intimate knowledge of the actual physical details.

When completed, the machine is expected to occupy the entire common room of the old fortress, largely because of the use of step-up vacuum tubes. In this connection, Seventeen describes how four electric dynamos were removed from Kenrube's old laboratories, their entire output channeled through the step-up tubes, with the result that a ninety-four percent improvement in efficiency was noted.

Seventeen goes on to state that orders for parts have been placed with various metal firms but, because of the defense program, deliveries are extremely slow. Professor Kenrube has resigned himself to the possibility that his invention will not be completed until 1944 or '45.

Seventeen, being a scientist in his own right, has become interested in the machine. In view of the fact that, if successful, it will insure measureless supplies of raw materials for our Reich, he urges that some effort be made to obtain priorities.

He adds that he has become quite friendly with Kenrube. He does not think that the Herr Professor suspects how closely he is connected with the Bureau of Science.

June 4, 1938

From      Gestapo
To        Reich and Prussian Minister of Science
Subject    10731—127—S—6

Raw materials! Why was I not informed before that Kenrube was expecting to produce raw materials? Why did you think I was taking an interest in this case, if not because Kenrube is a genius of the first rank; and therefore anything he does must be examined with the most minute care? But—raw materials! Are you all mad over there, or living in a world of pleasant dreams?

You will at once obtain from Herr Professor Kenrube the full plans, the full mathematics of his work, with photographs of the machine as far as it has progressed. Have your scientists prepare a report for me as to the exact nature of the raw materials that Kenrube expects to obtain. Is this some transmutation affair, or what is the method?

Inform Kenrube that he must supply this information or he will obtain no further materials. If he satisfies our requirements, on the other hand, there will be a quickening of supplies. Kenrube is no fool. He will understand the situation.

As for your agent, Seventeen, I am at once sending an agent to act as his bodyguard. Friendly with Kenrube indeed!

Himmler.

June 28, 1938

From      Gestapo
To        Secretary, Bureau of Physics
Subject    Secret Six

Have you received the report from Kenrube? Himmler is most anxious to see this the moment it arrives.

K. Reissel.

July 4, 1938

From    Gestapo
To       Secretary, Bureau of Physics
Subject  Secret Six

What about the Kenrube report? Is it possible that your office does not clearly grasp how important we regard this matter? We have recently discovered that Professor Kenrube's grandfather once visited a very curious and involved revenge on a man whom he hated years after the event that motivated the hatred. Every conceivable precaution must be taken to see to it that the Kenrube machine can be duplicated, and the machine itself protected.

Please send the scientific report the moment it is available.

K. Reissel.

July 4, 1938

From    Secretary, Bureau of Physics
To       Chief, Science Branch, Gestapo
Subject  Professor Johann Kenrube

The report, for which you have been asking, has come to hand, and a complete transcription is being sent to your office under separate cover. As you will see, it is very elaborately prepared; and I have taken the trouble to have a précis made of our scientific board's analysis of the report for your readier comprehension.

G.L.

PRÉCIS
OF
SCIENTIFIC ANALYSIS OF KENRUBE'S REPORT
ON HIS INVENTION

General Statement of Kenrube's Theory: That there are two kinds of space in the universe, normal and hyperspace.

Only in normal space is the distance between star systems and galaxies great. It is essential to the nature of things, to the unity of material bodies, that intimate cohesion exist between every particle of matter, between, for instance, the earth and the universe as a whole.

Kenrube maintains that gravity does not explain the perfect and wonderful balance, the singleness of organism that is a galactic system. And that the theory of relativity merely evades the issue in stating that planets go around the sun because it is easier for them to do that than to fly off into space.

Kenrube's thesis, therefore, is that all the matter in the universe conjoins according to a rigid mathematical pattern, and that this conjunction presupposes the existence of hyperspace.

Object of Invention: To bridge the gap through hyperspace between the Earth and any planet, or any part of any planet. In effect, this means that it would not be necessary to drill for oil in a remote planet. The machine would merely locate the oil stratum, and tap it at any depth; the oil would flow from the orifice of the machine which, in the case of the machine now under construction, is ten feet in diameter.

A ten-foot flow of oil at a pressure of four thousand feet a minute would produce approximately six hundred thousand tons of oil every hour.

Similarly, mining could be carried on simply by locating the ore-bearing veins, and skimming from them the purest ores.

It should be pointed out that, of the distinguished scientists who have examined the report, only Herr Professor Goureit claims to be able to follow the mathematics proving the existence of hyperspace.

COPY ONLY                                    July 14, 1938

TRANSCRIPTION OF INTERVIEW BY HERR HIMMLER OF PROFESSOR H. KLEINBERG, CHAIRMAN OF THE SCIENTIFIC COMMITTEE OF SCIENCE BRANCH, GESTAPO, INVESTIGATING REPORT OF HERR PROFESSOR JOHANN KENRUBE.

Q. You have studied the drawings and examined the mathematics?

A. Yes.

Q. What is your conclusion?

A. We are unanimously agreed that some fraud is being perpetrated.

Q. Does your verdict relate to the drawings of the invention, or to the mathematics explaining the theory?

A. To both. The drawings are incomplete. A machine made from those blueprints would hum with apparent power and purpose, but it would be a fraudulent uproar; the power simply goes oftener through a vacuumized circuit before returning to its source.

Q. I have sent your report to Kenrube. His comment is that almost the whole of modern electrical physics is founded on some variation of electricity being forced through a vacuum. What about that?

A. It is a half truth.

Q. What about the mathematics?

A. There is the real evidence. Since Descartes—

Q. Please abstain from using these foreign names.

A. Pardon me. Since Llibniz, number has been a function, a variable idea. Kenrube treats of number as an existing *thing*. Mathematics, he says, has living and being. You have to be a scientist to realize how incredible, impossible, ridiculous, such an idea is.

WRITTEN COMMENT ON THE ABOVE

I am not a scientist. I have no set ideas on the subject of mathematics or invention. I am, however, prepared to accept the theory that Kenrube is withholding information, and for this reason order that:

1. All further materials for the main machine be withheld.
2. Unlimited assistance be given Kenrube to build a model of his machine in the great government labora-

tories at Dresden. When, and not until, this model is in
operation, permission will be given for the larger machine to be completed.

3. Meanwhile, Gestapo scientists will examine the machine at Gribe Schloss, and Gestapo construction experts will, if necessary, reinforce the building, which
must have been damaged by the settling of the hill on
which it stands.

4. Gestapo agents will hereafter guard Gribe Schloss.

Himmler.

December 2, 1938

From     Secretary, Bureau of Physics
To       Chief, Science Branch, Gestapo
Subject   Herr Professor Kenrube

Inclosed is the quarterly précis of the reports of our
Agent Seventeen.

For your information, please.

August Buehnen

Author's Note: *Buehnen, a party man who was educated in one of the Nazi two-year Science Schools,
replaced G.L. as secretary of the Bureau of Physics
about September, 1938.*

*It is not known exactly what became of Lesser, who
was a strong party man. There was a Brigadier General
G. Lesser, a technical expert attached to the Fuehrer's
headquarters at Smolensk. This man, and there is some
evidence that he is the same, was killed in the first
battle of Moscow.*

QUARTERLY PRÉCIS OF REPORTS

OF

AGENT SEVENTEEN

1. Herr Professor Kenrube is working hard on the model.
He has at no time expressed bitterness over the en-
forced cessation of work on the main machine, and
apparently accepts readily the explanation that the gov-

ernment cannot afford to allot him material until the model proves the value of his work.

2. The model will have an orifice of six inches. This compares with the ten-foot orifice of the main machine. Kenrube's intention is to employ it for the procuration of liquids, and believes that the model will of itself go far to reducing the oil shortage in the Reich.

3. The machine will be in operation sometime in the summer of 1939. We are all eager and excited.

February 7, 1939

From      Secretary, Bureau of Physics
To        Gestapo
Subject   Secret Six

The following precautions have been taken with the full knowledge and consent of Herr Professor Kenrube:

1. A diary in triplicate is kept of each day's progress. Two copies are sent daily to our office here. As you know, the other copy is submitted by us to your office.

2. Photographs are made of each part of the machine before it is installed, and detailed plans of each part are kept, all in triplicate, the copies distributed as described above.

3. From time to time independent scientists are called in. They are invariably impressed by Kenrube's name, and suspicious of his mathematics and drawings.

For your information, please.

August Buehnen.

March 1, 1939

From      Reich and Prussian Minister of Science
To        Herr Heinrich Himmler, Gestapo
Subject   The great genius, Herr Professor Kenrube

It is my privilege to inform Your Excellency that the world-shaking invention of Herr Professor Johann Kenrube went into operation yesterday, and has already shown fantastic results.

The machine is not a pretty one, and some effort must be made to streamline future reproductions of this model, with an aim toward greater mobility. In its present condition, it is strung out over the floor in a most ungainly fashion. Rough metal can be very ugly.

Its most attractive feature is the control board, which consists of a number of knobs and dials, the operator of which, by an arrangement of mirrors, can peer into the orifice, which is located on the right side of the control board, and faces away from it. (I do not like these awkward names, orifice and hyperspace. We must find a great name for this wonderful machine and its vital parts.)

When Buehnen and I arrived, Professor Kenrube was busy opening and shutting little casements in various parts of that sea of dull metal. He took out and examined various items.

At eleven forty-five, Kenrube stationed himself at the control board, and made a brief speech comparing the locator dials of the board to the dial on a radio which tunes in stations. His dials, however, tuned in planets; and, quite simply, that is what he proceeded to do.

It appears that the same planets are always on exactly the same gradation of the main dial; and the principle extends down through the controls which operate to locate sections of planets. Thus it is always possible to return to any point of any planet. You will see how important this is.

The machine had already undergone its first tests, so Kenrube now proceeded to turn to various planets previously selected; and a fascinating show it was.

Gazing through the six-inch orifice is like looking through a glassless window. What a great moment it will be when the main machine is in operation, and we can *go* through the ten-foot orifice.

The first planet was a desolate, frozen affair, dimly lighted by a remote red sun. It must have been airless because there was a whistling sound, as the air rushed out of our room into that frigid space. Some of that deadly cold came trickling through, and we quickly switched below the surface of the planet.

Fantastic planet! It must be an incredibly heavy world,

for it is a treasure house of the heavier metals. Everywhere we turned, the soil formation showed a shifting pattern of gold, silver, zinc, iron, tin—thousands of millions of tons.

At Professor Kenrube's suggestion, I put on a pair of heavy gloves, and removed a four-inch rock of almost pure gold. It simply lay there in a gray shale, but it was so cold that the moisture of the room condensed on it, forming a thick hoarfrost. How many ages that planet must have frozen for the cold to penetrate so far below the surface!

The second planet was a vast expanse of steaming swamps and tropical forests, much as Earth must have been forty million years ago. However, we found not a single trace of animal, insect, reptile, or other non-floral life.

The third, fourth, and fifth planets were devoid of any kind of life, either plant or animal. The sixth planet might have been Earth, except that its green forests, its rolling plains showed no sign of animal or intelligent life. But it is on this planet that oil had been located by Kenrube and Seventeen in their private tests. When I left, a pipeline, previously rigged up, had been attached to the orifice, and was vibrating with oil at the colossal flow speed of nearly one thousand miles per hour.

This immense flow has now been continuous for more than twenty-four hours; and I understand it has already been necessary to convert the great water reservoir in the south suburbs to storage space for oil.

It may be *nouveau riche* to be storing oil at great inconvenience, when the source can be tapped at will. But I personally will not be satisfied until we have a number of these machines in action. It is better to be childish and have the oil than logical and have regrets.

I cannot conceive what could go wrong now. Because of our precautions, we have numerous and complete plans of the machines. It is necessary, of course, to ensure that our enemies do not learn our secret, and on this point I would certainly appreciate your most earnest attention.

The enormous potentialities of this marvelous instrument expand with every minute spent in thinking about it. I scarcely slept a wink last night.

                                        March 1, 1939
From     Chief, Criminal Investigation Branch, Gestapo
To       Reich and Prussian Minister of Science
Subject  Secret Six

Will you please inform this office without delay of the name of every scientist or other person who has any knowledge, however meager, of the Kenrube machine?
                                        Reinhard Heydrich

Author's Note: *This is the Heydrich, handsome, ruthless Heydrich, who in 1941 bloodily repressed the incipient Czech revolt, who after the notorious Himmler became Minister of the Interior, succeeded his former master as head of the Gestapo, and who was subsequently assassinated.*

                                        March 2, 1939
From     Secretary, Bureau of Physics
To       R. Heydrich
Subject  Secret Six

The list of names for which you asked is herewith attached.
                                        August Buehnen

COMMENT AT BOTTOM OF LETTER

In view of the importance of this matter, some changes should be made in the precautionary plan drawn up a few months ago with respect to these personages. Two, not one, of our agents must be assigned to keep secret watch on each of these individuals. The rest of the plan can be continued as arranged with one other exception: In the event that any of these men suspect that they are

being watched, I must be informed at once. I am prepared to explain to such person, within limits, the truth
of the matter, so that he may not be personally worried.
The important thing is we do not want these people
suddenly to make a run for the border.

Himmler.

SPECIAL DELIVERY
PERSONAL

From　　Reich and Prussian Minister of Science
To　　　Herr Heinrich Himmler
Subject　Professor Johann Kenrube

I this morning informed the Fuehrer of the Kenrube
machine. He became very excited. The news ended his
indecision about the Czechs. The army will move to
occupy.

For your advance information, please.

March 13, 1939

From　　Gestapo
To　　　Reich and Prussian Minister of Science
Subject　The Dresden Explosion

The incredibly violent explosion of the Kenrube
model must be completely explained. A board of discovery should be set up at Dresden with full authority.
I must be informed day by day of the findings of this
court.

This is a very grim business. Your agent, Seventeen,
is among those missing. Kenrube is alive, which is
very suspicious. There is no question of arresting him;
the only thing that matters is to frustrate future
catastrophes of this kind. His machine has proved
itself so remarkable that he must be conciliated at all
costs until we can be sure that everything is going
right.

Let me know *everything*.

Himmler.

PRELIMINARY REPORT OF AUGUST BUEHNEN

When I arrived at the scene of the explosion, I noticed immediately that a solid circle, a remarkably precise circle, of the wall of the fifth floor of the laboratories—where the Kenrube machine is located—had been sliced out as by some inconceivable force.

Examining the edges of this circle, I verified that it could not have been heat which performed so violent an operation. Neither the brick nor the exposed steel was in any way singed or damaged by fire.

The following facts have been given to me of what transpired:

It had been necessary to cut the flow of oil because of the complete absence of further storage space. Seventeen, who was in charge—Professor Kenrube during this whole time was at Gribe Schloss working on the main machine—was laboriously exploring other planets in search of rare metals.

The following is an extract from my interview with Jacob Schmidt, a trusted laboratory assistant in the government service:

Q. You say, Herr—(Seventeen) took a piece of ore to the window to examine it in the light of the sun?

A. He took it to the window, and stood there looking at it.

Q. This placed him directly in front of the orifice of the machine?

A. Yes.

Q. Who else was in front of the orifice?

A. Dobelmanns, Minster, Freyburg, Tousand-freind.

Q. These were all fellow assistants of yours?

A. Yes.

Q. What happened then?

A. There was a very loud click from the machine, followed by a roaring noise.

Q. Was anyone near the control board?

A. No, sir.

Q. It was an automatic action of the machine?

A.   Yes. The moment it happened we all turned to face the machine.

Q.   All of you? Herr—(Seventeen), too?

A.   Yes, he looked around with a start, just as Minster cried out that a blue light was coming from the orifice.

Q.   A blue light. What did this blue light replace?

A.   A soil formation of a planet, which we had numbered 447–711–Gradation A–131–8, which is simply its location on the dials. It was from this soil that Herr—(Seventeen) had taken the ore sample.

Q.   And then, just like that, there was the blue light?

A.   Yes. And for a few instants that was all there was, the blue light, the strange roaring sound, and us standing there half paralyzed.

Q.   Then it flared forth?

A.   It was terrible. It was such an intense blue it hurt my eyes, even though I could only see it in the mirror over the orifice. I have not the faintest impression of heat. But the wall was gone, and all the metal around the orifice.

Q.   And the men?

A.   Yes, and the men, all five of them.

March 18, 1939

From        Secretary, Bureau of Physics
To          Chief, Science Branch, Gestapo
Subject     Dresden Explosion


I am inclosing a précis of the report of the Court of Inquiry, which has just come to hand. The report will be sent to you as soon as a transcription has been typed.

For your information, please.

August Buehnen

PRÉCIS OF REPORT OF COURT OF INQUIRY

1. It has been established:
   (A) That the destruction was preceded by a clicking sound.

(B) That this click came from the machine.

(C) That the machine is fitted with automatic finders.

2. The blue flame was the sole final cause of the destruction.

3. No theory exists, or was offered, to explain the blue light. It should be pointed out that Kenrube was not called to testify.

4. The death of Herr—(Seventeen) and of his assistants was entirely due to the momentary impulse that had placed them in the path of the blue fire.

5. The court finds that the machine could have been tampered with, that the click that preceded the explosion could have been the result of some automatic device previously set to tamper with the machine. No other evidence of sabotage exists, and no one in the room at the time was to blame for the accident.

COPY ONLY

FOR MINISTRY OF SCIENCE                    March 19, 1939

From      Major H. L. Guberheit
To        Minister for Air
Subject   Destruction of plane, type JU-88

I have been asked to describe the destruction of a plane under unusual circumstances, as witnessed by several hundred officers and men under my command.

The JU-88, piloted by Cadet Pilot Herman Kiesler, was approaching the runway for a landing, and was at the height of about five hundred feet when there was a flash of intense blue—and the plane vanished.

I cannot express too strongly the violence, the intensity, the blue vastness of the explosion. It was titanic. The sky was alive with light reflections. And though a bright sun was shining, the entire landscape grew brilliant with that blue tint.

There was no sound of explosion. No trace of this machine was subsequently found, no wreckage. The time of the accident was approximately 10:30 A.M., March 13th.

There has been great uneasiness among the students during the past week.

For your information, please.

H. L. Guberheit
Major, C. Air Station 473

COMMENT AT BOTTOM OF LETTER

Excellency—I wish most urgently to point out that the time of this unnatural accident coincides with the explosion of "blue" light from the orifice of the Kenrube machine.

I have verified that the orifice was tilted ever so slightly upward, and that the angle would place the beam at a height of five hundred feet near the airport in question.

The staggering feature is that the airport referred to is *seventy-five miles* from Dresden. The greatest guns ever developed can scarcely fire that distance, and yet the incredible power of the blue energy showed no diminishment. Literally, it disintegrated metal and flesh—everything.

I do not dare to think what would have happened if that devastating flame had been pointed not away from but at the ground.

Let me have your instructions at once, because here is beyond doubt the weapon of the ages.

August Buehnen

March 19, 1939

From      Chief, Science Branch, Gestapo
To        Reich and Prussian Minister of Science
Subject   Secret Six

In perusing the report of the inquiry board, we were amazed to note that Professor Kenrube was not questioned in this matter.

Be assured that there is no intention here of playing up to this man. We absolutely require an explanation from him. Send Herr Buehnen to see Kenrube and instruct him to employ the utmost firmness if necessary.

K. Reissel

March 21, 1939

From      Secretary, Bureau of Physics
To        Chief, Science Branch, Gestapo
Subject   Dresden Explosion

As per your request, I talked with Kenrube at Gribe Schloss.

It was the second time I had seen him, the first time being when I accompanied his Excellency, the Minister of Science, to Dresden to view the model; and I think I should point out here that Herr Professor Kenrube's physical appearance is very different from what I had been led to expect from the description recorded in File Secret Six. I had pictured him a lean, fanatic-eyed type. He *is* tall, but he must have gained weight in recent years, for his body is well filled out, and his face and eyes are serene, with graying hair to crown the effect of a fine, scholarly, middle-aged man.

It is unthinkable to me that this is some madman plotting against the Reich.

The first part of his explanation of the blue light was a most curious reference to the reality of mathematics, and, for a moment, I almost thought he was attempting to credit the accident to this *actuality* of his incomprehensible number system.

Then he went on to the more concrete statement that a great star must have intruded into the plane of the planet under examination. The roaring sound that was heard he attributed to the fact that the component elements of the air in the laboratory were being sucked into the sun, and destroyed.

The sun, of course, would be in a state of balance all its own, and therefore would not come into the room until the balance had been interfered with by the air of the room.

(I must say my own explanation would be the reverse of this; that is, the destruction of the air would possibly create a momentary balance, a barrier, during which time nothing of the sun came into the room except light reflections. However, the foregoing is what Kenrube said, and I presume it is based on his own mathematics. I can only offer it for what it is worth.)

Abruptly, the balance broke down. For a fraction of an instant, then, before the model hyperspace machine was destroyed, the intolerable energies of a blue-white sun poured forth.

It would have made no difference if the airplane that was caught in the beam of blue light had been farther away from Dresden than seventy-five miles—that measureless force would have reached seven thousand five hundred miles just as easily, or seventy-five thousand.

The complete absence of visible heat is no evidence that it was not a sun. At forty million degrees Fahrenheit, heat, as we know it, does not exist.

The great man went on to say that he had previously given some thought to the danger from suns, and that in fact he was in the late mathematical stage of developing an attachment that would automatically reject bodies larger than ten thousand miles in diameter.

In his opinion, efforts to control the titanic energies of suns should be left to a later period, and should be carried out on uninhabited planets by scientists who have gone through the orifice and who have been then cut off from contact with earth.

August Buehnen

COMMENT ATTACHED

Kenrube's explanation sounds logical, and it does seem incredible that he would meddle with such forces, though it is significant that the orifice was tilted "slightly upward." We can dispense with his advice as to when and how we should experiment with sun energies. The extent of the danger seems to be a momentary discharge of inconceivable forces, and then destruction of the machine. If at the moment of discharge the orifice was slightly tilted toward London or New York, and if a sufficient crisis existed, the loss of one more machine would be an infinitesimal cost.

As for Kenrube's fine, scholarly appearance, I think

Buehnen has allowed himself to be carried away by the greatness of the invention. The democrats of Germany are not necessarily madmen, but here, as abroad, they are our remorseless enemies.

We must endeavor to soften Kenrube by psychological means.

I cannot forget that *there is not now a working model of the Kenrube machine in existence.* Until there is, all the fine, scholarly-looking men in the world will not convince me that what happened was entirely an accident.

The deadly thing about all this is that we have taken an irrevocable step with respect to the Czechs; and war in the west is now inevitable.

Himmler

May 1, 1939

From      Chief, Science Branch, Gestapo
To        Reich and Prussian Minister of Science
Subject   Secret Six

The Fuehrer has agreed to exonerate completely August Kenrube, the brother of Herr Professor Kenrube. As you will recall, August Kenrube was killed in the sacred purge of June, 1934. It will now be made clear that his death was an untimely accident, and that he was a true German patriot.

This is in line with our psychological attack on Professor Kenrube's suspected anti-Nazism.

K. Reissel.

June 17, 1939

From      Secretary, Bureau of Physics
To        Chief, Science Branch, Gestapo
Subject   Professor Johann Kenrube

In line with our policy to make Kenrube realize his oneness with the community of German peoples, I had him address the convention of mathematicians. The speech, of which I inclose a copy, was a model one; three thousand words of glowing generalities, giving not a hint as to his true opinions on anything. However, he received the ovation of his life; and I think he was pleased in spite of himself.

Afterward, I saw to it—without, of course, appearing directly—that he was introduced to Fräulein Ilse Weber.

As you know, the Fräulein is university educated, a mature, modern young woman; and I am sure that she is merely taking on one of the many facets of her character in posing to Kenrube as a young woman who has decided quite calmly to have a child, and desires the father to be biologically of the highest type.

I cannot see how any human male, normal or abnormal, could resist the appeal of Fräulein Weber.

August Buehnen.

July 11, 1939

From      Chief, Science Branch, Gestapo
To        Secretary, Bureau of physics.
Subject   Secret Six

Can you give me some idea when the Kenrube machine will be ready to operate? What about the duplicate machines which we agreed verbally would be built without Kenrube's knowledge? Great decisions are being made. Conversations are being conducted that will shock the world, and, in a general way, the leaders are relying on the Kenrube machine.

In this connection please submit as your own some variation of the following memorandum. It is from the Fuehrer himself, and therefore I need not stress its urgency.

K. Reissel.

MEMORANDUM OF ADOLF HITLER

Is it possible to tune the Kenrube machine to our own earth?

July 28, 1939

From      Secretary, Bureau of Physics
To        Chief, Science Branch, Gestapo
Subject   Secret Six

I enclose the following note from Kenrube, which is self-explanatory. We have retained a copy.

August Buehnen

NOTE FROM KENRUBE

Dear Herr Buehnen:

The answer to your memorandum is yes.

In view of the international anxieties of the times, I offer the following suggestions as to weapons that can be devised from the hyperspace machine:

1. Any warship can be rendered noncombatant at critical moments by draining of its oil tanks.

2. Similarly, enemy oil-storage supplies can be drained at vital points. Other supplies can be blown up or, if combustible, set afire.

3. Troops, tanks, trucks, and all movable war materials can be transported to any point on the globe, behind enemy lines, into cities, by the simple act of focussing the orifice at the desired destination—and driving it and them through. I need scarcely point out that my machine renders railway and steamship transport obsolete. The world shall be transformed.

4. It might even be possible to develop a highly malleable, delicately adjusted machine, which can drain the tanks of airplanes in full flight.

5. Other possibilities, too numerous to mention, suggest themselves with the foregoing as a basis.

Kenrube.

COMMENT ATTACHED

This machine is like a dream. With it, the world is ours, for what conceivable combination of enemies could fight an army that appeared from nowhere on their flank, in the centers of their cities, in London, New York, in the Middlewest plains of America, in the Ural Mountains, in the Caucasus? Who can resist us?

K. Reissel.

ADDITIONAL COMMENT

My dear Reissel:

Your enthusiasm overlooks the fact that the machine is still only in the building stage. What worries me is that our hopes are being raised to a feverish height—what greater revenge could there be than to lift us to the ultimate peak of confidence, and then smash it in a single blow?

Every day that passes we are involving ourselves more deeply, decisions are being made from which there is already no turning back. When, oh, when will this machine be finished?

H.

July 29, 1939

From      Secretary, Bureau of Physics
To        Chief, Science Branch, Gestapo
Subject   Secret Six

The hyperspace machine at Gribe Schloss will be completed in February, 1941. No less than five duplicate machines are under construction, unknown to Kenrube. What is done is that, when he orders an installation for the *Gribe Schloss* machine, the factory turns out five additional units from the same plans.

In addition, a dozen model machines are being secretly constructed from the old plans, but, as they must be built entirely from drawings and photographs, they will take not less, but more, time to build than the larger machines.

August Buehnen

August 2, 1939

From    Secretary, Bureau of Physics
To      Herr Heinrich Himmler
Subject Professor Johann Kenrube


I have just now received a telegram from Fräulein
Ilse Weber that she and the Herr Professor were married this morning, and that Kenrube will be a family
man by the middle of next summer.

August Buehnen


COMMENT WRITTEN BELOW

This is great news indeed. One of the most dangerous aspects of the Kenrube affair was that he was a
bachelor without ties. Now, we have him. He has committed himself to the future.

Himmler.


FURTHER COMMENT

I have advised the Fuehrer, and our great armies will
move into Poland at the end of this month.

H.

August 8, 1939

From    Gestapo
To      Reich and Prussian Minister of Science
Subject Secret Six


I have had second thought on the matter of Fräulein
Ilse Weber, now Frau Kenrube. In view of the fact that
a woman, no matter how intelligent or objective, becomes emotionally involved with the man who is the
father of her children, I would advise that Frau Kenrube
be appointed to some great executive post in a war
industry. This will keep her own patriotism at a high
level, and thus she will continue to have exemplary
influence on her husband. Such influence cannot be
overestimated.

Himmler.

January 3, 1940

From     Secretary, Bureau of Physics
To         Chief, Science Branch, Gestapo

In glancing through the correspondence, I notice that I have neglected to inform you that our Agent Twelve has replaced Seventeen as Kenrube's chief assistant.

Twelve is a graduate of Munich, and was for a time attached to the General Staff in Berlin as a technical expert.

In my opinion, he is a better man for our purpose than was Seventeen, in that Seventeen, it seemed to me, had toward the end a tendency to associate himself with Kenrube in what might be called a scientific comradeship, an intellectual fellowship. He was in a mental condition where he quite unconsciously defended Kenrube against our suspicion.

Such a situation will not arise with Twelve. He is a practical man to the marrow. He and Kenrube have nothing in common.

Kenrube accepted Twelve with an attitude of what-does-it-matter-who-they-send. It was so noticeable that it is now clear that he is aware that these men are agents of ours.

Unless Kenrube had some plan of revenge which is beyond all precautions, the knowledge that he is being watched should exercise a restraint on any impulses to evil that he may have.

August Buehnen

Author's Note: *Most of the letters written in the year 1940 were of a routine nature, consisting largely of detailed reports as to the progress of the machine. The following document, however, was an exception:*

December 17, 1940

From     Reich and Prussian Minister of Science
To         Herr Heinrich Himmler
Subject  Secret Six

The following work has now been completed on the fortress *Gribe Schloss*, where the Kenrube machine is nearing completion:

1. Steel doors have been fitted throughout.
2. A special, all-steel chamber has been constructed, from which, by an arrangement of mirrors, the orifice of the machine can be watched without danger to the watchers.
3. This watching post is only twenty steps from a paved road which runs straight up out of the valley.
4. A concrete pipeline for the transportation of oil is nearing completion.

August Buehnen.

MEMO AT BOTTOM OF LETTER

To Reinhard Heydrich:
Please make arrangements for me to inspect personally the reconstructed *Gribe Schloss*. It is Hitler's intention to attend the official opening.

The plan now is to invade England via the Kenrube machine possibly in March, not later than April. In view of the confusion that will follow the appearance of vast armies in every part of the country, this phase of the battle of Europe should be completed by the end of April.

In May, Russia will be invaded. This should not require more than two months. The invasion of the United States is set for July or August.

Himmler.

January 31, 1941

From      Secretary, Bureau of Physics
To        Chief, Science Branch, Gestapo
Subject   Secret Six

It will be impossible to complete the five extra Kenrube machines at the same time as the machine at *Gribe Schloss*. Kenrube has changed some of the designs, and our engineers do not know how to fit the sections together until they have studied Kenrube's method of connection.

I have personally asked Kenrube the reason for the changes. His answer was that he was remedying weak-

nesses that he had noticed in the model. I am afraid that
we shall have to be satisfied with this explanation, and
complete the duplicate machines after the official opening, which is not now scheduled until March 20th. The
delay is due to Kenrube's experimentation with design.

If you have any suggestions, please let me hear them.
I frankly do not like this delay, but what to do about it
is another matter.

August Buehnen.

February 3, 1941

From       Chief, Science Branch, Gestapo
To         Secretary, Bureau of Physics
Subject    Secret Six

Himmler says to do nothing. He notes that you are
still taking the precaution of daily photographs, and that
your agent, Twelve, who replaced Seventeen, is keeping a diary in triplicate.

There has been a meeting of leaders, and this whole
matter discussed very thoroughly, with special empha-
sis on critical analysis of the precautions taken, and of
the situation that would exist if Kenrube should prove
to be planning some queer revenge.

You will be happy to know that not a single additional
precaution was thought of, and that our handling of the
affair was commended.

K. Reissel.

February 18, 1941

From       Gestapo
To         Reich and Prussian Minister of Science
Subject    Secret Six

In view of our anxieties, the following information,
which I have just received, will be welcome:

Frau Kenrube, formerly our Ilse Weber, has reserved
a private room in the maternity ward of the Prussian
State Hospital for May 7th. This will be her second
child, another hostage to fortune by Kenrube.

K. Reissel.

COPY ONLY
MEMO                                    March 11, 1941

I have today examined *Gribe Schloss* and environs
and found everything according to plan.

                                            Himmler

                                    March 14, 1941

From      Secretary, Bureau of Physics
To        Herr Himmler, Gestapo
Subject   Secret Six

You will be relieved to know the reason for the
changes in design made by Kenrube.

The first reason is rather unimportant; Kenrube refers
to the mathematical structure involved, and states that,
for his own elucidation, he designed a functional instrument whose sole purpose was to defeat the mathematical
reality of the machine. This is very obscure, but he had
referred to it before, so I call it to your attention.

The second reason is that there are now two orifices,
not one. The additional orifice is for focussing. The
following illustration will clarify what I mean:

Suppose we had a hundred thousand trucks in Berlin,
which we wished to transfer to London. Under the old
method, these trucks would have to be driven all the way
to the *Gribe Schloss* before they could be transmitted.

With the new two-orifice machine, one orifice would
be focussed in Berlin, the other in London. The trucks
would drive through from Berlin to London.

Herr Professor Kenrube seems to anticipate our needs
before we realize them ourselves.

                                    August Buehnen.

                                    March 16, 1941

From      Gestapo
To        Secretary, Bureau of Physics
Subject   Secret Six

The last sentence of your letter of March 14th to the
effect that Kenrube seems to anticipate our needs made

me very uncomfortable, because the thought that follows naturally is: Is he also anticipating our plans?

I have accordingly decided at this eleventh hour that we are dealing with a man who may be our intellectual superior in every way. Have your agent advise us the moment the machine has undergone its initial tests. Decisive steps will be taken immediately.

Himmler.

March 19, 1941

DECODED TELEGRAM

KENRUBE MACHINE WAS TESTED TODAY AND WORKED PERFECTLY.

AGENT TWELVE.

COPY ONLY
MEMO                                      March 19, 1941
To    Herr Himmler:

This is to advise that Professor Johann Kenrube was placed under close arrest, and has been removed to Gestapo Headquarters, Berlin.

R. Heydrich.

March 19, 1941

DECODED TELEGRAM

REPLYING TO YOUR TELEPHONE INSTRUCTIONS, WISH TO STATE ALL AUTOMATIC DEVICES HAVE BEEN REMOVED FROM KENRUBE MACHINE. NONE SEEMED TO HAVE BEEN TAMPERED WITH. MADE PERSONAL TEST OF MACHINE. IT WORKED PERFECTLY.

TWELVE

COMMENT WRITTEN BELOW

I shall recommend that Kenrube be retired under guard to his private laboratories, and not allowed near a hyperspace machine until after the conquest of the United States.

And with this, I find myself at a loss for further precautions. In my opinion, all thinkable possibilities have been covered. The only dangerous man has been removed from the zone where he can be actively dangerous; a careful examination has been made to ascertain that he has left no automatic devices that will cause havoc. And, even if he has, five other large machines and a dozen small ones are nearing completion, and it is impossible that he can have tampered with them.

If anything goes wrong now, thoroughness is a meaningless word.

Himmler.

March 21, 1941

From      Gestapo
To        Secretary, Bureau of Physics
Subject   Secret Six


Recriminations are useless. What I would like to know is: What in God's name happened?

Himmler.

March 22, 1941

From      Secretary, Bureau of Physics
To        Herr Heinrich Himmler
Subject   Secret Six


The reply to your question is being prepared. The great trouble is the confusion among the witnesses, but it should not be long before some kind of coherent reply is ready.

Work is being rushed to complete the duplicate machines on the basis of photographs and plans that were made from day to day. I cannot see how anything can be wrong in the long run.

As for Number One, shall we send planes over with bombs?

August Buehnen.

COPY ONLY
MEMO                                    March 23, 1941

From     Detention Branch, Gestapo

The four agents, Gestner, Luslich, Heinreide, and Muemmer, who were guarding Herr Professor Johann Kenrube, report that he was under close arrest at our Berlin headquarters until 6 P.M., March 21st. At 6 P.M., he abruptly vanished.

                                         S. Duerner

COMMENT WRITTEN BELOW

Kenrube was at *Gribe Schloss* before 2 P.M., March 21st. This completely nullifies the 6 P.M. story. Place these scoundrels under arrest, and bring them before me at eight o'clock tonight.

                                         Himmler.

COPY ONLY
EXAMINATION BY HERR HIMMLER OF F. GESTNER

Q.   Your name?
A.   Gestner. Fritz Gestner. Long service.
Q.   Silence. If we want to know your service, we'll check it in the record.
A.   Yes, sir.
Q.   That's a final warning. You answer my questions, or I'll have your tongue.
A.   Yes, sir.
Q.   You're one of the stupid fools set to guard Kenrube?
A.   I was one of the four guards, sir.
Q.   Answer yes or no.
A.   Yes, sir.
Q.   What was your method of guarding Kenrube?
A.   By twos. Two of us at a time were in the great white cell with him.
Q.   Why weren't the four of you there?
A.   We thought—

Q. You thought! Four men were ordered to guard Kenrube and— By God, there'll be dead men around here before this night is over. I want to get this clear: There was never a moment when two of you were not in the cell with Kenrube?

A. Always two of us.

Q. Which two were with Kenrube at the moment he disappeared?

A. I was. I and Johann Luslich.

Q. Oh, you know Luslich by his first name. An old friend of yours, I suppose?

A. No, sir.

Q. You knew Luslich previously, though?

A. I met him for the first time when we were assigned to guard Herr Kenrube.

Q. Silence! Answer yes or no. I've warned you about that.

A. Yes, sir.

Q. Ah, you admit knowing him?

A. No, sir. I meant—

Q. Look here, Gestner, you're in a very bad spot. Your story is a falsehood on the face of it. Tell me the truth. Who are your accomplices?

A. None, sir.

Q. You mean you were working this alone?

A. No, sir.

Q. You damned liar! Gestner, we'll get the truth out of you if we have to tear you apart.

A. I am telling the truth, Excellency.

Q. Silence, you scum. What time did you say Kenrube disappeared?

A. About six o'clock.

Q. Oh, he did, eh? Well, never mind that. What was Kenrube doing just before he vanished?

A. He was talking to Luslich and me.

Q. What right had you to talk to the prisoner?

A. Sir, he mentioned an accident he expected to happen at some official opening somewhere.

Q. He what?

A.  Yes, sir; and I was desperately trying to find out where, so that I could send a warning.

Q.  Now, the truth is coming. So you do know about this business, you lying rat! Well, let's have the story you've rigged up.

A.  The dictaphone will bear out every word.

Q.  Oh, the dictaphone was on.

A.  Every word is recorded.

Q.  Oh, why wasn't I told about this in the first place?

A.  You wouldn't lis—

Q.  Silence, you fool! By God, the cooperation I get around this place. Never mind. Just what was Kenrube doing at the moment he disappeared?

A.  He was sitting—talking.

Q.  Sitting? You'll swear to that?

A.  To the Fuehrer himself.

Q.  He didn't move from his chair? He didn't walk over to an orifice?

A.  I don't know what you mean, Excellency.

Q.  So you pretend, anyway. But that's all for the time being. You will remain under arrest. Don't think we're through with you. That goes also for the others.

AUTHOR'S NOTE:

*The baffled fury expressed by the normally calm Himmler in this interview is one indication of the dazed bewilderment that raged through high Nazi circles. One can imagine the accusation and counter-accusation and then the slow, deadly realization of the situation.*

March 24, 1941

From      Gestapo
To         Reich and Prussian Minister of Science
Subject   Secret Six

Inclosed is the transcription of a dictaphone record which was made by Professor Kenrube. A careful study of these deliberate words, combined with what he said at *Gribe Schloss*, may reveal his true purpose, and may also explain the incredible thing that happened.

I am anxiously awaiting your full report.

Himmler

TRANSCRIPTION OF DICTAPHONE RECORD P–679–423–1; CONVERSATION OF PROFESSOR JOHANN KENRUBE IN WHITE CELL 26, ON 3/21/41.

(Note: K. refers to Kenrube, G. to any of the guards.)

K.  A glass of water, young man.

G.  I believe there is no objection to that. Here.

K.  It must be after five.

G.  There is no necessity for you to know the time.

K.  No, but the fact that it is late is very interesting. You see, I have invented a machine. A very queer machine it is going to seem when it starts to react according to the laws of real as distinct from functional mathematics. You have the dictaphone on, I hope?

G.  What kind of a smart remark is that?

K.  Young man, that dictaphone had better be on. I intend talking about my invention, and your masters will skin you alive if it's not recorded. Is the dictaphone on?

G.  Oh, I suppose so.

K.  Good. I may be able to finish what I have to say. I may not.

G.  Don't worry. You'll be here to finish it. Take your time.

K.  I had the idea before my brother was killed in the purge, but I thought of the problem then as one of education. Afterward, I saw it as revenge. I hated the Nazis and all they stood for.

G.  Oh, you did, eh? Go on.

K.  My plan after my brother's murder was to build for the Nazis the greatest weapon the world will ever know, and then have them discover that only I, who understood and who accordingly *fitted in* with

the immutable laws involved—only I could ever
operate the machine. And I would have to be
present physically. That way I would prove my
indispensability and so transform the entire world
to my way of thinking.

G.  We've got ways of making indispensables work.

K.  Oh, that part is past. I've discovered what is going
to happen—to me as well as to my invention.

G.  Plenty is going to happen to you. You've already
talked yourself into a concentration camp.

K.  After I discovered that, my main purpose was sim-
plified. I wanted to do the preliminary work on the
machine and, naturally, I had to do that under the
prevailing system of government—by cunning and
misrepresentation. I had no fear that any of the
precautions they were so laboriously taking would
give them the use of the machine, not this year,
not this generation, not ever. The machine simply
cannot be used by people who think as they do.
For instance, the model that—

G.  Model! What are you talking about?

K.  Silence, please. I am anxious to clarify for the
dictaphone what will seem obscure enough under
any circumstances. The reason the model worked
perfectly was because I fitted in mentally and physically. Even after I left, it continued to carry out
the task I had set it, but as soon as Herr—(Seventeen)
made a change, it began to yield to other pres-
sures. The accident—

G.  Accident!

K.  Will you shut up? Can't you see that I am trying to
give information for the benefit of future generations? I have no desire that my secret be lost. The
whole thing is in understanding. The mechanical
part is only half the means. The mental approach is
indispensable. Even Herr—(Seventeen), who was
beginning to be *sympathique* could not keep the
machine sane for more than an hour. His death, of
course, was inevitable, whether it looked like an
accident or not.

G.  Whose death?

K.  What it boils down to is this. My invention does
    not fit into our civilization. It's *the next*, the com-
    ing age of man. Just as modern science could not
    develop in ancient Egypt because the whole men-
    tal, emotional, and physical attitude was wrong, so
    my machine cannot be used until the thought struc-
    ture of man changes. Your masters will have some
    further facts soon to bear me out.

G.  Look! You said something before about something
    happening. What?

K.  I've just been telling you: I don't know. The law of
    averages says it won't be another sun, but there
    are a thousand deadly things that can happen.
    When Nature's gears snag, no imaginable horror
    can match the result.

G.  But something is going to happen?

K.  I really expected it before this. The official open-
    ing was set for half-past one. Of course, it doesn't
    really matter. If it doesn't happen today, it will
    take place tomorrow.

G.  Official opening! You mean an accident is going to
    happen at some official opening?

K.  Yes, and my body will be *attracted*. I—

G.  What— Good God! He's gone!

    (Confusion. Voices no longer audible.)

March 25, 1941

From      Reich and Prussian Minister of Science
To        Herr Himmler
Subject   Destruction of *Gribe Schloss*

The report is still not ready. As you were not present, I have asked the journalist, Polermann, who was
with Hitler, to write a description of the scene. His
account is enclosed, with the first page omitted.

You will note that in a number of paragraphs he
reveals incomplete knowledge of the basic situation,
but except for this, his story is, I believe, the most
accurate we have.

The first page of his article was inadvertently destroyed. It was simply a preliminary.

For your information.

DESCRIPTION OF DESTRUCTION OF *GRIBE SCHLOSS* BY HERR POLERMANN

—The first planet came in an unexpected fashion. I realized that as I saw Herr—(Twelve) make some hasty adjustments on one of his dials.

Still dissatisfied, he connected a telephone plug into a socket somewhere in his weird-looking asbestos suit, thus establishing telephone communication with the Minister of Science, who was in the steel inclosure with us. I heard His Excellency's reply:

"Night! Well, I suppose it has to be night some time on other planets. You're not sure it's the same planet? I imagine the darkness is confusing."

It was. In the mirror, the night visible through the orifice showed a bleak, gray, luminous landscape, incredibly eerie and remote, an unnatural world of curious shadows, and not a sign of movement anywhere.

And that, after an instant, struck us all with an appalling effect, the dark consciousness of that great planet, swinging somewhere around a distant sun, an uninhabited waste, a lonely reminder that life is rarer than death in the vast universe. Herr—(Twelve) made an adjustment on a dial; and, instantly, the great orifice showed that we were seeing the interior of the planet. A spotlight switched on, and picked out a solid line of red earth that slowly, as the dial turned, became clay; then a rock stratum came into view, and was held in focus.

An asbestos-clothed assistant of Herr—(Twelve) dislodged a piece of rock with a pick. He lifted it, and started to bring it toward the steel inclosure, apparently for the Fuehrer's inspection.

And abruptly vanished.

We blinked our eyes. But he was gone, and the rock with him. Herr—(Twelve) switched on his telephone hurriedly. There was a consultation, in which the Fuehrer participated. The decision finally was that it had been a mistake to examine a doubtful planet, and that the accident had happened because the rock had been removed. Accordingly, no further effort would be made to remove anything.

Regret was expressed by the Fuehrer that the brave assistant should have suffered such a mysterious fate.

We resumed our observant positions, more alert now, conscious of what a monstrous instrument was here before our eyes. A man whisked completely out of our space simply because he had touched a rock from a planet in hyperspace.

The second planet was also dark. At first it, too, looked a barren world, enveloped in night; and then— wonder. Against the dark, towering background of a great hill, a city grew. It spread along the shore of a moonlit sea, ablaze with ten million lights. It clung there for a moment, a crystalline city, alive with brilliant streets. Then it faded. Swiftly it happened. The lights seemed literally to slide off into the luminous sea. For a moment, the black outline of the city remained, then that, too, vanished into the shadows. Astoundingly, the hill that had formed an imposing background for splendor, distorted like a picture out of focus, and was gone with the city.

A flat, night-wrapped beach spread where a moment before there had been a world of lights, a city of another planet, the answer to ten million questions about life on other worlds—gone like a secret wind into the darkness.

It was plain to see that the test, the opening, was not according to schedule. Once more, Herr—(Twelve) spoke through the telephone to His Excellency, the Minister of Science.

His Excellency turned to the Fuehrer, and said, "He states that he appears to have no control over the order of appearance. Not once has he been able to tune in a planet which he had previously selected to show you."

There was another consultation. It was decided that

this second planet, though it had reacted in an abnormal manner, had not actually proved dangerous. Therefore, one more attempt would be made. No sooner was this decision arrived at, than there was a very distinctly audible click from the machine. And, though we did not realize it immediately, the catastrophe was upon us.

I cannot describe the queer loudness of that clicking from the machine. It was not a metallic noise. I have since been informed that only an enormous snapping of energy in motion could have made that unusual, unsettling sound.

My own sense of uneasiness was quickened by the sight of Herr—(Twelve) frantically twisting dials. But nothing happened for a few seconds. The planet on which we had seen the city continued to hold steady in the orifice. The darkened beach spread there in the half-light shed by a moon we couldn't see. And then—

A figure appeared in the orifice. I cannot recall all my emotions at the sight of that manlike being. There was a wild thought that here was some supercreature who, dissatisfied with the accidents he had so far caused us, was now come to complete our destruction. That thought ended as the figure came out onto the floor and one of the assistants swung a spotlight on him. The light revealed him as a tall, well-built, handsome man, dressed in ordinary clothes.

Beside me, I heard someone exclaim: "Why, it's Professor Kenrube!"

For most of those present, everything must have, in that instant, been clear. I, however, did not learn until later that Kenrube was one of the scientists assigned to assist Herr—(Twelve) in building the machine, and that he turned out to be a traitor. He was suspected in the destruction of an earlier model, but as there was no evidence and the suspicion not very strong, he was permitted to continue his work.

Suspicion had arisen again a few days previously, and he had been confined to his quarters, from whence, apparently, he had now come forth to make sure that his skillful tampering with the machine had worked out.

This, then, was the man who stood before us. My impression was that he should not have been allowed to utter his blasphemies, but I understand the leaders were anxious to learn the extent of his infamy, and thought he might reveal it in his speech. Although I do not profess to understand the gibberish, I have a very clear memory of what was said, and set it down here for what it is worth.

Kenrube began: "I have no idea how much time I have, and as I was unable to explain clearly to the dictaphone all that I had to say, I must try to finish here." He went on, "I am not thinking now in terms of revenge, though God knows my brother was very dear to me. But I want the world to know the way of this invention."

The poor fool seemed to be laboring under the impression that the machine was his. I did not, and do not, understand his reference to a dictaphone. Kenrube went on:

"My first inkling came through psychology, the result of meditating on the manner in which the soil of different parts of the earth influences the race that lives there. This race-product was always more than simply the end-shape of a seacoast, or a plains, or a mountain environment. Somehow, beneath adaptations, peculiar and unsuspected relationships existed between the properties of matter and the phenomena of life. And so my search was born. The idea of revenge came later.

I might say that in all history there has never been a revenge as complete as mine. Here is your machine. It is all there; yours to use for any purpose—provided you first change your mode of thinking to conform to the reality of the relationship between matter and life.

"I have no doubt you can build a thousand duplicates, but beware—every machine will be a Frankenstein monster. Some of them will distort time, as seems to have happened in the time of my arrival here. Others will feed you raw material that will vanish even as you reach forth to seize it. Still others will pour obscene things into our green earth; and others will blaze with terrible energies, but you will never know what is coming, you will never satisfy a single desire.

"You may wonder why everything will go wrong. Herr—(Twelve) has, I am sure, been able to make brief, successful tests. That will be the result of my earlier presence, and will not recur now that so many alien presences have affected its—sanity!

"It is not that the machine has will. It reacts to laws, which you must learn, and in the learning it will re-shape your minds, your outlook on life. It will change the world. Long before that, of course, the Nazis will be destroyed. They have taken irrevocable steps that will insure their destruction.

"Revenge! Yes, I have it in the only way that a decent human being could desire it. I ask any reason-able being how else these murderers could be wiped from the face of the earth, except by other nations, who would never act until *they* had acted first?

"I have only the vaguest idea what the machine will do with me—it matters not. But I should like to ask you, my great Fuehrer, one question: Where now will you obtain your raw material?"

He must have timed it exactly. For, as he finished, his figure dimmed. Dimmed! How else describe the blur that his body became? And he was gone, merged with the matter with which, he claimed, his life force was attuned.

The madman had one more devastating surprise for us. The dark planet, from which the city had disap-peared, was abruptly gone from the orifice. In its place appeared another dark world. As our vision grew accus-tomed to this new night, we saw that this was a world of restless water; to the remote, dim horizon was a blue-black, heaving sea. The machine switched below the surface. It must have been at least ten hellish miles below it, judging from the pressure, I have since been informed.

There was a roar that seemed to shake the earth.

Only those who were with the Fuehrer in the steel room succeeded in escaping. Twenty feet away a great army truck stood with engines churning—it was not the first time that I was thankful that some car engines are always left running wherever the Fuehrer is present.

The water swelled and surged around our wheels as we raced up the newly paved road, straight up out of the valley. It was touch and go. We looked back in sheer horror. Never in the world has there been such a titanic torrent, such a whirlpool.

The water rose four hundred feet in minutes, threatened to overflow the valley sides, and then struck a balance. The great new river is still there, raging toward the Eastern Sea.

Author's Note: *This is not quite the end of the file. A few more letters exist, but it is unwise to print more, as it might be possible for the GPU to trace the individual who actually removed the file Secret Six from its cabinet.*

*It is scarcely necessary to point out that we subsequently saw the answer that Hitler made to Professor Kenrube's question: "Where now will you obtain your raw materials?"*

*On June 22nd, three months almost to the day after the destruction of* Gribe Schloss, *the Nazis began their desperate invasion of Russia. By the end of 1941, their diplomacy bankrupt, they were at war with the United States.*

When the history of the twentieth century comes to be written, the figure of Adolf Hitler will undoubtedly stand unrivaled. As a mass killer, only Stalin and Mao bear comparison, and their bloodlettings were largely confined to the boundaries of their own states. The dogmas of Marxism at least pretend to a certain link to rationality, to the nineteenth century ideals of prosperity and progress. Marxism's bastard offspring National Socialism made no such pretence; it was nakedly a reaction against the basic concepts of the Enlightenment. And while Adolf Hitler created very little, the synthesis that found its form in the NSDAP was uniquely his own. The Cold War is the legacy of his defeat, and the only good that can be said of that long bloodsoaked travail is that it is infinitely better than the world Hitler's victory would have brought. Only science fiction could produce a suitable punishment for such a man as Adolf Hitler . . .

# MY NAME IS LEGION

## Lester del Rey

Bresseldorf lay quiet under the late-morning sun—
too quiet. In the streets there was no sign of activity,
though a few faint banners of smoke spread upward
from the chimneys, and the dropped tools of agriculture
lay all about, scattered as if from sudden flight. A thin
pig wandered slowly and suspiciously down Friedrichstrasse, turned into an open door cautiously, grunted in
grudging satisfaction, and disappeared within. But there
were no cries of children, no bustle of men in the
surrounding fields, nor women gossiping or making preparations for the noon meal. The few shops, apparently
gutted of foodstuffs, were bare, their doors flopping
open. Even the dogs were gone.

Major King dropped the binoculars to his side, tight
lines about his eyes that contrasted in suspicion with his
ruddy British face. "Something funny here, Wolfe. Think
it's an ambush?"

Wolfe studied the scene. "Doesn't smell like it, Major," he answered. "In the Colonials, we developed
something of a sixth sense for that, and I don't get a

151

hunch here. Looks more like a sudden and complete retreat to me, sir."

"We'd have had reports from the observation planes if even a dozen men were on the roads. I don't like this." The major put the binoculars up again. But the scene was unchanged, save that the solitary pig had come out again and was rooting his way down the street in lazy assurance that nothing now menaced him. King shrugged, flipped his hand forward in a quick jerk, and his command moved ahead again, light tanks in front, troop cars and equipment at a safe distance behind, but ready to move forward instantly to hold what ground the tanks might gain. In the village, nothing stirred.

Major King found himself holding his breath as the tanks reached antitank-fire distance, but as prearranged, half of them lumbered forward at a deceptive speed, maneuvered to two abreast to shuttle across Friedrichstrasse toward the village square, and halted. Still, there was no sign of resistance. Wolfe looked at the quiet houses along the street and grinned sourly.

"If it's an ambush, Major, they've got sense. They're waiting until we send in our men in the trucks to pick them off then, and letting the tanks alone. But I still don't believe it; not with such an army as he could throw together."

"Hm-m-m." King scowled, and again gave the advance signal.

The trucks moved ahead this time, traveling over the rough road at a clip that threatened to jar the teeth out of the men's heads, and the remaining tanks swung in briskly as a rear guard. The pig stuck his head out of a door as the major's car swept past, squealed, and slipped back inside in haste. Then all were in the little square, barely big enough to hold them, and the tanks were arranged facing out, their thirty-seven-millimeters raking across the houses that bordered, ready for an instant's notice. Smoke continued to rise peacefully, and the town slumbered on, unmindful of this strange invasion.

"Hell!" King's neck felt tense, as if the hair were

standing on end. He swung to the men, moved his hands outward. "Out and search! And remember—take him alive if you can! If you can't, plug his guts and save his face—we'll have to bring back proof!"

They broke into units and stalked out of the square toward the houses with grim efficiency and rifles ready, expecting guerrilla fire at any second; none came. The small advance guard of the Army of Occupation kicked open such doors as were closed and went in and sidewise, their comrades covering them. No shots came, and the only sound was the cries of the men as they reported "Empty!"

Then, as they continued around the square, one of the doors opened quietly and a single man came out, glanced at the rifles centered on him, and threw up his hands, a slight smile on his face. "*Kamerad!*" he shouted toward the major; then in English with only the faintest of accents: "There is no other here, in the whole village."

Holding onto the door, he moved aside slightly to let a search detail go in, waited for them to come out. "You see? I am alone in Bresseldorf; the Leader you seek is gone, and his troops with him."

Judging by the man's facial expression that he was in no condition to come forward, King advanced; Wolfe was at his side, automatic at ready. "I'm Major King, Army of Occupation. We received intelligence from some of the peasants who fled from here yesterday that your returned Fuehrer was hiding here. You say—"

"That he is quite gone, yes; and that you will never find him, though you comb the earth until eternity, Major King. I am Karl Meyers, once of Heidelberg."

"When did he leave?"

"A matter of half an hour or so—what matter? I assure you, sir, he is too far now to trace. Much too far!"

"In half an hour?" King grimaced. "You underestimate the covering power of a modern battalion. Which direction?"

"Yesterday," Meyers answered, and his drawn face

lighted slightly. "But tell me, did the peasants report but one Fuehrer?"

King stared at the man in surprise, taking in the basically pleasant face, intelligent eyes, and the pride that lay, somehow, in the bent figure; this was no ordinary villager, but a man of obvious breeding. Nor did he seem anything but completely frank and honest. "No," the major conceded, "there were stories. But when a band of peasants reports a thousand Fuehrers heading fifty thousand troops, we'd be a little slow in believing it, after all."

"Quite so, major. Peasant minds exaggerate." Again there was the sudden lighting of expression. "Yes, so they did—the troops. And in other ways, rather than exaggerating, they minimized. But come inside, sirs, and I'll explain over a bottle of the rather poor wine I've found here. I'll show you the body of the Leader, and even explain why he's gone—and when."

"But you said—" King shrugged. Let the man be as mysterious as he chose, if his claim of the body was correct. He motioned Wolfe forward with him and followed Meyers into a room that had once been kitchen and dining room, but was now in wild disarray, its normal holdings crammed into the corners to make room for a small piece of mechanism in the center and a sheeted bundle at one side. The machine was apparently in the process of being disassembled.

Meyers lifted the sheet. "Der Fuehrer," he said, simply, and King dropped with a gasp to examine the dead figure revealed.

There were no shoes, and the calluses on the feet said quite plainly that it was customary; such few clothes as remained had apparently been pieced together from odds and ends of peasant clothing, sewed crudely. Yet on them, pinned over the breast, were the two medals that the Leader alone bore. One side of the head had been blown away by one of the new issue German explosive bullets, and what remained was incredibly filthy, matted hair falling below the shoulders, scraggy, tangled beard covering all but the eye and nose. On the left cheek, however, the irregular reversed question-mark scar from the recent attempt at assassination showed plainly, but faded and blended with the normal skin where it should have been still sharp after only two months' healing.

"An old, old man, wild as the wind and dirty as a hog wallow," King thought, "yet, somehow, clearly the man I was after."

Wolfe nodded slowly at his superior's glance. "Sure, why not? I'll cut his hair and give him a shave and a wash. When we're about finished here, we can fire a shot from the gun on the table, if it's still loaded . . . good! Report that Meyers caught him and held him for us; then, while we were questioning him, he went crazy, and Meyers took a shot at him."

"Hm-m-m." King's idea had been about the same. "Men might suspect something, but I can trust them. He'd never stand a careful inspection, of course, without a lot of questions about such things as those feet, but the way things are, no really competent medical inspection will be made. It'll be a little hard to explain those rags, though."

Meyers nodded to a bag against the wall. "You'll find sufficient of his clothes there, Major; we couldn't pack out much luggage, but that much we brought." He sank back into a rough chair slowly, the hollow in his cheeks deepening, but a grim humor in his eyes. "Now, you'll want to know how it happened, no doubt? How he died? Suicide—murder; they're one and the same here. He died insane."

The car was long and low. European by its somewhat unrounded lines and engine housing, muddy with the ruck that sprayed up from its wheels and made the road almost impassable. Likewise, it was stolen, though that had no bearing on the matter at hand. Now, as it rounded an ill-banked curve, the driver cursed softly, jerked at the wheel, and somehow managed to keep all four wheels on the road and the whole pointed forward. His foot came down on the gas again, and it churned forward through the muck, then miraculously maneuvered another turn, and they were on a passable road and he could relax.

"Germany, my Leader," he said simply, his large hands gripping at the wheel with now needless ferocity. "Here, of all places, they will least suspect you."

The Leader sat hunched forward, paying little attention to the road or the risks they had taken previously. Whatever his enemies might say of his lack of bravery in the first war, there was no cowardice about him now; power, in unlimited quantity, had made him unaware of personal fear. He shrugged faintly, turned his face to the driver, so that the reversed question-mark scar showed up, running from his left eye down toward the almost comic little mustache. But there was nothing comic about him, somehow; certainly not to Karl Meyers.

"Germany," he said, tonelessly. "Good. I was a fool, Meyers, ever to leave it. Those accursed British—the loutish Russians—ungrateful French—trouble-making Americans—bombs, retreats, uprisings, betrayals—and the two I thought were my friends advising me to flee to Switzerland before my people— Bah, I was a fool. Now those two friends would have me murdered in my bed, as this letter you brought testifies. And the curs stalk the Reich, such as remains of it, and think they have beaten me. Bonaparte was beaten once, and in a hundred days, except for the stupidity of fools and the tricks of weather, even he might have regained his empire. . . . Where?"

"Bresseldorf. My home is near there, and the equipment, also. Besides, when we have—the legion with us, Bresseldorf will feed us, and the clods of peasants will offer little resistance. Also, it is well removed from the areas policed by the Army of Occupation. Thank God, I finished the machine in time."

Meyers swung the car into another little used, but passable, road, and opened it up, knowing it would soon be over. This mad chase had taken more out of him than he'd expected. Slipping across into Switzerland, tracking, playing hunches, finally locating the place where the Fuehrer was hidden had used almost too much time, and the growth within him that would not wait was killing him day by day. Even after finding the place, he'd been forced to slip past the guards who were half-protecting, half-imprisoning the Leader and use half a hundred tricks to see him. Convincing him of the conspiracy of his "friends" to have him shot was not hard; the Leader knew something of the duplicity of men in power, or fearful of their lives. Convincing him of the rest of the plan had been harder, but on the coldly logical argument that there was nothing else, the Fuehrer had come. Somehow they'd escaped—he still could give no details of that—and stolen this car, to run out into the rain and the night over the mountain roads, through the back ways, and somehow out unnoticed and into Germany again.

The Leader settled more comfortably into the seat with an automatic motion, his mind far from body comforts. "Bresseldorf? And near it—yes, I remember that clearly now—within fifteen miles of there, there's a small military depot those damned British won't have found yet. There was a new plan—but that doesn't matter now; what matters are the tanks, and better, the ammunition. This machine—will it duplicate tanks, also? And ammunition?"

Meyers nodded. "Tanks, cars, equipment, all of them. But not ammunition or petrol, since once used, they're not on the chain any longer to be taken."

"No matter. God be praised, there's petrol and ammunition enough there, until we can reach the others; and a few men, surely, who are still loyal. I was beginning to doubt loyalty, but tonight you've shown it does exist. Some day, Karl Meyers, you'll find I'm not ungrateful."

"Enough that I serve you," Meyers muttered. "Ah, here we are; good time made, too, since it's but ten in the morning. That house is mine, inside you'll find wine and food, while I dispose of this car in the little lake yonder. Fortunately, the air is still thick here, even though it's not raining. There'll be none to witness."

\*   \*   \*

The Leader had made no move to touch the food when Meyers returned. He was pacing the floor, muttering to himself, working himself up as Meyers had seen him do often before on the great stands in front of the crowds, and the mumbled words had a hysterical drive to them that bordered on insanity. In his eyes, though, there was only the insanity that drives men remorselessly to rule, though that ruling may be under a grimmer sword than that of Damocles. He stopped as he saw Meyers, and one of his rare and sudden smiles flashed out, unexpectedly warm and human, like a small, bewildered boy peering out from the chinks of the man's armor. This was the man who had cried when he saw his soldiers dying, then sent them on again, sure they should honor him for the right to die; and like all those most loved or hated by their fellow men, he was a paradox of conflictions, unpredictable.

"The machine, Karl," he reminded the other gently. "As I remember, the Jew—Christ—cast a thousand devils out of one man; well, let's see you cast the thousand out of me—and devils they'll be to those who fetter the Reich! This time I think we'll make no words of secret weapons, but annihilate them first, eh? After that—there'll be a day of atonement for those who failed me, and a new and greater Germany—master of a world!"

"Yes, my Leader."

Meyers turned and slipped through the low door, back into a part of the building that had once been a stable, but was now converted into a workshop, filled with a few pieces of fine machinery and half a hundred makeshifts, held together, it seemed, with hope and prayer. He stopped before a small affair slightly larger than a suitcase, only a few dials and control knobs showing on the panel, the rest covered with a black housing. From it, two small wires led to a single storage battery.

"This?" The Fuehrer looked at it doubtfully.

"This, Leader. This is one case where brute power has little to do, and the proper use everything. A few tubes, coils, condensers, two little things of my own, and perhaps five watts of power feeding in—no more. Just as the cap that explodes the bomb may be small and weak, yet release forces that bring down the very mountains. Simple in design, yet there's no danger of them finding it."

"So? And it works in what way?"

Meyers scowled, thinking. "Unless you can think in a plenum, my Leader, I can't explain," he began diffidently. "Oh, mathematicians believe they can—but they think in symbols and terms, not in the reality. Only by thinking in the plenum itself can this be understood, and with due modesty, I alone in the long years since I gave up work at Heidelberg have devoted the time and effort—with untold pure luck—to master such thought. It isn't encompassed in mere symbols on paper."

"What," the Leader wanted to know, "is a plenum?"

"A complete universe, stretching up and forward and sidewise—and durationally; the last being the difficulty. The plenum is—well, the composite whole of all that is and was and will be—it is everything and everywhen, all existing together as a unit, in which time does not move, but simply is, like length or thickness. As an example, years ago in one of those American magazines, there was a story of a man who saw himself. He came through a woods somewhere and stumbled on a machine, got in, and it took him three days back in time. Then, he lived foward again, saw himself get in the machine and go back. Therefore, the time machine was never made, since he always took it back, let it stay three days, and took it back again. It was a closed circle, uncreated, but existent in the plenum. By normal nonplenar thought, impossible."

"Someone had to make it." The Leader's eyes clouded suspiciously.

Meyers shook his head. "Not so. See, I draw this line upon the paper, calling the paper now a plenum. It starts here, follows here, ends here. That is like life, machines, and so forth. We begin, we continue, we end. Now, I draw a circle—where does it begin or end? Yes, followed by a two-dimensional creature, it would be utter madness, continuing forever without reason or beginning—to us, simply a circle. Or, here I have a pebble—do you see at one side the energy, then the molecules, then the compounds, then the stone, followed by breakdown products? No, simply a stone. And in a plenum, that time machine is simply a pebble—complete, needing no justification, since it was."

The Leader nodded doubtfully, vaguely aware that he seemed to understand, but did not. If the machine worked, though, what matter the reason? "And—"

"And, by looking into the plenum as a unit, I obtain miracles, seemingly. I pull an object back from its future to stand beside its present. I multiply it in the present. As you might take a straight string and bend it into a series of waves or loops, so that it met itself repeatedly. For that, I need some power, yet not much. When I cause the bending from the future to the present, I cause nothing, since in a plenum, all that is, was and will be; when I bring you back, the mere fact that you are back means that you always have and always will exist in that manner. Seemingly then, if I did nothing, you would still multiply, but since my attempt to create such a condition is fixed in the plenum beside your multiplying at this time, therefore I must do so. The little energy I use, really, has only the purpose of not bringing you exactly within yourself, but separating individuals. Simple, is it not?"

"When I see an example, Meyers, I'll believe my eyes," the Leader answered.

Meyers grinned, and put a small coin on the ground, making quick adjustments of the dials. "I'll cause it to multiply from each two minutes," he said. "From each two minutes in the future, I'll bring it back to now. See!"

He depressed a switch, a watch in his hand. Instantly, there was a spreading out and multiplying, instantaneous or too rapid to be followed. As he released the switch, the Leader stumbled backward away from the small mountain of coins. Meyers glanced at him, consulted his watch, and moved another lever at the top. After a second or so, the pile disappeared, as quietly and quickly as it had come into being. There was a glint of triumph or something akin to it in the scientist's eyes as he turned back to the Fuehrer.

"I've tried it on myself, so it's safe to living things," he answered the unasked question.

The Leader nodded impatiently and stepped to the place where the coin had been laid. "Get on with it, then. The sooner the accursed enemies and traitors are driven out, the better it will be."

Meyers hesitated. "There's one other thing," he said doubtfully. "When those others are here, there might be a question of leadership, which would go ill with us. I mean no offense, my Leader, but—well, sometimes a man looks at things differently at different ages, and any disagreement would delay us. Fortunately, though, there's a curious by-product of the use of this machine; apparently, its action has some relation to thought, and I've found in my experiments that any strong thought on the part of the original will be duplicated in the others; I don't fully understand it myself, but it seems to work that way. The compulsion dissipates slowly and is gone in a day or so, but—"

"So?"

"So, if you'll think to yourself while you're standing there: 'I must obey my original implicitly; I must not cause trouble for my original or Karl Meyers,' then the problem will be cared for automatically. Concentrate on that, my Leader, and perhaps it would be wise to concentrate also on the thought that there should be no talking by our legion, except as we demand."

"Good. There'll be time for talk when the action is finished. Now, begin!"

The Leader motioned toward the machine and Meyers breathed a sigh of relief as the scarred face crinkled in concentration. From a table at the side, the scientist picked up a rifle and automatic, put them into the other's hands, and went to his machine.

"The weapons will be duplicated, also," he said, set-

ting the controls carefully. "Now, it should be enough if
I take you back from each twenty-four hours in the
future. And since there isn't room here, I'll assemble
the duplicates in rows outside. So."

He depressed the switch and a red bulb on the
control panel lighted. In the room, nothing happened,
for a few minutes; then the bulb went out, and Meyers
released the controls. "It's over. The machine has traced
ahead and brought back until there was no further
extension of yourself; living, that is, since I set it for
you in life only."

"But I felt nothing." The Leader glanced at the machine with a slight scowl, then stepped quickly to the
door for a hasty look. Momentarily, superstitious awe
flicked across his face, to give place to sharp triumph.
"Excellent, Meyers, most excellent. For this day, we'll
have the world at our feet, and that soon!"

In the field outside, a curious company was lined up
in rows. Meyers ran his eyes down the ranks, smiling
faintly, as he traced forward. Near, in almost exact
duplication of the man at his side, were several hundred; then, as his eyes moved backward, the resem-
blance was still strong, but differences began to creep
in. And farthest from him a group of old men stood,
their clothes faded and tattered, their faces hidden
under mangled beards. Rifles and automatics were
gripped in the hands of all the legion. There were also
other details, and Meyers nodded slowly to himself, but
he made no mention of them to the Fuehrer, who
seemed not to notice.

The Leader was looking ahead, a hard glow in his
eyes, his face contorted with some triumphant vision.
Then, slowly and softly at first, he began to speak and
to pace back and forth in front of the doorway, moving
his arms. Meyers only half listened, busy with his own
thoughts; but he could have guessed the words as they
came forth with mounting fury, worked up to a climax
and broke, to repeat it all again. Probably it was a great
speech the Leader was making, one that would have

swept a mob from their seats in crazy exultation in other days and set them screaming with savage applause. But the strange Legion of Later Leaders stood quietly, faces betraying varying emotions, mostly unreadable. Finally the speaker seemed to sense the difference and paused in the middle of one of his rising climaxes; he half-turned to Meyers, then suddenly swung back, decisively.

"But I speak to myselves," he addressed the legion again in a level, reasonable voice. "You who come after me know what is to be this day and in the days to come, so why should I tell you? And you know that my cause is just. The Jews, and Jew-lovers, the Pluto-democracies, the Bolsheviks, the treasonous cowards within and without the Reich must be put down! They shall be! Now, they are sure of victory, but tomorrow they'll be trembling in their beds and begging for peace. And soon, like a tide irresistible and without end, from the few we can trust many shall be made, and they shall sweep forward to victory. Not victory in a decade, nor a year, but in a month! We shall go north and south and east and west! We shall show them that our fangs are not pulled; that those which we lost were but our milk teeth, now replaced by a second and harder growth!

"And, for those who would have betrayed us, or bound us down in chains to feed the gold lust of the mad democracies, or denied us the room to live which is rightfully ours—for those, we shall find a proper place. This time, for once and for all, there shall be an end to the evils that corrupt the earth—the Jews and the Bolsheviks, and their friends, and friends' friends. Germany shall emerge, purged and cleansed, a new and greater Reich, whose domain shall not be Europe, nor this hemisphere, but the world!

"Many of you have seen all this in the future from which you come, and all of you must be ready to reassure yourselves of it today, that the glory of it may fill your tomorrow. Now, we march against a few peasants. Tomorrow, after quartering in Bresseldorf, we shall be in the secret depot, where those who remain loyal shall be privileged to multiply and join us, and where we shall multiply all our armament ten-thousand-fold! Into Bresseldorf, then, and if any of the peasants are disloyal, be merciless in removing the scum! Forward!"

One of the men in the front—the nearest—was crying openly, his face white, his hands clenched savagely around the rifle he held, and the Leader smiled at the display of fervor and started forward. Meyers touched his shoulder.

"My Leader, there is no need that you should walk, though these must. I have a small auto here, into which we can put the machine. Send the legion ahead, and we'll follow later; they'll have little trouble clearing out Bresseldorf for us. Then, when we've packed our duplicator and I've assembled spare parts for an emergency, we can join them."

"By all means, yes. The machine must be well handled." The Fuehrer nodded and turned back to the men. "Proceed to Bresseldorf, then, and we follow. Secure quarters for yourself and food, and a place for me and for Meyers; we stop there until I can send word to the depot during the night and extend my plans. To Bresseldorf!"

Silently, without apparent organization, but with only small confusion, the legion turned and moved off, rifles in hands. There were no orders, no beating of drums to announce to the world that the Leader was on the march again, but the movement of that body of men, all gradations of the same man, was impressive enough without fanfare as it turned into the road that led to Bresseldorf, only a mile away. Meyers saw a small cart coming toward them, watched it halt while the driver stared dumbly at the company approaching. Then, with a shriek that cut thinly over the distance, he was whipping his animal about and heading in wild flight toward the village.

"I think the peasants will cause no trouble, my Leader," the scientist guessed, turning back to the shop. "No, the legion will be quartered by the time we reach them."

\*     \*     \*

And when the little car drove up into the village square half an hour later and the two men got out, the legion was quartered well enough to satisfy all prophets. There was no sign of the peasants, but the men from the future were moving back and forth into the houses and shops along the street, carrying foodstuffs to be cooked. Cellars and stores had been well gutted, and a few pigs were already killed and being cut up— not skillfully, perhaps, but well enough for practical purposes.

The Leader motioned toward one of the amateur butchers, a copy of himself who seemed perhaps two or three years older, and the man approached with frozen face. His knuckles, Meyers noted, were white where his fingers clasped around the butcher knife he had been using.

"The peasants—what happened?"

The legionnaire's face set tighter, and he opened his mouth to say something; apparently he changed his mind after a second, shut it and shrugged. "Nothing," he answered. "We met a peasant on the road who went ahead shouting about a million troops, all the Leader. When we got here, there were a few children and women running off, and two men trying to drag away one of the pigs. They left it behind and ran off. Nothing happened."

"Stupid dolts! Superstition, no loyalty!" The Fuehrer twisted his lips, frowning at the man before him, apparently no longer conscious that it was merely a later edition of himself. "Well, show us to the quarters you've picked for us. And have someone send us food and wine. Has a messenger been sent to the men at the tank depot?"

"You did not order it."

"What— No, so I didn't. Well, go yourself, then, if you . . . but, of course, you know where it is, naturally. Tell Hauptmann Immenhoff to expect me tomorrow and not to be surprised at anything. You'll have to go on foot, since we need the car for the machine."

The legionnaire nodded indicating one of the houses on the square. "You quarter here. I go on foot, as I knew I would." He turned expressionlessly and plodded off to the north, grabbing up a half-cooked leg of pork as he passed the fire burning in the middle of the square.

The Leader and Meyers did not waste time following him with their eyes, but went into the house indicated, where wine and food were sent in to them shortly. With the help of one of the duplicates, space was quickly cleared for the machine, and a crude plank table drawn up for the map that came from the Leader's bag. But Meyers had little appetite for the food or wine, less for the dry task of watching while the other made marks on the paper or stared off into space in some rapt dream of conquest. The hellish tumor inside him was giving him no rest now, and he turned to his machine, puttering over its insides as a release from the pain. Outside, the legion was comparatively silent, only the occasional sound of a man walking past breaking the monotony. Darkness fell just as more food was brought in to them, and the scientist looked out to see the square deserted; apparently the men had moved as silently as ever to the beds selected for the night. And still, the Fuehrer worked over his plans, hardly touching the food at his side.

Finally he stirred. "Done," he stated. "See, Meyers, it is simple now. Tomorrow, probably from the peasants who ran off, the enemy will know we are here. With full speed, possibly they can arrive by noon, and though we start early, fifteen miles is a long march for untrained men; possibly they would catch us on the road. Therefore, we do not march. We remain here."

"Like rats in a trap? Remember, my Leader, while we have possibly ten thousand men with rifles, ammunition can be used but once—so that our apparently large supply actually consists of but fifty rounds at most."

"Even so, we remain, not like rats, but like cheese in a trap. If we move, they can strafe us from the air; if we remain, they send light tanks and trucks of men against us, since they travel fastest. In the morning, therefore, we'll send out the auto with a couple of older men—less danger of their being suspected—to the depot to order Immenhoff here with one medium tank, a crew, and trucks of ammunition and petrol. We allow an hour for the auto to reach Immenhoff and for his return here. Here, they are duplicated to a thousand tanks, perhaps, with crews, and fueled and made ready. Then, when the enemy arrives, we wipe them out, move on to the depot, clean out our supplies there, and strike north to the next. After that—"

He went on, talking now more to himself than to Meyers, and the scientist only pieced together parts of the plan. As might have been expected it was unexpected, audacious, and would probably work. Meyers was no military genius, had only a rough working idea of military operations, but he was reasonably sure that the Leader could play the cards he was dealing himself and come out on top, barring the unforeseen in large quantities. But now, having conquered Europe, the Leader's voice was lower, and what little was audible no longer made sense to the scientist, who drew out a cheap blanket and threw himself down, his eyes closed.

Still the papers and maps rustled, and the voice droned on in soft snatches, gradually falling to a whisper and then ceasing. There was a final rattling of the map, followed by complete silence, and Meyers could feel the other's eyes on his back. He made no move, and the Leader must have been satisfied by the regular breathing that the scientist was asleep, for he muttered to himself again as he threw another blanket on the floor and blew out the light.

"A useful man, Meyers, now. But after victory, perhaps his machine would be a menace. Well, that can wait."

Meyers smiled slightly in the darkness, then went back to forcing himself to sleep. As the Leader had said, such things could wait. At the moment, his major worry was that the Army of Occupation might come an hour too soon—but that also was nonsense; obviously, from the ranks of the legion, that could not be any part of the order of things. That which was would be, and he had nothing left to fear.

The Leader was already gone from the house when Meyers awoke. For a few minutes the scientist stood staring at the blanket of the other, then shrugged, looked at his watch, and made a hasty breakfast of wine and morphine; with cancer gnawing their vitals, men have small fear of drug addiction, and the opiate would make seeming normality easier for a time. There were still threads to be tied in to his own satisfaction, and little time left in which to do it.

Outside, the heavy dew of the night was long since gone, and the air was fully warmed by the sun. Most of the legion were gathered in the square, some preparing breakfast, others eating, but all in the same stiff silence that had marked their goings and comings since the first. Meyers walked out among them slowly, and their eyes followed him broodingly, but they made no other sign. One of the earlier ones who had been shaving with a straight razor stopped, fingering the blade, his eyes on the scientist's neck.

Meyers stopped before him, half smiling. "Well, why not say it? What are you thinking?"

"Why bother? You know." The legionnaire's fingers clenched around the handle, then relaxed, and he went on with his shaving, muttering as his unsteady hand made the razor nick his skin. "In God's will, if I could draw this once across your throat, Meyers, I'd cut my own for the right."

Meyers nodded. "I expected so. But you can't. Remember? You must obey your original implicitly; you must not cause trouble for your original or Karl Meyers; you must not speak to us or others except as we demand. Of course, in a couple of days, the compulsion would wear away slowly, but by that time we'll be out of reach of each other. . . . No, back! Stay where you are and continue shaving; from the looks of the others, you'll stop worrying about your hair shortly, but why hurry it?"

"Some day, somehow, I'll beat it! And then, a word to the original—or I'll track you down myself! God!" But the threatening scowl lessened, and the man went reluctantly back to his shaving, in the grip of the compulsion still. Meyers chuckled dryly.

"What was and has been—will be."

He passed down the line again, in and out among the mingled men who were scattered about without order, studying them carefully, noting how they ranged from trim copies of the Leader in field coat and well kept to what might have been demented scavengers picking from the garbage cans of the alleys and back streets. And yet, even the oldest and filthiest of the group was still the same man who had come closer to conquering the known world than anyone since Alexander. Satisfied at last, he turned back toward the house where his quarters were.

A cackling, tittering quaver at his right brought him around abruptly to face something that had once been a man, but now looked more like some animated scarecrow.

"You're Meyers," the old one accused him. "*Shh!* I know it. I remember. Hee-yee, I remember again. Oh, this is wonderful, wonderful, wonderful! Do you wonder how I can speak? Wonderful, wonderful, wonderful!"

Meyers backed a step and the creature advanced again, leering, half dancing in excitement. "Well, how can you speak? The compulsion shouldn't have worn off so soon."

"Hee! Hee-yee-yee! Wonderful!" The wreck of a man was dancing more frantically now, rubbing his hands together. Then he sobered sharply, laughter bubbling out of a straight mouth and tapering off, like the drippings from a closed faucet. "*Shh!* I'll tell you. Yes, tell you all about it, but you mustn't tell *him. He* makes me come here every day where I can eat, and I like to eat. If *he* knew, *he* might not let me come. This is my last day; did you know it? Yes, my last day. I'm the oldest. Wonderful, don't you think it's wonderful? I do."

"You're crazy!" Meyers had expected it, yet the realization of the fact was still a shock to him and to his Continental background of fear of mental unbalance.

The scarecrow figure bobbed its head in agreement. "I'm crazy, yes—crazy. I've been crazy almost a year now—isn't it wonderful? But don't tell *him*. It's nice to be crazy. I can talk now; I couldn't talk before—*he* wouldn't let me. And some of the others are crazy, too, and they talk to me; we talk quietly, and *he* doesn't know. . . . You're Meyers, I remember now. I've been watching you, wondering, and now I remember. There's something else I should remember—something I should do; I planned it all once, and it was *so* clever, but now I can't remember— You're Meyers. Don't I hate you?"

"No. No, Leader, I'm your friend." In spite of himself, Meyers was shuddering, wondering how to break away from the maniac. He was painfully aware that for some reason the compulsion on which he had counted no longer worked; insanity had thrown the normal rules overboard. If this person should remember fully— Again Meyers shuddered, not from personal fear, but the fear that certain things still undone might not be completed. "No, great Leader, I'm your real friend. Your best friend. I'm the one who told him to bring you here to eat."

"Yes? Oh, wonderful—I like to eat. But I'm not the Leader; *he* is . . . and *he* told me . . . what did *he* tell me? Hee! I remember again, *he* told me to find you; *he* wants you. And I'm the last. Oh, it's wonderful, wonderful, wonderful, wonderful. Now I'll remember it all, I will. Hee-yee-yee! Wonderful. You'd better go now, Meyers. *He* wants you. Isn't it wonderful?"

Meyers lost no time in leaving, glad for any excuse, but wondering why the Leader had sent for him, and how much the lunatic had told. He glanced at his watch again, and at the sun, checking mentally, and felt surer as he entered the quarters. Then he saw there was no reason to fear, for the Leader had his maps out again, and was nervously tapping his foot against the floor; but there was no personal anger in his glance.

"Meyers? Where were you?"

"Out among the legion, my Leader, making sure they were ready to begin operations. All is prepared."

"Good." The Leader accepted his version without doubt. "I, too, have been busy. The car was sent off almost an hour ago—more than an hour ago—to the depot, and Immenhoff should be here at any moment. No sign of the enemy yet; we'll have time enough. Then, let them come!"

He fell back to the chair beside the table, nervous fingers tapping against the map, feet still rubbing at the floor, keyed to the highest tension, like a cat about to leap at its prey. "What time is it? Hm-m-m. No sound of the tank yet. What's delaying that fool? He should be here now. Hadn't we best get the machine outside?"

"It won't be necessary," Meyers assured him. "I'll simply run out a wire from the receiver to the tank when it arrives; the machine will work at a considerable distance, just as long as the subject is under some part of it."

"Good. What's delaying Immenhoff? He should have made it long ago. And where's the courier I sent last night? Why didn't he report back? I—"

"Hee-yee! He's smart, Leader, just as I once was." The tittering voice came from the door of their quarters, and both men looked up to see the old lunatic standing there, running his fingers through his beard. "Oh, it was wonderful! Why walk all that long way back when he knew it made no difference where he was— the machine will bring him back, anyhow. Wonderful, don't you think it it was wonderful? You didn't tell him to walk back."

The Leader scowled, nodded. "Yes, I suppose it made no difference whether he came back or not. He could return with Immenhoff."

"Not he, not he! Not with Immenhoff!"

"Fool! Why not? And get out of here!"

But the lunatic was in no hurry to leave. He leaned against the doorway, snickering. "Immenhoff's dead— Immenhoff's dead. Wonderful! He's been dead a long time now. The Army of Occupation found him and he got killed. I remember it all now, how I found him all dead when I was the courier. So I didn't come back, because I was smart, and then I was back without walking. Wonderful, wonderful, wonderful! I remember everything now, don't I?"

"Immenhoff dead? Impossible!" The Leader was out of the chair, stalking toward the man, black rage on his face. "You're insane!"

"Hee! Isn't it wonderful? They always said I was and now I am. But Immenhoff's dead, and he won't come here, and there'll be no tanks. Oh, how wonderful, never to march at all, but just come here every day to eat. I like to eat. . . . No, don't touch me. I'll shoot, I will. I remember this is a gun, and I'll shoot, and the bullet will explode with noise, lots of noise. Don't come near me." He centered the automatic squarely on the Leader's stomach, smirking gleefully as he watched his original retreat cautiously back toward the table.

"You're mad at me because I'm crazy—" A sudden effort of concentration sent the smirk away to be replaced by cunning. "You know I'm crazy now! I didn't want you to know, but I told you. How sad, how sad, isn't it sad? No, it isn't sad, it's wonderful still, and I'm going to kill you. That's what I wanted to remember. I'm going to kill you, Leader. Now isn't that nice that I'm going to kill you?"

Meyers sat back in another chair, watching the scene as he might have a stage play, wondering what the next move might be, but calmly aware that he had no part to play in the next few moments. Then he noticed the Leader's hand drop behind him and grope back on the table for the automatic there, and his curiosity was satisfied. Obviously, the lunatic couldn't have killed his original.

The lunatic babbled on. "I remember my plan, Leader. I'll kill you, and then there won't be any you. And without you, there won't be any me. I'll never have to hunt for clothes, or keep from talking, or go crazy. I won't be at all, and it'll be wonderful. No more twenty years. Wonderful, isn't it wonderful? Hee-yee-yee! Oh, wonderful. But I like to eat, and dead men don't eat, do they? Do they? Too bad, too bad, but I had breakfast this morning, anyhow. I'm going to kill you the next time I say wonderful, Leader. I'm going to shoot, and there'll be noise, and you'll be dead. Wonder—"

His lips went on with the motion, even as the Leader's hand whipped out from behind him and the bullet exploded in his head with a sudden crash that split his skull like a melon and threw mangled bits of flesh out through the door, leaving half a face and a tattered old body to slump slowly toward the floor with a last spasmodic kick. With a wry face, the Fuehrer tossed the gun back on the table and rolled the dead figure outside the door with his foot.

Meyers collected the gun quietly, substituting his watch, face up where he could watch the minute hand. "That was yourself you shot, my Leader," he stated as the other turned back to the table.

"Not myself, a duplicate. What matter, he was useless, obviously, with his insane babble of Immenhoff's death. Or— The tank should have been here long before! But Immenhoff couldn't have been discovered!"

Meyers nodded. "He was—all the 'secret' depots were; I knew of it. And the body you just tossed outside wasn't merely a duplicate—it was yourself as you will inevitably be."

"You— Treason!" Ugly horror and the beginnings of personal fear spread across the Leader's face, twisting the scar and turning it livid. "For that—"

Meyers covered him with the automatic. "For that," he finished, "you'll remain seated, Leader, with your hands on the table in clear view. Oh, I have no intention of killing you, but I could stun you quite easily; I assure you, I'm an excellent shot."

"What do you want? The reward of the invaders?"

"Only the inevitable, Leader, only what will be because it has already been. Here!" Meyers tossed a small leather wallet onto the table with his left hand, flipping it open to the picture of a woman perhaps thirty-five years old. "What do you see there?"

"A damned Jewess!" The Leader's eyes had flicked to the picture and away, darting about the room and back to it.

"Quite so. Now, to you, a damned Jewess, Leader." Meyers replaced the wallet gently, his eyes cold. "Once though, to me, a lovely and understanding woman, interested in my work, busy about our home, a good mother to my children; there were two of them, a boy and a girl—more damned Jews to you, probably. We were happy then. I was about to become a full professor at Heidelberg, we had our friends, our life, our home. Some, of course, even then were filled with hatred toward the Jewish people, but we could stand all that. Can you guess what happened? Not hard, is it?

"Some of your Youths. She'd gone to her father to stay with him, hoping it would all blow over and she could come back to me without her presence hurting me. They raided the shop one night, beat up her father, tossed her out of a third-story window, and made the children jump after her—mere sport, and patriotic sport! When I found her at the home of some friends, the children were dead and she was dying."

The Leader stirred again. "What did you expect? That we should coddle every Jew to our bosom and let them bespoil the Reich again? You were a traitor to your fatherland when you married her."

"So I found out. Two years in a concentration camp, my Leader, taught me that, well indeed. And it gave me time to think. No matter how much *you* beat a man down and make him grovel and live in filth, he still may be able to think, and his thoughts may still find you out—you should have thought of that. For two years, I thought about a certain field of mathematics, and at last I began to think about the thing instead of the symbols. And at last, when I'd groveled and humbled myself, sworn a thousandfold that I'd seen the light, and made myself something a decent man would spurn aside, they let me out again, ten years older for the two years there, and a hundred times wiser.

"So, I came finally to the little farm near Bresseldorf, and I worked as I could, hoping that, somehow, a just God would so shape things that I could use my discovery. About the time I'd finished, you fled, and I almost gave up hope; then I saw that in your escape lay my chances. I found you, persuaded you to return, and here you are. It sounds simple enough now, but I wasn't sure until I saw the legion. What would happen if I turned you over to the Army of Occupation?"

"Eh?" The Leader had been watching the door, hoping for some distracting event, but his eyes now swung back to Meyers. "I don't know. Is that what you plan?"

"Napoleon was exiled; Wilhelm died in bed at Dorn. Are the leaders who cause the trouble ever punished, my Leader? I think not. Exile may not be pleasant, but normally is not too hard a punishment—normal exile to another land. I have devised a slightly altered exile, and now I shall do nothing to you. What was—will be—and I'll be content to know that eventually you will kill yourself, after you've gone insane." Meyers glanced at the watch on the table, and his eyes gleamed savagely for a second before the cool, impersonal manner returned.

"The time is almost up, my Leader. I was fair to you; I explained to the best of my ability the workings of my invention. But instead of science, you wanted magic; you expected me to create some pseudo-duplicate of yourself, yet leave the real self unaltered. You absorbed the word 'plenum' as an incantation, but gave no heed to the reality. Remember the example I gave—a piece of string looped back on itself? In front of you is a string from some peasant's dress; now, conceive that piece of string—it loops back, starts out again, and is again drawn back—it does not put forth new feelers that do the returning to base for it, but must come back by itself, and never gets beyond a certain distance from itself. The coins that you saw in the pile disappeared—

not because I depressed a dummy switch, but because the two-minute interval was finished, and they were forced to return again to the previous two minutes."

Escape thoughts were obviously abandoned in the mind of the Leader now, and he was staring fixedly at Meyers while his hands played with the raveling from a peasant's garment, looping and unlooping it. "No," he said at last, and there was a tinge of awe and pleading in his voice, the beginning of tears in his eyes. "That is insane. Karl Meyers, you are a fool. Release me from this and even now, with all that has happened, you'll still find me a man who can reward his friends; release me, and still I'll reconquer the world, half of which shall be yours. Don't be a fool, Meyers."

Meyers grinned. "There's no release, Leader. How often must I tell you that what is now will surely be; you have already been on the wheel—you must continue. And—the time is almost here!"

He watched the tensing of the Fuehrer's muscles with complete calm, dropping the automatic back on his lap. Even as the Leader leaped from his chair in a frenzied effort and dashed toward him he made no move. There was no need. The minute hand of the watch reached a mark on the face, and the leaping figure of the world's most feared man was no longer there. Meyers was alone in the house, and alone in Bresseldorf.

He tossed the gun on the table, patting the pocket containing his wallet, and moved toward the dead figure outside the door. Soon, if the Leader had been right, the Army of Occupation would be here. Before then, he must destroy his machine.

One second he was dashing across the room toward the neck of Karl Meyers, the next, without any feeling of change, he was standing in the yard of the house of Meyers, near Bresseldorf, and ranging from him and behind him were rows of others. In his hands, which had been empty a second before, he clutched a rifle. At his side was belted one of the new-issue automatics. And before him, through the door of the house that had been Karl Meyers', he could see himself coming forward, Meyers at a few paces behind.

For the moment there were no thoughts in his head, only an endless refrain that went: "I must obey my original implicitly; I must not cause trouble for my original or Karl Meyers; I must not speak to anyone unless one of those two commands. I must obey my original implicitly; I must not cause trouble—" By an effort, he stopped the march of the words in his head, but the force of them went on, an undercurrent to all his thinking, an endless and inescapable order that must be obeyed.

Beside him, those strange others who were himself waited expressionlessly while the original came out into the doorway and began to speak to them. "Soldiers of the Greater Reich that is to be. . . . Let us be merciless in avenging. . . . The fruits of victory. . . ." Victory! Yes, for Karl Meyers. For the man who stood there beside the original, a faint smile on his face, looking out slowly over the ranks of the legion.

"But I speak to myselves. You who come after me know what is to be this day and in the days to come, so why should I tell you? And you know that my cause is just. The Jews, the Jew lovers—" The words of the original went maddeningly on, words that were still fresh in his memory, words that he had spoken only twenty-four hours before.

And now, three dead Jews and a Jew lover had brought him to this. Somehow, he must stop this mad farce, cry out to the original that it was treason and madness, that it was far better to turn back to the guards in Switzerland, or to march forth toward the invaders. But the words were only a faint whisper, even to himself, and the all-powerful compulsion choked even the whisper off before he could finish it. He must not speak to anyone unless one of those two commanded.

Still the words went on. "Not victory in a decade, nor a year, but in a month! We shall go north and south and east and west! We shall show them that our fangs are not pulled; that those which we lost were but our milk teeth, now replaced by a second and harder growth!

"And for those who would have betrayed us, or bound us down in chains to feed the gold lust of the mad democracies, or denied us the room to live which is rightfully ours—for those, we shall find a proper place. This time, for once and for all, there shall be an end to the evils that corrupt the earth—the Jews and the Bolsheviks, and their friends, and friends' friends. Germany shall emerge, purged and cleansed, a new and greater Reich, whose domain shall not be Europe, nor this hemisphere, but the world!

"Many of you have seen all this in the future from which you come, and all of you must be ready to reassure yourselves of it today, that the glory of it may fill your tomorrow. Now, we march against a few peasants. Tomorrow, after quartering in Bresseldorf, we shall be in the secret depot, where those who remain loyal shall be privileged to multiply and join us, and where we shall multiply all our armament ten-thousand-fold! Into Bresseldorf, then, and if any of the peasants are disloyal, be merciless in removing the scum! Forward!"

His blood was pounding with the mockery of it, and his hands were clutched on the rifle. Only one shot from the gun, and Karl Meyers would die. One quick move, too sudden to defeat, and he would be avenged. Yet, as he made the first effort toward lifting the rifle, the compulsion surged upward, drowning out all other orders of his mind. He must not cause trouble for his original or Karl Meyers!

He could feel the futile tears on his face as he stood there, and the mere knowledge of their futility was the hardest blow of all. Before him, his original was smiling at him and starting forward, to be checked by Meyers, and to swing back after a few words.

"Proceed to Bresseldorf, then, and we follow. Secure quarters for yourself and food, and a place for me and for Meyers; we stop there until I can send word to the depot during the night and extend my plans. To Bresseldorf!"

Against his will, his feet turned then with the others, out across the yard and into the road, and he was headed toward Bresseldorf. His eyes swept over the group, estimating them to be six or seven thousand in number; and that would mean twenty years, at one a day— Twenty years of marching to Bresseldorf, eating, sleeping, eating again, being back at the farm, hearing the original's speech, and marching to Bresseldorf. Finally—from far down the line, a titter from the oldest and filthiest reached him—finally that; madness, and death at the hands of himself, while Karl Meyers stood by, watching and gloating. He no longer doubted the truth of the scientist's statements; what had been, would be.

For twenty years! For more than seven thousand days, each the same day, each one step nearer madness. God!

*The great strength of religions such as Christianity and Buddhism is that they promise no victory in this world; hence their longevity, as all earthly suffering can be interpreted as punishment for sin or preparation for heaven/nirvana. Islam, whose founder was a ruler and conqueror as well as a prophet, has yet to really recover from the trauma of Western domination. Communism and National Socialism both promise inevitable victory in the here and now; neither is well-equipped to survive defeat. Many of Hitler's followers remained loyal up to the Leader's death, but after that the occupation forces found: "Nazis? Only one in our town, and he died last year." The following grisly little tale shows one who remained faithful to the Master's vision . . .*

# BARBAROSSA

## Edward Wellen

The submarine rises slowly. The Commander stands on the hatchway ladder. He puts his hand on the hatch-securing wheel. Rust bites his palm and flakes away as he takes a firmer grip. From the hydrophone comes, "All clear." The submarine rises to ten fathoms. The Commander gives the order for release. "Surface!" Compressed air hisses into the tanks. The depth gauge in the conning tower starts moving; it accelerates. "Hatchway free!" shouts the chief engineer. "Pressure equalized."

Above and ahead, a rowboat with makeshift sail tattering itself on an oar jury-rigged as a mast rides low in the water. The outboard motor has long ago sputtered itself out. The people aboard forget to bail when the monster rips up through their wake.

Fear leaves their faces when they see the U-999 does not bear Cuban markings.

The Commander raises the conning-tower hatch and climbs out onto the bridge. The senior watch-officer follows, carrying a submachine gun.

Fresh air! The Commander's long beard streams in the spume like an oriflamme.

The people in the rowboat gape at the Commander. When he lowers his nose they point toward Key West and smile and nod and jabber.

The Commander does not shift his gaze toward where they gesture. He is looking them over. They are three men, two of military age, one pushing sixty; a boy of thirteen; two women, one in her early twenties, the other in her late fifties; and a baby. The Commander lets the breeze carry his voice over his shoulder.

"Bring the two young men and the boy aboard."

It takes a boarding party to tear the three males from the others and across to the bridge of the U-999.

The Commander watches a petty officer shove the three through the hatchway. Now he has a full complement again. He strokes his beard. He has dyed the flowing white beard red. Barbarossa. In his youth he had learned the legend of the redbearded Emperor Frederick I, who sleeps in his Kyffhäuser mountain cave till he shall come forth to rescue Germany and make her chief of nations.

Without needing a word the boarding party seizes the refugee craft's spare jerricans of petrol and passes them down the conning-tower hatch. Fueling the U-999 is a standing problem. At least now they will have hot meals for some time to come.

The two men and the boy stumble down the ladder. The foulness of the air smacks them at once, the scene waits for their eyes to adapt to the dim flicker.

The U-999 is not what she was. The damp causes vital electrical parts to fail. The woodwork has rotted badly. Condensation steadily drips down the bulkheads. Bunks and linen are always damp. Everything is black with diesel exhaust which, because the water pressure has grown too great for the exhaust valves, backs up. When he can spare the hands the Commander puts them to work on spit and polish but it is a losing battle. Just to keep the boat operating is enough to busy the crew. Not in a long while has the Commander given the order "Full speed ahead!" He knows the old engines cannot stand that strain for long.

By now the three refugees have seen the ratings lying on bunks. They look like corpses in the oily haze that fills this dank coffin. When they are not on watch the ratings, for the most part, simply lie on their bunks in a dead stupor. They are chained to the bunks; the chains lie neatly, as if the men have learned not to entangle their long fetters. Those of the crew in the engine room are worst off. They are always bathed in oil and sweat.

A petty officer jabs the three males aft into the engine room. He handcuffs them to pipes for now. Once the U-999 dives and shapes course there will be time to fit and weld the neck and leg irons in place.

The three hear a burst of submachine-gun fire outside the hull.

The Commander secures the hatch and climbs down into the control room. It is too bad about the women. But from the first he has made it a rule never to take the women aboard. It is hard enough to maintain discipline as it is. Woman's place is in church, in the kitchen, in the nursery. Not aboard a U-boat. As for the baby, if it had been a boy child he might have considered sparing it. He could have brought it up to serve in the crew one day.

One day. Der Tag. When will that come? What will happen when it comes?

Sometimes he forgets who he is and why he sails under the seas. But he is not mad. Give him time; it always comes back to him. He is Kapitän-Leutnant Helmut Niemans and he is waiting for the Party to come again to power—to *surface*, as it were.

Meanwhile, he stays in hiding and watches the Amis and the Russkis play Chicken-of-the-Sea. He smiles in his beard thinking of Der Tag. One torpedo salvo fore and one aft; one for an Ami ship, one for a Russki. Each side will blame the other. Then it will all take up where it left off.

He was a mere twenty-two long ago in 1945. On Tuesday, May 1st, of that year, Hamburg radio announced that Adolf Hitler was dead. Grand Admiral Karl Doenitz took over as Der Fuehrer and began trying to arrange a surrender—to the Western Allies, but not to Russia. To show his good faith, Doenitz broadcast on the night of May 4th an order to every German warship to cease hostilities and return to port.

U-999 did not acknowledge the order.

It fought to break through to the open sea. It backed into its own wake to confound surface ships' detection devices. (The around-the-clock ping! ping! ping! of sound gear searching for submarines was enough to drive one mad!) It churned up knuckles of water with its propellers so that sonarmen heard a U-boat that wasn't there and chased after that. Finally, it shot flotsam (an officer's cap, escape lungs, life jackets, abandon-ship kits, planking, the top of a chart table, a jack-staff) through torpedo tubes. German Naval records carry the U-999 as "missing and probably sunk." But one day the U-999 will radio to Berlin in the old code that it is still here, still ready for action.

It has not been easy to keep the U-999 watertight and functional and the tin fish primed. The Commander is now in his eighties. All but 12 of his original crew of 55 have died. Some went naturally, some were shot trying to jump ship, others killed themselves. Once there was a near-mutiny, but he has put that out of his mind.

The 43 replacements are a motley lot. Few of them understand or speak German. He has had to teach them an international language of signs and kicks. It is like a little U.N. He sighs. Yes, he has a full complement now, but he knows he will soon have to jettison the black cook. The hull of the U-999 has closed in on the man and he has the long stare. But that can wait. The Commander knows how to wait.

He gives the conn to his mate and goes to his quarters. He puts on a gramophone record and listens to the old songs that remind him of home.

*Alternate history is science fiction's answer to the historical novel, examining what might have been as a counterpoint to what might be in the future. World War II is a favorite subject for such treatment. It has innumerable attractions ranging from the discreditable—fetishistic use of Nazi trappings—through the merely lazy—in an alternate history the writer can use the ultimate prepackaged villain, the SS-man, yet again—to the artistically serious: showing by a consideration of alternatives the precise moral implications of what did happen. "Two Dooms" deals with a tendency which sheltered North Americans must always be wary of: imagining that the first horror they stub their moral toes on is necessarily the worst possible in a world far less suburbanly pleasant than they have been reared to believe. Much has been written on the moral dilemmas of those who worked on the Manhattan project; below is a cautionary tale reminding us of why the Project was launched in the first place . . .*

# TWO DOOMS

## C. M. Kornbluth

*". . . why should we be tender*
*To let an arrogant piece of flesh threat us,*
*Play judge and executioner all himself?"*
      —CYMBELINE, IV, 2

## I

It was May, not yet summer by five weeks, but the afternoon heat under the corrugated roofs of Manhattan Engineer District's Los Alamos Laboratory was daily less bearable. Young Dr. Edward Royland had lost fifteen pounds from an already meager frame during his nine-month hitch in the desert. He wondered every day while the thermometer crawled up to its 5:45 peak whether he had made a mistake he would regret the rest of his life in accepting work with the laboratory rather than letting the local draft board have his carcass and do what they pleased with it. His University of Chicago classmates were glamorously collecting ribbons and wounds from Saipan to Brussels; one of them, a

187

first-rate mathematician named Hatfield, would do no more first-rate mathematics. He had gone down, burning, in an Eighth Air Force Mitchell bomber ambushed over Lille.

"And what, Daddy, did you do in the war?"

"Well, kids it's a little hard to explain. They had this stupid atomic bomb project that never came to anything, and they tied up a lot of us in a Godforsaken place in New Mexico. We figured and we calculated and we fooled with uranium and some of us got radiation burns and then the war was over and they sent us home."

Royland was not amused by this prospect. He had heat rash under his arms and he was waiting, not patiently, for the Computer Section to send him his figures on Phase 56c, which was the (goddam childish) code designation for Element Assembly Time. Phase 56c was Royland's own particular baby. He was under Rotschmidt, supervisor of WEAPON DESIGN TRACK III, and Rotschmidt was under Oppenheimer, who bossed the works. Sometimes a General Groves came through, a fine figure of a man, and once from a window Royland had seen the venerable Henry L. Stimson, Secretary of War, walking slowly down their dusty street, leaning on a cane and surrounded by young staff officers. That's what Royland was seeing of the war.

Laboratory! It had sounded inviting, cool, bustling but quiet. So every morning these days he was blasted out of his cot in a barracks cubicle at seven by "Oppie's whistle," fought for a shower and shave with thirty-seven other bachelor scientists in eight languages, bolted a bad cafeteria breakfast and went through the barbed-wire Restricted Line to his "office"—another matchboard-walled cubicle, smaller and hotter and noisier, with talking and typing and clack of adding machines all around him.

Under the circumstances he was doing good work, he supposed. He wasn't happy about being restricted to his one tiny problem, Phase 56c, but no doubt he was happier than Hatfield had been when his Mitchell got it.

Under the circumstances . . . they included a weird haywire arrangement for computing. Instead of a decent differential analyzer machine they had a human sea of office girls with Burroughs desk calculators; the girls screamed "Banzai!" and charged on differential equations and swamped them by sheer volume; they clicked them to death with their little adding machines. Royland thought hungrily of Conant's huge, beautiful analog differentiator up at M.I.T.; it was probably tied up by whatever the mysterious "Radiation Laboratory" there was doing. Royland suspected that the "Radiation Laboratory" had as much to do with radiation as his own "Manhattan Engineer District" had to do with Manhattan engineering. And the world was supposed to be trembling on the edge these days of a New Dispensation of Computing which would obsolete even the M.I.T. machine—tubes, relays and binary arithmetic at blinding speed instead of the suavely turning cams and the smoothly extruding rods and the elegant scribed curves of Conant's masterpiece. He decided that he wouldn't like that; he would like it even less than he liked the little office girls clacking away, pushing lank hair from their dewed brows with undistracted hands.

He wiped his own brow with a sodden handkerchief and permitted himself a glance at his watch and the thermometer. Five-fifteen and 103 Fahrenheit respectively.

He thought vaguely of getting out, of fouling up just enough to be released from the project and drafted. No; there was the post-war career to think of. But one of the big shots, Teller, had been irrepressible; he had rambled outside of his assigned mission again and again until Oppenheimer let him go; now Teller was working with Lawrence at Berkeley on something that had reputedly gone sour at a reputed quarter of a billion dollars—

A girl in khaki knocked and entered. "Your material from the Computer Section, Dr. Royland. Check them and sign here, please." He counted the dozen sheets, signed the clipboarded form she held out and plunged into the material for thirty minutes.

When he sat back in his chair, the sweat dripped into his eyes unnoticed. His hands were shaking a little, though he did not know that either. Phase 56c of WEAPON DESIGN TRACK III was finished, over, done, successfully accomplished. The answer to the question "Can $U_{235}$ slugs be assembled into a critical mass within a physically feasible time?" was in. The answer was "Yes."

Royland was a theory man, not a Wheatstone or a Kelvin; he liked the numbers for themselves and had no special passion to grab for wires, mica and bits of graphite so that what the numbers said might immediately be given flesh in a wonderful new gadget. Nevertheless he could visualize at once a workable atomic bomb assembly within the framework of Phase 56c. You have so many microseconds to assemble your critical mass without it boiling away in vapor; you use them by blowing the subassemblies together with shaped charges; lots of microseconds to spare by that method; practically foolproof. Then comes the Big Bang.

Oppie's whistle blew; it was quitting time. Royland sat still in his cubicle. He should go, of course, to Rotschmidt and tell him; Rotschmidt would probably clap him on the back and pour him a jigger of Bols Geneva from the tall clay bottle he kept in his safe. Then Rotschmidt would go to Oppenheimer. Before sunset the project would be redesigned! TRACK I, TRACK II, TRACK IV and TRACK V would be shut down and their people crammed into TRACK III, the one with the paydirt! New excitement would boil through the project; it had been torpid and souring for three months. Phase 56c was the first good news in at least that long; it had been one damned blind alley after another. General Groves had looked sour and dubious last time around.

Desk drawers were slamming throughout the corrugated, sun-baked building; doors were slamming shut on cubicles; down the corridor, somebody roared with laughter, strained laughter. Passing Royland's door somebody cried impatiently: "*—aber was kan Man tun?*"

Royland whispered to himself: "You damned fool, what are you thinking of?"

But he knew—he was thinking of the Big Bang, the Big Dirty Bang, and of torture. The judicial torture of the old days, incredibly cruel by today's lights, stretched the whole body, or crushed it, or burned it, or shattered the fingers and legs. But even that old judicial torture carefully avoided the most sensitive parts of the body, the generative organs, though damage to these, or a real threat of damage to these, would have produced quick and copious confessions. You have to be more or less crazy to torture somebody that way; the sane man does not think of it as a possibility.

An M.P. corporal tried Royland's door and looked in. "Quitting time, professor," he said.

"Okay," Royland said. Mechanically he locked his desk drawers and his files, turned his window lock and set out his wastepaper basket in the corridor. Click the door; another day, another dollar.

Maybe the project *was* breaking up. They did now and then. The huge boner at Berkeley proved that. And Royland's barracks was light two physicists now; their cubicles stood empty since they had been drafted to M.I.T. for some anti-submarine thing. Groves had *not* looked happy last time around; how did a general make up his mind anyway? Give them three months, then the axe? Maybe Stimson would run out of patience and cut the loss, close the District down. Maybe F.D.R. would say at a cabinet meeting, "By the way, Henry, what ever became of—?" and that would be the end if old Henry could say only that the scientists appear to be optimistic of eventual success, Mr. President, but that as yet there seems to be nothing *concrete*—

He passed through the barbed wire of the Line under scrutiny of an M.P. lieutenant and walked down the barracks-edged company street of the maintenance troops to their motor pool. He wanted a jeep and a trip ticket; he wanted a long desert drive in the twilight; he wanted a dinner of *frijoles* and egg plant with his old friend Charles Miller Nahataspe, the medicine man of the

adjoining Hopi reservation. Royland's hobby was anthropology; he wanted to get a little drunk on it—he
hoped it would clear his mind.


II


Nahataspe welcomed him cheerfully to his hut; his
million wrinkles all smiled. "You want me to play infor-
mant for a while?" he grinned. He had been to Carlyle
in the 1880's and had been laughing at the white man
ever since; he admitted that physics was funny, but for
a real joke give him cultural anthropology every time.
"You want some nice unsavory stuff about our institu-
tionalized homosexuality? Should I cook us a dog for
dinner? Have a seat on the blanket, Edward."

"What happened to your chairs? And the funny picture of McKinley? And—and everything?" The hut was
bare except for cooking pots that simmered on the
stone-curbed central hearth.

"I gave the stuff away," Nahataspe said carelessly.
"You get tired of things."

Royland thought he knew what that meant. Nahataspe
believed he would die quite soon; these particular Indians did not believe in dying encumbered by possessions. Manners, of course, forbade discussing death.

The Indian watched his face and finally said: "Oh, it's
all right for *you* to talk about it. Don't be embarrassed."

Royland asked nervously: "Don't you feel well?"

"I feel terrible. There's a snake eating my liver. Pitch
in and eat. You feel pretty awful yourself, don't you?"

The hard-learned habit of security caused Royland to
evade the question. "You don't mean that literally about
the snake, do you Charles?"

"Of course I do," Miller insisted. He scooped a steaming gourd full of stew from the pot and blew on it.
"What would an untutored child of nature know about
bacteria, viruses, toxins and neoplasms? What would I
know about break-the-sky medicine?"

Royland looked up sharply; the Indian was blandly

eating. "Do you hear any talk about break-the-sky medicine?" Royland asked.

"No talk, Edward. I've had a few dreams about it." He pointed with his chin toward the Laboratory. "You fellows over there shouldn't dream so hard; it leaks out."

Royland helped himself to stew without answering. The stew was good, far better than the cafeteria stuff, and he did not *have* to guess the source of the meat in it.

Miller said consolingly: "It's only kid stuff, Edward. Don't get so worked up about it. We have a long dull story about a horned toad who ate some loco-weed and thought he was the Sky God. He got angry and he tried to break the sky but he couldn't so he slunk into his hole ashamed to face all the other animals and died. But they never knew he tried to break the sky at all."

In spite of himself Royland demanded: "Do you have any stories about anybody who did break the sky?" His hands were shaking again and his voice almost hysterical. Oppie and the rest of them were going to break the sky, kick humanity right in the crotch, and unleash a prowling monster that would go up and down by night and day peering in all the windows of all the houses in the world, leaving no sane man ever unterrified for his life and the lives of his kin. Phase 56c, God damn it to blackest hell, made sure of that! Well done, Royland; you earned your dollar today!

Decisively the old Indian set his gourd aside. He said: "We have a saying that the only good paleface is a dead paleface, but I'll make an exception for you, Edward. I've got some strong stuff from Mexico that will make you feel better. I don't like to see my friends hurting."

"Peyote? I've tried it. Seeing a few colored lights won't make me feel better, but thanks."

"Not peyote, this stuff. It's God Food. I wouldn't take it myself without a month of preparation; otherwise the Gods would scoop me up in a net. That's because my people see clearly, and your eyes are clouded." He was busily rummaging through a claychinked wicker box as he spoke; he came up with a covered dish. "You people have your sight cleared just a little by the God Food, so it's safe for you."

Royland thought he knew what the old man was talking about. It was one of Nahataspe's biggest jokes that Hopi children understood Einstein's relativity as soon as they could talk—and there was some truth to it. The Hopi language—and thought—had no tenses and therefore no concept of time-as-an-entity; it had nothing like the Indo-European speech's subjects and predicates, and therefore no built-in metaphysics of cause and effect. In the Hopi language and mind all things were frozen together forever into one great relationship, a crystalline structure of space-time events that simply were because they were. So much for Nahataspe's people "seeing clearly." But Royland gave himself and any other physicist credit for seeing as clearly when they were working a four-dimensional problem in the X Y Z space variables and the T time variable.

He could have spoiled the old man's joke by pointing that out, but of course he did not. No, no; he'd get a jag and maybe a bellyache from Nahataspe's herb medicine and then go home to his cubicle with his problem unresolved: to kick or not to kick?

The old man began to mumble in Hopi, and drew a tattered cloth across the door-frame of his hut; it shut out the last rays of the setting sun, long and slanting on the desert, pink-red against the adobe cubes of the Indian settlement. It took a minute for Royland's eyes to accommodate to the flickering light from the hearth and the indigo square of the ceiling smoke hole. Now Nahataspe was "dancing," doing a crouched shuffle around the hut holding the covered dish before him. Out of the corner of his mouth, without interrupting the rhythm, he said to Royland: "Drink some hot water now." Royland sipped from one of the pots on the hearth; so far it was much like peyote ritual, but he felt calmer.

Nahataspe uttered a loud scream, added apologetically: "Sorry, Edward," and crouched before him whipping the cover off the dish like a headwaiter. So God Food was dried black mushrooms, miserable, wrinkled little things. "You swallow them all and chase them with hot water," Nahataspe said.

Obediently Royland choked them down and gulped from the jug; the old man resumed his dance and chanting.

A little old self-hypnosis, Royland thought bitterly. Grab some imitation sleep and forget about old 56c, as if you could. He could see the big dirty one now, a hell of a fireball, maybe over Munich, or Cologne, or Tokyo, or Nara. Cooked people, fused cathedral stone, the bronze of the big Buddha running like water, perhaps lapping around the ankles of a priest and burning his feet off so he fell prone into the stuff. He couldn't see the gamma radiation, but it would be there, invisible sleet doing the dirty unthinkable thing, coldly burning away the sex of men and women, cutting short so many fans of life at their points of origin. Phase 56c could snuff out a family of Bachs, or five generations of Bernoullis, or see to it that the great Huxley-Darwin cross did not occur.

The fireball loomed, purple and red and fringed with green—

The mushrooms were reaching him, he thought fuzzily. He could really see it. Nahataspe, crouched and treading, moved through the fireball just as he had the last time, and the time before that. Déjà vu, extraordinarily strong, stronger than ever before, gripped him. Royland knew all this had happened to him before, and remembered perfectly what would come next; it was on the very tip of his tongue, as they say—

The fireballs began to dance around him and he felt his strength drain suddenly out; he was lighter than a feather; the breeze would carry him away; he would be blown like a dust-mote into the circle that the circling fireballs made. And he knew it was wrong. He croaked with the last of his energy, feeling himself slip out of the world: "Charlie! Help!"

Out of the corner of his mind as he slipped away he

sensed that the old man was pulling him now under the arms, trying to tug him out of the hut, crying dimly into his ear: "You should have told me you did not see through smoke! You see clear; I never knew; I nev—"

And then he slipped through into blackness and silence.

III

Royland awoke sick and fuzzy; it was morning in the hut; there was no sign of Nahataspe. Well. Unless the old man had got to a phone and reported to the Laboratory, there were now jeeps scouring the desert in search of him and all hell was breaking loose in Security and Personnel. He would catch some of that hell on his return, and avert it with his news about assembly time.

Then he noticed that the hut had been cleaned of Nahataspe's few remaining possessions, even to the door cloth. A pang went through him; had the old man died in the night? He limped from the hut and looked around for a funeral pyre, a crowd of mourners. They were not there; the adobe cubes stood untenanted in the sunlight, and more weeds grew in the single street than he remembered. And his jeep, parked last night against the hut, was missing.

There were no wheeltracks, and uncrushed weeds grew tall where the jeep had stood.

Nahataspe's God Food had been powerful stuff. Royland's hand crept uncertainly to his face. No; no beard.

He looked about him, looked hard. He made the effort necessary to see details. He did not glance at the hut and because it was approximately the same as it had always been, conclude that it was unchanged, eternal. He looked and saw changes everywhere. Once-sharp adobe corners were rounded; protruding roof beams were bleached bone-white by how many years of desert sun? The wooden framing of the deep fortress-like windows had crumbled; the third building from him had

wavering soot-stains above its window-holes and its beams
were charred.

He went to it, numbly thinking: Phase 56c at least is
settled. Not old Rip's baby now. They'll know me from
fingerprints, I guess. One year? Ten? I *feel* the same.

The burnt-out house was a shambles. In one corner
were piled dry human bones. Royland leaned dizzily
against the doorframe; its charcoal crumbled and streaked
his hand. Those skulls were Indian—he was anthropolo-
gist enough to know that. Indian men, women and
children, slain and piled in a heap. Who kills Indians?
There should have been some sign of clothes, burnt
rags, but there were none. Who strips Indians naked
and kills them?

Signs of a dreadful massacre were everywhere in the
house. Bulletpocks in the walls, high and low. Savage
nicks left by bayonets—and swords? Dark stains of blood;
it had run two inches high and left its mark. Metal
glinted in a rib cage across the room. Swaying, he
walked to the boneheap and thrust his hand into it. The
thing bit him like a razor blade; he did not look at it as
he plucked it out and carried it to the dusty street.
With his back turned to the burnt house he studied his
find. It was a piece of swordblade six inches long,
hand-honed to a perfect edge, with a couple of nicks in
it. It had stiffening ribs and the usual blood gutters. It
had a perceptible curve that would fit into only one
shape: the Samurai sword of Japan.

However long it had taken, the war was obviously
over.

He went to the village well and found it choked with
dust. It was while he stared into the dry hole that he
first became afraid. Suddenly it all was real; he was no
more an onlooker but a frightened and very thirsty
man. He ransacked the dozen houses of the settlement
and found nothing to his purpose—a child's skeleton
here, a couple of cartridge cases there.

There was only one thing left, and that was the road,
the same earth track it had always been, wide enough
for one jeep or the rump-sprung station wagon of the

Indian settlement that once had been. Panic invited him to run; he did not yield. He sat on the well-curb, took off his shoes to meticulously smooth wrinkles out of his khaki G.I. socks, put the shoes on and retied the laces loosely enough to allow for swelling, and hesitated a moment. Then he grinned, selected two pebbles carefully from the dust and popped them in his mouth. "Beaver Patrol, forward march," he said, and began to hike.

Yes, he was thirsty; soon he would be hungry and tired; what of it? The dirt road would meet state-maintained blacktop in three miles and then there would be traffic and he'd hitch a ride. Let them argue with his fingerprints if they felt like it. The Japanese had got as far as New Mexico, had they? Then God help their home islands when the counterblow had come. Americans were a ferocious people when trespassed on. Conceivably, there was not a Japanese left alive . . .

He began to construct his story as he hiked. In large parts it was a repeated "I don't know." He would tell them: "I don't expect you to believe this, so my feelings won't be hurt when you don't. Just listen to what I say and hold everything until the F.B.I. has checked my fingerprints. My name is—" And so on.

It was midmorning then, and he would be on the highway soon. His nostrils, sharpened by hunger, picked up a dozen scents on the desert breeze: the spice of sage, a whiff of acetylene stink from a rattler dozing on the shaded side of a rock, the throat-tightening reek of tar suggested for a moment on the air. That would be the highway, perhaps a recent hotpatch on a chuck hole. Then a startling tang of sulfur dioxide drowned them out and passed on, leaving him stung and sniffling and groping for a handkerchief that was not there. What in God's name had that been, and where from? Without ceasing to trudge he studied the horizon slowly and found a smoke pall to the far west dimly smudging the sky. It looked like a small city's, or a fair-sized factory's, pollution. A city or a factory where "in his time"—he formed the thought reluctantly—there had been none.

Then he was at the highway. It had been improved; it was a two-laner still, but it was nicely graded now, built up by perhaps three inches of gravel and tar beyond its old level, and lavishly ditched on either side.

If he had a coin he would have tossed it, but you went for weeks without spending a cent at Los Alamos Laboratory; Uncle took care of everything, from cigarettes to tombstones. He turned left and began to walk westward toward that sky-smudge.

I am a reasonable animal, he was telling himself, and I will accept whatever comes in a spirit of reason. I will control what I can and try to understand the rest—

A faint siren scream began behind him and built up fast. The reasonable animal jumped for the ditch and hugged it for dear life. The siren howled closer, and motors roared. At the ear-splitting climax Royland put his head up for one glimpse, then fell back into the ditch as if a grenade had exploded in his middle.

The convoy roared on, down the *center* of the two-lane highway, straddling the white line. First the three little recon cars with the twin-mount machine guns, each filled brimful with three helmeted Japanese soldiers. Then the high-profiled, armored car of state, six-wheeled, with a probably ceremonial gun turret astern—nickel-plated gunbarrels are impractical—and the Japanese admiral in the fore-and-aft hat taking his lordly ease beside a rawboned, hatchet-faced SS officer in gleaming black. Then, diminuendo, two more little recon jobs . . .

"We've lost," Royland said in his ditch meditatively. "Ceremonial tanks with glass windows—we lost a *long* time ago." Had there been a Rising Sun insignia or was he now imagining that?

He climbed out and continued to trudge westward on the improved blacktop. You couldn't say "I reject the universe"; not when you were as thirsty as he was.

He didn't even turn when the put-putting of a westbound vehicle grew loud behind him and then stopped at his side.

"Zeegail," a curious voice said. "What are you doing here?"

The vehicle was just as odd in its own way as the ceremonial tank. It was minimum motor transportation, a kid's sled on wheels, powered by a noisy little air-cooled outboard motor. The driver sat with no more comfort than a cleat to back his coccyx against, and behind him were two twenty-five-pound flour sacks that took up all the remaining room the little buckboard provided. The driver had the leathery Southwestern look; he wore a baggy blue outfit that was obviously a uniform and obviously unmilitary. He had a name-tape on his breast above an incomprehensible row of dull ribbons: MARTFIELD, E., 1218824, P/7 NQOTD43. He saw Royland's eyes on the tape and said kindly: "My name is Martfield—Paymaster Seventh, but there's no need to use my rank here. Are you all right, my man?"

"Thirsty," Royland said. "What's the NQOTD43 for?"

"You can read!" Martfield said, astounded. "Those clothes—"

"Something to drink, please," Royland said. For the moment nothing else mattered in the world. He sat down on the buckboard like a puppet with cut strings.

"See here, fellow!" Martfield snapped in a curious, strangled way, forcing the words through his throat with a stagy, conventional effect of controlled anger. "You can stand until I invite you to sit!"

"Have you any water?" Rowland asked dully.

With the same bark: "Who do you think you are?"

"I happen to be a theoretical physicist—" tiredly arguing with a dim seventh-carbon-copy imitation of a drill sergeant.

"Oh-*hoh!*" Martfield suddenly laughed. His stiffness vanished; he actually reached into his baggy tunic and brought out a pint canteen that gurgled. He then forgot all about the canteen in his hand, rogueishly dug Rowland in the ribs and said: "I should have suspected. You scientists! Somebody was supposed to pick you up—but he was another scientist, eh? Ah-hah-hah-hah!"

Royland took the canteen from his hand and sipped. So a scientist was supposed to be an idiot savant, eh? Never mind now; drink. People said you were not supposed to fill your stomach with water after great thirst; it sounded to him like one of those puritanical rules people make up out of nothing because they sound reasonable. He finished the canteen while Martfield, Paymaster Seventh, looked alarmed, and wished only that there were three or four more of them.

"Got any food?" he demanded.

Martfield cringed briefly. "Doctor, I regret extremely that I have nothing with me. However if you would do me the honor of riding with me to my quarters—"

"Let's go," Royland said. He squatted on the flour sacks and away they chugged at a good thirty miles an hour; it was a fair little engine. The Paymaster Seventh continued deferential, apologizing over his shoulder because there was no windscreen, later dropped his cringing entirely to explain that Royland was seated on flour—"*white* flour, understand?" An over-the-shoulder wink. He had a friend in the bakery at Los Alamos. Several buckboards passed the other way as they traveled. At each encounter there was a peering examination of insignia to decide who saluted. Once they met a sketchily-enclosed vehicle which furnished its driver with a low seat instead of obliging him to sit with legs straight out, and Paymaster Seventh Martfield almost dislocated his shoulder saluting first. The driver of that one was a Japanese in a kimono. A long curved sword lay across his lap.

Mile after mile the smell of sulfur and sulfides increased; finally there rose before them the towers of a Frasch Process layout. It looked like an oilfield, but instead of ground-laid pipelines and bassdrum storage tanks there were foothills of yellow sulfur. They drove between them—more salutes from baggily-uniformed workers with shovels and yard-long Stillson wrenches. Off to the right were things that might have been

Solvay Process towers for sulfuric acid, and a glittering horror of a neo-Roman administration-and-labs building. The Rising Sun banner fluttered from its central flagstaff.

Music surged as they drove deeper into the area; first it was a welcome counterirritant to the pop-pop of the two-cycle buckboard engine, and then a nuisance by itself. Royland looked, annoyed, for the loudspeakers, and saw them everywhere—on power poles, buildings, gateposts. Schmaltzy Strauss waltzes bathed them like smog, made thinking just a little harder, made communication just a little more blurry even after you had learned to live with the noise.

"I miss music in the wilderness," Martfield confided over his shoulder. He throttled down the buckboard until they were just rolling; they had passed some line unrecognized by Royland beyond which one did not salute everybody—just the occasional Japanese walking by in business suit with blueprint-roll and slide rule, or in kimono with sword. It was a German who nailed Royland, however: a classic jackbooted German in black broadcloth, black leather and plenty of silver trim. He watched them roll for a moment after exchanging salutes with Martfield, made up his mind, and said: "Halt."

The Paymaster Seventh slapped on the brake, killed the engine and popped to attention beside the buckboard. Royland more or less imitated him. The German said, stiffly but without accent: "Whom have you brought here, Paymaster?"

"A scientist, sir. I picked him up on the road returning from Los Alamos with personal supplies. He appears to be a minerals prospector who missed a rendezvous, but naturally I have not questioned the Doctor."

The German turned to Royland contemplatively. "So, Doctor. Your name and specialty."

"Dr. Edward Royland," he said. "I do nuclear power research." If there was no bomb he'd be damned if he'd invent it now for these people.

"So? that is very interesting, considering that there is no such thing as nuclear power research. Which camp

are you from?" The German threw an aside to the
Paymaster Seventh, who was literally shaking with fear
at the turn things had taken. "You may go, Paymaster.
Of course you will report yourself for harboring a
fugitive."

"At once, sir," Martfield said in a sick voice. He
moved slowly away pushing the little buckboard before
him. The Strauss waltz oom-pah'd its last chord and
instantly the loudspeakers struck up a hoppity-hoppity
folk dance.

"Come with me," the German said, and walked off,
not even looking behind to see whether Royland was
obeying. This itself demonstrated how unlikely any dis-
obedience was to succeed. Royland followed at his heels,
which of course were garnished with silver spurs. Royland
had not seen a horse so far that day.

IV

A Japanese stopped them politely inside the administration building, a rimless-glasses, office-manager type
in a grey suit. "How nice to see you again, Major
Kappel! Is there anything I might do to help you?"

The German stiffened. "I didn't want to bother your
people, Mr. Ito. This fellow appears to be a fugitive
from one of our camps; I was going to turn him over to
our liaison group for examination and return."

Mr. Ito looked at Royland and slapped his face hard.
Royland, by the insanity of sheer reflex, cocked his fist
as a red-blooded boy should, but the German's reflexes
operated also. He had a pistol in his hand and pressed
against Royland's ribs before he could throw the punch.

"All right," Royland said, and put down his hand.

Mr. Ito laughed. "You are at least partly right, Major
Kappel; he certainly is not from one of *our* camps!
But do not let me delay you further. May I hope for a
report on the outcome of this?"

"Of course, Mr. Ito," said the German. He holstered
his pistol and walked on, trailed by the scientist. Royland

heard him grumble something that sounded like "Damned extraterritoriality!"

They descended to a basement level where all the door signs were in German, and in an office labeled WISSENSCHAFTSLICHESICHERHEITSLIAISON Royland finally told his story. His audience was the major, a fat officer deferentially addressed as Colonel Biederman, and a bearded old civilian, a Dr. Piqueron, called in from another office. Royland suppressed only the matter of bomb research, and did it easily with the old security habit. His improvised cover story made the Los Alamos Laboratory a research center only for the generation of electricity.

The three heard him out in silence. Finally, in an amused voice, the colonel asked: "Who was this Hitler you mentioned?"

For that Royland was not prepared. His jaw dropped.

Major Kappel said: "Oddly enough, he struck on a name which does figure, somewhat infamously, in the annals of the Third Reich. One Adolf Hitler was an early Party agitator, but as I recall it he intrigued against the Leader during the War of Triumph and was executed."

"An ingenious madman," the colonel said. "Sterilized, of course?"

"Why, I don't know. I suppose so. Doctor, would you—?"

Dr. Piqueron quickly examined Royland and found him all there, which astonished them. Then they thought of looking for his camp tattoo number on the left bicep, and found none. Then, thoroughly upset, they discovered that he had no birth number above his left nipple either.

"And," Dr. Piqueron stammered, "his shoes are odd, sir—I just noticed. Sir, how long since you've seen sewn shoes and braided laces?"

"You must be hungry," the colonel suddenly said. "Doctor, have my aide get something to eat for—for the doctor."

"Major," said Royland, "I hope no harm will come to the fellow who picked me up."

"Have no fear, er, Doctor," said the major. "Such humanity! You are of German blood?"

"Not that I know of; it may be."

"It *must* be!" said the colonel.

A platter of hash and a glass of beer arrived on a tray. Royland postponed everything. At last he demanded: "Now. Do you believe me? There must be fingerprints to prove my story still in existence."

"I feel like a fool," the major said. "You still could be hoaxing us. Dr. Piqueron, did not a German scientist establish that nuclear power is a theoretical and practical impossibility, that one always must put more into it than one can take out?"

Piqueron nodded and said reverently: "Heisenberg, 1953, during the War of Triumph. His group was then assigned to electrical weapons research and produced the blinding bomb. But this fact does not invalidate the doctor's story; he says only that his group was *attempting* to produce nuclear power."

"We've got to research this," said the colonel. "Dr. Piqueron, entertain this man, whatever he is, in your laboratory."

Piqueron's laboratory down the hall was a place of astounding simplicity, even crudeness. The sinks, reagents and balance were capable only of simple qualitative and quantitative analyses; various works in progress testified that they were not even strained to their modest limits. Samples of sulfur and its compounds were analyzed here. It hardly seemed to call for a "doctor" of anything, and hardly even for a human being. Machinery should be continuously testing the products as they flowed out; variations should be scribed mechanically on a moving tape; automatic controls should at least stop the processes and signal an alarm when variation went beyond limits; at most it might correct whatever was going wrong. But here sat Piqueron every day, titrating, precipitating and weighing, entering results by hand in a ledger and telephoning them to the works!

Piqueron looked about proudly. "As a physicist you wouldn't understand all this, of course," he said. "Shall I explain?"

"Perhaps later, doctor, if you'd be good enough. If you'd first help me orient myself—"

So Piqueron told him about the War of Triumph (1940–1955) and what came after.

## V

In 1940 the realm of der Fuehrer (Herr Goebbels, of course—that strapping blond fellow with the heroic jaw and eagle's eye whom you can see in the picture there) was simultaneously and treacherously invaded by the misguided French, the sub-human Slavs and the perfidious British. The attack, for which the shocked Germans coined the name *blitzkrieg*, was timed to co-incide with an internal eruption of sabotage, well-poisoning and assassination by the *Zigeunerjuden*, or Jewpsies, of whom little is now known; there seem to be none left.

By Nature's ineluctable law, the Germans had necessarily to be tested to the utmost so that they might fully respond. Therefore Germany was overrun from East and West, and Holy Berlin itself was taken; but Goebbels and his court withdrew like Barbarossa into the mountain fastnesses to await their day. It came unexpectedly soon. The deluded Americans launched a million-man amphibious attack on the homeland of the Japanese in 1945. The Japanese resisted with almost Teutonic courage. Not one American in twenty reached shore alive, and not one in a hundred got a mile inland. Particularly lethal were the women and children who lay in camouflaged pits hugging artillery shells and air-craft bombs, which they detonated when enough invaders drew near to make it worth while.

The second invasion attempt, a month later, was

made up of second-line troops scraped up from everywhere, including occupation duty in Germany.

"Literally," Piqueron said, "the Japanese did not know how to surrender so they did not. They could not conquer, but they could and did continue suicidal resistance, consuming manpower of the allies and their own womanpower and childpower—a shrewd bargain for the Japanese! The Russians refused to become involved in the Japanese war; they watched with apish delight while two future enemies, as they supposed, were engaged in mutual destruction.

"A third assault wave broke on Kyushu and gained the island at last. What lay ahead? Only another assault on Honshu, the main island, home of the Emperor and the principal shrines. It was 1946; the volatile, childlike Americans were war-weary and mutinous; the best of them were gone by then. In desperation the Anglo-American leaders offered the Russians an economic sphere embracing the China coast and Japan as the price of participation."

The Russians grinned and assented; they would take that—at *least* that. They mounted a huge assault for the spring of 1947; they would take Korea and leap off from there for Northern Honshu while the Anglo-American forces struck in the south. Surely this would provide at last a symbol before which the Japanese might without shame bow down and admit defeat!

And then, from the mountain fastnesses, came the radio voice: "Germans! Your Leader calls upon you again!" Followed the Hundred Days of Glory during which the German Army reconstituted itself and expelled the occupation troops—by then, children without combat experience, and leavened by not-quite-disabled veterans. Followed the seizure of the airfields; the Luftwaffe in business again. Followed the drive, almost a dress parade, to the Channel Coast, gobbling up immense munition dumps awaiting shipment to the Pacific Theater, millions of warm uniforms, good boots, mountains of rations, piles of shells and explosive that lined the French roads for scores of miles, thousands of two-and-a-half-ton trucks, and lakes of gasoline to fuel them. The shipyards of Europe, from Hamburg to Toulon, had been turning out, furiously, invasion barges for the Pacific. In April of 1947 they sailed against England in their thousands.

Halfway around the world, the British Navy was pounding Tokyo, Nagasaki, Kobe, Hiroshima, Nara. Three quarters of the way across Asia the Russian Army marched stolidly on; let the decadent British pickle their own fish; the glorious motherland at last was gaining her long-sought, long-denied warm-water seacoast. The British, tired women without their men, children fatherless these eight years, old folks deathly weary, deathly worried about their sons, were brave but they were not insane. They accepted honorable peace terms; they capitulated.

With the Western front secure for the first time in history, the ancient Drive to the East was resumed; the immemorial struggle of Teuton against Slav went on.

His spectacles glittering with rapture, Dr. Piqueron said: "We were worthy in those days of the Teutonic Knights who seized Prussia from the sub-men! On the ever-glorious Twenty-First of May, Moscow was ours!"

Moscow and the monolithic state machinery it controlled, and all the roads and rail lines and communication wires which led only to—and from—Moscow. Detroit-built tanks and trucks sped along those roads in the fine, bracing spring weather; the Red Army turned 180 degrees at last and countermarched halfway across the Eurasian landmass, and at Kazan it broke exhausted against the Frederik Line.

Europe at last was One and German. Beyond Europe lay the dark and swarming masses of Asia, mysterious and repulsive folk whom it would be better to handle through the non-German, but chivalrous, Japanese. The Japanese were reinforced with shipping from Birkenhead, artillery from the Putilov Works, jet fighters from Chateauroux, steel from the Ruhr, rice from the Po valley, herring from Norway, timber from Sweden, oil from Romania and laborers from India.

American forces were driven from Kyushu in the winter of 1948, and bloodily back across their chain of island stepping-stones during the half-decade that followed.

Surrender they would not; it was a monstrous affront that shield-shaped North America dared to lie there between the German Atlantic and the Japanese Pacific threatening both. The affront was wiped out in 1955.

For 150 years now the Germans and the Japanese had uneasily eyed each other across the banks of the Mississippi. Their orators were fond of referring to that river as a vast frontier unblemished by a single fortification.

There was even, in fact, some interpenetration; a Japanese colony fished out of Nova Scotia on the very rim of German America; a sulfur mine which was part of the Farben system lay in New Mexico, the very heart of Japanese America—this was where Dr. Edward Royland found himself, being lectured to by Dr. Piqueron, Dr. Gaston Pierre Piqueron, true-blue German.

VI

"Here, of course," Dr. Piqueron said gloomily, "we are so damned provincial. Little ceremony and less manners. Well, it would be too much to expect them to assign *German* Germans to this dreary outpost, so we French Germans must endure it somehow."

"You're all French?" Royland asked, startled.

"French *Germans*," Piqueron stiffly corrected him. "Colonel Biederman happens to be a French German also; Major Kappel is—hrrmph—an Italian German." He sniffed to show what he thought of that.

The Italian German entered at that point, not in time to shut off the question: "And you all come from Europe?"

They looked at him in bafflement. "My grandfather did," Dr. Piqueron said. Royland remembered; so Roman legions used to guard their empire—Romans born and raised in Britain, or on the Danube, Romans who would never in their lives see Italy or Rome.

Major Kappel said affably: "Well, this needn't concern us. I'm afraid, my dear fellow, that your little hoax has not succeeded." He clapped Royland merrily on the back. "I admit you've tricked us all nicely; now may we have the facts?"

Piqueron said, surprised: "His story is false? The shoes? The missing *geburtsnummer*? And he appears to understand some chemistry!"

"Ah-h-h—but he said his specialty was *physics*, doctor! Suspicious in itself!"

"Quite so. A discrepancy. But the rest—?"

"As to his birth number, who knows? As to his shoes, who cares? I took some inconspicuous notes while he was entertaining us and have checked thoroughly. There *was* no Manhattan Engineering District. There *was* no Dr. Oppenheimer, or Fermi, or Bohr. There *is* no theory of relativity, or equivalence of mass and energy. Uranium has one use only—coloring glass a pretty orange. There is such a thing as an isotope but it has nothing to do with chemistry; it is the name used in Race Science for a permissable variation within a subrace. And what have you to say to *that*, my dear fellow?"

Royland wondered first, such was the positiveness with which Major Kappel spoke, whether he had slipped into a universe of different physical properties and history entirely, one in which Julius Caeser discovered Peru and the oxygen molecule was lighter than the hydrogen atom. He managed to speak. "How did you find all that out, Major?"

"Oh, don't think I did a skimpy job," Kappel smiled. "I looked it all up in the *big* encyclopedia."

Dr. Piqueron, chemist, nodded grave approval of the major's diligence and thorough grasp of the scientific method.

"You still don't want to tell us?" Major Kappel asked coaxingly.

"I can only stand by what I said."

Kappel shrugged. "It's not my job to persuade you; I

wouldn't know how to begin. But I can and will ship you off forthwith to a work camp."

"What—is a work camp?" Royland unsteadily asked.

"Good heavens, man, a camp where one works! You're obviously an *ungleichgeschaltling* and you've got to be *gleichgerschaltet.*" He did not speak these words as if they were foreign; they were obviously part of the everyday American working vocabulary. *Gleichgeschaltet* meant to Royland something like "coordinated, brought into tune with." So he would be brought into tune—with what, and how?

The major went on: "You'll get your clothes and your bunk and your chow, and you'll work, and eventually your irregular vagabondish habits will disappear and you'll be turned loose on the labor market. And you'll be damned glad we took the trouble with you." His face fell. "By the way, I was too late with your friend the Paymaster. I'm sorry. I sent a messenger to Disciplinary Control with a stop order. After all, if you took us in for an hour, why should you not have fooled a Pay-Seventh?"

"Too late? He's *dead*? For picking up a *hitchhiker*?"

"I don't know what that last word means," said the Major. "If it's dialect for 'vagabond', the answer is ordinarily 'yes.' The man, after all, was a Pay-Seventh; he could read. Either you're keeping up your hoax with remarkable fidelity or you've been living in isolation. Could that be it? Is there a tribe of you somewhere? Well, the interrogators will find out; that's their job."

"The Dogpatch legend!" Dr. Piqueron burst out, thunderstruck. "He may be an Abnerite!"

"By Heaven," Major Kappel said slowly, "that might be it. What a feather in my cap to find a living Abnerite."

"*Whose* cap?" demanded Dr. Piqueron coldly.

"I think I'll look the Dogpatch legend up," said Kappel, heading for the door and probably the big encyclopedia.

"So will I," Dr. Piqueron announced firmly. The last Royland saw of them they were racing down the corridor, neck and neck.

Very funny. And they had killed simple minded Paymaster Martfield for picking up a hitchhiker. The Nazis always had been pretty funny—fat Hermann pretending he was young Seigfried. As blond as Hitler, as slim as Goering and as tall as Goebbels. Immature guttersnipes who hadn't been able to hang a convincing frame on Dimitrov for the Reichstag fire; the world had roared at their bungling. Huge, corny party rallies with let's-play-detectives nonsense like touching the local flags to that hallowed banner on which the martyred Horst Wessel had had a nosebleed. And they had rolled over Europe, and they killed people. . . .

One thing was certain: life in the work camp would at least bore him to death. He was supposed to be an illiterate simpleton, so things were excused him which were not excused an exalted Pay-Seventh. He poked through a closet in the corner of the laboratory—he and Piqueron were the same size—

He found a natty change of uniform and what must be a civilian suit, somewhat baggy pants and a sort of tunic with the neat, sensible Russian collar. Obviously it would be all right to wear it because here it was; just as obviously, it was all wrong for him to be dressed in chinos and a flannel shirt. He did not know exactly what this made him, but Martfield had been done to death for picking up a man in chinos and a flannel shirt. Royland changed into the civilian suit, stuffed his own shirt and pants far back on the top shelf of the closet; this was probably concealment enough from those murderous clowns. He walked out, and up the stairs, and through the busy lobby, and into the industrial complex. Nobody saluted him and he saluted nobody. He knew where he was going—to a good, sound Japanese laboratory where there were no Germans.

Royland had known Japanese students at the University and admired them beyond words. Their brains, frugality, doggedness and good humor made them, as far as he was concerned, the most sensible people he had ever known. Tojo and his warlords were not, as far as Royland was concerned, essentially Japanese but just more damfool soldiers and politicians. The real Japanese would courteously listen to him, calmly check the facts—

He rubbed his cheek and remembered Mr. Ito and his slap in the face. Well, presumably Mr. Ito was a damfool soldier and politician—and demonstrating for the German's benefit in a touchy border area full of jurisdictional questions.

At any rate, he would *not* go to a labor camp and bust rocks or refinish furniture until those imbeciles decided he was *gleichgeschaltet;* he would go mad in a month.

Royland walked to the Solvay towers and followed the glass pipes containing their output of sulfuric acid along the ground until he came to a bottling shed where beetle-browed men worked silently filling great wicker-basketed carboys and heaving them outside. He followed other men who levered them up onto handtrucks and rolled them in one door of a storage shed. Out the door at the other end more men loaded them onto enclosed trucks which were driven up from time to time.

Royland settled himself in a corner of the storage shed behind a barricade of carboys and listened to the truck dispatcher swear at his drivers and the carboy handlers swear at their carboys.

"Get the goddam Frisco shipment *loaded,* stupid! I don't *care* if you gotta go, we gotta get it out by *midnight!*"

So a few hours after dark Royland was riding west, without much air, and in the dangerous company of one thousand gallons of acid. He hoped he had a careful driver.

VII

A night, a day, and another night on the road. The truck never stopped except to gas up; the drivers took turns and ate sandwiches at the wheel and dozed off shift. It rained the second night. Royland, craftily and perhaps a little crazily, licked the drops that ran down the tarpaulin flap covering the rear. At the first crack of dawn, hunched between two wicker carcasses, he saw they were rolling through irrigated vegetable fields, and the water in the ditches was too much for him. He heard the transmission shift down to slow for a curve, swarmed over the tailgate and dropped to the road. He was weak and limp enough to hit like a sack.

He got up, ignoring his bruises, and hobbled to one of the brimming five-foot ditches; he drank, and drank, and drank. This time puritanical folklore proved right; he lost it all immediately, or what had not been greedily absorbed by his shriveled stomach. He did not mind; it was bliss enough to *stretch*.

The field crop was tomatoes, almost dead ripe. He was starved for them; as he saw the rosy beauties he knew that tomatoes were the only thing in the world he craved. He gobbled one so that the juice ran down his chin; he ate the next two delicately, letting his teeth break the crispness of their skin and the beautiful taste ravish his tongue. There were tomatoes as far as the eye could see, on either side of the road, the green of the vines and the red dots of the ripe fruit graphed by the checkerboard of silvery ditches that caught the first light. Nevertheless he filled his pockets with them before he walked on.

Royland was happy.

Farewell to the Germans and their sordid hash and murderous ways. *Look* at these beautiful fields! The Japanese are an innately artistic people who bring beauty to every detail of daily life. And they make damn good physicists, too, Confined in their stony home, cramped as he had been in the truck, they grew twisted and painful; why should they not have reached out for more room to grow, and what other way is there to reach but to make war? He could be very understanding about any people who had planted these beautiful tomatoes for him.

A dark blemish the size of a man attracted his attention. It lay on the margin of one of the swirling five-foot ditches out there to his right. And then it rolled slowly into the ditch with a splash, floundered a little and proceeded to drown.

In a hobbling run Royland broke from the road and across the field. He did not know whether he was limber enough to swim. As he stood panting on the edge of the ditch, peering into the water, a head of hair surfaced near him. He flung himself down, stretched wildly and grabbed the hair—and yet had detachment enough to feel a pang when the tomatoes in his tunic pocket smashed.

"Steady," he muttered to himself, yanked the head toward him, took hold with his other hand and lifted. A surprised face confronted him and then went blank and unconscious.

For half an hour Royland, weak as he was, struggled, cursed feebly, and sweated to get that body out of the water. At last he plunged in himself, found it only chest-deep, and shoved the carcass over the mudslick bank. He did not know by then whether the man was alive or dead or much care. He knew only that he couldn't walk away and leave the job half-finished.

The body was that of a fat, middle-aged Oriental, surely Chinese rather than Japanese, though Royland could not say why he thought so. His clothes were soaked rags except for a leather wallet the size of a cigar box which he wore on a wide cloth belt. Its sole content was a handsome blue-glazed porcelain bottle. Royland sniffed at it and reeled. Some kind of super-gin! He sniffed agin, and then took a conservative gulp of the stuff. While he was still coughing he felt the bottle being removed from his hand. When he looked he saw the Chinese, eyes still closed, accurately guiding the neck of the bottle to his mouth. The Chinese drank and drank and drank, then returned the bottle to the wallet and finally opened his eyes.

"Honorable sir," said the Chinese in flat, California American speech, "you have deigned to save my unworthy life. May I supplicate your honorable name?"

"Ah, Royland. Look, take it easy. Don't try to get up; you shouldn't even talk."

Somebody screamed behind Royland: "There has been thieving of tomatoes! There has been smasheeng and deestruction of thee vines! Chil-dren you, will bee weet-ness be-fore the Jappa-neese!"

Christ, now what?

Now a skinny black man, not a Negro, in a dirty loin-cloth, and beside him like a pan-pipes five skinny black loinclothed offspring in descending order. All were capering, pointing and threatening. The Chinese groaned, fished in his tattered robes with one hand and pulled out a soggy wad of bills. He peeled one off, held it out and said: "Begone pestilential barbarians from beyond Tian-Shang. My master and I give you alms, not tribute."

The Dravidian, or whatever he was, grabbed the bill and keened: "Een-suffee-cient for the terrible dommage! The Jappa-neese—"

The Chinese waved them away boredly. He said: "If my master will condescend to help me arise?"

Royland uncertainly helped him up. The man was wobbly, whether from the near-drowning or the terrific belt of alcohol he'd taken there was no knowing. They proceeded to the road, followed by shrieks to be careful about stepping on the vines.

On the road, the Chinese said: "My unworthy name is Li Po. Will my master deign to indicate in which direction we are to travel?"

"What's this master business?" Royland demanded. "If you're grateful, swell, but I don't *own* you."

"My master is pleased to jest," said Li Po. Politely, face-saving and third-personing Royland until hell wouldn't have it, he explained that Royland, having meddled with the Celestial decree that Li Po should, while drunk, roll into the irrigation ditch and drown, now had Li Po on his hands, for the Celestial Ones had washed theirs of him. "As my master of course will recollect in a moment or two." Understandingly, he expressed his sympathy with Royland's misfortune in acquiring him as an obligation, especially since he had a hearty appetite, was known to be dishonest, and suffered from fainting fits and spasms when faced with work.

"I don't *know* about all this," Royland said fretfully. "Wasn't there another Li Po? A poet?"

"Your servant prefers to venerate his namesake as one of the greatest drunkards the Flowery Kingdom has ever known," the Chinese observed. And a moment later he bent over, clipped Royland behind the knees so that he toppled forward and bumped his head, and performed the same obeisance himself, more gracefully.

A vehicle went sputtering and popping by on the road as they kowtowed.

Li Po said reproachfully: "I humbly observe that my master is unaware of the etiquette our noble overlords exact. Such negligence cost the head of my insignificant elder brother in his twelfth year. Would my master be pleased to explain how he can have reached his honorable years without learning what babes in their cradles are taught?"

Royland answered with the whole truth. Li Po politely begged clarification from time to time, and a sketch of his mental horizons emerged from his questioning. That "Magic" had whisked Royland forward a century or more he did not doubt for an instant, but he found it difficult to understand why the proper *fung shui* precautions had not been taken to avert a disastrous outcome to the God Food experiment. He suspected, from a description of Nahataspe's hut, that a simple wall at right angles to the door would have kept all really important demons out. When Royland described his escape from German territory to Japanese, and why he had effected it, he was very bland and blank. Royland judged that Li Po privately thought him not very bright for having left *any* place to come here.

And Royland hoped he was not right. "Tell me what it's like," he said.

"This realm," said Li Po, "under our benevolent and noble overlords, is the haven of all whose skin is not the bleached-bone hue which indicates the undying curse of the Celestial Ones. Hither flock men of Han like my unworthy self, and the sons of Hind beyond the Tian-Shang that we may till new soil and raise up sons, and sons of sons to venerate us when we ascend."

"What was that bit," Royland demanded, "about the bleached bones? Do they shoot, ah, white men on sight here, or do they not?"

Li Po said evasively: "We are approaching the village where I unworthily serve as fortune teller, doctor of *fung shui*, occasional poet and story teller. Let my master have no fear about his color. This humble one will roughen his master's skin, tell a circumstantial and artistic lie or two, and pass his master off as merely a leper."

### VIII

After a week in Li Po's village Royland knew that life was good there. The place was a wattle-and-clay settlement of about two hundred souls on the bank of an irrigation ditch large enough to be dignified by the name of "canal". It was situated nobody knew just where; Royland thought it must be the San Fernando Valley. The soil was thick and rich and bore furiously the year round. A huge kind of radish was the principal crop. It was too coarse to be eaten by man; the villagers understood that it was feed for chickens somewhere up north. At any rate they harvested the stuff, fed it through a great hand-powered shredder and shade-cured the shreds. Every few days a Japanese of low caste would come by in a truck, they would load tons of the stuff onto it, and wave their giant radish goodbye forever. Presumably the chickens ate it and Japanese then ate the chickens.

The villagers ate chicken too, but only at weddings and funerals. The rest of the time they ate vegetables which they cultivated, a quarter-acre to a family, the way other craftsmen facet diamonds. A single cabbage might receive, during its ninety days from planting to maturity, one hundred work-hours from grandmother, grandfather, son, daughter, eldest grandchild and on down to the smallest toddler. Theoretically the entire family line should have starved to death, for there are not one hundred energy-hours in a cabbage; somehow they did not. They merely stayed thin and cheerful and hardworking and fecund.

They spoke English by Imperial decree; the reasoning seemed to be that they were as unworthy to speak Japanese as to paint the Imperial Chrysanthemum Seal on their houses, and that to let them cling to their old languages and dialects would have been politically unwise.

They were a mixed lot of Chinese, Hindus, Dravidians and, to Royland's surprise, low-caste and outcaste Japanese; he had not known there were such things. Village tradition had it that a *samurai* named Ugetsu long ago said, pointing at the drunk tank of a Hong Kong jail, "I'll have that lot," and "that lot" had been the ancestors of these villagers transported to America in a foul hold practically as ballast and settled here by the canal with orders to start making their radish quota. The place was at any rate called the Ugetsu Village, and if some of the descendants were teetotallers, others like Li Po gave color to the legend of their starting point.

After a week the cheerful pretense that he was a sufferer from Hansen's disease evaporated and he could wash the mud off his face. He had merely to avoid the upper-caste Japanese and especially the *samurai*. This was not exactly a stigma; in general it was a good idea for *everybody* to avoid the *samurai*.

In the village Royland found his first love and his first religion both false.

He had settled down; he was getting used to the Oriental work rhythm of slow, repeated, incessant effort; it did not surprise him any longer that he could count his ribs. When he ate a bowl of artfully-arranged vegetables, the red of pimiento played off against the yellow of parsnip, a slice of pickled beet adding visual and olfactory tang to the picture, he felt full enough; he *was* full enough for the next day's feeble work in the field. It was pleasant enough to play slowly with a wooden mattock in the rich soil; did not people once buy sand so their children might do exactly what he did, and envy their innocent absorption? Royland was innocently absorbed, then, and the radish truck had collected six times since his arrival, when he began to feel stirrings of lust. On the edge of starvation (but who knew this? For everybody was) his mind was dulled, but not his loins. They burned, and he looked about him in the fields, and the first girl he saw who was not repulsive he felt abysmally in love with.

Bewildered, he told Li Po, who was also Ugetsu Village's go-between. The storyteller was delighted; he waddled off to seek information and returned. "My master's choice is wise. The slave on whom his lordly eye deigned to rest is known as Vashti, daughter of Hari Bose, the distiller. She is his seventh child and so no great dowry can be expected (I shall ask for fifteen kegs toddy, but would settle for seven), but all this humble village knows that she is a skilled and willing worker in the hut as in the fields. I fear she has the customary lamentable Hindu talent for concocting curries, but a dozen good beatings at the most should cause her to reserve it to appropriate occasions, such as visits from her mother and sisters."

So, according to the sensible custom of Ugetsu, Vashti came that night to the hut which Royland shared with Li Po, and Li Po visited with cronies by his master's puzzling request. He begged humbly to point out that it would be dark in the hut, so this talk of lacking privacy was inexplicable to say the least. Royland made it an order, and Li Po did not really object, so he obeyed it.

It was a damnably strange night during which Royland learned all about India's national sport and most highly developed art-form. Vashti, if she found him weak on the theory side, made no complaints. On the contrary, when Royland woke she was doing something or other to his feet.

"More?" he thought incredulously. "With *feet*?" He

asked what she was doing. Submissively she replied: "Worshipping my lord husband-to-be's big toe. I am a pious and old-fashioned woman."

So she painted his toe with red paint and prayed to it, and then she fixed breakfast—curry, and excellent. She watched him eat, and then modestly licked his leavings from the bowl. She handed him his clothes, which she had washed while he still slept, and helped him into them after she helped him wash. Royland thought incredulously: "It's not possible! It must be a show, to sell me on marrying her—as if I had to be sold!" His heart turned to custard as he saw her, without a moment's pause, turn from dressing him to polishing his wooden rake. He asked that day in the field, round-about-fashion, and learned that this was the kind of service he could look forward to for the rest of his life after marriage. If the woman got lazy he'd have to beat her, but this seldom happened more than every year or so. We have good girls here in Ugetsu Village.

So an Ugetsu Village peasant was in some ways better off than anybody from "his time" who was less than a millionaire!

His starved dullness was such that he did not realize this was true for only half the Ugetsu Village peasants.

Religion sneaked up on him in similar fashion. He went to the part-time Taoist priest because he was a little bored with Li Po's current after-dinner saga. He could have sat like all the others and listened passively to the interminable tale of the glorious Yellow Emperor, and the beautiful but wicked Princess Emerald, and the virtuous but plain Princess Moon Blossom; it just happened that he went to the priest of Tao and got hooked hard.

The kindly old man, a toolmaker by day, dropped a few pearls of wisdom which, in his foggy starvation-daze, Royland did not perceive to be pearls of undemonstrable nonsense, and showed Royland how to meditate. It worked the first time. Royland bunged right smack through into a 200-proof state of *samadhi*—the Eastern version of self-hypnotized Enlightenment—that made him feel wonderful and all-knowing and left him without a hangover when it wore off. He had despised, in college, the type of people who took psychology courses and so had taken none himself; he did not know a thing about self-hypnosis except as just demonstrated by this very nice old gentleman. For several days he was offensively religious and kept trying to talk to Li Po about the Eightfold Way, and Li Po kept changing the subject.

It took murder to bring him out of love and religion.

At twilight they were all sitting and listening to the storyteller as usual. Royland had been there just one month and for all he knew would be there forever. He soon would have his bride officially; he knew he had discovered The Truth About the Universe by way of Tao meditation; why should he change? Changing demanded a furious outburst of energy, and he did not have energy on that scale. He metered out his energy day and night; one had to save so much for tonight's love-play, and then one had to save so much for tomorrow's planting. He was a poor man; he could not afford to change.

Li Po had reached a rather interesting bit where the Yellow Emperor was declaiming hotly: "Then she shall die! Whoever dare transgress Our divine will—"

A flashlight began to play over their faces. They perceived that it was in the hand of a *samurai* with kimono and sword. Everybody hastily kowtowed, but the *samurai* shouted irritably (all *samurai* were irritable, all the time): "Sit up, you fools! I want to see your stupid faces. I hear there's a peculiar one in this flea-bitten dung-heap you call a village."

Well, by now Royland knew his duty. He rose and with downcast eyes asked: "Is the noble protector in search of my unworthy self?"

"Ha!" the *samurai* roared. "It's true! Big nose!" He hurled the flashlight away (all *samurai* were nobly contemptuous of the merely material), held his scabbard in his left hand and swept out the long curved sword with his right.

Li Po stepped forward and said in his most enchanting voice: "If the Heaven-born would only deign to heed a word from his humble—" What he must have known would happen happened. With a contemptuous backhand sweep of the blade the *samurai* beheaded him and Li Po's debt was paid.

The trunk of the storyteller stood for a moment and then fell stiffly forward. The *samurai* stooped to wipe his blade clean on Li Po's ragged robes.

Royland had forgotten much, but not everything. With the villagers scattering before him he plunged forward and tackled the *samurai* low and hard. No doubt the *Samurai* was a Brown Belt judo master; if so he had nobody but himself to blame for turning his back. Royland, not remembering that he was barefoot, tried to kick the *samurai's* face in. He broke his worshipful big toe, but its untrimmed horny nail removed the left eye of the warrior and after that it was no contest. He never let the *samurai* get up off the ground; he took out his other eye with the handle of a rake and then killed him an inch at a time with his hands, his feet, and the clownish rustic's traditional weapon, a flail. It took easily half an hour, and for the final twenty minutes the *samurai* was screaming for his mother. He died when the last light left the western sky, and in darkness Royland stood quite alone with the two corpses. The villagers were gone.

He assumed, or pretended, that they were within earshot and yelled at them brokenly: "I'm sorry, Vashti. I'm sorry, all of you. I'm going. Can I make you understand?

"Listen. You aren't living. This isn't life. You're not making anything but babies, you're not changing, you're not growing up. That's not enough! You've got to read and write. You can't pass on anything but baby-stories like the Yellow Emperor by word of mouth. The village is growing. Soon your fields will touch the fields of Sukoshi Village to the west, and then what happens? You won't know what to do, so you'll fight with Sukoshi Village.

"Religion. No! It's just getting drunk the way you do

it. You're set up for it by being half-starved and then you go into *samadhi* and you feel better so you think you understand everything. No! You've got to *do* things. If you don't grow up, you die. All of you.

"Women. *That's* wrong. It's good for the men, but it's wrong. Half of you are slaves, do you understand? Women are people too, but you use them like animals and you've convinced them it's right for them to be old at thirty. For God's sake, can't you try to think of yourselves in their place?

"The breeding, the crazy breeding—it's got to stop. You frugal Orientals! But you aren't frugal; you're crazy drunken sailors. You're squandering the whole world. Every mouth you breed has got to be fed by the land, and the land isn't infinite.

"I hope some of you understood. Li Po would have, a little, but he's dead.

"I'm going away now. You've been kind to me and all I've done is make trouble. I'm sorry."

He fumbled on the ground and found the *samurai's* flashlight. With it he hunted the village's outskirts until he found the Japanese's buckboard car. He started the motor with its crank and noisily rolled down the dirt track from the village to the highway.

### IX

Royland drove all night, still westward. His knowledge of southern California's geography was inexact, but he hoped to hit Los Angeles. There might be a chance of losing himself in a great city.

He had long since abandoned hope of finding present-day counterparts of his old classmates like Jimmy Ichimura; obviously they had lost out. Why shouldn't they have lost? The soldier-politicians had won the war by happenstance, so all power to the soldier-politicians! Reasoning under the great natural law *post hoc ergo propter hoc*, Tojo and his crowd had decided: fanatic feudalism won the war; therefore fanatic feudalism is a

good thing, and it necessarily follows that the more
fanatical and feudal it is, the better a thing it is. So you
had Sukoshi Village, and Ugetsu Village; Ichi Village,
Ni Village, San Village, Shi Village, dotting that part of
Great Japan formerly known as North America, breeding with the good old fanatic feudalism and so feudally
averse to new thought and innovations that it made you
want to scream at them—which he had.

The single weak headlight of his buckboard passed
few others on the road; a decent feudal village is
self-contained.

Damn them and their suicidal cheerfulness! It was a
pleasant trait; it was a fool in a canoe approaching the
rapids saying: "Chin up! Everything's going to be all
right if we just keep smiling."

The car ran out of gas when false dawn first began to
pale the sky behind him. He pushed it into the road-
side ditch and walked on; by full light he was in a
tumbledown, planless, evil-smelling, paper-and-galvan-
ized-iron city whose name he did not know. There was
no likelihood of him being noticed as a "white" man by
anyone not specifically looking for him. A month of
outdoor labor had browned him, and a month of artisti-
cally-composed vegetable plates had left him gaunt.

The city was carpeted with awakening humanity. Its
narrow streets were paved with sprawled-out men,
women and children beginning to stir and hawk up
phlegm and rub their rheumy eyes. An open sewer-
latrine running down the center of each street was
casually used, ostrich-fashion—the users hid their own
eyes while in action.

Every mangled variety of English rang in Royland's
ears as he trod between bodies.

There had to be something more, he told himself.
This was the shabby industrial outskirts, the lowest
marginal-labor area. Somewhere in the city there was
beauty, science, learning!

He walked aimlessly plodding until noon, and found
nothing of the sort. These people in the cities were
food-handlers, food-traders, food-transporters. They took

in one another's washing and sold one another chop suey. They made automobiles (Yes! There were one-family automobile factories which probably made six buckboards a year, filing all metal parts by hand out of bar stock!) and orange crates and baskets and coffins; abacuses, nails and boots.

The Mysterious East has done it again, he thought bitterly. The Indians-Chinese-Japanese won themselves a nice sparse area. They could have laid things out neatly and made it pleasant for everybody instead of for a minute speck of aristocracy which he was unable even to detect in this human soup . . . but they had done it again. They had bred irresponsibly just as fast as they could until the land was *full*. Only famines and pestilence could "help" them now.

He found exactly one building which owned some clear space around it and which would survive an earthquake or a flicked cigarette butt. It was the German Consulate.

I'll give them the Bomb, he said to himself. Why not? None of this is mine. And for the Bomb I'll exact a price of some comfort and dignity for as long as I live. *Let* them blow one another up! He climbed the consulate steps.

To the black-uniformed guard at the swastika-trimmed bronze doors he said: "*Wenn die Licht-staerke der von einer Flaeche kommenden Strahlung dem Cosinus des Winkels zwischen Strahlrichtung und Flaechennormalen proportional ist, so nennen wir die Flaeche eine volkommen streunde Flaeche.*" Lambert's Law, Optics I. All the Goethe he remembered happened to rhyme, which might have made the guard suspicious.

Naturally the German came to attention and said apologetically: "I don't speak German. What is it, sir?"

"You may take me to the consul," Royland said, affecting boredom.

"Yes, sir. At once, sir. Er, you're an *agent* of course, sir?"

Royland said witheringly: "*Sicherheit, bitte!*"

X

The consul was a considerate, understanding gentleman. He was somewhat surprised by Royland's true tale, but said from time to time: "I see; I see. Not impossible. Please go on."

Royland concluded: "Those people at the sulfur mine were, I hope, unrepresentative. One of them at least complained that it was a dreary sort of backwoods assignment. I am simply gambling that there is intelligence in your Reich. I ask you to get me a real physicist for twenty minutes of conversation. You, Mr. Consul, will not regret it. I am in a position to turn over considerable information on—atomic power." So he had not been able to say it after all; the Bomb was still an obscene kick below the belt.

"This has been very interesting, Dr. Royland," said the Consul gravely. "You referred to your enterprise as a gamble. I too shall gamble. What have I to lose by putting you en rapport with a scientist of ours if you prove to be a plausible lunatic?" He smiled to soften it. "Very little indeed. On the other hand, what have I to gain if your extraordinary story is quite true? A great deal. I will go along with you, Doctor. Have you eaten?"

The relief was tremendous. He had lunch in a basement kitchen with the Consulate guards—a huge lunch, a rather nasty lunch of stewed *lungen* with a floured gravy, and cup after cup of coffee. Finally one of the guards lit up an ugly little spindle-shaped cigar, the kind Royland had only seen before in the caricatures of George Grosz, and as an afterthought offered one to him.

He drank in the rank smoke and managed not to cough. It stung his mouth and cut the greasy aftertaste of the stew satisfactory. One of the blessings of the Third Reich, one of its gross pleasures. They were just people, after all—a certain censorious, busybody type of person with altogether too much power, but they were human. By which he meant, he supposed, members of Western Industrial Culture like him.

After lunch he was taken by truck from the city to an airfield by one of the guards. The plane was somewhat bigger than a B-29 he had once seen, and lacked propellers. He presumed it was one of the "jets" Dr. Piqueron had mentioned. His guard gave his dossier to a Luftwaffe sergeant at the foot of the ramp and said cheerfully: "Happy landings, fellow. It's all going to be all right."

"Thanks," he said. "I'll remember you, Corporal Collins. You've been very helpful." Collins turned away.

Royland climbed the ramp into the barrel of the plane. A bucket-seat job, and most of the seats were filled. He dropped into one on the very narrow aisle. His neighbor was in rags; his face showed signs of an old beating. When Royland addressed him he simply cringed away and began to sob.

The Luftwaffe sergeant came up, entered and slammed the door. The "jets" began to wind up, making an unbelievable racket; further conversation was impossible. While the plane taxied, Royland peered through the windowless gloom at his fellow-passengers. They all looked poor.

God, were they so quickly and quietly airborne? They were. Even in the bucket seat, Royland fell asleep.

He was awakened, he did not know how much later, by the sergeant. The man was shaking his shoulder and asking him: "Any joolery hid away? Watches? Got some nice fresh water to sell to people that wanna buy it."

Royland had nothing and would not take part in the miserable little racket if he had. He shook his head indignantly and the man moved on with a grin. He would not last long!—petty chiselers were leaks in the efficient dictatorship; they were rapidly detected and stopped up. Mussolini made the trains run on time, after all. (But naggingly Royland recalled mentioning this to a Northwestern University English professor, one Bevans. Bevans had coldly informed him that from 1931 to 1936 he had lived under Mussolini as a student and tourist guide, and therefore had extraordinary opportunities for observing whether the trains ran on time or not, and could definitely state that they did not; that railway timetables under Mussolini were best regarded as humorous fiction.)

And another thought nagged at him, a thought connected with a pale, scarred face named Bloom. Bloom was a young refugee physical chemist working on WEAPONS DEVELOPMENT TTRACK I, and he was somewhat crazy, perhaps. Royland, on TRACK III, used to see little of him and could have done with even less. You couldn't say hello to the man without it turning into a lecture on the horrors of Nazism. He had wild stories about "gas chambers" and crematoria which no reasonable man could believe, and was a blanket slanderer of the German medical profession. He claimed that trained doctors, certified men, used human beings in experiments which terminated fatally. Once, to try and bring Bloom to reason, he asked what sort of experiments these were, but the monomaniac had heard that worked out, piffling nonsense about reviving mortally frozen men by putting naked women into bed with them! The man was probably sexually deranged to believe that; he naively added that one variable in the series of experiments was to use women immediately after sexual intercourse, one hour after sexual intercourse, etcetera. Royland had blushed for him and violently changed the subject.

But that was not what he was groping for. Neither was Bloom's crazy story about the woman who made lampshades from the tattooed skin of concentration camp prisoners; there were people capable of such things, of course, but under no regime whatever do they rise to positions of authority; they simply can't do the work required in positions of authority because their insanity gets in the way.

"Know your enemy," of course—but making up pointless lies? At least Bloom was not the conscious prevaricator. He got letters in Yiddish from friends and relations in Palestine, and these were laden with the latest wild rumors supposed to be based on the latest word from "escapees."

Now he remembered. In the cafeteria about three months ago Bloom had been sipping tea with somewhat shaking hand and rereading a letter. Royland tried to pass him with only a nod, but the skinny hand shot out and held him.

Bloom looked up with tears in his eyes: "It's cruel, I'm tellink you, Royland, it's cruel. They're not givink them the right to scream, to strike a futile blow, to sayink prayers *Kiddush ha Shem* like a Jew should when he is dyink for Consecration of the Name! They trick them, they say they go to farm settlements, to labor camps, so four-five of the stinking bastards can handle a whole trainload Jews. They trick the clothes off of them at the camps, they sayink, they delouse them. They trick them into room says showerbath over the door and then is too late to sayink prayers; *then goes on the gas.*"

Bloom had let go of him and put his head on the table between his hands. Royland had mumbled something, patted his shoulder and walked on, shaken. For once the neurotic little man might have got some straight facts. That was a very circumstantial touch about expediting the handling of prisoners by systematic lies— always the carrot and the stick.

Yes, everybody had been so goddamn agreeable since he climbed the Consulate steps! The friendly door guard, the Consul who nodded and remarked that his story was not an impossible one, the men he'd eaten with— all that quiet optimism. "Thanks. I'll remember you, Corporal Collins. You've been very helpful." He had felt positively benign toward the corporal, and now remembered that the corporal had turned around *very* quickly after he spoke. *To hide a grin?*

The guard was working his way down the aisle again and noticed that Royland was awake. "Changed your mind by now?" he asked kindly. "Got a good watch, maybe I'll find a piece of bread for you. You won't need a watch where you're going, fella."

"What do you mean?" Royland demanded.

The guard said soothingly: "Why, they got clocks all

over them work camps, fella. Everybody knows what time it is in them work camps. You don't need no watches there. Watches just get in the way at them work camps." He went on down the aisle, quickly.

Royland reached across the aisle and, like Bloom, gripped the man who sat opposite him. He could not see much of him; the huge windowless plane was lit only by half a dozen stingy bulbs overhead. "What are you here for?" he asked.

The man said shakily: "I'm a Laborer Two, see? A Two. Well, my father he taught me to read, see, but he waited until I was ten and knew the score, see? So I figured it was a family tradition, so I taught my own kid to read because he was a pretty smart kid, ya know? I figured he'd have some fun reading like I did, no harm done, who's to know, ya know? But I should of waited a couple years, I guess, because the kid was too young and got to bragging he could read, ya know how kids do? I'm from St. Louis, by the way. I should of said first I'm from St. Louis a track maintenance man, see, so I hopped a string of returning empties for San Diego because I was scared like you get."

He took a deep sigh. "Thirsty," he said. "Got in with some Chinks, nobody to trouble ya ya stay outta the way, but then one of them cops-like seen me and he took me to the Consul place like they do, ya know? Had me scared, they always tole me illegal reading they bump ya off, but they don't ya know? Two years work camp, how about that?"

Yes, Royland wondered. How about it?

The plane decelerated sharply; he was thrown forward. Could they brake with those "jets" by reversing the stream or were the engines just throttling down? He heard gurgling and thudding; hydraulic fluid to the actuators letting down the landing gear. The wheels bumped a moment later and he braced himself; the plane was still and the motors cut off seconds later.

Their Luftwaffe sergeant unlocked hte door and bawled through it: "Shove that goddam ramp, willya?" The sergeant's assurance had dropped from him; he looked like a very scared man. He must have been a very brave one, really, to have let himself be locked in with a hundred doomed men, protected only by an eight-shot pistol and a chain of systematic lies.


XI


They were herded out of the plane onto a runway of what Royland immediately identified as the Chicago Municipal Airport. The same reek wafted from the stockyards; the row of airline buildings at the eastern edge of the field was ancient and patched but unchanged; the hangars though were now something that looked like inflated plastic bags. A good trick. Beyond the buildings surely lay the dreary red-brick and painted-siding wastes of Cicero, Illinois.

Luftwaffe men were yapping at them: "Form up, boys; make a line! Work means freedom! Look tall!" They shuffled and were shoved into columns of fours. A snappy majorette in shiny satin panties and white boots pranced out of an administration building twirling her baton; a noisy march blared from louvers in her tall fur hat. Another good trick.

"Forward march, boys," she shrilled at them. "Wouldn't y'all just like to follow me?" Seductive smile and a wiggle of the rump; a judas ewe. She strutted off in time to the music; she must have been wearing earstopples. They shuffled after her. At the airport gate they dropped their blue-coated Luftwaffe boys and picked up a waiting escort of a dozen black-coats with skulls on their high-peaked caps.

They walked in time to the music, hypnotized by it, through Cicero. Cicero had been bombed to hell and not rebuilt. To his surprise Royland felt a pang for the vanished Poles and Slovaks of Al's old bailiwick. There were *German* Germans, French Germans and even Italian Germans, but he knew in his bones that there were no Polish or Slovakian Germans. . . . And Bloom had been right all along.

Deathly weary after two hours of marching (the majorette was indefatigable) Royland looked up from the broken pavement to see a cockeyed wonder before him. It was a Castle; it was a Nightmare; it was the Chicago Parteihof. The thing abutted Lake Michigan; it covered perhaps sixteen city blocks. It frowned down on the lake at the east and at the tumbled acres of bombed-out Chicago at the north, west and south. It was made of steel-reinforced concrete grained and grooved to look like medieval masonry. It was walled, moated, portcullis-ed, towered, ramparted, crenellated. The death's-head guards looked at it reverently and the prisoners with fright. Royland wanted only to laugh wildly. It was a Disney production. It was as funny as Hermann Goering in full fig, and probably as deadly.

With a mumbo-jumbo of passwords, heils and salutes they were admitted, and the majorette went away, no doubt to take off her boots and groan.

The most bedecked of the death's-heads lined them up and said affably: "Hot dinner and your beds presently, my boys; first a selection. Some of you, I'm afraid, aren't well and should be in sick bay. Who's sick? Raise your hands, please."

A few hands crept up. Stooped old men.

"That's right. Step forward, please." Then he went down the line tapping a man here and there—one fellow with glaucoma, another with terrible varicose sores visible through the tattered pants he wore. Mutely they stepped forward. Royland he looked thoughtfully over. "You're thin, my boy," he observed. "Stomach pains? Vomit blood? Tarry stools in the morning?"

"Nossir!" Royland barked. The man laughed and continued down the line. The "sick bay" detail was marched off. Most of them were weeping silently; they knew. Everybody knew; everybody pretended that the terrible thing would not, might not, happen. It was much more complex than Royland had realized.

"Now," said the death's-head affably, "we require some competent cement workers—"

The line of remaining men went mad. They surged

forward almost touching the officer but never stepping over an invisible line surrounding him. "Me!" some yelled. "Me! Me!" Another cried: "I'm good with my hands, I can learn, I'm a machinist too, I'm strong and young, I can learn!" A heavy middle-aged one waved his hands in the air and boomed: "Grouting and tile-setting! Grouting and tile-setting!" Royland stood alone, horrified. They knew. They knew this was an offer of real work that would keep them alive for a while.

He knew suddenly how to live in a world of lies.

The officer lost his patience in a moment or two, and whips came out. Men with their faces bleeding struggled back into line. "Raise your hands, you cement people, and no lying, please. But you wouldn't lie, would you?" He picked half a dozen volunteers after questioning them briefly, and one of his men marched them off. Among them was the grouting-and-tile man, who looked pompously pleased with himself; such was the reward of diligence and virtue, he seemed to be proclaiming; pooh to those grasshoppers back there who neglected to learn A Trade.

"Now," said the officer casually, "we require some laboratory assistants." The chill of death stole down the line of prisoners. Each one seemed to shrivel into himself, become poker-faced, imply that he wasn't really involved in all this.

Royland raised his hand. The officer looked at him in stupefaction and then covered up quickly. "Splendid," he said. "Step forward, my boy. You," he pointed at another man. "You have an intelligent forehead; you look as if you'd make a fine laboratory assistant. Step forward."

"Please, no!" the man begged. He fell to his knees and clasped his hands in supplication. "Please no!" The officer took out his whip meditatively; the man groaned, scrambled to his feet and quickly stood beside Royland.

When there were four more chosen, they were marched off across the concrete yard into one of the absurd towers, and up a spiral staircase and down a corridor, and through the promenade at the back of an auditorium where a woman screamed German from the stage at an audience of women. And through a tunnel, and down the corridor of an elementary school with empty classrooms full of small desks on either side. And into a hospital area where the fake-masonry walls yielded to scrubbed white tile and the fake flagstones underfoot to composition flooring and the fake pinewood torches in bronze brackets that had lighted their way to fluorescent tubes.

At the door marked RASSENWISSENSCHAFT the guard rapped and a frosty-faced man in a laboratory coat opened up. "You requisitioned a demonstrator, Dr. Kalten," the guard said. "Pick any one of these."

Dr. Kalten looked them over. "Oh, this one, I suppose," he said. Royland. "Come in, fellow."

The Race Science Laboratory of Dr. Kalten proved to be a decent medical setup with an operating table, intricate charts of the races of men and their anatomical, mental and moral makeups. There was also a phrenological head diagram and a horoscope on the wall, and an arrangement of glittering crystals on wire which Royland recognized. It was a model of one Hans Hörbiger's crackpot theory of planetary formation, the *Welteislehre*.

"Sit there," the doctor said, pointing to a stool. "First I've got to take your pedigree. By the way, you might as well know that you're going to end up dissected for my demonstration in Race Science III for the Medical School, and your degree of cooperation will determine whether the dissection is performed under anesthesia or not. Clear?"

"Clear, doctor."

"Curious—no panic. I'll wager we find you're a proto-Hamitoidal hemi-Nordic of at *least* degree five . . . but let's get on. Name?"

"Edward Royland."

"Birthdate?"

"July second, 1923."

The doctor threw down his pencil. "If my previous explanation was inadequate," he shouted, "let me add that if you continue to be difficult I may turn you over to my good friend Dr. Herzbrenner. Dr. Herzbrenner happens to teach interrogation technique at the Gestapo School. *Do—you—now—understand?*"

"Yes, doctor. I'm sorry I cannot withdraw my answer."

Dr. Kalten turned elaborately sarcastic. "How then do you account for your remarkable state of preservation at your age of approximately 180 years?"

"Doctor, I am twenty-three years old. I have travelled through time."

"Indeed?" Kalten was amused. "And how was this done?"

Royland said steadily: "A spell was put on me by a satanic Jewish magician. It involved the ritual murder and desanguination of seven beautiful Nordic virgins."

Dr. Kalten gaped for a moment. Then he picked up his pencil and said firmly: "You will understand that my doubts were logical under the circumstances. Why did you not give me the sound scientific basis for your surprising claim at once? Go ahead; tell me all about it."

XII

He was Dr. Kalten's prize; he was Dr. Kalten's treasure. His peculiarities of speech, his otherwise-inexplicable absence of a birth-number over his left nipple, when they got around to it the gold filling in one of his teeth, his uncanny knowledge of Old America, now had a simple scientific explanation. He was from 1944. What was so hard to grasp about that? Any sound specialist knew about the lost Jewish Kabbalah magic, golems and such.

His story was that he had been a student Race Scientist under the pioneering master William D. Pully. (A noisy whack who used to barnstorm the chaw-and-gallus belt with the backing of Deutches Neues Buro; sure enough they found him in Volume VII of the standard *Introduction to a Historical Handbook of Race Science.*)

The Jewish fiends had attempted to ambush his master on a lonely road; Royland persuaded him to switch hats and coats; in the darkness the substitution was not noticed. Later, in their stronghold he was identified, but the Nordic virgins had already been ritually murdered and drained of their blood, and it wouldn't keep. The dire fate destined for the master had been visited upon the disciple.

Dr. Kalten loved that bit. It tickled him pink that the submen's "revenge" on their enemy had been to precipitate him into a world purged of the sub-men entirely, where a Nordic might breathe freely!

Kalten, except for discreet consultations with such people as Old America specialists, a dentist who was stupefied by the gold filling, and a dermatologist who established that there was not and never had been a *geburtsnummer* on the subject examined, was playing Royland close to his vest. After a week it became apparent that he was reserving Royland for a grand unveiling which would climax the reading of a paper. Royland did not want to be unveiled; there were too many holes in his story. He talked with animation about the beauties of Mexico in the spring, its fair mesas, cactus and mushrooms. Could they make a short trip there? Dr. Kalten said they could not. Royland was becoming restless? Let him study, learn, profit by the matchless arsenal of the sciences available here in Chicago Parteihof. Dear old Chicago boasted distinguished exponents of the World Ice Theory, the Hollow World Theory, Dowsing, Homeopathic Medicine, Curative Folk Botany—

That last did sound interesting. Dr. Kalten was pleased to take his prize to the Medical School and introduce him as a protege to Professor Albiani, of Folk Botany.

Albiani was a bearded gnome out of the Arthur Rackham illustrations for *Das Rheingold*. He loved his subject. "Mother Nature, the all-bounteous one! Wander the fields, young man, and with a seeing eye in an hour's stroll you will find the ergot that aborts, the dill that cools fever, the tansy that strengthens the old, the poppy that soothes the fretful teething babe!"

"Do you have any hallucinogenic Mexican mushrooms?" Royland demanded.

"We may," Albiani said, surprised. They browsed through the Folk Botany museum and pored over dried vegetation under glass. From Mexico there were peyote, the buttons and the root, and there was marihuana root, stem, seed and stalk. No mushrooms.

"They may be in the storeroom," Albiani muttered.

All the rest of the day Royland mucked through the storeroom where specimens were waiting for exhibit space on some rotation plan. He went to Albiani and said, a little wild-eyed: "They're not there."

Albiani had been interested enough to look up the mushrooms in question in the reference books. "See?" he said happily, pointing to a handsome color plate of the mushroom: growing, mature, sporing and dried. He read: " '. . . superstitiously called "God Food," ' " and twinkled through his beard at the joke.

"They're not there," Royland said.

The professor, annoyed at last, said: "There might be some uncatalogued in the basement. Really, we don't have room for everything in our limited display space—just the *interesting* items."

Royland pulled himself together and charmed the location of the department's basement storage space out of him, together with permission to inspect it. And left alone for a moment, ripped the color plate from the professor's book and stowed it away.

That night Royland and Dr. Kalten walked out on one of the innumerable tower-tops for a final cigar. The moon was high and full; its light turned the cratered terrain that had been Chicago into another moon. The sage and his disciple from another day leaned their elbows on a crenellated rampart two hundred feet above Lake Michigan.

"Edward," said Dr. Kalten, "I shall read my paper tomorrow before the Chicago Academy of Race Science." The words were a challenge; something was wrong. He went on: "I shall expect you to be in the wings of the auditorium, and to appear at my command to answer a few questions from me and, if time permits, from our audience."

"I wish it could be postponed," Royland said.

"No doubt."

"Would you explain your unfriendly tone of voice, doctor?" Royland demanded. "I think I've been completely cooperative and have opened the way for you to win undying fame in the annals of Race Science."

"Cooperative, yes. Candid—I wonder? You see, Edward, a dreadful thought struck me today. I have always thought it amusing that the Jewish attack on Reverend Pully should have been for the purpose of precipitating him into the future and that it should have misfired." He took something out of his pocket: a small pistol. He aimed it casually at Royland. "Today I began to wonder *why* they should have done so. Why did they not simply murder him, as they did thousands, and dispose of him in their secret crematoria, and permit no mention in their controlled newspapers and magazines of the disappearance?

"Now, the blood of seven Nordic virgins can have been no cheap commodity. One pictures with ease Nordic men patrolling their precious enclaves of humanity, eyes roving over every passing face, noting who bears the stigmata of the sub-men, and following those who do most carefully indeed lest race-defilement be committed with a look or an 'accidental' touch in a crowded street. Nevertheless the thing was done; your presence here is proof of it. It must have been done at enormous cost; hired Slavs and Negroes must have been employed to kidnap the virgins, and many of them must have fallen before Nordic rage.

"This merely to silence one small voice crying in the wilderness? *I—think—not.* I think, Edward Royland, or whatever your real name may be, that Jewish arrogance sent you, a Jew yourself, into the future as a greeting from the Jewry of that day to what it foolishly thought would be the triumphant Jewry of this. At any rate, the public questioning tomorrow will be conducted by my friend Dr. Hertzbrunner, whom I have mentioned to you. If you have any little secrets, they will not remain secrets long. No, no! Do not move towards me. I shall shoot you disablingly in the knee if you do."

Royland moved toward him and the gun went off; there was an agonizing hammer blow high on his left shin. He picked up Kalten and hurled him, screaming, over the parapet two hundred feet into the water. And collapsed. The pain was horrible. His shinbone was badly cracked if not broken through. There was not much bleeding; maybe there would be later. He need not fear that the shot and scream would rouse the castle. Such sounds were common in the Medical Wing.

He dragged himself, injured leg trailing, to the doorway of Kalten's living quarters; he heaved himself into a chair by the signal bell and threw a rug over his legs. He rang for the diener and told him very quietly: "Go to the medical storeroom for a leg U-brace and whatever is necessary for a cast, please. Dr. Kalten has an interesting idea he wishes to work out."

He should have asked for a syringe of morphine—no he shouldn't. It might affect the time-distortion.

When the man came back he thanked him and told him to turn in for the night.

He almost screamed getting his shoe off; his trouser leg he cut away. The gauze had arrived just in time; the wound was beginning to bleed more copiously. Pressure seemed to stop it. He constructed a sloppy walking cast on his leg. The directions on the several five-pound cans of plaster helped.

His leg was getting numb; good. His cast probably pinched some major nerve, and a week in it would cause permanent paralysis; who cared about *that*?

He tried it out and found he could get across the floor inefficiently. With a strong-enough bannister he could get down stairs but not, he thought, up them. That was all right. He was going to the basement.

God-damning the medieval Nazis and their cornball castle every inch of the way, he went to the basement; there he had a windfall. A dozen drunken SS men were

living it up in a corner far from the censorious eyes of
their company commander; they were playing a game
which might have been called Spin the Corporal. They
saw Royland limping and wept sentimental tears for poor
ol' doc with a bum leg; they carried him two winding miles
to the storeroom he wanted, and shot the lock off for
him. They departed, begging him to call on ol' Company
K any time, bes' fellas in Chicago, doc. Ol' Bruno here
can tear the arm off a Litvak shirker with his bare
hands, honest, doc! Jus' the way you twist a drumstick
off a turkey. You wan' us to get a Litvak an' show you?

He got rid of them at last, clicked on the light and began
his search. His leg was now ice cold, painfully so. He
rummaged through the uncatalogued botanicals and found
after what seemed like hours a crate shipped from Jalasca.
Royland opened it by beating its corners against the concrete floor. It yielded and spilled plastic envelopes;
through the clear material of one he saw the wrinkled
black things. He did not even compare them with the
color plate in his pocket. He tore the envelope open
and crammed them into his mouth, and chewed and
swallowed.

Maybe there had to be a Hopi dancing and chanting,
maybe there didn't have to be. Maybe one had to be
calm, if bitter, and fresh from a day of hard work at
differential equations which approximated the Hopi mode
of thought. Maybe you only had to fix your mind savagely
on what you desired, as his was fixed now. Last time he
had hated and shunned the Bomb; what he wanted was
a world without the Bomb. He had got it, all right!

. . . his tongue was thick and the fireballs were beginning to dance around him, the circling circles . . .

XIII

Charles Miller Nahataspe whispered: "Close. Close.
I was so frightened."

Royland lay on the floor of the hut, his leg unsplinted,
unfractured, but aching horribly. Drowsily he felt his

ribs; he was merely slender now, no longer gaunt. He mumbled: "You were working to pull me back from this side?"

"Yes. You, you were there?"

"I was there. God, let me sleep."

He rolled over heavily and collapsed into complete unconsciousness.

When he awakened it was still dark and his pains were gone. Nahataspe was crooning a healing song very softly. He stopped when he saw Royland's eyes open. "Now you know about break-the-sky medicine," he said.

"Better than anybody. What time is it?"

"Midnight."

"I'll be going then." They clasped hands and looked into each other's eyes.

The jeep started easily. Four hours earlier, or possibly two months earlier, he had been worried about the battery. He chugged down the settlement road and knew what would happen next. He wouldn't wait until morning; a meteorite might kill him, or a scorpion in his bed. He would go directly to Rotschmidt in his apartment, defy Vrow Rotschmidt and wake her man up to tell him about 56c, tell him we have the Bomb.

We have a symbol to offer the Japanese now, something to which they can and will surrender.

Rotschmidt would be philosphical. He would probably sigh about the Bomb: "Ah, do we ever act responsibly? Do we ever know what the consequences of our decisions will be?"

And Royland would have to try to avoid answering him very sharply: "Yes. This once we damn well do."

If there is a single character who stands to our century as a ready-made popular icon of Good, in the same way as Adolf Hitler stands for Evil, then Mohandas Gandhi, called the Mahatma, would be it. Gandhi has appealed to the intellectuals of the West in a way few others in this century have, particularly those unwilling to bow down to the bloodstained altars of the God That Failed. He fought oppression, yet without violence; he expressed what passed for exotic Eastern Wisdom (actually largely reworded Thoreau in a dhoti) in a language thoroughly Western. Without succumbing to idolatry, even the harshest critic must admit Gandhi's keen intelligence, massive integrity, and complete indifference to danger. Yet as this story reminds us, the greatest hero is a product of his times—and his enemy. Gandhi won moral victories over a peculiarly moralistic people, the British. Bernard Shaw once called the English the most dangerous people in the world because they could convince themselves that whatever they wanted to do was morally correct. Gandhi, the brilliant product of the centuries-long interaction of England and India, saw that the way to disarm the Raj was to unconvince the English. Against a different opponent, different consequences . . .

# THE LAST ARTICLE

## Harry Turtledove

*Nonviovlence is the first article of my faith. It is also the last article of my creed.*

—Mohandas Gandhi

*The one means that wins the easiest victory over reason: terror and force.*

—Adolf Hitler, *Mein Kampf*

The tank rumbled down the Rajpath, past the ruins of the Memorial Arch, toward the India Gate. The gateway arch was still standing, although it had taken a couple of shell hits in the fighting before New Delphi fell. The Union Jack fluttered above it.

British troops lined both sides of the Rajpath, watching silently as the tank rolled past them. Their khaki uniforms were filthy and torn; many wore bandages. They had the weary, past-caring stares of beaten men, though the Army of India had fought until flesh and munitions gave out.

The India Gate drew near. A military band, smartened

up for the occasion, began to play as the tank went past.
The bagpipes sounded thin and lost in the hot, humid
air.

A single man stood waiting in the shadow of the gate.
Field Marshal Walther Model leaned down into the
cupola of the Panzer IV. "No one can match the British
at ceremonies of this sort," he said to his aide.

Major Dieter Lasch laughed, a bit unkindly. "They've
had enough practice, sir," he answered, raising his
voice to be heard over the flatulent roar of the tank's
engine.

"What is that tune?" the field marshal asked. "Does
it have a meaning?"

"It's called 'The World Turned Upside Down,' " said
Lasch, who had been involved with his British opposite
number in planning the formal surrender: "Lord Corn-
wallis's army musicians played it when he yielded to
the Americans at Yorktown."

"Ah, the Americans." Model was for a moment so
lost in his own thoughts that his monocle threatened to
slip from his right eye. He screwed it back in. The
single lens was the only thing he shared with the clichéd
image of a high German officer. He was no lean, hawk-
faced Prussian. But his rounded features were unyielding, and his stocky body sustained the energy of his will
better than the thin, dyspeptic frames of so many aris-
tocrats. "The Americans," he repeated. "Well, that will
be the next step, won't it? But enough. One thing at a
time."

The panzer stopped. The driver switched off the engine. The sudden quiet was startling. Model leaped
nimbly down. He had been leaping down from tanks for
eight years now, since his days as a staff officer for the
IV Corps in the Polish campaign.

The man in the shadows stepped forward, saluted.
Flashbulbs lit his long, tired face as German photogra-
phers recorded the moment for history. The Englishman
ignored cameras and cameramen alike. "Field Marshal
Model," he said pointedly. He might have been about
to discuss the weather.

Model admired his sangfroid. "Field Marshal Auchinleck," he replied, returning the salute and giving Auchinleck a last few seconds to remain his equal. Then he came back to the matter at hand. "Field Marshal, have you signed the instrument of surrender of the British Army of India to the forces of the Reich?"

"I have," Auchinleck replied. He reached into the left pocket of his battle dress, removed a folded sheet of paper. Before handing it to Model, though, he said, "I should like to request your permission to make a brief statement at this time."

"Of course, sir. You may say what you like, at whatever length you like." In victory, Model could afford to be magnanimous. He had even granted Marshal Zhukov leave to speak in the Soviet capitulation at Kuibyshev, before the marshal was taken out and shot.

"I thank you," Auchinleck stiffly dipped his head. "I will say, then, that I find the terms I have been forced to accept to be cruelly hard on the brave men who have served under my command."

"That is your privilege, sir." But Model's round face was no longer kindly, and his voice had iron in it as he replied, "I must remind you, however, that my treating with you at all under the rules of war is an act of mercy for which Berlin may yet reprimand me. When Britain surrendered in 1941, all Imperial forces were also ordered to lay down their arms. I daresay you did not expect us to come so far, but I would be within my rights in reckoning you no more than so many bandits."

A slow flush darkened Auchinleck's cheeks. "We gave you a bloody good run, for bandits."

"So you did." Model remained polite. He did not say he would ten times rather fight straight-up battles than deal with the partisans who to this day harassed the Germans and their allies in occupied Russia. "Have you anything further to add?"

"No, sir, I do not." Auchinleck gave the German the signed surrender, handed him his sidearm. Model put the pistol in the empty holster he wore for the occasion. It did not fit well; the holster was made for a Walther

P38, not this man-killing brute of a Webley and Scott. That mattered little, though—the ceremony was almost over.

Auchinleck and Model exchanged salutes for the last time. The British field marshal stepped away. A German lieutenant came up to lead him into captivity.

Major Lasch waved his left hand. The Union Jack came down from the flagpole on the India Gate. The swastika rose to replace it.

Lasch tapped discreetly on the door, stuck his head into the field marshal's office. "That Indian politician is here for his appointment with you, sir."

"Oh yes. Very well, Dieter, send him in." Model had been dealing with Indian politicians even before the British surrender, and with hordes of them now that resistance was over. He had no more liking for the breed than for Russian politicians, or even German ones. No matter what pious principles they spouted, his experience was that they were all out for their own good first.

The small, frail brown man the aide showed in made him wonder. The Indian's emaciated frame and the plain white cotton loincloth that was his only garment contrasted starkly with the Victorian splendor of the Viceregal Palace from which Model was administering the Reich's new conquest. "Sit down, *Herr* Gandhi," the field marshal urged.

"I thank you very much, sir." As he took his seat, Gandhi seemed a child in an adult's chair: it was much too wide for him, and its soft, overstuffed cushions hardly sagged under his meager weight. But his eyes, Models saw, were not child's eyes. They peered with disconcerting keenness through his wire-framed spectacles as he said, "I have come to inquire when we may expect German troops to depart from our country."

Model leaned forward, frowning. For a moment he thought he had misunderstood Gandhi's Gujarati-flavored English. When he was sure he had not, he said, "Do you think perhaps we have come all this way as tourists?"

"Indeed I do not." Gandhi's voice was sharp with disapproval. "Tourists do not leave so many dead behind them."

Model's temper kindled. "No, tourists do not pay such a high price for the journey. Having come regardless of that cost, I assure you we shall stay."

"I am very sorry, sir; I cannot permit it."

"*You* cannot?" Again, Model had to concentrate to keep his monocle from falling out. He had heard arrogance from politicians before, but this scrawny old devil surpassed belief. "Do you forget I can call my aide and have you shot behind this building? You would not be the first, I assure you."

"Yes, I know that," Gandhi said sadly. "If you have that fate in mind for me, I am an old man. I will not run."

Combat had taught Model a hard indifference to the prospect of injury or death. He saw the older man possessed something of the same sort, however he had acquired it. A moment later he realized his threat had not only failed to frighten Gandhi, but had actually amused him. Disconcerted, the field marshal said, "Have you any serious issues to address?"

"Only the one I named just now. We are a nation of more than 300 million; it is no more just for Germany to rule us than for the British."

Model shrugged. "If we are able to, we will. We have the strength to hold what we have conquered, I assure you."

"Where there is no right, there can be no strength," Gandhi said. "We will not permit you to hold us in bondage."

"Do you think to threaten me?" Model growled. In fact, though, the Indian's audacity surprised him. Most of the locals had fallen over themselves, fawning on their new masters. Here, at least, was a man out of the ordinary.

Gandhi was still shaking his head, although Model saw he had still not frightened him (a man out of the ordinary indeed, thought the field marshal, who respected courage when he found it). "I make no threats, sir, but I will do what I believe to be right."

"Most noble," Model said, but to his annoyance the words came out sincere rather than with the sardonic edge he had intended. He had heard such canting phrases before, from Englishmen, from Russians, yes, and from Germans as well. Somehow, though, this Gandhi struck him as one who always meant exactly what he said. He rubbed his chin, considering how to handle such an intransigent.

A large green fly came buzzing into the office. Model's air of detachment vanished the moment he heard that malignant whine. He sprang from his seat, swatted at the fly. He missed. The insect flew around awhile longer, then settled on the arm of Gandhi's chair. "Kill it," Model told him. "Last week one of those accursed things bit me on the neck, and I still have the lump to prove it."

Gandhi brought his hand down, but several inches from the fly. Frightened, it took off. Gandhi rose. He was surprisingly nimble for a man nearing eighty. He chivied the fly out of the office, ignoring Model, who watched his performance in openmouthed wonder.

"I hope it will not trouble you again," Gandhi said, returning as calmly as if he had done nothing out of the ordinary. "I am one of those who practice ahimsa: I will do no injury to any living thing."

Model remembered the fall of Moscow, and the smell of burning bodies filling the chilly autumn air. He remembered machine guns knocking down cossack cavalry before they could close, and the screams of the wounded horses, more heartrendering than any woman's. He knew of other things, too, things he had not seen for himself and of which he had no desire to learn more.

"*Herr* Gandhi," he said, "how do you propose to bend to your will someone who opposes you, if you will not use force for the purpose?"

"I have never said I will not use force, sir." Gandhi's smile invited the field marshal to enjoy with him the distinction he was making. "I will not use violence. If my people refuse to cooperate in any way with yours, how can you compel them? What choice will you have but to grant us leave to do as we will?"

Without the intelligence estimates he had read, Model would have dismissed the Indian as a madman. No madman, though, could have caused the British so much trouble. But perhaps the decadent Raj simply had not made him afraid. Model tried again. "You understand that what you have said is treason against the Reich," he said harshly.

Gandhi bowed in his seat. "You may, of course, do what you will with me. My spirit will in any case survive among my people."

Model felt his face heat. Few men were immune to fear. Just his luck, he thought sourly, to have run into one of them. "I warn you, *Herr* Gandhi, to obey the authority of the officials of the Reich, or it will be the worse for you."

"I will do what I believe to be right, and nothing else. If you Germans exert yourselves toward the freeing of India, joyfully will I work with you. If not, then I regret we must be foes."

The field marshal gave him one last chance to see reason. "Were it you and I alone, there might be some doubt as to what would happen." Not much, he thought, not when Gandhi was twenty-odd years older and thin enough to break like a stick. He fought down the irrelevance, went on, "But where, *Herr* Gandhi, is your *Wehrmacht?*"

Of all things, he had least expected to amuse the Indian again. Yet Gandhi's eyes unmistakably twinkled behind the lenses of his spectacles. "Field Marshal, I have an army, too."

Model's patience, never of the most enduring sort, wore thin all at once. "Get out!" he snapped.

Gandhi stood, bowed, and departed. Major Lasch stuck his head into the office. The field marshal's glare drove him out again in a hurry.

*       *       *

"Well?" Jawaharlal Nehru paced back and forth. Tall, slim, and saturnine, he towered over Gandhi without dominating him. "Dare we use the same policies against the Germans that we employed against the English?"

"If we wish our land free, dare we do otherwise?" Gandhi replied. "They will not grant our wish of their own volition. Model struck me as a man not much different from various British leaders whom we have succeeded in vexing in the past." He smiled at the memory of what passive resistance had done to officials charged with combating it.

"Very well, satyagraha it is." But Nehru was not smiling. He had less humor than his older colleague.

Gandhi teased him gently: "Do you fear another spell in prison, then?" Both men had spent time behind bars during the war, until the British released them in a last, vain effort to rally the support of the Indian people to the Raj.

"You know better." Nehru refused to be drawn, and persisted, "The rumors that come out of Europe frighten me."

"Do you tell me you take them seriously?" Gandhi shook his head in surprise and a little reproof. "Each side in any war will always paint its opponents as blackly as it can."

"I hope you are right, and that that is all. Still, I confess I would feel more at ease with what we plan to do if you found me one Jew, officer or other rank, in the army now occupying us."

"You would be hard-pressed to find any among the forces they defeated. The British have little love for Jews, either."

"Yes, but I daresay it could be done. With the Germans, they are banned by law. The English would never make such a rule. And while the laws are vile enough, I think of the tales that man Wiesenthal told, the one who came here the gods know how across Russia and Persia from Poland."

"Those I do not believe," Gandhi said firmly. "No

nation could act in that way and hope to survive. Where could men be found to carry out such horrors?"

"*Azad Hind*," Nehru said, quoting the "Free India" motto of the locals who had fought on the German side.

But Gandhi shook his head. "They are only soldiers, doing as soldiers have always done. Wiesenthal's claims are for an entirely different order of bestiality, one that could not exist without destroying the fabric of the state that gave it birth."

"I hope very much you are right," Nehru said.

Walther Model slammed the door behind him hard enough to make his aide, whose desk faced away from the field marshal's office, jump in alarm. "Enough of this twaddle for one day," Model said. "I need schnapps, to get the taste of these Indians out of my mouth. Come along if you care to, Dieter."

"Thank you, sir." Major Lasch threw down his pen, eagerly got to his feet. "I sometimes think conquering India was easier than ruling it will be."

Model rolled his eyes. "I *know* it was. I would ten times rather be planning a new campaign than sitting here bogged down in pettifogging details. The sooner Berlin sends me people trained in colonial administration, the happier I will be."

The bar might have been taken from an English pub. It was dark, quiet, and paneled in walnut; a dartboard still hung on the wall. But a German sergeant in field gray stood behind the bar, and, despite the lazily turning ceiling fan, the temperature was close to thirty-five Celsius. The one might have been possible in occupied London, the other not.

Model knocked back his first shot at a gulp. He sipped his second more slowly, savoring it. Warmth spread through him, warmth that had nothing to do with the heat of the evening. He leaned back in his chair, steepled his fingers. "A long day," he said.

"Yes, sir," Lasch agreed. "After the effrontery of that Gandhi, any day would seem a long one. I've rarely seen you so angry." Considering Model's temper, that was no small statement.

"Ah yes, Gandhi." Model's tone was reflective rather than irate; Lasch looked at him curiously. The field marshal said, "For my money, he's worth a dozen of the ordinary sort."

"Sir?" The aide no longer tried to hide his surprise.

"He is an honest man. He tells me what he thinks, and he will stick by that. I may kill him—I may have to kill him—but he and I will both know why, and I will not change his mind." Model took another sip of schnapps. He hesitated, as if unsure whether to go on. At last he did. "Do you know, Dieter, after he left I had a vision."

"Sir?" Now Lasch was alarmed.

The field marshal might have read his aide's thoughts. He chuckled wryly. "No, no, I am not about to swear off eating beefsteak and wear sandals instead of my boots, that I promise. But I saw myself as a Roman procurator, listening to the rantings of some early Christian priest."

Lasch raised an eyebrow. Such musings were unlike Model, who was usually direct to the point of bluntness and altogether materialistic—assets in the makeup of a general officer. The major cautiously sounded these unexpected depths: "How do you suppose the Roman felt, facing that kind of man?"

"Bloody confused, I suspect," Model said, which sounded more like him. "And because he and his comrades did not know how to handle such fanatics, you and I are Christians today, Dieter."

"So we are." The major rubbed his chin. "Is that a bad thing?"

Model laughed and finished his drink. "From your point of view or mine, no. But I doubt that old Roman would agree with us, any more than Gandhi agrees with me over what will happen next here. But then, I have two advantages over the dead procurator." He raised his finger; the sergeant hurried over to fill his glass.

At Lasch's nod, the young man also poured more

schnapps for him. The major drank, then said, "I should hope so. We are more civilized, more sophisticated, than the Romans ever dreamed of being."

But Model was still in that fey mood. "Are we? My procurator was such a sophisticate that he tolerated anything, and never saw the danger in a foe who would not do the same. Our Christian God, though, is a jealous god who puts up with no rivals. And one who is a National Socialist serves also the *Volk,* to whom he owes sole loyalty. I am immune to Gandhi's virus in a way the Roman was not to the Christian's."

"Yes, that makes sense," Lach agreed after a moment. "I had not thought of it in that way, but I see it is so. And what is our other advantage over the Roman procurator?"

Suddenly the field marshal looked hard and cold, much the way he had looked leading the tanks of Third Panzer against the Kremlin compound. "The machine gun," he said.

The rising sun's rays made the sandstone of the Red Fort seem even more the color of blood. Gandhi frowned and turned his back on the fortress, not caring for that thought. Even at dawn the air was warm and muggy.

"I wish you were not here," Nehru told him. The younger man lifted his trademark fore-and-aft cap, scratched his graying hair, and glanced at the crowd growing around them. "The Germans' orders forbid assemblies, and they will hold you responsible for this gathering."

"I am, am I not?" Gandhi replied. "Would you have me send my followers into a danger I do not care to face myself? How would I presume to lead them afterward?"

"A general does not fight in the front ranks," Nehru came back. "If you are lost to our cause, will we be able to go on?"

"If not, then surely the cause is not worthy, yes? Now let us be going."

Nehru threw his hands in the air. Gandhi nodded, satisfied, and worked his way toward the head of the crowd. Men and women stepped aside to let him through. Still shaking his head, Nehru followed.

The crowd slowly began to march east up Chandni Chauk, the Street of Silversmiths. Some of the fancy shops had been wrecked in the fighting, more looted afterward. But others were opening up, their owners as happy to take German money as they had been to serve the British before.

One of the proprietors, a man who had managed to stay plump even through the past year of hardship, came rushing out of his shop when he saw the procession go by. He ran to the head of the march and spotted Nehru, whose height and elegant dress singled him out.

"Are you out of your mind?" the silversmith shouted. "The Germans have banned assemblies. If they see you, something dreadful will happen."

"Is it not dreadful that they take away the liberty that properly belongs to us?" Gandhi asked. The silversmith spun round. His eyes grew wide when he recognized the man who was speaking to him. Gandhi went on, "Not only is it dreadful, it is wrong. And so we do not recognize the German's right to ban anything we may choose to do. Join us, will you?"

"Great-souled one, I—I—," the silversmith spluttered. Then his glance slid past Gandhi. "The Germans!" he squeaked. He turned and ran.

Gandhi led the procession toward the approaching squad. The Germans stamped down Chandni Chauk as if they expected the people in front of them to melt from their path. Their gear, Gandhi thought, was not that much different from what British soldiers wore: ankle boots, shorts, and open-necked tunics. But their coal-scuttle helmets gave them a look of sullen, beetle-browed ferocity the British tin hat did not convey. Even for a man of Gandhi's equanimity, it was daunting, as no doubt it was intended to be.

"Hello, my friends," he said. "Do any of you speak English?"

"I speak it, a little," one of them replied. His shoulder straps had the twin pips of a sergeant major: he was the squad leader, then. He hefted his rifle, not menacingly, Gandhi thought, but to emphasize what he was saying. "Go to your homes back. This coming together is *verboten.*"

"I am sorry, but I must refuse to obey your order," Gandhi said. "We are walking peacefully on our own street in our own city. We will harm no one, no matter what; this I promise you. But walk we will, as we wish." He repeated himself until he was sure the sergeant major understood.

The German spoke to his comrades in his own language. One of the soldiers raised his gun and with a nasty smile pointed it at Gandhi. The Indian nodded politely. The German blinked to see him unafraid. The sergeant major slapped the rifle down. One of his men had a field telephone on his back. The sergeant major cranked it, waited for a reply, spoke urgently into it.

Nehru caught Gandhi's eye. His dark, tired gaze was full of worry. Somehow that nettled Gandhi more than the Germans' arrogance in ordering about his people. He began to walk forward again. The marchers followed him, flowing around the German squad like water flowing round a boulder.

The soldier who had pointed his rifle at Gandhi shouted in alarm. He brought up the weapon again. The sergeant major barked at him. Reluctantly, he lowered it.

"A sensible man," Gandhi said to Nehru. "He sees we do no injury to him or his, and so does none to us."

"Sadly, though, not everyone is so sensible," the younger man replied, "as witness his lance corporal there. And even a sensible man may not be well inclined to us. You notice he is still on the telephone."

The phone on Field Marshal Model's desk jangled. He jumped and swore; he had left orders he was to be disturbed only for an emergency. He had to find time to work. He picked up the phone. "This had better be good," he growled without preamble.

He listened, swore again, slammed the receiver down. "Lasch!" he shouted.

It was his aide's turn to jump. "Sir?"

"Don't just sit there on your fat arse," the field marshal said unfairly. "Call out my car and driver, and quickly. Then belt on your sidearm and come along. The Indians are doing something stupid. Oh yes, order out a platoon and have them come after us. Up on Chandni Chauk, the trouble is."

Lasch called for the car and the troops, then hurried after Model. "A riot?" he asked as he caught up.

"No, no." Model moved his stumpy frame along so fast that the taller Lasch had to trot beside him. "Some of Gandhi's tricks, damn him."

The field marshal's Mercedes was waiting when he and his aide hurried out of the Viceregal Palace. "Chandni Chauk," Model snapped as the driver held the door open for him. After that he sat in furious silence as the powerful car roared up Irwin Road, round a third of Connaught Circle, and north on Chelmsford Road past the bombed-out railway station until, for no reason Model could see, the street's name changed to Qutb Road.

A little later the driver said, "Some kind of disturbance up ahead, sir."

"Disturbance?" Lasch echoed, leaning forward to peer through the windscreen. "It's a whole damned regiment's worth of Indians coming at us. Do't they know better than that? And what the devil," he added, his voice rising, "are so many of our men doing ambling along beside them? Don't they know they're supposed to break up this sort of thing?" In his indignation he did not notice he was repeating himself.

"I suspect they don't," Model said dryly. "Gandhi, I gather, can have that effect on people who aren't ready for his peculiar brand of stubbornness. That, however, does not include me." He tapped the driver on the shoulder. "Pull up about two hundred meters in front of the first rank of them, Joachim."

"Yes, sir."

Even before the car had stopped moving, Model jumped out of it. Lasch, hand on his pistol, was close behind, protesting, "What if one of those fanatics has a gun?"

"Then Colonel General Weidling assumes command, and a lot of Indians end up dead." Model strode toward Gandhi, ignoring the German troops who were drawing themselves to stiff, horrified attention at the sight of his field marshal's uniform. He would deal with them later. For the moment, Gandhi was more important.

He had stopped—which meant the rest of the marchers did, too—and was waiting politely for Model to approach. The German commandant was not impressed. He thought Gandhi sincere, and could not doubt his courage, but none of that mattered at all. He said harshly, "You were warned against this sort of behavior."

Gandhi looked him in the eye. They were very much of a height. "And I told you, I do not recognize your right to give such orders. This is our country, not yours, and if some of us choose to walk on our streets, we will do so."

From behind Gandhi, Nehru's glance flicked worriedly from one of the antagonists to the other. Model noticed him only peripherally; if Nehru was already afraid, he could be handled whenever necessary. Gandhi was a tougher nut. The field marshal waved at the crowd behind the old man. "You are responsible for all these people. If harm come to them, you will be to blame."

"Why should harm come to them? They are not soldiers. They do not attack your men. I told that to one of your sergeants, and he understood it, and refrained from hindering us. Surely you, sir, an educated, cultured man, can see that what I say is self-evident truth."

Model turned his head to speak to his aide in German: "If we did not have Goebbels, this would be the one for his job." He shuddered to think of the propaganda victory Gandhi would win if he got away with flouting German ordinances. The whole countryside would be boiling with partisans in a week. And he had already managed to hoodwink some Germans into letting him do it!

Then Gandhi surprised him again. "*Ich danke Ihnen, Herr General-feldmarschall, aber das glaube ich kein Kompliment zu sein,*" he said in slow but clear German: "I thank you, Field Marshal, but I believe that to be no compliment."

Having to hold his monocle in place helped Model keep his face straight. "Take it however you like," he said. "Get these people off the street, or they and you will face the consequences. We will do what you force us to."

"I force you to nothing. As for these people who follow, each does so of his or her own free will. We are free, and will show it, not by violence, but through firmness in truth."

Now Model listened with only half an ear. He had kept Gandhi talking long enough for the platoon he had ordered out to arrive. Half a dozen SdKfz 251 armored personnel carriers came clanking up. The men piled out of them. "Give me a firing line, three ranks deep," Model shouted. As the troopers scrambled to obey, he waved the half-tracks into position behind them, all but blocking Qutb Road. The half-tracks' commanders swiveled the machine guns at the front of the vehicles' troop compartments so they bore on the Indians.

Gandhi watched these preparations as calmly as if they had nothing to do with him. Again Model had to admire his calm. Gandhi's followers were less able to keep fear from their faces. Very few, though, used the pause to slip away. Gandhi's discipline was a long way from the military sort, but effective all the same.

"Tell them to disperse now, and we can still get away without bloodshed," the field marshal said.

"We will shed no one's blood, sir. But we will continue on our pleasant journey. Moving carefully, we will, I think, be able to get between your large lorries there." Gandhi turned to wave his people forward once more.

"You insolent—" Rage choked Model, which was as well, for it kept him from cursing Gandhi like a fishwife. To give him time to master his temper, he plucked his monocle from his eye and began polishing the lens with a silk handkerchief. He replaced the monocle, started to jam the handkerchief back into his trouser pocket, then suddenly had a better idea.

"Come, Lasch," he said, and started toward the waiting German troops. About halfway to them, he dropped the handkerchief on the ground. He spoke in loud, simple German so his men and Gandhi could both follow: "If any Indians come past this spot, I wash my hands of them."

He might have known Gandhi would have a comeback ready. "That is what Pilate said also, you will recall, sir."

"Pilate washed his hands to evade responsibility," the field marshal answered steadily; he was in control of himself again. "I accept it: I am responsible to my Führer and to the *Oberkommando-Wehrmacht* for maintaining Reichs control over India, and will do what I see fit to carry out that obligation."

For the first time since they had come to know each other, Gandhi looked sad. "I too, sir, have my responsibilities." He bowed slightly to Model.

Lasch chose that moment to whisper in his commander's ear: "Sir, what of our men over there? Had you planned to leave them in the line of fire?"

The field marshal frowned. He had planned to do just that; the wretches deserved no better, for being taken in by Gandhi. But Lasch had a point. The platoon might balk at shooting countrymen, if it came to that. "You men," Model said sourly, jabbing his marshal's baton at them, "fall in behind the armored personnel carriers, at once."

The Germans' boots pounded on the macadam as they dashed to obey. They were still all right, then, with a clear order in front of them. Something, Model thought, but not much.

He had also worried that the Indians would take advantage of the moment of confusion to press forward, but they did not. Gandhi and Nehru and a couple of other men were arguing among themselves. Model nodded once. Some of them knew he was earnest, then. And Gandhi's followers' discipline, as the field marshal had thought a few minutes ago, was not of the military sort. He could not simply issue an order and know his will would be done.

"I issue no orders," Gandhi said. "Let each man follow his conscience as he will—what else is freedom?"

"They will follow *you* if you go forward, great-souled one," Nehru replied, "and that German, I fear, means to carry out his threat. Will you throw your life away, and those of your countrymen?"

"I will not throw my life away," Gandhi said, but before the men around him could relax, he went on, "I will gladly give it, if freedom requires that. I am but one man. If I fall, others will surely carry on; perhaps the memory of me will serve to make them more steadfast."

He stepped forward.

"Oh damnation," Nehru said softly, and followed.

For all his vigor, Gandhi was far from young. Nehru did not need to nod to the marchers close by him; of their own accord, they hurried ahead of the man who had led them for so long, forming with their bodies a barrier between him and the German guns.

He tried to go faster. "Stop! Leave me my place! What are you doing?" he cried, though in his heart he understood only too well.

"This once, they will not listen to you," Nehru said.

"But they must!" Gandhi peered through eyes dimmed now by tears as well as age. "Where is that stupid handkerchief? We must be almost to it!"

"For the last time, I warn you to halt!" Model shouted. The Indians still came on. The sound of their feet, sandal-clad or bare, was like a growing murmur on the pavement, very different from the clatter of German boots. "Fools!" the field marshal muttered under his breath. He turned to his men. "Take your aim!"

The advance slowed when the rifles came up; of that Model was certain. For a moment he thought that ultimate threat would be enough to bring the marchers to their senses. But then they advanced again. The Polish cavalry had shown that same reckless bravery, charging with lances and sabers and carbines against the German tanks. Model wondered whether the inhabitants of the *Reichsgeneralgouvernement* of Poland thought the gallantry worthwhile.

A man stepped on the field marshal's handkerchief. "Fire!" Model said.

A second passed, two. Nothing happened. Model scowled at his men. Gandhi's deviltry had got into them; sneaky as a Jew, he was turning the appearance of weakness into a strange kind of strength. But then trained discipline paid its dividend. One finger tightened on a Mauser trigger. A single shot rang out. As if it were a signal that recalled the other men to their duty, they, too, began to fire. From the armored personnel carriers, the machine guns started their deadly chatter. Model heard screams above the gunfire.

The volley smashed into the front ranks of marchers at close range. Men fell. Others ran, or tried to, only to be held by the power of the stream still advancing behind them. Once begun, the Germans methodically poured fire into the column of Indians. The march dissolved into a panic-stricken mob.

Gandhi still tried to press forward. A fleeing wounded man smashed into him, splashing him with blood and knocking him to the ground. Nehru and another man immediately lay down on top of him.

"Let me up! Let me up!" he shouted.

"No," Nehru screamed in his ear. "With shooting like this, you are in the safest spot you can be. We need you, and need you alive. Now we have martyrs around whom to rally our cause."

"Now we have dead husbands and wives, fathers and mothers. Who will tend to their loved ones?"

Gandhi had no time for more protest. Nehru and the

other man hauled him to his feet and dragged him away. Soon they were among their people, all running now from the German guns. A bullet struck the back of the unknown man who was helping Gandhi escape. Gandhi heard the slap of the impact, felt the man jerk. Then the strong grip on him loosened as the man fell.

He tried to tear free from Nehru. Before he could, another Indian laid hold of him. Even at that horrid moment, he felt the irony of his predicament. All his life he had championed individual liberty, and here his own followers were robbing him of his. In other circumstances, it might have been funny.

"In here," Nehru shouted. Several people had already broken down the door to a shop and, Ghandi saw a moment later, the rear exit as well. Then he was hustled into the alley behind the shop, and through a maze of lanes that reminded him of the old Delhi, which, unlike its British-designed sister city, was an Indian town through and through.

At last the nameless man with Gandhi and Nehru knocked on the back door of a tearoom. The woman who opened it gasped to recognize her unexpected guests, then pressed her hands together in front of her and stepped aside to let them in. "You will be safe here," the man said, "at least for a while. Now I must see to my own family."

"From the bottom of our hearts, we thank you," Nehru replied as the fellow hurried away. Gandhi said nothing. He was winded, battered, and filled with anguish at the failure of the march and at the suffering it had brought to so many marchers and to their kinsfolk.

The woman sat the two fugitive leaders at a small table in the kitchen, served them tea and cakes. "I will leave you now, best ones," she said gently, "lest those out front wonder why I neglect them for so long."

Gandhi left the cake on his plate. He sipped the tea. Its warmth began to restore them physically, but the wound in his spirit would never heal. "The Armritsar massacre pales beside this," he said, setting down the empty cup. "There the British panicked and opened fire. This had nothing of panic about it. Model told me what he would do, and he did it." He shook his head, still hardly believing what he had just been through.

"So he did." Nehru had gobbled his cake like a starving wolf, and ate his companion's when he saw Gandhi did not want it. His once immaculate white jacket and pants were torn, filthy, and blood-spattered; his cap sat awry on his head. But his eyes, usually so somber, were lit with a fierce glow. "And by his brutality, he has delivered himself into our hands. No one now can imagine the Germans have anything but their own interests at heart. We will gain followers all over the country. After this, not a wheel will turn in India."

"Yes, I will declare the satyagraha campaign," Gandhi said. "Noncooperation will show how we reject foreign rule, and will cost the Germans dear because they will not be able to exploit us. The combination of nonviolence and determined spirit will surely shame them into granting us our liberty."

"There—you see." Encouraged by his mentor's rally, Nehru rose and came round the table to embrace the older man. "We will triumph yet."

"So we will," Gandhi said, and sighed heavily. He had pursued India's freedom for half his long life, and this change of masters was a setback he had not truly planned for, even after England and Russia fell. The British were finally beginning to listen to him when the Germans swept them aside. Now he had to begin anew. He sighed again. "It will cost our poor people dear, though."

"Cease firing," Model said. Few good targets were left on Qutb Road; almost all the Indians in the procession were down or had run from the guns.

Even after the bullets stopped, the street was far from silent. Most of the people the German platoon had shot were alive and shrieking; as if he needed more proof, the Russian campaign had taught the field marshal how hard human beings were to kill outright.

Still, the din distressed him, and evidently Lasch as

well. "We ought to put them out of their misery," the major said.

"So we should." Model had a happy inspiration. "And I know just how. Come with me."

The two men turned their backs on the carnage and walked around the row of armored personnel carriers. As they passed the lieutenant commanding the platoon, Model nodded to him and said, "Well done."

The lieutenant saluted. "Thank you, sir." The soldiers in earshot nodded at one another: nothing bucked up the odds of getting promoted like performing under the commander's eye.

The Germans behind the armed vehicles were not so proud of themselves. They were the ones who had let the march get this big and come this far in the first place. Model slapped his boot with his field marshal's baton. "You all deserve courts-martial," he said coldly, glaring at them. "You know the orders concerning native assemblies, yet there you were tagging along, more like sheepdogs than soldiers." He spat in disgust.

"But sir—," began one of them—a sergeant major, Model saw. He subsided in a hurry when Model's gaze swung his way.

"Speak," the field marshal urged. "Enlighten me— tell me what possessed you to act in the disgraceful way you did. Was it some evil spirit, perhaps? This country abounds with them, if you listen to the natives—as you all too obviously have been."

The sergeant major flushed under Model's sarcasm, but finally burst out, "Sir, it didn't look to me as if they were up to any harm, that's all. The old man heading them up swore they were peaceful, and he looked too feeble to be anything but, if you take my meaning."

Model's smile had all the warmth of a Moscow December night. "And so in your wisdom you set aside the commands you had received. The results of that wisdom you hear now." The field marshal briefly let himself listen to the cries of the wounded, a sound the war had taught him to screen out. "Now then, come with me—yes, you, Sergeant Major, and the rest of your shirkers, too, or those of you who wish to avoid a court."

As he had known they would, they all trooped after him. "There is your handiwork," he said, pointing to the shambles in the street. His voice hardened. "You are responsible for those people lying there—had you acted as you should have, you would have broken up that march long before it ever got so far or so large. Now the least you can do is give those people their release." He set hands on hips, waited.

No one moved. "Sir?" the sergeant major said faintly. He seemed to have become the group's spokesman.

Model made an impatient gesture. "Go on, finish them. A bullet in the back of the head will quiet them once and for all."

"In cold blood, sir?" The sergeant major had not wanted to understand him before. Now he had no choice.

The field marshal was inexorable. "They—and you—disobeyed Reich's commands. They made themselves liable to capital punishment the moment they gathered. You at least have the chance to atone, by carrying out this just sentence."

"I don't think I can," the sergeant major muttered.

He was probably just talking to himself, but Model gave him no chance to change his mind. He turned to the lieutenant of the platoon that had broken the march. "Place this man under arrest." After the sergeant major had been seized, Model turned his chill, monocled stare at the rest of the reluctant soldiers. "Any others?"

Two more men let themselves be arrested rather than draw their weapons. The field marshal nodded to the others. "Carry out your orders." He had an afterthought. "If you find Gandhi or Nehru out there, bring them to me alive."

The Germans moved out hesitantly. They were no *Einsatzkommandos*, and not used to this kind of work. Some looked away as they administered the first coup de grace; one missed as a result, and had his bullet ricochet off the pavement and almost hit a comrade.

But as the soldiers worked their way up Qutb Road, they became quicker, more confident, and more competent. War was like that, Model thought. So soon one became used to what had been unimaginable.

After a while the flat cracks died away, but from lack of targets rather than reluctance. A few at a time, the soldiers returned to Model. "No sign of the two leaders?" he asked. They all shook their heads.

"Very well—dismissed. And obey your orders like good Germans henceforward."

"No further reprisals?" Lasch asked as the relieved troopers hurried away.

"No, let them go. They carried out their part of the bargain, and I will meet mine. I am a fair man, after all, Dieter."

"Very well, sir."

Gandhi listened with undisguised dismay as the shopkeeper babbled out his tale of horror. "This is madness!" he cried.

"I doubt Field Marshal Model, for his part, understands the principle of ahimsa," Nehru put in. Neither Gandhi nor he knew exactly where they were: a safe house somewhere not far from the center of Delhi was the best guess he could make. The men who brought the shopkeeper were masked. What one did not know, one could not tell the Germans if captured.

"Neither do you," the older man replied, which was true; Nehru had a more pragmatic nature than Gandhi. Gandhi went on, "Rather more to the point, neither do the British. And Model, to speak to, seemed no different from any high-ranking British military man. His specialty has made him harsh and rigid, but he is not stupid and does not appear unusually cruel."

"Just a simple soldier, doing his job." Nehru's irony was palpable.

"He must have gone insane," Gandhi said; it was the only explanation that made even the slightest sense of the massacre of the wounded. "Undoubtedly he will be censured when the news of this atrocity reaches Berlin, as General Dyer was by the British after Armritsar."

"Such is to be hoped." But again Nehru did not sound hopeful.

"How could it be otherwise, after such an appalling action? What government, what leaders could fail to be filled with humiliation and remorse at it?"

Model strode into the mess. The officers stood and raised their glasses in salute. "Sit, sit," the field marshal growled, using gruffness to hide his pleasure.

An Indian servant brought him a fair imitation of roast beef and Yorkshire pudding: better than they were eating in London these days, he thought. The servant was silent and unsmiling, but Model would only have noticed more about him had he been otherwise. Servants were supposed to assume a cloak of invisibility.

When the meal was done, Model took out his cigar case. The *Waffen-SS* officer on his left produced a lighter. Model leaned forward, puffed a cigar into life. "My thanks, *Brigadeführer*," the field marshal said. He had little use for SS titles of rank, but brigade commander was at least recognizably close to brigadier.

"Sir, it is my great pleasure," Jürgen Stroop declared. "You could not have handled things better. A lesson for the Indians—less than they deserve, too; (he also took no notice of the servant) "and a good one for your men as well. We train ours harshly, too."

Model nodded. He knew about SS training methods. No one denied the daring of the *Waffen-SS* divisions. No one (except the SS) denied that the *Wehrmacht* had better officers.

Stroop drank. "A lesson," he repeated in a pedantic tone that went oddly with the SS's reputation for aggressiveness. "Force is the only thing the racially inferior can understand. Why, when I was in Warsaw—"

That had been four or five years ago, Model suddenly recalled. Stroop had been a *Brigadeführer* then, too, if memory served; no wonder he was still one now, even after all the hard fighting since. He was lucky not to be a buck private. Imagine letting a pack of desperate, starving Jews chew up the finest troops in the world.

And imagine, afterward, submitting a seventy-five-page operations report bound in leather and grandiosely called "The Warsaw Ghetto Is No More." And imagine, with all that, having the crust to boast about it afterward. No wonder the man sounded like a pompous ass. He *was* a pompous ass, and an inept butcher to boot. Model had done enough butchery before today's work—anyone who fought in Russia learned all about butchery—but he had never botched it.

He did not revel in it, either. He wished Stroop would shut up. He thought about telling the *Brigade-führer* he would sooner have been listening to Gandhi. The look on the fellow's face, he thought, would be worth it. But no. One could never be sure who was listening. Better safe.

The shortwave set crackled to life. It was in a secret cellar, a tiny, dark, hot room lit only by the glow of its dial and by the red end of the cigarette in its owner's mouth. The Germans had made not turning in a radio a capital crime. Of course, Gandhi thought, harboring him was also a capital crime. That weighed on his conscience. But the man knew the risk he was taking.

The fellow (Gandhi knew him only as Lal) fiddled with the controls. "Usually we listen to the Americans," he said. "There is some hope of truth from them. But tonight you want to hear Berlin."

"Yes," Gandhi said. "I must learn what action is to be taken against Model."

"If any," Nehru added. He was once again impeccably attired in white, which made him the most easily visible object in the cellar.

"We have argued this before," Ghandi said tiredly. "No government can uphold the author of a cold-blooded slaughter of wounded men and women. The world would cry out in abhorrence."

Lal said, "That government controls too much of the world already." He adjusted the tuning knob again.

After a burst of static, the strains of a Strauss waltz filled the little room. Lal grunted in satisfaction. "We are a little early yet."

After a few minutes the incongruously sweet music died away. "This is Radio Berlin's English-language channel," an announcer declared. "In a moment, the news program." Another German tune rang out: the *Horst Wessel* song. Gandhi's nostrils flared with distaste.

A new voice came over the air. "Good day. This is William Joyce." The nasal Oxonian accent was that of the archetypal British aristocrat, now vanished from India as well as England. It was the accent that flavored Gandhi's own English, and Nehru's as well. In fact, Gandhi had heard Joyce was a New York-born rabble-rouser of Irish blood who also happened to be a passionately sincere Nazi. The combination struck the Indian as distressing.

"What did the English used to call him?" Nehru murmured. "Lord Haw-Haw?"

Gandhi waved his friends to silence. Joyce was reading the news, or what the Propaganda Ministry in Berlin wanted to present to English-speakers as the news.

Most of it was on the dull side: a trade agreement between Manchukuo, Japanese-dominated China, and Japanese-dominated Siberia; advances by German-supported French troops against American-supported French troops in a war by proxy in the African jungles. Slightly more interesting was the German warning about American interference in the East Asia Co-Prosperity Sphere.

One day soon, Gandhi thought sadly, the two mighty powers of the Old World would turn on the one great nation that stood between them. He feared the outcome. Thinking herself secure behind ocean barriers, the United States had stayed out of the European war. Now the war was bigger than Europe, and the ocean barriers no longer, but highways for her foes.

Lord Haw-Haw droned on and on. He gloated over the fate of rebels hunted down in Scotland: they were publicly hanged. Nehru leaned forward. "Now," he guessed. Gandhi nodded.

But the commentator passed on to unlikely sounding boasts about the prosperity of Europe under the New Order. Against his will, Gandhi felt anger rise in him. Were Indians too insignificant to the Reich even to be mentioned?

More music came from the radio: the first bars of the other German anthem, *"Deutschland über alles."* William Joyce said solemnly, "And now, a special announcement from the Ministry for Administration of Acquired Territories. *Reichsminister* Reinhard Heydrich commends Field Marshal Walther Model's heroic suppression of insurrection in India, and warns that his leniency will not be repeated."

"Leniency!" Nehru and Gandhi burst out together, the latter making it into as much of a curse as he allowed himself.

As if explaining to them, the voice on the radio went on, "Henceforward, hostages will be taken at the slightest sound of disorder, and will be executed forthwith if it continues. Field Marshal Model had also placed a reward of fifty thousand rupees on the capture of the criminal revolutionary Gandhi, and twenty-five thousand on the capture of his henchman Nehru."

*"Deutschland über alles"* rang out again, to signal the end of the announcement. Joyce went on to the next piece of news. "Turn that off," Nehru said after a moment. Lal obeyed, plunging the cellar into complete darkness. Nehru surprised Gandhi by laughing. "I have never before been the henchman of a criminal revolutionary."

The older man might as well not have heard him. "They commended him," he said. "Commended!" Disbelief put the full tally of his years in his voice, which usually sounded much stronger and younger.

"What will you do?" Lal asked quietly. A match flared, dazzling in the dark, as he lit another cigarette.

"They shall not govern India in this fashion," Gandhi snapped. "Not a soul will cooperate with them from now on. We outnumber them a thousand to one; what can they accomplish without us? We shall use that to full advantage."

"I hope the price is not more than the people can pay," Nehru said.

"The British shot us down, too, and we were on our way toward prevailing," Gandhi said stoutly. As he would not have a few days before, though, he added, "So do I."

Field Marshal Model scowled and yawned at the same time. The pot of tea that should have been on his desk was nowhere to be found. His stomach growled. A plate of rolls should have been beside the teapot.

"How am I supposed to get anything done without breakfast?" he asked rhetorically (no one was in the office to hear him complain). Rhetorical complaint was not enough to satisfy him. "Lasch!" he shouted.

"Sir?" the aide came rushing in.

Model jerked his chin at the empty space on his desk where the silver tray full of good things should have been. "What's become of what's his name? Naoroji, that's it. If he's home with a hangover, he could have had the courtesy to let us know."

"I will inquire with the liaison officer for native personnel, sir, and also have the kitchen staff send you up something to eat." Lasch picked up a telephone, spoke into it. The longer he talked, the less happy he looked. When he turned back to the field marshal, his expression was a good match for the stony one Model often wore. He said, "None of the locals has shown up for work today, sir."

"What? None?" Model's frown made his monocle dig into his cheek. He hesitated. "I will feel better if you tell me some new hideous malady has broken out among them."

Lasch spoke with the liaison officer again. He shook his head. "Nothing like that, sir—or at least," he corrected himself with the caution that made him a good aide, "nothing Captain Wechsler knows about."

Model's phone rang again. It startled him; he jumped. "*Bitte?*" he growled into the mouthpiece, embarrassed at starting even though only Lash had seen. He listened. Then he growled again, in good earnest this time. He slammed the phone down. "That was our railway officer. Hardly any natives are coming into the station."

The phone rang again. "*Bitte?*" This time it was a swearword. Model snarled, cutting off whatever the man on the other end was saying, and hung up. "The damned clerks are staying out, too," he shouted at Lasch, as if it were the major's fault. "I know what's wrong with the blasted locals, by God—an overdose of Gandhi, that's what."

"We should have shot him down in that riot he led," Lash said angrily.

"Not for lack of effort that we didn't," Model said. Now that he saw where his trouble was coming from, he began thinking like a General Staff-trained officer again. That discipline went deep in him. His voice was cool and musing as he corrected his aide: "It was no riot, Dieter. That man is a skilled agitator. Armed with no more than words, he gave the British fits. Remember that the Führer started out as an agitator, too."

"Ah, but the Führer wasn't above breaking heads to back up what he said." Lasch smiled reminiscently, and raised a fist. He was a Munich man, and wore on his sleeve the harsh mark that showed party membership before 1933.

But the field marshal said, "You think Gandhi doesn't? His way is to break them from the inside out, to make his foes doubt themselves. Those soldiers who took courts rather than obey their commanding officer had their heads broken, wouldn't you say? Think of him as a Russian tank commander, say, rather than as a political agitator. He is fighting us every bit as much as the Russians did."

Lasch thought about it. Plainly he did not like it. "A coward's way of fighting."

"The weak cannot use the weapons of the strong," Model shrugged. "He does what he can, and skillfully. But I can make his backers doubt themselves, too: see if I don't."

"Sir?"

"We'll start with the railway workers. They are the most essential to have back on the job, yes? Get a list of names. Cross off every twentieth one. Send a squad to each of those homes, haul the slackers out, and shoot them in the street. If the survivors don't report tomorrow, do it again. Keep at it every day until they go back to work or no workers are left."

"Yes, sir." Lasch hesitated. At last he asked, "Are you sure, sir?"

"Have you a better idea, Dieter? We have a dozen divisions here; Grandhi has the whole subcontinent. I have to convince them in a hurry that obeying me is a better idea than obeying him. Obeying is what counts. I don't care a pfennig as to whether they love me. *Oderint, dum metuant.*"

"Sir?" The major had no Latin.

" 'Let them hate, so long as they fear.' "

"Ah," Lasch said. "Yes, I like that." He fingered his chin as he thought. "In aid of which, the Muslims hereabouts like the Hindus none too well. I daresay we could use them to help hunt Gandhi down."

"Now that *I* like," Model said. "Most of our Indian Legion lads are Muslims. They will know people, or know people who know people. And"—the field marshal chuckled cynically—"the reward will do no harm, either. Now get those feelers in motion—and if they pay off, you'll probably have earned yourself a new pip on your shoulder boards."

"Thank you very much, sir!"

"My pleasure. As I say, you'll have earned it. So long as things go as they should, I am a very easy man to get along with. Even Gandhi could, if he wanted to. He will end up having caused a lot of people to be killed because he does not."

"Yes, sir," Lasch agreed. "If only he would see that, since we have won India from the British, we will not turn around and tamely yield it to those who could not claim it for themselves."

"You're turning into a political philosopher now, Dieter?"

"Ha! Not likely." But the major looked pleased as he picked up the phone.

* * *

"My dear friend, my ally, my teacher, we are losing," Nehru said as the messenger scuttled away from this latest in a series of what were hopefully called safe houses. "Day by day, more people return to their jobs."

Gandhi shook his head, slowly as if the motion caused him physical pain. "But they must not. Each one who cooperated with the Germans sets back the day of his own freedom."

"Each one who fails to ends up dead," Nehru said dryly. "Most men lack your courage, great-souled one. To them, that carries more weight than the other. Some are willing to resist, but would rather take up arms than the restraints of satyagraha."

"If they take up arms, they will be defeated. The British could not beat the Germans with guns and tanks and planes; how shall we? Besides, if we shoot a German here and there, we give them the excuse they need to strike at us. When one of their lieutenants was waylaid last month, their bombers leveled a village in reprisal. Against those who fight through nonviolence, they have no such justification."

"They do not seem to need one, either," Nehru pointed out.

Before Gandhi could reply to that, a man burst into the hovel where they were hiding. "You must flee!" he cried. "The Germans have found this place! They are coming. Out with me, quick! I have a cart waiting."

Nehru snatched up the canvas bag in which he carried his few belongings. For a man used to being something of a dandy, the haggard life of a fugitive came hard. Gandhi had never wanted much. Now that he had nothing, that did not disturb him. He rose calmly, followed the man who had come to warn them.

"Hurry!" the fellow shouted as they scrambled into his oxcart while the humpbacked cattle watched indifferently with their liquid brown eyes. When Gandhi and Nehru were lying in the cart, the man piled blankets and straw mats over them. He scrambled up to take the reins, saying, "*Inshallah*, we shall be safely away from here before the platoon arrives." He flicked a switch over the backs of the cattle. They lowed indignantly. The cart rattled away.

Lying in the sweltering semidarkness under the concealment the man had draped on him, Gandhi peered through chinks, trying to figure out where in Delhi he was going next. He had played the game more than once these past few weeks, though he knew doctrine said he should not. The less he knew, the less he could reveal. Unlike most men, though, he was confident he could not be made to talk against his will.

"We are using the technique the American Poe called the 'purloined letter,' I see," he remarked to Nehru. "We will be close by the German barracks. They will not think to look for us there."

The younger man frowned. "I did not know we had safe houses there," he said. Then he relaxed, as well as he could when folded into too small a space. "Of course, I do not pretend to know everything there is to know about such matters. It would be dangerous if I did."

"I was thinking much the same myself, though with me as subject of the sentence." Gandhi laughed quietly. "Try as we will, we always have ourselves at the center of things, don't we?"

He had to raise his voice to finish. An armored personnel carrier came rumbling and rattling toward them, getting louder as it approached. The silence when the driver suddenly killed the engine was a startling contrast to the previous racket. Then there was noise again, as soldiers shouted in German.

"What are they saying?" Nehru asked.

"Hush," Gandhi said absently: not from ill manners, but out of the concentration he needed to follow German at all. After a moment he resumed, "They are swearing at a black-bearded man, asking why he flagged them down."

"Why would anyone flag down German sol—," Nehru began, then stopped in abrupt dismay. The fellow who burst into their hiding place wore a bushy black beard. "Now we better get out of—" Again Nehru broke off in mid-sentence, this time because the oxcart driver was throwing off the coverings that concealed his two passengers.

Nehru started to get to his feet so he could try to scramble out and run. Too late—a rifle barrel that looked wide as a tunnel was shoved in his face as a German came dashing up to the cart. The big curved magazine said the gun was one of the automatic assault rifles that had wreaked such havoc among the British infantry. A burst would turn a man into bloody hash. Nehru sank back in despair.

Gandhi, less spry than his friend, had only sat up in the bottom of the cart. "Good day, gentlemen," he said to the Germans peering down at him. His tone took no notice of their weapons.

"Down." The word was in such gutturally accented Hindi that Gandhi hardly understood it, but the accompanying gesture with a rifle was unmistakable.

His face a mask of misery, Nehru got out of the cart. A German helped Gandhi descend. *"Danke,"* he said. The soldier nodded gruffly. He pointed the barrel of his rifle—toward the armored personnel carrier.

"My rupees!" the black-bearded man shouted.

Nehru turned on him, so quickly he almost got shot for it. "Your thirty pieces of silver, you mean," he cried.

"Ah, a British education," Gandhi murmured. No one was listening to him.

"My rupees," the man repeated. He did not understand Nehru; so often, Gandhi thought sadly, that was at the root of everything.

"You'll get them," promised the sergeant leading the German squad. Gandhi wondered if he was telling the truth. Probably so, he decided. The British had had centuries to build a network of Indian clients. Here but a matter of months, the Germans would need all they could find.

"In." The soldier with a few words of Hindi nodded to the back of the armored personnel carrier. Up close, the vehicle took on a war-battered individuality its kind had lacked when they were just big, intimidating shapes rumbling down the highway. It was bullet-scarred and patched in a couple of places, with sheets of steel crudely welded on.

Inside, the jagged lips of the bullet holes had been hammered down so they did not gouge a man's back. The carrier smelled of leather, sweat, tobacco, smokeless powder, and exhaust fumes. It was crowded, all the more so with the two Indians added to its usual contingent. The motor's roar when it started up challenged even Gandhi's equanimity.

Not, he thought with uncharacteristic bitterness, that that equanimity had done him much good.

"They are here, sir," Lasch told Model, then, at the field marshal's blank look, amplified: "Gandhi and Nehru."

Model's eyebrow came down toward his monocle. "I won't bother with Nehru. Now that we have him, take him out and give him a noodle"—army slang for a bullet in the back of the neck—"but don't waste any time over him. Gandhi, now, is interesting. Fetch him in."

"Yes, sir," the major sighed. Model smiled. Lasch did not find Gandhi interesting. Lasch would never carry a field marshal's baton, not if he lived to be ninety.

Model waved away the soldiers who escorted Gandhi into his office. Either of them could have broken the little Indian like a stick. "Have a care," Gandhi said. "If I am the desperate criminal bandit you have styled me, I may overpower you and escape."

"If you do, you will have earned it," Model retorted. "Sit, if you care to."

"Thank you." Gandhi sat. "They took Jawaharlal away. Why have you summoned me instead?"

"To talk for a while, before you join him." Model saw that Gandhi knew what he meant, and that the old man remained unafraid. Not that that would change anything, Model thought, although he respected his opponent's courage the more for his keeping it in the last extremity.

"I will talk, in the hope of persuading you to have mercy on my people. For myself I ask nothing."

Model shrugged. "I was as merciful as the circumstances of war allowed, until you began your campaign against us. Since then I have done what I needed to restore order. When it returns, I may be milder again."

"You seem a decent man," Gandhi said, puzzlement in his voice. "How can you so callously massacre people who have done you no harm?"

"I never would have, had you not urged them to folly."

"Seeking freedom is not folly."

"Is it when you cannot gain it—and you cannot. Already your people are losing their stomach for—what do you call it? Passive resistance? A silly notion. A passive resister simply ends up dead, with no chance to hit back at his foe.

That hit a nerve, Model thought. Gandhi's voice was less detached as he answered, "Satyagraha strikes the oppressor's soul, not his body. You must be without honor or conscience, to fail to feel your victim's anguish."

Nettled in turn, the field marshal snapped, "I have honor. I follow the oath of obedience I swore with the army to the Führer and through him to the Reich. I need consider nothing past that."

Now Gandhi's calm was gone. "But he is a madman! What has he done to the Jews of Europe?"

"Removed them," Model said matter-of-factly; *Einsatzgruppe* B had followed Army Group central to Moscow and beyond. "They were capitalists or Bolsheviks, and either way enemies of the Reich. When an enemy falls into a man's hands, what else is there to do but destroy him, lest he revive to turn the tables one day?"

Gandhi had buried his face in his hands. Without looking at Model, he said, "Make him a friend."

"Even the British knew better than that, or they would not have held India as long as they did," the field marshal snorted. "They must have begun to forget, though, or your movement would have got what it deserves long ago. You first made the mistake of confusng us with them long ago, by the way." He touched a fat dossier on his desk.

"When was that?" Gandhi asked indifferently. The man was beaten now, Model thought with a touch of pride: he had succeeded where a generation of degenerate, decadent Englishmen had failed. Of course, the field marshal told himself, he had beaten the British, too.

He opened the dossier, riffled through it. "Here we are," he said, nodding in satisfaction. "It was after *Kristallnacht*, eh, in 1938, when you urged the German Jews to play at the same game of passive resistance you were using here. Had they been fools enough to try it, we would have thanked you, you know: it would have let us bag the enemies of the Reich all the more easily."

"Yes, I made a mistake," Gandhi said. Now he was looking at the field marshal, looking at him with such fierceness that for a moment Model thought he would attack him despite advanced age and effete philosophy. But Gandhi only continued sorrowfully, "I made the mistake of thinking I faced a regime ruled by conscience, one that could at the very least be shamed into doing that which is right."

Model refused to be baited. "We do what is right for our *Volk*, for our Reich. We are meant to rule, and rule we do—as you see." The field marshal tapped the dossier again. "You could be sentenced to death for this earlier meddling in the affairs of the fatherland, you know, even without these later acts of insane defiance you have caused."

"History will judge us," Gandhi warned as the field marshal rose to have him taken away.

Model smiled then. "Winners write history." He watched the two strapping German guards lead the old man off. "A very good morning's work," the field marshal told Lasch when Gandhi was gone. "What's on the menu for lunch?"

"Blood sausage and sauerkraut, I believe."

"Ah, good. Something to look forward to." Model sat down. He went back to work.

**Fantasy: The Golden Age**
## Only at Baen

**Unknown**—The best of John W. Campbell's fantasy magazine, described by **Isaac Asimov** to be "the best fantasy magazine that ever existed or, in my opinion, is likely to exist . . .".
69785-4 ∗ $3.50

**The Complete Compleat Enchanter**—Together at last: *all* of the Harold Shea stories of L. Sprague de Camp and Fletcher Pratt! Over 500 pages of first class fantasy.
69809-5 ∗ $4.50

**John the Balladeer**—Pulitzer Prize winning author Manly Wade Wellman makes the hills of North Carolina come alive—literally—in these timeless tales. Collected in one volume for the first time, the stories of Silver John are not to be missed!
65418-7 ∗ $3.50

☐ **Unknown**    ☐ **John the Balladeer**
☐ **The Complete Compleat Enchanter**

*Name* _____

*Address* _____

_____

*Available at your local bookstore, or just send this coupon and the cover price(s) to: Baen Books, Dept. BA, 260 Fifth Ave., New York, NY 10001.*